EX LIBRIS

VINTAGE CLASSICS

ALSO BY GRAHAM GREENE

NOVELS

The Man Within
It's a Battlefield
A Gun for Sale
Brighton Rock
The Confidential Agent
The Ministry of Fear
The Third Man
The End of the Affair
Loser Takes All
The Quiet American
A Burnt-out Case
Travels with my Aunt
Dr Fischer of Geneva or
The Bomb Party
The Human Factor
The Tenth Man
England Made Me
Stamboul Train
The Power and the Glory
The Heart of the Matter
The Fallen Idol
Our Man in Havana
The Comedians
The Honorary Consul
Monsignor Quixote
The Captain and the Enemy

PLAYS

Collected Plays

SHORT STORIES

Collected Stories
Twenty-One Stories
The Last Word and Other Stories
May We Borrow Your Husband?

TRAVEL

Journey Without Maps
The Lawless Roads
In Search of a Character
Getting to Know the General

ESSAYS

Yours etc.
Reflections
Mornings in the Dark
Collected Essays

AUTOBIOGRAPHY

A Sort of Life
Ways of Escape
Fragments of an Autobiography
A World of my Own

BIOGRAPHY

Lord Rochester's Monkey
An Impossible Woman

CHILDREN'S BOOKS

The Little Train
The Little Horse-Bus
The Little Steamroller
The Little Fire Engine

GRAHAM GREENE
DUEL DUET

Selected Stories

EDITED AND WITH AN INTRODUCTION BY
Yiyun Li

VINTAGE CLASSICS

1 3 5 7 9 10 8 6 4 2

Vintage Classics is part of the Penguin Random House group of companies

Vintage, Penguin Random House UK, One Embassy Gardens,
8 Viaduct Gardens, London SW11 7BW

penguin.co.uk/vintage-classics
global.penguinrandomhouse.com

Copyright © Graham Greene 1954, 1963, 1967, 1990, 2005.
For further details, see p. 383
Introduction copyright © Yiyun Li 2025

The moral right of the author has been asserted

This edition published in Vintage Classics in 2025

Penguin Random House values and supports copyright. Copyright fuels creativity, encourages diverse voices, promotes freedom of expression and supports a vibrant culture. Thank you for purchasing an authorised edition of this book and for respecting intellectual property laws by not reproducing, scanning or distributing any part of it by any means without permission. You are supporting authors and enabling Penguin Random House to continue to publish books for everyone. No part of this book may be used or reproduced in any manner for the purpose of training artificial intelligence technologies or systems. In accordance with Article 4(3) of the DSM Directive 2019/790, Penguin Random House expressly reserves this work from the text and data mining exception.

A CIP catalogue record for this book is available from the British Library

ISBN 9781529946512

Typeset in 12/14.75pt Bembo Book MT Pro by Jouve (UK), Milton Keynes
Printed and bound in Great Britain by Clays Ltd, Elcograf S.p.A.

The authorised representative in the EEA is Penguin Random House Ireland,
Morrison Chambers, 32 Nassau Street, Dublin D02 YH68

Penguin Random House is committed to a sustainable future
for our business, our readers and our planet. This book is made
from Forest Stewardship Council® certified paper.

Contents

Introduction: Return to the Home Key	1
Dream of a Strange Land	11
The News in English	26
The End of the Party	39
The Case for the Defence	49
The Basement Room	55
A Day Saved	84
Across the Bridge	91
A Drive in the Country	102
The Innocent	121
The Destructors	127
Men at Work	147
A Little Place Off the Edgware Road	154
A Visit to Morin	163
The Hint of an Explanation	180
Cheap in August	197
The Moment of Truth	225

The Root of All Evil	235
A Branch of the Service	249
Two Gentle People	267
Church Militant	276
The Other Side of the Border	285
Under the Garden	318
Publication History	383

Introduction

Return to the Home Key

Two moments in Graham Greene's published life have often returned to me in the past twenty years. This may sound strange: an ideal reader should refrain from crossing the boundary between a writer's work and his life. And yet it is inevitable: rarely does an author have the luxury of having no known biography. Greene, having written about his life and having had his life extensively written about by others, remains near when one reads his work – not insistently dominating or distracting, as some writers may prove to be, but as a presence often felt and at times caught by a side glance.

The first moment appears in Greene's memoir *Ways of Escape*. In a chapter about *Brighton Rock*, which Greene called a labour of love, he explains the original inspiration for the novel with a reminiscence about the first film he saw at age six – a silent film about a kitchen maid turned queen, with live music played offscreen – he writes, 'Her march was accompanied by an old lady on a piano, but the tock-tock-tock of untuned wires stayed in my memory when other melodies faded . . . That was the kind of book I always wanted to write: the high romantic tale, capturing us in youth with hopes that prove illusions, to which we return again in age in order to escape the sad reality.'*

The second moment appears in *Graham Greene: An Intimate Portrait by His Closest Friend and Confidant* by Leopoldo Duran.

---

* *Ways of Escape*, Simon and Schuster, 1980, p. 82.

In 1983, Father Duran accompanied Greene on a journey to Spain for the filming of his novel *Monsignor Quixote*. At a Trappist monastery, Father Duran noticed an elderly monk, Father Juan. 'I saw him, standing discreetly apart, at the entrance to the porter's lodge, learning on this walking stick, chin in both hands, and totally absorbed by these people and the strange things they were doing ... With seventy years' experience of Trappist rule behind him, Father Juan did not want to go to heaven without seeing how films were made.'*

To say that these two moments encapsulate Greene's work for me is an irresponsible cliche: the point of literature is not to be put into capsules, a trick good only for pharmaceutical manufacturers. Rather, the two moments provide a home key whenever I read Greene's work. There are multiple pairings of twos in both scenes: a duel or a duet; who can say which is the more apt noun here?

In the first, the heroine, a kitchen maid and a queen within one being, offers a fairytale setting for some confrontations: reality versus fantasy, past versus future, entrapment versus freedom – variations of these appear in many of Greene's novels. But a more interesting pairing is the beautiful image of a silent woman on the screen and the old lady plinking-plonking off stage: which of them is more dramatic, more romantic, more illusory and yet more permanent? And of course, in that same passage, there is also Greene the author (in his mid-seventies, going by the publication date of the book) and Greene the six-year-old boy. The mature man feels the young boy's emotions – in Greene's own words, 'to live again the follies and sentimentalities and exaggerations of the distant time, and to

---

* *Graham Greene: An Intimate Portrait by His Closest Friend and Confidant*, HarperSanFrancisco, p. 229.

feel them, as I felt them then, without irony'.* The younger self, in carving into his memory feelings he's not yet capable of articulating or even understanding, is nevertheless an equal partner: here is the source of a writer's sense and sensibility, like the initial vibration that makes the sound; what comes after are echoes and reverberations.

In the second moment, again the illusory cinematic art appears. Father Juan, with his seventy years of Trappist history, must never have watched a film, and there he stands, witnessing what would remain a mysterious process to most audiences in the cinema. The clash and the harmony between the holy and the secular, believing and make-believing, faith and entertainment, the pending death of Monsignor Quixote – a fictional character, whose Sancho in the novel is an ex-mayor, a communist – and the pending death of Father Juan in the not too distant future: one has a sense that one enters, at that moment, the quintessential Greene-land.

There is defiance that comes only with youth and inexperience, the refusal to accept life as it is: no one says a kitchen maid cannot also be a warrior queen; no one says a child cannot have the emotions that would put the world, which is often indifferent, to shame. There is also a defiance that comes with old age when the world seems no longer new: surely there is still something more to ponder, even if you've lived close to God in a Trappist cell for seventy years. And those who understand both kinds of defiance, one suspects, will be the right readers for Greene.

There are different ways to talk about Greene's work. We can focus on the amphitheatre of history, where wars, revolutions and colonial intrigues play impersonal gods to the mortals.

---

* *A Sort of Life,* Vintage Classics, p. xi.

We can scrutinise the mundane settings waiting for major and minor human dramas to happen – the streets and alleyways of Brighton and Saigon, the un-aired offices of London ministry buildings, the manicured suburban gardens, the well-lit casinos and much-visited seaside resorts, the jungles and rivers of Africa and South America. We can also step away from those external settings and enter the interior landscapes of many of his characters, some of them with God on their side, others without; some have time on their side, others not; some with friends or loves or even enemies on their side, others not. But all of them have memories and dreams on their side – a blessing, even if it sometimes masks itself as a curse. And all of them, it seems to me, are only half of a duel or half of a duet, their partners sometimes visible and other times invisible.

In 'A Day Saved', an unnamed narrator follows an unnamed man, with a detailed plan to kill him and yet with the horror that he knows nothing about the man, not even his name. This seems a classic Greene dilemma, where one man's despair and (partial) knowledge and another man's innocence and faith in the ordinary (if he takes a flight instead of a train, he will save a day) constitute the quicksand for the reader: surely we are in a worse situation than the two characters; there is no choice for us but to be both of them at the same time. 'A day saved . . . Save it from what, for what?' We may as well ask ourselves every day, for the rest of our lives, without knowing the answer.

In 'The Basement Room', a child – temporarily orphaned (his parents are out of town) – and the butler of the house, whom the child loves genuinely, are set on a course from page one to betray each other in the most fatal manner, and nothing will help them or save them. All the same, for as long as they go on being gentle and tender towards each other, we readers hold on to wishful thinking: of course, life will not take their sides, but perhaps – just perhaps – because of that, they will end up on the same side, two partners in a perpetual duet rather than being pitched against each other in a duel. But wishful thinking neither saves the butler nor the child nor us.

There is a general belief that short stories are better read one at a time – one sees some sense in that. But stories (and novels, too) are like people. For a writer with a long career, chances are, many stories and novels have their duet or duel partners in other stories and novels. In selecting the stories for this collection and ordering the sequence, I have taken the liberty of ignoring the chronology of publication. Instead, I have allowed myself to be guided by this thought: rather than to be read one at a time, the stories in this selection may be more interesting and illuminating if read two at a time.

For instance, 'Dream of a Strange Land' and 'The News in English'. The former is set in unnamed countryside near 'the capital', where a 'Herr Colonel' is requisitioning the house of a 'Herr Professor' for one night and converting it into a Monte Carlo casino for a 'Herr General'. The transformation, a strange dream for the professor, becomes a stranger dream for a patient of his, who is trying to reach the house after dark on a life-and-death matter. 'The wrong house? But this is not the wrong house; it is the wrong country,' the patient ponders. The two men meet at an existential bleakness that is more than a momentary despair – but only fleetingly. They are not engaged in a proper duel, though one of them dies after that encounter; they are not in a proper duet, either, though their music, like the untuned piano music that went on living in Greene's recollection, has never faded in my memory. The echo of that music easily intertwines with another tune from 'The News in English', in which a husband, a POW in the Second World War, broadcasts German propaganda in English to England, but only his young wife recognises the real messages conveyed. Is she imagining it, or is it that he and she live on a higher plane of consciousness and understanding that is so extraordinary and unfathomable to the world at large? Like the patient and the professor in the previous story, these two also form a duet, though its music remains unheard, and the meaning of the music dwarfs wars and history.

In 'The End of the Party', twin boys hold hands in the dark, as though they were back in the womb together, waiting to be found in a game of hide-and-seek, and yet only one of them will be born again this time. In 'The Case for the Defence', twins, having lived to adulthood, face the same situation: one of them must save the other through their twinhood – a pair of identical twins can destroy the most waterproof legal case merely by looking like each other. Does it work? A little better than for the pair of boys, though not much.

I have placed the two long stories, 'Under the Garden' and 'The Other Side of the Border', at the end of this selection. Both are novelistic (Greene called the latter manuscript one of his 'abandoned novels'), and there was a moment when I was reading them side by side when I had an eerie feeling of their merging in my imagination into a novel: one has to shake one's head decisively to dispel that (mis)apprehension.

I could go on, though that would be to spoil the pleasure that awaits. A better way is for a reader to read these stories closely, two at a time.

I must admit that the stories, arranged according to my understanding, may offer other insights to readers, who may then want to reorder the stories according to their own liking. That would be even better: a rearranged piece of music sometimes speaks of discoveries. And Greene has offered sufficiently for each of his readers to come up with his or her arrangement.

Is there any fundamental difference between a duel and a duet? In each, a connection pre-dates the actual event. What comes after – understanding or misunderstanding, agreement or disagreement, harmony or dissonance, conversation or argument, life or death – may surprise us, but it is because human relationships are by nature surprising; what comes after may feel inevitable, and that too is what human relationships are about.

I started to read Greene when I was a young writer; twenty years later, he remains among a handful of writers I reread. His work keeps one's mind on tiptoe. Illusions beget disillusions but also hopes; hopes beget illusions but also clarities.

As I was writing this introduction, I looked for *Ways of Escape* on my bookshelf, wanting to revisit the cinema scene with the six-year-old Greene. It would be like a return to the home key, I thought, but among over twenty books by Greene (a few in duplicates) and still more about him, the one book I was looking for was absent! So much for the wish to see my previous annotations in the book and to have a duet with my younger self. And that missed connection, I must admit, is surprising and inevitable, like a tree standing inconspicuously and yet meaningfully in Greene-land.

Yiyun Li, 2025

**Dream of a
Strange Land**

*The News
in English*

Dream of a Strange Land

1

The house of the Herr Professor was screened on every side by the plantation of fir-trees which grew among great grey rocks. Although it was only twenty minutes' ride from the capital and then a few minutes from the main road to the north, a visitor had the impression that he was in deep country; he felt himself to be hundreds of miles away from the cafés, the kiosks, the opera-houses and the theatres.

The Herr Professor had virtually retired two years ago when he reached the age of sixty-five. His appointment at the hospital had been filled, he had closed his consulting-room in the capital, and if he continued to work it was only for a few favoured patients who were compelled to drive out to see him, or if they were poor (for he had not clung to a few rich patients only) to take a bus which landed them about ten minutes' walk away at the edge of the trees and the rocks.

It was one of these poorer patients who stood now in the doctor's study listening to his doom. The study had folding pitch-pine doors leading to the living-room, which the patient had never seen. A heavy dark bookcase stood against the wall full of heavy dark books, all obviously medical in character (no one had ever seen the Herr Professor with any lighter literature, nor heard him give an opinion of even the most respected classic. Once questioned on Madame Bovary's poisoning, he had professed complete ignorance of the book, and another time he had shown himself to be equally ignorant of Ibsen's treatment of syphilis in *Ghosts*). The desk was as heavy and dark as the bookcase; it was only a desk as heavy which could have borne without cracking the massive bronze paperweight more than a foot high which represented Prometheus chained to his rock with a hovering eagle thrusting its beak into his liver. (Sometimes, when breaking the news to a patient with cirrhosis, the Professor had referred to his paperweight with dry humour.)

The patient wore a shabby-genteel suit of dark cloth; the cuffs had frayed and been repaired. He wore stout boots which had seen just as long a service, and through the open door in the hall behind him hung an overcoat and an umbrella, while a pair of goloshes stood in the steel trough under the umbrella, the snow not yet melted from their uppers. He was a man past fifty who had spent all his adult years behind the counter of a bank and by patient labour and courtesy he had risen to the position of second cashier. He would never be first cashier, for the first cashier was at least five years younger.

The Herr Professor had a short grey beard and he wore old-fashioned glasses, steel-rimmed, for his short sight. His rather hairy hands were scattered with grave-marks. As he seldom smiled one had very little opportunity to see his strong and perfect teeth. He said firmly, caressing Prometheus as he spoke, 'I warned you when you first came that my treatment might have started too late – to arrest the disease. Now the smear-test shows . . .'

'But, Herr Professor, you have been treating me all these months. No one knows about it. I can go on working at the bank. Can't you continue to treat me a little longer?'

'I would be breaking the law,' the Herr Professor explained, making a motion as though his thumb and forefinger clutched a chalk. 'Contagious cases must always go to the hospital.'

'But you yourself, Herr Professor, have said that it is one of the most difficult of all diseases to catch.'

'And yet you caught it.'

'How? How?' the patient asked himself with the weariness of a man who has confronted the same question time without mind.

'Perhaps it was when you were working on the coast. There are many contacts in a port.'

'Contacts?'

'I assume you are a man like other men.'

'But that was seven years ago.'

'One has known the disease to take ten years to develop.'

'It will be the end of my work, Herr Professor. The bank will never take me back. My pension will be very small.'

'You take an exaggerated view. After a certain period . . . Hansen's disease is eventually curable.'

'Why don't you call it by its proper name?'

'The International Congress decided five years ago to change the name.'

'The world hasn't changed the name, Herr Professor. If you send me to that hospital, everyone will know that I am a leper.'

'I have no choice. But I assure you you will find it very comfortable. There is television, I believe, in every room, and a golf-course.'

The Herr Professor showed no impatience at all, unless the fact that he did not ask the patient to sit and stood himself, stiff and straight-backed behind Prometheus and the eagle, was a sign of it.

'Herr Professor, I implore you. I will not breathe a word to a soul. You can treat me just as well as the hospital can. You've said yourself that the risk of contagion is very small, Herr Professor. I have my savings – they are not very great, but I will give them all . . .'

'My dear sir, you must not try to bribe me. It is not only insulting, it is a gross error of taste. I am sorry. I must ask you to go now. My time is very much occupied.'

'Herr Professor, you have no idea what it means to me. I lead a very simple life, but if a man is alone in the world he grows to love his habits. I go to a café by the lake every day at seven o'clock and stay there till eight. They all know me in the café. Sometimes I play a game of checkers. On Sunday I take the lake steamer to—'

'Your habits will have to be interrupted for a year or two,' the Herr Professor said sharply.

'Interrupted? You say interrupted? But I can never go back. Never. Leprosy is a word — it isn't a disease. They'll never believe leprosy can be cured. You can't cure a word.'

'You will be getting a certificate signed by the hospital authorities,' the Herr Professor said.

'A certificate! I might just as well carry a bell.'

He moved to the door, the hall, his umbrella and the goloshes; the Herr Professor, with a sigh of relief which was almost inaudible beyond the room, seated himself at his desk. But again the patient had turned back. 'Is it that you don't trust me to keep quiet, Herr Professor?'

'I have every belief, I can assure you, that you would keep quiet. For your own sake. But you cannot expect a doctor of my standing to break the law. A sensible and necessary law. If it had not been infringed somewhere by someone you would not be standing here today. Good-bye, Herr—', but the patient had already closed the outer door and had begun to walk back amongst the rocks and firs towards the road, the bus-stop and the capital. The Herr Professor went to the window to make sure that he was truly gone and saw him among the snow-flakes which drifted lightly between the trees; he paused once and gesticulated with his hands as though a new argument had occurred to him which he was practising on a rock. Then he padded on and disappeared from sight.

The Herr Professor opened the sliding doors of the dining-room and made his accurate way to the sideboard, which was heavy like his desk. Instead of the Prometheus there stood on it a large silver flagon inscribed with the Herr Professor's name and a date more than forty years past – an award for fencing – and beside it lay a large silver epergne, also inscribed, a present from the staff of the hospital on his retirement. The Herr Professor took a hard green apple and walked back to his study. He sat down at his desk again and his teeth went crunch, crunch, crunch.

2

Later that morning the Herr Professor received another caller, but this one arrived before the house in a Mercedes-Benz car and the Herr Professor went himself to the door to show him in.

'Herr Colonel,' he said as he pulled forward the only chair of any comfort to be found in his study, 'this I hope is only a friendly call and not a professional one.'

'I am never ill,' the Colonel said with a look of irritated amusement at the very idea. 'My blood-pressure is normal, my weight is what it should be, and my heart's sound. I function like a machine. Indeed I find it difficult to believe that this machine need ever wear out. I have no worries, my nervous system is perfectly adjusted . . .'

'Then I'm relieved to know, Herr Colonel, that this is a social call.'

'The army,' the Colonel went on, crossing his long slim legs encased in English tweed, 'is the most healthy profession possible – naturally I mean in a neutral country like ours. The annual manoeuvres do one a world of good, brace the system, clean the blood . . .'

'I wish I could recommend them to my patients.'

'Oh, we can't have sick men in the army.' The Colonel added with a dry laugh, 'We leave that to the warring nations. They can never have our efficiency.'

The Herr Professor offered the Colonel a cigar. The Colonel took a cutter from a little leather case and prepared the cigar. 'You have met the Herr General?' he asked.

'On one or two occasions.'

'He is celebrating his seventieth birthday tonight.'

'Really? A very well preserved man.'

'Naturally. Now his friends – of whom I count myself the chief – have been arranging a very special occasion for him. You know, of course, his favourite hobby?'

'I can't say . . .'

'The tables. For the last fifty years he has spent most of his leaves at Monte Carlo.'

'He too must have a good nervous system.'

'Of course. Now it occurred to his friends, since he cannot spend his birthday at Monte Carlo for reasons of a quite temporary indisposition, to bring, as it were, the tables to him.'

'How can that be possible?'

'Everything was satisfactorily arranged. A croupier from Cannes and two assistants. All the necessary equipment. One of my friends was to have lent us his house in the country. You understand that everything has to be very discreet because of our absurd laws. You would think the police on such an occasion would turn a blind eye, but among the higher officials there is a great jealousy of the army. I once heard the Commissioner remark – at a party to which I was surprised to see that he had been invited – that the only wars in which our country had ever been engaged were fought by *his* men.'

'I don't follow.'

'Oh, he was referring to crime. An absurd comparison. What has crime to do with war?'

The Herr Professor said, 'You were telling me that everything had been satisfactorily arranged . . . ?'

'With the Herr General Director of the National Bank. But suddenly today he telephoned to say that a child – a girl as one might expect – had developed scarlatina. The household therefore is in quarantine.'

'The Herr General will be disappointed.'

'The Herr General knows nothing of all this. He understands that a party is being given in his honour in the country – that is all.'

'And you come to me,' the Herr Professor said, trying to hide mystification which he regarded as a professional weakness, 'in case I can suggest . . . ?'

'I come to you, Herr Professor, quite simply to borrow your house for this evening. The problem can be reduced to very simple terms. The house has to be in the country – I have explained to you why. It must have a *salon* of a certain size – to receive the tables; we can hardly have less than three, since the guests will number about a hundred. And the owner of the house must naturally be acceptable to the Herr General. There are houses a great deal larger than yours that the General could not be expected to enter as a guest. We can hardly, in this case, requisition.'

'I am honoured, of course, Herr Colonel, but . . .'

'These doors slide back, I suppose, and can form a room sufficiently large . . . ?'

'Yes, but . . .'

'Pardon me. You were saying?'

'I had the impression that the party was for tonight?'

'Yes.'

'I don't see how there could be time . . .'

'A matter of logistics, Herr Professor. Leave logistics to the army.' He took a notebook from his pocket and wrote down 'lights'. He explained to the Herr Professor, 'We shall have to hang chandeliers. A casino is unthinkable without chandeliers. May I see the other room, please?'

He paced it with his long tweed-clad legs. 'It will make a fine *salle privée* with the doors folded back and the chandeliers substituted for these – forgive me for saying so – rather commonplace centre lights. Your furniture we can store upstairs? Of course we will bring our own chairs. This sideboard, however, can serve as a bar. I see you were a fencer in your time, Herr Professor?'

'Yes.'

'The Herr General used to be very keen on fencing. Now tell me, where do you think we could put the orchestra?'

'Orchestra?'

'My regiment will supply the musicians. If the worst came to the worst I suppose they could play on the stairs.' He stood at the window of the *salon,* looking out at the wintry garden bounded by the dark wood of fir-trees. 'Is that a summerhouse?'

'Yes.'

'The oriental touch is very suitable. If they played there, and if we left a window a little open, the music will surely carry faintly . . .'

'The cold . . .'

'You have a fine stove and the curtains are heavy.'

'The summerhouse is altogether unheated.'

'The men can wear their military overcoats. And then for a fiddler, you know, the exercise . . .'

'And all this for tonight?'

'For tonight.'

The Herr Professor said, 'I have never before violated the law,' and then smiled a quick false smile to cover his failure of nerve.

'You could hardly do so in a better cause,' the Herr Colonel replied.

3

Long before dark the furniture-vans began to arrive. The chandeliers came first, with the wine-glasses, and remained crated in the hall until the electricians drove up, and then the waiters arrived simultaneously with the van that contained seventy-four small gilt chairs. The mover's men had beer in the kitchen with the Herr Professor's housekeeper, waiting for a lorry to turn up with the three roulette-tables. The roulette-wheels, the cloths and the boxes of plastic tokens, of varying colours and shapes according to value, were brought later in a smart private car with the three croupiers, serious men in black suits. The Herr Professor had never seen so many cars parked before his house. He felt a stranger, a guest, and lingered at his bedroom-window, afraid to go out on the stairs and meet the workmen. The long passage outside his room became littered with the furniture from below.

As the red winter sun sank in early afternoon below the black firs the cars began to multiply upon the drive. First a fleet of taxis arrived one behind the other, all bright yellow in colour like an amber chain, and out of these scrambled many burly men in military overcoats carrying musical instruments, which too often stuck in the doors and had to be extricated with care and difficulty: it was hard indeed to understand how the 'cello had ever fitted in – the neck came out first like a dressmaker's dummy and then the shoulders proved too wide. The men in overcoats stood around holding violin-bows like rifles at the ready, and a small man with a triangle shouted advice. Presently they had all disappeared from the front of the house and discordant sounds of tuning came across the snow from the summerhouse built in oriental taste. Something broke in the passage outside, and the Herr Professor, looking out, saw that it was one of the central lamps criticized by the Herr Colonel, which had fallen off the occasional table on which it had been propped. The passage was nearly blocked by the heavy desk from the study, the glass-fronted bookcase and his three filing cabinets. The Herr Professor salvaged Prometheus and carried the bronze into his bedroom for safety, though it was the least fragile thing in all the house. There was a sound of hammers below and the Herr Colonel's voice could be heard giving orders. The Herr Professor went back into his bedroom. He sat on the bed and read a little Schopenhauer to soothe himself.

It was some three-quarters of an hour later that the Herr Colonel found him there. He came briskly in, wearing regimental evening-dress, which made his legs thinner and longer than ever. 'Zero hour approaches,' he said, 'and we are all but ready. You would not recognize your house, Herr Professor. It is quite transformed. The Herr General will feel himself in a sunnier and more liberal clime. The musicians will play a pot-pourri of Strauss and Offenbach with a little of Lehar, which the Herr General finds more easy to recognize. I've seen to it that suitable paintings hang on the walls. You will realize when you come down and see the *salle privée* that this has been no ordinary military exercise. A care for detail marks a good soldier. Tonight, Herr Professor, your house has become a casino, by the Mediterranean. I had thought of masking the trees in some way, but there was no way of getting rid of the snow which continues to fall.'

'Astonishing,' the Herr Professor said. 'Quite astonishing.' From the distant summerhouse he could hear a melody from *La Belle Hélène*, and on the drive outside cars continually braked. He felt far from home as though he were living in a strange country.

'If you will excuse me,' he said, 'I will leave everything tonight in your hands. I hardly know the Herr General. I will have a sandwich quietly in my room.'

'Quite impossible,' the Herr Colonel said. 'You are the host. By this time the Herr General knows your name, although of course he hardly expects the sight which will greet . . . Ah, the guests are now beginning to arrive. I asked them to come early so that by the time the Herr General puts in his appearance everything will be in full swing, the wheels turning, the stakes laid, the croupiers calling . . . the field of battle stretched before him, *rouge et noir*. Come, Herr Professor, a little flutter at the tables – it is time for the two of us to open the ball.'

4

The road was treacherous under the thin and new-fallen snow; the bus from the capital proceeded at a pace no smarter than a practice-runner who is unwilling to strain a muscle before the great race. The patient's feet felt chilled even through his goloshes, or perhaps it was the cold of his errand, a fool's errand. There was a lot of traffic on the road that night: yellow taxis frequently passed the bus, and small sports-cars full of young men in uniform or evening-dress, laughing or singing, and once at a particularly imperious siren – which might have been that of a police-car or an ambulance – the bus slithered awkwardly to a stop beside the blue heaps of snow on the margin, and a large Mercedes went by; in it the patient saw an old man sitting stiffly upright with a long grey moustache which might have dated from the neutrality of 1914, wearing an old-fashioned uniform with a fur hat on his head, pulled down over his ears.

The patient alighted at a halt beside the road; the moon was nearly full, but he still required the pocket-torch which he carried with him to show the way through the woods: no headlights of cars helped him now on the private drive to the Herr Professor's house. As he walked through the loose snow at the edge of the road he tried to practise his final appeal. If that failed there was nothing for him but the hospital, unless he could summon enough courage to enter the icy water of the lake and never to return. He felt very little hope, and, for some reason that he could not understand, when he tried to visualize the Herr Professor at his desk – angry and impatient at this so late and unforeseen a visit – he could see only the half-spread wings of the bronze eagle and the jutting beak fastened in the intestines of the prisoner.

He pleaded in an undertone beneath the trees, 'There would be no danger to anyone at all, Herr Professor. I have always been a lonely man. I have no parents. My only sister died last year. I see no one, speak to no one except the clients in the bank. An occasional game of checkers in the café perhaps – that is all. I would cut myself off even further, Herr Professor, if you thought it wiser. As for the bank, I have always been in the habit of wearing gloves when I handle the notes – so many are filthy. I will take any precaution you suggest if you will go on treating me in private, Herr Professor. I am a law-abiding man, but surely the spirit is more important than the letter. I will abide by the spirit.'

The eagle gripped Prometheus with its unrelenting beak, and the patient said sadly as though to prevent the repetition of a phrase he could not bear to hear again, 'I don't like television, Herr Professor – it makes my eyes water, and I have never played golf.'

He halted under the trees, and a lump of snow from a burdened branch fell with a plomp upon his umbrella. It seemed very unlikely, but he thought that he heard strains of distant music borne on a gust of wind and borne away again. He even thought he recognized the melody, something from *La Vie Parisienne*, a waltz sounding for a moment from where the darkness and the snow lay all around. He had seen this place before only in daylight; the snow touched his face, and the stars crackled overhead between the firs; he felt as though he must have missed his path and entered a strange estate where perhaps a dance was in progress . . .

But when he reached the circular drive before the house he recognized the portico, the shape of the windows, the steep slope of the roof from which at intervals the snow slid with a crunch like the sound of a man eating apples. It was all that he could recognize, for he had never seen the house like this, ablaze with light and noisy with voices. Perhaps two neighbouring estates had been built by the same architect, and somehow in the wood he had taken the wrong turning. To make sure, he approached the windows, the hard snow breaking like biscuits under his goloshes.

Two young officers, who were obviously the worse for drink, staggered out from the open doorway. 'I have been betrayed by nineteen,' one of them said, 'that confounded nineteen.'

'And I by zero. I have been faithful to zero for an hour but not once . . .'

The first young man took a revolver from the holster at his side and waved it in the moonlight. 'All that is required now,' he said, 'is a suicide. The atmosphere is imperfect without one.'

'Be careful. It might be loaded.'

'It *is* loaded. Who is that man?'

'I don't know. The gardener probably. Don't fool about with that thing.'

'More bubbly is required,' the first man said. He tried to put his revolver back into the holster, but it slid down into the snow and he carefully secured the empty holster. 'More bubbly,' he repeated, 'before the dream fades.' They moved erratically back into the house. The dark object made a pocket in the snow.

The patient went up to the window, which should, if he had taken the right path, have been the window of the Herr Professor's study, but now he realized for certain that in the darkness he had come to the wrong house. Instead of a small square room with heavy desk and heavy bookcase and steel filing-cabinets was a long room brilliantly lit with cut-glass chandeliers, the walls hung with pictures of dubious taste – young women in diaphanous nightgowns leaning over waterfalls or paddling among water-lilies in a stooping position. A crowd of men wearing uniform and evening-dress swarmed around three roulette tables, and the croupiers' cries came thinly out into the night, *'Faites vos jeux, messieurs, faites vos jeux,'* while somewhere in the black garden an orchestra was playing 'The Blue Danube'. The patient stood motionless in the snow, with his face pressed to the glass, and he thought, The wrong house? But this is not the wrong house; it is the wrong country. He felt that he could never find his way home from here – it was too far away.

At one of the tables, on the right of the croupier, sat the old man whom he had seen pass in the Mercedes. One hand was playing with his moustache, the other with a pile of tokens before him, counting and rearranging them while the ball span and jumped and span, and one foot beat in time to the tune from *The Merry Widow*. A champagne cork from the bar shot diagonally up and struck the chandelier while the croupiers cried again, *'Faites vos jeux, messieurs,'* and the stem of a glass went crack in somebody's fingers.

Then the patient saw the Herr Professor standing with his back to the window at the other end of the great room, beyond the second chandelier, and they regarded each other, with the laughter and cries and glitter of light between them.

The Herr Professor could not properly see the patient – only the outline of a face pressed to the exterior of the pane, but the patient could see the Herr Professor very clearly between the tables, in the light of the chandelier. He could even see his expression, the lost look on his face like that of someone who has come to the wrong party. The patient raised his hand, as though to indicate to the other that he was lost too, but of course the Herr Professor could not see the gesture in the dark. The patient realized quite clearly that, though they had once been well known to each other, it was quite impossible for them to meet, in this house to which they had both strayed by some strange accident. There was no consulting-room here, no file on his case, no desk, no Prometheus, no doctor even to whom he could appeal. *'Faites vos jeux, messieurs,'* the croupiers cried, *'faites vos jeux.'*

5

The Herr Colonel said, 'My dear Herr Professor, after all, you are the host. You should at least lay one stake upon the table.' He took the Herr Professor by his sleeve and led him to the board where the Herr General sat, beating tip, tap, tip to the music of Lehar.

'The Herr Professor wishes to follow your fortune, Herr General.'

'I have little luck tonight, but let him . . .' and the General's fingers wove a design over the cloth. 'At the same time guard yourself with the zero.'

The ball span and jumped and span and came to rest. 'Zero,' the croupier announced and began to rake the other stakes in.

'At least you have not lost, Herr Professor,' the Herr General said. Somewhere far away behind the voices there was a faint explosion.

'The corks are popping,' the Herr Colonel said. 'Another glass of champagne, Herr General?'

'I had hoped it was a shot,' the Herr General said with a rather freezing smile. 'Ah, the old days . . . I remember once in Monte Carlo . . .'

The Herr Professor looked at the window, where he had thought a moment ago that someone looked in as lost as himself, but no one was there.

The News in English

Tonight Lord Haw-Haw of Zeesen was off the air.

All over England the new voice was noticed; precise and rather lifeless, it was the voice of a typical English don.

In his first broadcast he referred to himself as a man young enough to sympathize with what he called 'the resurgence of youth all over the new Germany', and that was the reason – combined with the pedantic tone – he was at once nicknamed Dr Funkhole.

It is the tragedy of such men that they are never alone in the world.

Old Mrs Bishop was knitting by the fire at her house in Crowborough when young Mrs Bishop tuned in to Zeesen. The sock was khaki: it was as if she had picked up at the point where she had dropped a stitch in 1918. The grim comfortable house stood in one of the long avenues, all spruce and laurel and a coating of snow, which are used to nothing but the footsteps of old retired people. Young Mrs Bishop never forgot that moment; the wind beating up across Ashdown Forest against the blacked-out window, and her mother-in-law happily knitting, and the sense of everything waiting for this moment. Then the voice came into the room from Zeesen in the middle of a sentence, and old Mrs Bishop said firmly, 'That's David.'

Young Mary Bishop made a hopeless protest – 'It can't be,' but she knew.

'I know my son if you don't know your husband.'

It seemed incredible that the man speaking couldn't hear them, that he should just go on, reiterating for the hundredth time the old lies, as if there were nobody anywhere in the world who knew him – a wife or a mother.

Old Mrs Bishop had stopped knitting. She said, 'Is that the man they've been writing about – Doctor Funkhole?'

'It must be.'

'It's David.'

The voice was extraordinarily convincing: he was going into exact engineering details – David Bishop had been a mathematics don at Oxford. Mary Bishop twisted the wireless off and sat down beside her mother-in-law.

'They'll want to know who it is,' Mrs Bishop said.

'We mustn't tell them,' said Mary.

The old fingers had begun on the khaki sock. She said, 'It's our duty.' Duty, it seemed to Mary Bishop, was a disease you caught with age: you ceased to feel the tug-tug of personal ties; you gave yourself up to the great tides of patriotism and hate. She said, 'They must have made him do it. We don't know what threats—'

'That's neither here nor there.'

She gave weakly in to hopeless wishes. 'If only he'd got away in time. I never wanted him to give that lecture course.'

'He always was stubborn,' said old Mrs Bishop.

'He said there wouldn't be a war.'

'Give me the telephone.'

'But you see what it means,' said Mary Bishop. 'He may be tried for treason if we win.'

'*When* we win,' old Mrs Bishop said.

The nickname was not altered, even after the interviews with the two Mrs Bishops, even after the sub-acid derogatory little article about David Bishop's previous career. It was suggested now that he had known all along that war was coming, that he had gone to Germany to evade military service, leaving his wife and his mother to be bombed. Mary Bishop fought, almost in vain, with the reporters for some recognition that he might have been forced – by threats or even physical violence. The most one paper would admit was that if threats had been used Bishop had taken a very unheroic way out. We praise heroes as though they are rare, and yet we are always ready to blame another man for lack of heroism. The name Dr Funkhole stuck.

But the worst of it to Mary Bishop was old Mrs Bishop's attitude. She turned a knife in the wound every evening at 9.15. The radio set must be tuned in to Zeesen, and there she sat listening to her son's voice and knitting socks for some unknown soldier on the Maginot Line. To young Mrs Bishop none of it made sense – least of all that flat, pedantic voice with its smooth, well-thought-out, elaborate lies. She was afraid to go out now into Crowborough: the whispers in the post office, the old faces watching her covertly in the library. Sometimes she thought almost with hatred, *why has David done this to me? Why?*

Then suddenly she got her answer.

The voice for once broke new ground. It said, 'Somewhere back in England my wife may be listening to me. I am a stranger to the rest of you, but she knows that I am not in the habit of lying.'

A personal appeal was too much. Mary Bishop had faced her mother-in-law and the reporters – she couldn't face her husband. She began to cry, sitting close beside the radio set like a child beside its doll's house when something has been broken in it which nobody can repair. She heard the voice of her husband speaking as if he were at her elbow from a country which was now as distant and as inaccessible as another planet.

'The fact of the matter is—'

The words came slowly out as if he were emphasizing a point in a lecture, and then he went on – to what would concern a wife. The low price of food, the quantity of meat in the shops. He went into great detail, giving figures, picking out odd, irrelevant things – like Mandarin oranges and toy zebras – perhaps to give an effect of richness and variety.

Suddenly Mary Bishop sat up with a jerk as if she had been asleep. She said, 'Oh, God, where's that pencil?' and upset one of the too many ornaments looking for one. Then she began to write, but in no time at all the voice was saying, 'Thank you for having listened to me so attentively,' and Zeesen had died out on the air. She said, 'Too late.'

'What's too late?' said old Mrs Bishop sharply. 'Why did you want a pencil?'

'Just an idea,' Mary Bishop said.

She was led next day up and down the cold, unheated corridors of a War Office in which half the rooms were empty, evacuated. Oddly enough, her relationship to David Bishop was of use to her now, if only because it evoked some curiosity and a little pity. But she no longer wanted the pity, and at last she reached the right man.

He listened to her with great politeness. He was not in uniform. His rather good tweeds made him look as if he had just come up from the country for a day or two, to attend to the war. When she had finished he said, 'It's rather a tall story, you know, Mrs Bishop. Of course it's been a great shock to you – this – well – action of your husband's.'

'I'm proud of it.'

'Just because in the old days you had this – scheme, you really believe—?'

'If he was away from me and he telephoned "The fact of the matter is," it always meant, "This is all lies, but take the initial letters which follow." ... Oh, Colonel, if you only knew the number of unhappy weekends I've saved him from – because, you see, he could always telephone to me, even in front of his host.' She said with tears in her voice, 'Then I'd send him a telegram...'

'Yes. But still – you didn't get anything this time, did you?'

'I was too late. I hadn't a pencil. I only got this – I know it doesn't seem to make sense.' She pushed the paper across. 'SOSPIC. I know it might easily be coincidence – that it does seem to make a kind of word.'

'An odd word.'

'Mightn't it be a man's name?'

The officer in tweeds was looking at it, she suddenly realized, with real interest – as if it was a rare kind of pheasant. He said, 'Excuse me a moment,' and left her. She could hear him telephoning to somebody from another room: the little ting of the bell, silence, and then a low voice she couldn't overhear. Then he returned, and she could tell at once from his face that all was well.

He sat down and fiddled with a fountain-pen – he was obviously embarrassed. He started a sentence and stopped it. Then he brought out in an embarrassed gulp, 'We'll have to apologize to your husband.'

'It meant something?'

He was obviously making his mind up about something difficult and out of the way – he was not in the habit of confiding in members of the public. But she had ceased to be a member of the public.

'My dear Mrs Bishop,' he said, 'I've got to ask a great deal from you.'

'Of course. Anything.'

He seemed to reach a decision and stopped fiddling. 'A neutral ship called the *Pic* was sunk this morning at 4.00 a.m., with a loss of two hundred lives. SOS *Pic*. If we'd had your husband's warning, we could have got destroyers to her in time. I've been speaking to the Admiralty.'

Mary Bishop said in a tone of fury, 'The things they are writing about David. Is there one of them who'd have the courage—?'

'That's the worst part of it, Mrs Bishop. They must go on writing. Nobody must know, except my department and yourself.'

'His mother?'

'You mustn't even tell her.'

'But can't you make them just leave him alone?'

'This afternoon I shall ask them to intensify their campaign – in order to discourage others. An article on the legal aspect of treason.'

'And if I refuse to keep quiet?'

'Your husband's life won't be worth much, will it?'

'So he's just got to go on?'

'Yes. Just go on.'

He went on for four weeks. Every night now she tuned in to Zeesen with a new horror – that he would be off the air. The code was a child's code. How could they fail to detect it? But they did fail. Men with complicated minds can be deceived by simplicity. And every night, too, she had to listen to her mother-in-law's indictment; every episode which she thought discreditable out of a child's past was brought out – the tiniest incident. Women in the last war had found a kind of pride in 'giving' their sons: this, too, was a gift on the altar of a warped patriotism. But now young Mrs Bishop didn't cry: she just held on – it was relief enough to hear his voice.

It wasn't often that he had information to give – the phrase 'the fact of the matter is' was a rare one in his talks. Sometimes there were the numbers of the regiments passing through Berlin, or of men on leave – very small details, which might be of value to military intelligence, but to her seemed hardly worth the risk of a life. If this was all he could do, why, why hadn't he allowed them simply to intern him?

At last she could bear it no longer. She visited the War Office again. The man in tweeds was still there, but this time for some reason he was wearing a black tail coat and a black stock as if he had been to a funeral. He must have been to a funeral, and she thought with more fear than ever of her husband.

'He's a brave man, Mrs Bishop,' he said.

'You needn't tell me that,' she cried bitterly.

'We shall see that he gets the highest possible decoration . . .'

'Decorations!'

'What do you want, Mrs Bishop? He's doing his duty.'

'So are other men. But they come home on leave. Sometime. He can't go on for ever. Soon they are bound to find out.'

'What can we do?'

'You can get him out of there. Hasn't he done enough for you?'

He said gently, 'It's beyond our power. How can we communicate with him?'

'Surely you have agents.'

'Two lives would be lost. Can't you imagine how they watch him?'

Yes. She could imagine all that clearly. She had spent too many holidays in Germany – as the Press had not failed to discover – not to know how men were watched, telephone lines tapped, table companions scrutinized.

He said, 'If there was some way we could get a message to him, it *might* be managed. We do owe him that.'

Young Mrs Bishop said quickly before he could change his mind, 'Well, the code works both ways. The fact of the matter is—! We have news broadcast in German. He might one day listen in.'

'Yes. There's a chance.'

She became privy to the plan because again they needed her help. They wanted to attract his notice first by some phrase peculiar to her. For years they had spoken German together on their annual holiday. That phrase was to be varied in every broadcast, and elaborately they worked out a series of messages which would convey to him the same instructions – to go to a certain station on the Cologne–Wesel line and contact there a railway worker who had already helped five men and two women to escape from Germany.

Mary Bishop felt she knew the place well – the small country station which probably served only a few dozen houses and a big hotel where people went in the old days for cures. The opportunity was offered him, if he could only take it, by an elaborate account of a railway accident at that point – so many people killed – sabotage – arrests. It was plugged in the news as relentlessly as the Germans repeated the news of false sinkings, and they answered indignantly back that there had been no accident.

It seemed more horrible than ever to Mary Bishop – those nightly broadcasts from Zeesen. The voice was in the room with her, and yet he couldn't know whether any message for which he risked his life reached home, and she couldn't know whether their message to him just petered out unheard or unrecognized.

Old Mrs Bishop said, 'Well, we can do without David tonight, I should hope.' It was a new turn in her bitterness – now she would simply wipe him off the air. Mary Bishop protested. She said she must hear – then at least she would know that he was well.

'It serves him right if he's not well.'

'I'm going to listen,' Mary Bishop persisted.

'Then I'll go out of the room. I'm tired of his lies.'

'You're his mother, aren't you?'

'That's not my fault. I didn't choose – like you did. I tell you I won't listen to it.'

Mary Bishop turned the knob. 'Then stop your ears,' she cried in a sudden fury, and heard David's voice coming over.

'The lies,' he was saying, 'put over by the British capitalist Press. There has not even been a railway accident – leave alone any sabotage – at the place so persistently mentioned in the broadcasts from England. Tomorrow I am leaving myself for the so-called scene of the accident, and I propose in my broadcast the day after tomorrow to give you an impartial observer's report, with records of the very railwaymen who are said to have been shot for sabotage. Tomorrow, therefore, I shall not be on the air . . .'

'Oh, thank God, thank God,' Mary Bishop said.

The old woman grumbled by the fire. 'You haven't much to thank Him for.'

All next day she found herself praying, although she didn't much believe in prayer. She visualized that station 'on the Rhine not far from Wesel' – and not far either from the Dutch frontier. There must be some method of getting across – with the help of that unknown worker – possibly in a refrigerating van. No idea was too fantastic to be true. Others had succeeded before him.

All through the day she tried to keep pace with him – he would have to leave early, and she imagined his cup of ersatz coffee and the slow wartime train taking him south and west. She thought of his fear and of his excitement – he was coming home to her. Ah, when he landed safely, what a day that would be! The papers then would have to eat their words – no more Dr Funkhole and no more of this place, side by side with his unloving mother.

At midday, she thought, he has arrived: he has his black discs with him to record the men's voices, he is probably watched, but he will find his chance – and now he is not alone. He has someone with him helping him. In one way or another he will miss his train home. The freight train will draw in – perhaps a signal will stop it outside the station. She saw it all so vividly, as the early winter dark came down and she blacked the windows out, that she found herself thankful he possessed, as she knew, a white mackintosh. He would be less visible waiting there in the snow.

Her imagination took wings, and by dinnertime she felt sure that he was already on the way to the frontier. That night there was no broadcast from Dr Funkhole, and she sang as she bathed and old Mrs Bishop beat furiously on her bedroom floor above.

In bed she could almost feel herself vibrating with the heavy movement of *his* train. She saw the landscape going by outside – there must be a crack in any van in which he lay hid, so that he could mark the distances. It was very much the landscape of Crowborough – spruces powdered with snow, the wide dreary waste they called a forest, dark avenues – she fell asleep.

When she woke she was still happy. Perhaps before night she would receive a cable from Holland, but if it didn't come she would not be anxious because so many things in wartime might delay it. It didn't come.

That night she made no attempt to turn on the radio, so old Mrs Bishop changed her tactics again. 'Well,' she said, 'aren't you going to listen to your husband?'

'He won't be broadcasting.' Very soon now she could turn on his mother in triumph and say, *There, I knew it all the time, my husband's a hero*.

'That was last night.'

'He won't be broadcasting again.'

'What do you mean? Turn it on and let me hear.'

There was no harm in proving that she knew – she turned it on.

A voice was talking in German – something about an accident and English lies, she didn't bother to listen. She felt too happy. 'There,' she said, 'I told you. It's not David.'

And then David spoke.

He said, 'You have been listening to the actual voices of the men your English broadcasters have told you were shot by the German police. Perhaps now you will be less inclined to believe the exaggerated stories you hear of life inside Germany today.'

'There,' old Mrs Bishop said, 'I told you.'

And all the world, she thought, *will go on telling me now, for ever – Dr Funkhole. He never got those messages. He's there for keeps.* David's voice said with curious haste and harshness, 'The fact of the matter is—'

He spoke rapidly for about two minutes as if he were afraid they would fade him at any moment, and yet it sounded harmless enough – the old stories about plentiful food and how much you could buy for an English pound – figures. But some of the examples this time, she thought with dread, are surely so fantastic that even the German brain will realize something is wrong. How had he ever dared to show this copy to his chiefs?

She could hardly keep pace with her pencil, so rapidly did he speak. The words grouped themselves on her pad: *Five U's refuelling hodie noon 53.23 by 10.5. News reliable source Wesel so returned. Talk unauthorized. The end.*

'This order. Many young wives I feel enjoy giving one' – he hesitated – 'one's day's butter in every dozen –' the voice faded, gave out altogether. She saw on her pad: *To my wife, goodbye d—*

The end, goodbye, the end – the words rang on like funeral bells. She began to cry, sitting as she had done before, close up against the radio set. Old Mrs Bishop said with a kind of delight, 'He ought never to have been born. I never wanted him. The coward,' and now Mary Bishop could stand no more of it.

'Oh,' she cried to her mother-in-law across the little overheated over-furnished Crowborough room, 'if only he were a coward, if only he were. But he's a hero, a damned hero, a hero, a hero—' she cried hopelessly on, feeling the room reel round her, and dimly supposing behind all the pain and horror that one day she would have to feel, like other women, pride.

*The End of
the Party*

*The Case for
the Defence*

The End of the Party

Peter Morton woke with a start to face the first light. Rain tapped against the glass. It was January the fifth.

He looked across a table on which a night-light had guttered into a pool of water, at the other bed. Francis Morton was still asleep, and Peter lay down again with his eyes on his brother. It amused him to imagine it was himself whom he watched, the same hair, the same eyes, the same lips and line of cheek. But the thought palled, and the mind went back to the fact which lent the day importance. It was the fifth of January. He could hardly believe a year had passed since Mrs Henne-Falcon had given her last children's party.

Francis turned suddenly upon his back and threw an arm across his face, blocking his mouth. Peter's heart began to beat fast, not with pleasure now but with uneasiness. He sat up and called across the table, 'Wake up.' Francis's shoulders shook and he waved a clenched fist in the air, but his eyes remained closed. To Peter Morton the whole room seemed to darken, and he had the impression of a great bird swooping. He cried again, 'Wake up,' and once more there was silver light and the touch of rain on the windows. Francis rubbed his eyes. 'Did you call out?' he asked.

'You are having a bad dream,' Peter said. Already experience had taught him how far their minds reflected each other. But he was the elder, by a matter of minutes, and that brief extra interval of light, while his brother still struggled in pain and darkness, had given him self-reliance and an instinct of protection towards the other who was afraid of so many things.

'I dreamed that I was dead,' Francis said.

'What was it like?' Peter asked.

'I can't remember,' Francis said.

'You dreamed of a big bird.'

'Did I?'

The two lay silent in bed facing each other, the same green eyes, the same nose tilting at the tip, the same firm lips, and the same premature modelling of the chin. The fifth of January, Peter thought again, his mind drifting idly from the image of cakes to the prizes which might be won. Egg-and-spoon races, spearing apples in basins of water, blind man's buff.

'I don't want to go,' Francis said suddenly. 'I suppose Joyce will be there . . . Mabel Warren.' Hateful to him, the thought of a party shared with those two. They were older than he. Joyce was eleven and Mabel Warren thirteen. The long pigtails swung superciliously to a masculine stride. Their sex humiliated him, as they watched him fumble with his egg, from under lowered scornful lids. And last year . . . he turned his face away from Peter, his cheeks scarlet.

'What's the matter?' Peter asked.

'Oh, nothing. I don't think I'm well. I've got a cold. I oughtn't to go to the party.' Peter was puzzled. 'But Francis, is it a bad cold?'

'It will be a bad cold if I go to the party. Perhaps I shall die.'

'Then you mustn't go,' Peter said, prepared to solve all difficulties with one plain sentence, and Francis let his nerves relax, ready to leave everything to Peter. But though he was grateful he did not turn his face towards his brother. His cheeks still bore the badge of a shameful memory, of the game of hide and seek last year in the darkened house, and of how he had screamed when Mabel Warren put her hand suddenly upon his arm. He had not heard her coming. Girls were like that. Their shoes never squeaked. No boards whined under the tread. They slunk like cats on padded claws.

When the nurse came in with hot water Francis lay tranquil leaving everything to Peter. Peter said, 'Nurse, Francis has got a cold.'

The tall starched woman laid the towels across the cans and said, without turning, 'The washing won't be back till tomorrow. You must lend him some of your handkerchiefs.'

'But, Nurse,' Peter asked, 'hadn't he better stay in bed?'

'We'll take him for a good walk this morning,' the nurse said. 'Wind'll blow away the germs. Get up now, both of you,' and she closed the door behind her.

'I'm sorry,' Peter said. 'Why don't you just stay in bed? I'll tell mother you felt too ill to get up.' But rebellion against destiny was not in Francis's power. If he stayed in bed they would come up and tap his chest and put a thermometer in his mouth and look at his tongue, and they would discover he was malingering. It was true he felt ill, a sick empty sensation in his stomach and a rapidly beating heart, but he knew the cause was only fear, fear of the party, fear of being made to hide by himself in the dark, uncompanioned by Peter and with no night-light to make a blessed breach.

'No, I'll get up,' he said, and then with sudden desperation, 'But I won't go to Mrs Henne-Falcon's party. I swear on the Bible I won't.' Now surely all would be well, he thought. God would not allow him to break so solemn an oath. He would show him a way. There was all the morning before him and all the afternoon until four o'clock. No need to worry when the grass was still crisp with the early frost. Anything might happen. He might cut himself or break his leg or really catch a bad cold. God would manage somehow.

He had such confidence in God that when at breakfast his mother said, 'I hear you have a cold, Francis,' he made light of it. 'We should have heard more about it,' his mother said with irony, 'if there was not a party this evening,' and Francis smiled, amazed and daunted by her ignorance of him. His happiness would have lasted longer if, out for a walk that morning, he had not met Joyce. He was alone with his nurse, for Peter had leave to finish a rabbit-hutch in the woodshed. If Peter had been there he would have cared less; the nurse was Peter's nurse also, but now it was as though she were employed only for his sake, because he could not be trusted to go for a walk alone. Joyce was only two years older and she was by herself.

She came striding towards them, pigtails flapping. She glanced scornfully at Francis and spoke with ostentation to the nurse. 'Hello, Nurse. Are you bringing Francis to the party this evening? Mabel and I are coming.' And she was off again down the street in the direction of Mabel Warren's home, consciously alone and self-sufficient in the long empty road. 'Such a nice girl,' the nurse said. But Francis was silent, feeling again the jump-jump of his heart, realizing how soon the hour of the party would arrive. God had done nothing for him, and the minutes flew.

They flew too quickly to plan any evasion, or even to prepare his heart for the coming ordeal. Panic nearly overcame him when, all unready, he found himself standing on the doorstep, with coat-collar turned up against a cold wind, and the nurse's electric torch making a short trail through the darkness. Behind him were the lights of the hall and the sound of a servant laying the table for dinner, which his mother and father would eat alone. He was nearly overcome by the desire to run back into the house and call out to his mother that he would not go to the party, that he dared not go. They could not make him go. He could almost hear himself saying those final words, breaking down for ever the barrier of ignorance which saved his mind from his parents' knowledge. 'I'm afraid of going. I won't go. I daren't go. They'll make me hide in the dark, and I'm afraid of the dark. I'll scream and scream and scream.' He could see the expression of amazement on his mother's face, and then the cold confidence of a grown-up's retort.

'Don't be silly. You must go. We've accepted Mrs Henne-Falcon's invitation.' But they couldn't make him go; hesitating on the doorstep while the nurse's feet crunched across the frost-covered grass to the gate, he knew that. He would answer: 'You can say I'm ill. I won't go. I'm afraid of the dark.' And his mother: 'Don't be silly. You know there's nothing to be afraid of in the dark.' But he knew the falsity of that reasoning; he knew how they taught also that there was nothing to fear in death, and how fearfully they avoided the idea of it. But they couldn't make him go to the party. 'I'll scream. I'll scream.'

'Francis, come along.' He heard the nurse's voice across the dimly phosphorescent lawn and saw the yellow circle of her torch wheel from tree to shrub. 'I'm coming,' he called with despair; he couldn't bring himself to lay bare his last secrets and end reserve between his mother and himself, for there was still in the last resort a further appeal possible to Mrs Henne-Falcon. He comforted himself with that, as he advanced steadily across the hall, very small, towards her enormous bulk. His heart beat unevenly, but he had control now over his voice, as he said with meticulous accent, 'Good evening, Mrs Henne-Falcon. It was very good of you to ask me to your party.' With his strained face lifted towards the curve of her breasts, and his polite set speech, he was like an old withered man. As a twin he was in many ways an only child. To address Peter was to speak to his own image in a mirror, an image a little altered by a flaw in the glass, so as to throw back less a likeness of what he was than of what he wished to be, what he would be without his unreasoning fear of darkness, footsteps of strangers, the flight of bats in dusk-filled gardens.

'Sweet child,' said Mrs Henne-Falcon absent-mindedly, before, with a wave of her arms, as though the children were a flock of chickens, she whirled them into her set programme of entertainments: egg-and-spoon races, three-legged races, the spearing of apples, games which held for Francis nothing worse than humiliation. And in the frequent intervals when nothing was required of him and he could stand alone in corners as far removed as possible from Mabel Warren's scornful gaze, he was able to plan how he might avoid the approaching terror of the dark. He knew there was nothing to fear until after tea, and not until he was sitting down in a pool of yellow radiance cast by the ten candles on Colin Henne-Falcon's birthday cake did he become fully conscious of the imminence of what he feared. He heard Joyce's high voice down the table, 'After tea we are going to play hide and seek in the dark.'

'Oh, no,' Peter said, watching Francis's troubled face, 'don't let's. We play that every year.'

'But it's in the programme,' cried Mabel Warren. 'I saw it myself. I looked over Mrs Henne-Falcon's shoulder. Five o'clock tea. A quarter to six to half past, hide and seek in the dark. It's all written down in the programme.'

Peter did not argue, for if hide and seek had been inserted in Mrs Henne-Falcon's programme, nothing which he could say would avert it. He asked for another piece of birthday cake and sipped his tea slowly. Perhaps it might be possible to delay the game for a quarter of an hour, allow Francis at least a few extra minutes to form a plan, but even in that Peter failed, for children were already leaving the table in twos and threes. It was his third failure, and again he saw a great bird darken his brother's face with its wings. But he upbraided himself silently for his folly, and finished his cake encouraged by the memory of that adult refrain, 'There's nothing to fear in the dark.' The last to leave the table, the brothers came together to the hall to meet the mustering and impatient eyes of Mrs Henne-Falcon.

'And now,' she said, 'we will play hide and seek in the dark.'

Peter watched his brother and saw the lips tighten. Francis, he knew, had feared this moment from the beginning of the party, had tried to meet it with courage and had abandoned the attempt. He must have prayed for cunning to evade the game, which was now welcomed with cries of excitement by all the other children. 'Oh, do let's.' 'We must pick sides.' 'Is any of the house out of bounds?' 'Where shall home be?'

'I think,' said Francis Morton, approaching Mrs Henne-Falcon, his eyes focused unwaveringly on her exuberant breasts, 'it will be no use my playing. My nurse will be calling for me very soon.'

'Oh, but your nurse can wait, Francis,' said Mrs Henne-Falcon, while she clapped her hands together to summon to her side a few children who were already straying up the wide staircase to upper floors. 'Your mother will never mind.'

That had been the limit of Francis's cunning. He had refused to believe that so well-prepared an excuse could fail. All that he could say now, still in the precise tone which other children hated, thinking it a symbol of conceit, was, 'I think I had better not play.' He stood motionless, retaining, though afraid, unmoved features. But the knowledge of his terror, or the reflection of the terror itself, reached his brother's brain. For the moment, Peter Morton could have cried aloud with the fear of bright lights going out, leaving him alone in an island of dark surrounded by the gentle lappings of strange footsteps. Then he remembered that the fear was not his own, but his brother's. He said impulsively to Mrs Henne-Falcon, 'Please, I don't think Francis should play. The dark makes him jump so.' They were the wrong words. Six children began to sing, 'Cowardy cowardy custard,' turning torturing faces with the vacancy of wide sunflowers towards Francis Morton.

Without looking at his brother, Francis said, 'Of course I'll play. I'm not afraid, I only thought . . .' But he was already forgotten by his human tormentors. The children scrambled round Mrs Henne-Falcon, their shrill voices pecking at her with questions and suggestions. 'Yes, anywhere in the house. We will turn out all the lights. Yes, you can hide in the cupboards. You must stay hidden as long as you can. There will be no home.'

Peter stood apart, ashamed of the clumsy manner in which he had tried to help his brother. Now he could feel, creeping in at the corners of his brain, all Francis's resentment of his championing. Several children ran upstairs, and the lights on the top floor went out. Darkness came down like the wings of a bat and settled on the landing. Others began to put out the lights at the edge of the hall, till the children were all gathered in the central radiance of the chandelier, while the bats squatted round on hooded wings and waited for that, too, to be extinguished.

'You and Francis are on the hiding side,' a tall girl said, and then the light was gone, and the carpet wavered under his feet with the sibilance of footfalls, like small cold draughts, creeping away into corners.

'Where's Francis?' he wondered. 'If I join him he'll be less frightened of all these sounds.' 'These sounds' were the casing of silence: the squeak of a loose board, the cautious closing of a cupboard door, the whine of a finger drawn along polished wood.

Peter stood in the centre of the dark deserted floor, not listening but waiting for the idea of his brother's whereabouts to enter his brain. But Francis crouched with fingers on his ears, eyes uselessly closed, mind numbed against impressions, and only a sense of strain could cross the gap of dark. Then a voice called 'Coming,' and as though his brother's self-possession had been shattered by the sudden cry, Peter Morton jumped with his fear. But it was not his own fear. What in his brother was a burning panic was in him an altruistic emotion that left the reason unimpaired. 'Where, if I were Francis, should I hide?' And because he was, if not Francis himself, at least a mirror to him, the answer was immediate. 'Between the oak book-case on the left of the study door, and the leather settee.' Between the twins there could be no jargon of telepathy. They had been together in the womb, and they could not be parted.

Peter Morton tiptoed towards Francis's hiding-place. Occasionally a board rattled, and because he feared to be caught by one of the soft questers through the dark, he bent and untied his laces. A tag struck the floor and the metallic sound set a host of cautious feet moving in his direction. But by that time he was in his stockings and would have laughed inwardly at the pursuit had not the noise of someone stumbling on his abandoned shoes made his heart trip. No more boards revealed Peter Morton's progress. On stockinged feet he moved silently and unerringly towards his object. Instinct told him he was near the wall, and, extending a hand, he laid the fingers across his brother's face.

Francis did not cry out, but the leap of his own heart revealed to Peter a proportion of Francis's terror. 'It's all right,' he whispered, feeling down the squatting figure until he captured a clenched hand. 'It's only me. I'll stay with you.' And grasping the other tightly, he listened to the cascade of whispers his utterance had caused to fall. A hand touched the book-case close to Peter's head and he was aware of how Francis's fear continued in spite of his presence. It was less intense, more bearable, he hoped, but it remained. He knew that it was his brother's fear and not his own that he experienced. The dark to him was only an absence of light; the groping hand that of a familiar child. Patiently he waited to be found.

He did not speak again, for between Francis and himself was the most intimate communion. By way of joined hands thought could flow more swiftly than lips could shape themselves round words. He could experience the whole progress of his brother's emotion, from the leap of panic at the unexpected contact to the steady pulse of fear, which now went on and on with the regularity of a heart-beat. Peter Morton thought with intensity, 'I am here. You needn't be afraid. The lights will go on again soon. That rustle, that movement is nothing to fear. Only Joyce, only Mabel Warren.' He bombarded the drooping form with thoughts of safety, but he was conscious that the fear continued. 'They are beginning to whisper together. They are tired of looking for us. The lights will go on soon. We shall have won. Don't be afraid. That was someone on the stairs. I believe it's Mrs Henne-Falcon. Listen. They are feeling for the lights.' Feet moving on a carpet, hands brushing a wall, a curtain pulled apart, a clicking handle, the opening of a cupboard door. In the case above their heads a loose book shifted under a touch. 'Only Joyce, only Mabel Warren, only Mrs Henne-Falcon,' a crescendo of reassuring thought before the chandelier burst, like a fruit-tree, into bloom.

The voices of the children rose shrilly into the radiance. 'Where's Peter?' 'Have you looked upstairs?' 'Where's Francis?' but they were silenced again by Mrs Henne-Falcon's scream. But she was not the first to notice Francis Morton's stillness, where he had collapsed against the wall at the touch of his brother's hand. Peter continued to hold the clenched fingers in an arid and puzzled grief. It was not merely that his brother was dead. His brain, too young to realize the full paradox, wondered with an obscure self-pity why it was that the pulse of his brother's fear went on and on, when Francis was now where he had always been told there was no more terror and no more darkness.

The Case for the Defence

It was the strangest murder trial I ever attended. They named it the Peckham murder in the headlines, though Northwood Street, where the old woman was found battered to death, was not strictly speaking in Peckham. This was not one of those cases of circumstantial evidence in which you feel the jurymen's anxiety – because mistakes *have* been made – like domes of silence muting the court. No, this murderer was all but found with the body; no one present when the Crown counsel outlined his case believed that the man in the dock stood any chance at all.

He was a heavy stout man with bulging bloodshot eyes. All his muscles seemed to be in his thighs. Yes, an ugly customer, one you wouldn't forget in a hurry – and that was an important point because the Crown proposed to call four witnesses who hadn't forgotten him, who had seen him hurrying away from the little red villa in Northwood Street. The clock had just struck two in the morning.

Mrs Salmon in 15 Northwood Street had been unable to sleep; she heard a door click shut and thought it was her own gate. So she went to the window and saw Adams (that was his name) on the steps of Mrs Parker's house. He had just come out and he was wearing gloves. He had a hammer in his hand and she saw him drop it into the laurel bushes by the front gate. But before he moved away, he had looked up – at her window. The fatal instinct that tells a man when he is watched exposed him in the light of a street-lamp to her gaze – his eyes suffused with horrifying and brutal fear, like an animal's when you raise a whip. I talked afterwards to Mrs Salmon, who naturally after the astonishing verdict went in fear herself. As I imagine did all the witnesses – Henry MacDougall, who had been driving home from Benfleet late and nearly ran Adams down at the corner of Northwood Street. Adams was walking in the middle of the road looking dazed. And old Mr Wheeler, who lived next door to Mrs Parker, at No. 12, and was wakened by a noise – like a chair falling – through the thin-as-paper villa wall, and got up and looked out of the window, just as Mrs Salmon had done, saw Adams's back and, as he turned, those bulging eyes. In Laurel Avenue he had been seen by yet another witness – his luck was badly out; he might as well have committed the crime in broad daylight.

'I understand,' counsel said, 'that the defence proposes to plead mistaken identity. Adams's wife will tell you that he was with her at two in the morning on February 14, but after you have heard the witnesses for the Crown and examined carefully the features of the prisoner, I do not think you will be prepared to admit the possibility of a mistake.'

It was all over, you would have said, but the hanging.

After the formal evidence had been given by the policeman who had found the body and the surgeon who examined it, Mrs Salmon was called. She was the ideal witness, with her slight Scotch accent and her expression of honesty, care and kindness.

The counsel for the Crown brought the story gently out. She spoke very firmly. There was no malice in her, and no sense of importance at standing there in the Central Criminal Court with a judge in scarlet hanging on her words and the reporters writing them down. Yes, she said, and then she had gone downstairs and rung up the police station.

'And do you see the man here in court?'

She looked straight at the big man in the dock, who stared hard at her with his pekingese eyes without emotion.

'Yes,' she said, 'there he is.'

'You are quite certain?'

She said simply, 'I couldn't be mistaken, sir.'

It was all as easy as that.

'Thank you, Mrs Salmon.'

Counsel for the defence rose to cross-examine. If you had reported as many murder trials as I have, you would have known beforehand what line he would take. And I was right, up to a point.

'Now, Mrs Salmon, you must remember that a man's life may depend on your evidence.'

'I do remember it, sir.'

'Is your eyesight good?'

'I have never had to wear spectacles, sir.'

'You are a woman of fifty-five?'

'Fifty-six, sir.'

'And the man you saw was on the other side of the road?'

'Yes, sir.'

'And it was two o'clock in the morning. You must have remarkable eyes, Mrs Salmon?'

'No, sir. There was moonlight, and when the man looked up, he had the lamplight on his face.'

'And you have no doubt whatever that the man you saw is the prisoner?'

I couldn't make out what he was at. He couldn't have expected any other answer than the one he got.

'None whatever, sir. It isn't a face one forgets.'

Counsel took a look round the court for a moment. Then he said, 'Do you mind, Mrs Salmon, examining again the people in court? No, not the prisoner. Stand up, please, Mr Adams,' and there at the back of the court with thick stout body and muscular legs and a pair of bulging eyes, was the exact image of the man in the dock. He was even dressed the same – tight blue suit and striped tie.

'Now think very carefully, Mrs Salmon. Can you still swear that the man you saw drop the hammer in Mrs Parker's garden was the prisoner – and not this man, who is his twin brother?'

Of course she couldn't. She looked from one to the other and didn't say a word.

There the big brute sat in the dock with his legs crossed, and there he stood too at the back of the court and they both stared at Mrs Salmon. She shook her head.

What we saw then was the end of the case. There wasn't a witness prepared to swear that it was the prisoner he'd seen. And the brother? He had his alibi, too; he was with his wife.

And so the man was acquitted for lack of evidence. But whether – if he did the murder and not his brother – he was punished or not, I don't know. That extraordinary day had an extraordinary end. I followed Mrs Salmon out of court and we got wedged in the crowd who were waiting, of course, for the twins. The police tried to drive the crowd away, but all they could do was keep the road-way clear for traffic. I learned later that they tried to get the twins to leave by a back way, but they wouldn't. One of them – no one knew which – said, 'I've been acquitted, haven't I?' and they walked bang out of the front entrance. Then it happened. I don't know how, though I was only six feet away. The crowd moved and somehow one of the twins got pushed on to the road right in front of a bus.

He gave a squeal like a rabbit and that was all; he was dead, his skull smashed just as Mrs Parker's had been. Divine vengeance? I wish I knew. There was the other Adams getting on his feet from beside the body and looking straight over at Mrs Salmon. He was crying, but whether he was the murderer or the innocent man nobody will ever be able to tell. But if you were Mrs Salmon, could you sleep at night?

The Basement Room

A Day Saved

The Basement Room

1

When the front door had shut the two of them out and the butler Baines had turned back into the dark and heavy hall, Philip began to live. He stood in front of the nursery door, listening until he heard the engine of the taxi die out along the street. His parents were safely gone for a fortnight's holiday; he was 'between nurses', one dismissed and the other not arrived; he was alone in the great Belgravia house with Baines and Mrs Baines.

He could go anywhere, even through the green baize door to the pantry or down the stairs to the basement living-room. He felt a happy stranger in his home because he could go into any room and all the rooms were empty.

You could only guess who had once occupied them: the rack of pipes in the smoking-room beside the elephant tusks, the carved wood tobacco jar; in the bedroom the pink hangings and the pale perfumes and three-quarter finished jars of cream which Mrs Baines had not yet cleared away for her own use; the high glaze on the never-opened piano in the drawing-room, the china clock, the silly little tables and the silver. But here Mrs Baines was already busy, pulling down the curtains, covering the chairs in dust-sheets.

'Be off out of here, Master Philip,' and she looked at him with her peevish eyes, while she moved round, getting everything in order, meticulous and loveless and doing her duty.

Philip Lane went downstairs and pushed at the baize door; he looked into the pantry, but Baines was not there, then he set foot for the first time on the stairs to the basement. Again he had the sense: this is life. All his seven nursery years vibrated with the strange, the new experience. His crowded brain was like a city which feels the earth tremble at a distant earthquake shock. He was apprehensive, but he was happier than he had ever been. Everything was more important than before.

Baines was reading a newspaper in his shirt-sleeves. He said, 'Come in, Phil, and make yourself at home. Wait a moment and I'll do the honours,' and going to a white cleaned cupboard he brought out a bottle of ginger-beer and half a Dundee cake. 'Half past eleven in the morning,' Baines said. 'It's opening time, my boy,' and he cut the cake and poured out the ginger-beer. He was more genial than Philip had ever known him, more at his ease, a man in his own home.

'Shall I call Mrs Baines?' Philip asked, and he was glad when Baines said no. She was busy. She liked to be busy, so why interfere with her pleasure?

'A spot of drink at half past eleven,' Baines said, pouring himself out a glass of ginger-beer, 'gives an appetite for chop and does no man any harm.'

'A chop?' Philip asked.

'Old Coasters,' Baines said, 'they call all food chop.'

'But it's not a chop?'

'Well, it might be, you know, if cooked with palm oil. And then some paw-paw to follow.'

Philip looked out of the basement window at the dry stone yard, the ash-can and the legs going up and down beyond the railings.

'Was it hot there?'

'Ah, you never felt such heat. Not a nice heat, mind, like you get in the park on a day like this. Wet,' Baines said, 'corruption.' He cut himself a slice of cake. 'Smelling of rot,' Baines said, rolling his eyes round the small basement room, from clean cupboard to clean cupboard, the sense of bareness, of nowhere to hide a man's secrets. With an air of regret for something lost he took a long draught of ginger-beer.

'Why did father live out there?'

'It was his job,' Baines said, 'same as this is mine now. And it was mine then too. It was a man's job. You wouldn't believe it now, but I've had forty niggers under me, doing what I told them to.'

'Why did you leave?'

'I married Mrs Baines.'

Philip took the slice of Dundee cake in his hand and munched it round the room. He felt very old, independent and judicial; he was aware that Baines was talking to him as man to man. He never called him Master Philip as Mrs Baines did, who was servile when she was not authoritative.

Baines had seen the world; he had seen beyond the railings. He sat there over his ginger pop with the resigned dignity of an exile; Baines didn't complain; he had chosen his fate, and if his fate was Mrs Baines he had only himself to blame.

But today – the house was almost empty and Mrs Baines was upstairs and there was nothing to do – he allowed himself a little acidity.

'I'd go back tomorrow if I had the chance.'

'Did you ever shoot a nigger?'

'I never had any call to shoot,' Baines said. 'Of course I carried a gun. But you didn't need to treat them bad. That just made them stupid. Why,' Baines said, bowing his thin grey hair with embarrassment over the ginger pop, 'I loved some of those damned niggers. I couldn't help loving them. There they'd be laughing, holding hands; they liked to touch each other; it made them feel fine to know the other fellow was around. It didn't mean anything we could understand; two of them would go about all day without loosing hold, grown men; but it wasn't love; it didn't mean anything we could understand.'

'Eating between meals,' Mrs Baines said. 'What would your mother say, Master Philip?'

She came down the steep stairs to the basement, her hands full of pots of cream and salve, tubes of grease and paste. 'You oughtn't to encourage him, Baines,' she said, sitting down in a wicker armchair and screwing up her small ill-humoured eyes at the Coty lipstick, Pond's cream, the Leichner rouge and Cyclax powder and Elizabeth Arden astringent.

She threw them one by one into the wastepaper basket. She saved only the cold cream. 'Tell the boy stories,' she said. 'Go along to the nursery, Master Philip, while I get lunch.'

Philip climbed the stairs to the baize door. He heard Mrs Baines's voice like the voice in a nightmare when the small Price light has guttered in the saucer and the curtains move; it was sharp and shrill and full of malice, louder than people ought to speak, exposed.

'Sick to death of your ways, Baines, spoiling the boy. Time you did some work about the house,' but he couldn't hear what Baines said in reply. He pushed open the baize door, came up like a small earth animal in his grey flannel shorts into a wash of sunlight on a parquet floor, the gleam of mirrors dusted and polished and beautified by Mrs Baines.

Something broke downstairs, and Philip sadly mounted the stairs to the nursery. He pitied Baines; it occurred to him how happily they could live together in the empty house if Mrs Baines were called away. He didn't want to play with his Meccano sets; he wouldn't take out his train or his soldiers; he sat at the table with his chin on his hands: this is life; and suddenly he felt responsible for Baines, as if he were the master of the house and Baines an ageing servant who deserved to be cared for. There was not much one could do; he decided at least to be good.

He was not surprised when Mrs Baines was agreeable at lunch; he was used to her changes. Now it was 'another helping of meat, Master Philip', or 'Master Philip, a little more of this nice pudding'. It was a pudding he liked, Queen's pudding with a perfect meringue, but he wouldn't eat a second helping lest she might count that a victory. She was the kind of woman who thought that any injustice could be counterbalanced by something good to eat.

She was sour, but she liked making sweet things; one never had to complain of a lack of jam or plums; she ate well herself and added soft sugar to the meringue and the strawberry jam. The half-light through the basement window set the motes moving above her pale hair like dust as she sifted the sugar, and Baines crouched over his plate saying nothing.

Again Philip felt responsibility. Baines had looked forward to this, and Baines was disappointed: everything was being spoilt. The sensation of disappointment was one which Philip could share; he could understand better than anyone this grief, something hoped for not happening, something promised not fulfilled, something exciting which turned dull. 'Baines,' he said, 'will you take me for a walk this afternoon?'

'No,' Mrs Baines said, 'no. That he won't. Not with all the silver to clean.'

'There's a fortnight to do it in,' Baines said.

'Work first, pleasure afterwards.'

Mrs Baines helped herself to some more meringue.

Baines put down his spoon and fork and pushed his plate away. 'Blast,' he said.

'Temper,' Mrs Baines said, 'temper. Don't you go breaking any more things, Baines, and I won't have you swearing in front of the boy. Master Philip, if you've finished you can get down.'

She skinned the rest of the meringue off the pudding.

'I want to go for a walk,' Philip said.

'You'll go and have a rest.'

'I want to go for a walk.'

'Master Philip,' Mrs Baines said. She got up from the table, leaving her meringue unfinished, and came towards him, thin, menacing, dusty in the basement room. 'Master Philip, you just do as you're told.' She took him by the arm and squeezed it; she watched him with a joyless passionate glitter and above her head the feet of typists trudged back to the Victoria offices after the lunch interval.

'Why shouldn't I go for a walk?'

But he weakened; he was scared and ashamed of being scared. This was life; a strange passion he couldn't understand moving in the basement room. He saw a small pile of broken glass swept into a corner by the wastepaper basket. He looked at Baines for help and only intercepted hate; the sad hopeless hate of something behind bars.

'Why shouldn't I?' he repeated.

'Master Philip,' Mrs Baines said, 'you've got to do as you're told. You mustn't think just because your father's away there's nobody here to—'

'You wouldn't dare,' Philip cried, and was startled by Baines's low interjection:

'There's nothing she wouldn't dare.'

'I hate you,' Philip said to Mrs Baines. He pulled away from her and ran to the door, but she was there before him; she was old, but she was quick.

'Master Philip,' she said, 'you'll say you're sorry.' She stood in front of the door quivering with excitement. 'What would your father do if he heard you say that?'

She put a hand out to seize him, dry and white with constant soda, the nails cut to the quick, but he backed away and put the table between them, and suddenly to his surprise she smiled; she became again as servile as she had been arrogant. 'Get along with you, Master Philip,' she said with glee, 'I see I'm going to have my hands full till your father and mother come back.'

She left the door unguarded and when he passed her she slapped him playfully. 'I've got too much to do today to trouble about you. I haven't covered half the chairs,' and suddenly even the upper part of the house became unbearable to him as he thought of Mrs Baines moving around shrouding the sofas, laying out the dust-sheets.

So he wouldn't go upstairs to get his cap but walked straight out across the shining hall into the street, and again, as he looked this way and looked that way, it was life he was in the middle of.

2

The pink sugar cakes in the window on a paper doily, the ham, the slab of mauve sausage, the wasps driving like small torpedoes across the pane caught Philip's attention. His feet were tired by pavements; he had been afraid to cross the road, had simply walked first in one direction, then in the other. He was nearly home now; the square was at the end of the street; this was a shabby outpost of Pimlico, and he smudged the pane with his nose looking for sweets, and saw between the cake and ham a different Baines. He hardly recognized the bulbous eyes, the bald forehead. This was a happy, bold and buccaneering Baines, even though it was, when you looked closer, a desperate Baines.

Philip had never seen the girl, but he remembered Baines had a niece. She was thin and drawn, and she wore a white mackintosh; she meant nothing to Philip; she belonged to a world about which he knew nothing at all. He couldn't make up stories about her, as he could make them up about withered Sir Hubert Reed, the Permanent Secretary, about Mrs Wince-Dudley who came up once a year from Penstanley in Suffolk with a green umbrella and an enormous black handbag, as he could make them up about the upper servants in all the houses where he went to tea and games. She just didn't belong. He thought of mermaids and Undine, but she didn't belong there either, nor to the adventures of Emil, nor to the Bastables. She sat there looking at an iced pink cake in the detachment and mystery of the completely disinherited, looking at the half-used pots of powder which Baines had set out on the marble-topped table between them.

Baines was urging, hoping, entreating, commanding, and the girl looked at the tea and the china pots and cried. Baines passed his handkerchief across the table, but she wouldn't wipe her eyes; she screwed it in her palm and let the tears run down, wouldn't do anything, wouldn't speak, would only put up a silent resistance to what she dreaded and wanted and refused to listen to at any price. The two brains battled over the tea-cups loving each other, and there came to Philip outside, beyond the ham and wasps and dusty Pimlico pane, a confused indication of the struggle.

He was inquisitive and he didn't understand and he wanted to know. He went and stood in the doorway to see better, he was less sheltered than he had ever been; other people's lives for the first time touched and pressed and moulded. He would never escape that scene. In a week he had forgotten it, but it conditioned his career, the long austerity of his life; when he was dying, rich and alone, it was said that he asked: 'Who is she?'

Baines had won; he was cocky and the girl was happy. She wiped her face, she opened a pot of powder, and their fingers touched across the table. It occurred to Philip that it might be amusing to imitate Mrs Baines's voice and to call 'Baines' to him from the door.

His voice shrivelled them; you couldn't describe it in any other way, it made them smaller, they weren't together any more. Baines was the first to recover and trace the voice, but that didn't make things as they were. The sawdust was spilled out of the afternoon; nothing you did could mend it, and Philip was scared. 'I didn't mean . . .' He wanted to say that he loved Baines, that he had only wanted to laugh at Mrs Baines. But he had discovered you couldn't laugh at Mrs Baines. She wasn't Sir Hubert Reed, who used steel nibs and carried a pen-wiper in his pocket; she wasn't Mrs Wince-Dudley; she was darkness when the night-light went out in a draught; she was the frozen blocks of earth he had seen one winter in a graveyard when someone said, 'They need an electric drill'; she was the flowers gone bad and smelling in the little closet room at Penstanley. There was nothing to laugh about. You had to endure her when she was there and forget about her quickly when she was away, suppress the thought of her, ram it down deep.

Baines said, 'It's only Phil,' beckoned him in and gave him the pink iced cake the girl hadn't eaten, but the afternoon was broken, the cake was like dry bread in the throat. The girl left them at once: she even forgot to take the powder. Like a blunt icicle in her white mackintosh she stood in the doorway with her back to them, then melted into the afternoon.

'Who is she?' Philip asked. 'Is she your niece?'

'Oh, yes,' Baines said, 'that's who she is; she's my niece,' and poured the last drops of water on to the coarse black leaves in the teapot.

'May as well have another cup,' Baines said.

'The cup that cheers,' he said hopelessly, watching the bitter black fluid drain out of the spout.

'Have a glass of ginger pop, Phil?'

'I'm sorry. I'm sorry, Baines.'

'It's not your fault, Phil. Why, I could really believe it wasn't you at all, but her. She creeps in everywhere.' He fished two leaves out of his cup and laid them on the back of his hand, a thin soft flake and a hard stalk. He beat them with his hand: 'Today,' and the stalk detached itself, 'tomorrow, Wednesday,

Thursday, Friday, Saturday, Sunday,' but the flake wouldn't come, stayed where it was, drying under his blows, with a resistance you wouldn't believe it to possess. 'The tough one wins,' Baines said.

He got up and paid the bill and out they went into the street. Baines said, 'I don't ask you to say what isn't true. But you needn't actually *tell* Mrs Baines you met us here.'

'Of course not,' Philip said, and catching something of Sir Hubert Reed's manner, 'I understand, Baines.' But he didn't understand a thing; he was caught up in other people's darkness.

'It was stupid,' Baines said. 'So near home, but I hadn't time to think, you see. I'd got to see her.'

'I haven't time to spare,' Baines said. 'I'm not young. I've got to see that she's all right.'

'Of course you have, Baines.'

'Mrs Baines will get it out of you if she can.'

'You can trust me, Baines,' Philip said in a dry important Reed voice; and then, 'Look out. She's at the window watching.' And there indeed she was, looking up at them, between the lace curtains, from the basement room, speculating. 'Need we go in, Baines?' Philip asked, cold lying heavy on his stomach like too much pudding; he clutched Baines's arm.

'Careful,' Baines said softly, 'careful.'

'But need we go in, Baines? It's early. Take me for a walk in the park.'

'Better not.'

'But I'm frightened, Baines.'

'You haven't any cause,' Baines said. 'Nothing's going to hurt you. You just run along upstairs to the nursery. I'll go down by the area and talk to Mrs Baines.' But he stood hesitating at the top of the stone steps pretending not to see her, where she watched between the curtains. 'In at the front door, Phil, and up the stairs.'

Philip didn't linger in the hall; he ran, slithering on the parquet

Mrs Baines had polished, to the stairs. Through the drawing-room doorway on the first floor he saw the draped chairs; even the china clock on the mantel was covered like a canary's cage. As he passed, it chimed the hour, muffled and secret under the duster. On the nursery table he found his supper laid out: a glass of milk and a piece of bread and butter, a sweet biscuit, and a little cold Queen's pudding without the meringue. He had no appetite; he strained his ears for Mrs Baines's coming, for the sound of voices, but the basement held its secrets; the green baize door shut off that world. He drank the milk and ate the biscuit, but he didn't touch the rest, and presently he could hear the soft precise footfalls of Mrs Baines on the stairs: she was a good servant, she walked softly; she was a determined woman, she walked precisely.

But she wasn't angry when she came in; she was ingratiating as she opened the night nursery door – 'Did you have a good walk, Master Philip?' – pulled down the blinds, laid out his pyjamas, came back to clear his supper. 'I'm glad Baines found you. Your mother wouldn't have liked your being out alone.' She examined the tray. 'Not much appetite, have you, Master Philip? Why don't you try a little of this nice pudding? I'll bring you up some more jam for it.'

'No, no, thank you, Mrs Baines,' Philip said.

'You ought to eat more,' Mrs Baines said. She sniffed round the room like a dog. 'You didn't take any pots out of the waste-paper basket in the kitchen, did you, Master Philip?'

'No,' Philip said.

'Of course you wouldn't. I just wanted to make sure.' She patted his shoulder and her fingers flashed to his lapel; she picked off a tiny crumb of pink sugar. 'Oh, Master Philip,' she said, 'that's why you haven't any appetite. You've been buying sweet cakes. That's not what your pocket money's for.'

'But I didn't,' Philip said, 'I didn't.'

She tasted the sugar with the tip of her tongue.

'Don't tell lies to me, Master Philip. I won't stand for it any more than your father would.'

'I didn't, I didn't,' Philip said. 'They gave it me. I mean Baines,' but she had pounced on the word 'they'. She had got what she wanted; there was no doubt about that, even when you didn't know what it was she wanted. Philip was angry and miserable and disappointed because he hadn't kept Baines's secret. Baines oughtn't to have trusted him; grown-up people should keep their own secrets, and yet here was Mrs Baines immediately entrusting him with another.

'Let me tickle your palm and see if you can keep a secret.' But he put his hand behind him; he wouldn't be touched. 'It's a secret between us, Master Philip, that I know all about them. I suppose she was having tea with him,' she speculated.

'Why shouldn't she?' he asked, the responsibility for Baines weighing on his spirit, the idea that he had got to keep her secret when he hadn't kept Baines's making him miserable with the unfairness of life. 'She was nice.'

'She was nice, was she?' Mrs Baines said in a bitter voice he wasn't used to.

'And she's his niece.'

'So that's what he said,' Mrs Baines struck softly back at him like the clock under the duster. She tried to be jocular. 'The old scoundrel. Don't you tell him I know, Master Philip.' She stood very still between the table and the door, thinking very hard, planning something. 'Promise you won't tell. I'll give you that Meccano set, Master Philip . . .'

He turned his back on her; he wouldn't promise, but he wouldn't tell. He would have nothing to do with their secrets, the responsibilities they were determined to lay on him. He was only anxious to forget. He had received already a larger dose of life than he had bargained for, and he was scared. 'A 2A Meccano set, Master Philip.' He never opened his Meccano set again, never built anything, never created anything, died the old dilettante, sixty years later with nothing to show rather than preserve the memory of Mrs Baines's malicious voice saying good night, her soft determined footfalls on the stairs to the basement, going down, going down.

3

The sun poured in between the curtains and Baines was beating a tattoo on the water-can. 'Glory, glory,' Baines said. He sat down on the end of the bed and said, 'I beg to announce that Mrs Baines has been called away. Her mother's dying. She won't be back till tomorrow.'

'Why did you wake me up so early?' Philip complained. He watched Baines with uneasiness; he wasn't going to be drawn in; he'd learnt his lesson. It wasn't right for a man of Baines's age to be so merry. It made a grown person human in the same way that you were human. For if a grown-up could behave so childishly, you were liable to find yourself in their world. It was enough that it came at you in dreams: the witch at the corner, the man with a knife. So 'It's very early,' he whined, even though he loved Baines, even though he couldn't help being glad that Baines was happy. He was divided by the fear and the attraction of life.

'I want to make this a long day,' Baines said. 'This is the best time.' He pulled the curtains back. 'It's a bit misty. The cat's been out all night. There she is, sniffing round the area. They haven't taken in any milk at 59. Emma's shaking out the mats at 63.' He said, 'This was what I used to think about on the Coast: somebody shaking mats and the cat coming home. I can see it today,' Baines said, 'just as if I was still in Africa. Most days you don't notice what you've got. It's a good life if you don't weaken.' He put a penny on the washstand. 'When you've dressed, Phil, run and get a *Mail* from the barrow at the corner. I'll be cooking the sausages.'

'Sausages?'

'Sausages,' Baines said. 'We're going to celebrate today.' He celebrated at breakfast, restless, cracking jokes, unaccountably merry and nervous. It was going to be a long, long day, he kept on coming back to that: for years he had waited for a long day, he had sweated in the damp Coast heat, changed shirts, gone down with fever, lain between the blankets and sweated, all in the hope of this long day, that cat sniffing round the area, a bit of mist, the mats beaten at 63. He propped the *Mail* in front of the coffee-pot and read pieces aloud. He said, 'Cora Down's been married for the fourth time.' He was amused, but it wasn't his idea of a long day. His long day was the Park, watching the riders in the Row, seeing Sir Arthur Stillwater pass beyond the rails ('He dined with us once in Bo; up from Freetown; he was governor there'), lunch at the Corner House for Philip's sake (he'd have preferred himself a glass of stout and some oysters at the York bar), the Zoo, the long bus ride home in the last summer light: the leaves in the Green Park were beginning to turn and the motors nuzzled out of Berkeley Street with the low sun gently glowing on their windscreens. Baines envied no one, not Cora Down, or Sir Arthur Stillwater, or Lord Sandale, who came out on to the steps of the Army and Navy and then went back again – he hadn't anything to do and might as well look at another paper. 'I said don't let me see you touch that black again.' Baines had led a man's life; everyone on top of the bus pricked his ears when he told Philip all about it.

'Would you have shot him?' Philip asked, and Baines put his head back and tilted his dark respectable manservant's hat to a better angle as the bus swerved round the Artillery Memorial.

'I wouldn't have thought twice about it. I'd have shot to kill,' he boasted, and the bowed figure went by, the steel helmet, the heavy cloak, the down-turned rifle and the folded hands.

'Have you got the revolver?'

'Of course I've got it,' Baines said. 'Don't I need it with all the burglaries there've been?' This was the Baines whom Philip loved: not Baines singing and carefree, but Baines responsible, Baines behind barriers, living his man's life.

All the buses streamed out from Victoria like a convoy of aeroplanes to bring Baines home with honour. 'Forty blacks under me,' and there waiting near the area steps was the proper reward, love at lighting-up time.

'It's your niece,' Philip said, recognizing the white mackintosh, but not the happy sleepy face. She frightened him like an unlucky number; he nearly told Baines what Mrs Baines had said; but he didn't want to bother, he wanted to leave things alone.

'Why, so it is,' Baines said. 'I shouldn't wonder if she was going to have a bit of supper with us.' But he said, they'd play a game, pretend they didn't know her, slip down the area steps, 'and here,' Baines said, 'we are,' lay the table, put out the cold sausages, a bottle of beer, a bottle of ginger pop, a flagon of harvest burgundy. 'Everyone his own drink,' Baines said. 'Run upstairs, Phil, and see if there's been a post.'

Philip didn't like the empty house at dusk before the lights went on. He hurried. He wanted to be back with Baines. The hall lay there in quiet and shadow prepared to show him something he didn't want to see. Some letters rustled down and someone knocked. 'Open in the name of the Republic.' The tumbrils rolled, the head bobbed in the bloody basket. Knock, knock, and the postman's footsteps going away. Philip gathered the letters. The slit in the door was like the grating in a jeweller's window. He remembered the policeman he had seen peer through. He had said to his nurse, 'What's he doing?' and when she said, 'He's seeing if everything's all right,' his brain immediately filled with images of all that might be wrong. He ran to the baize door and the stairs. The girl was already there and Baines was kissing her. She leant breathless against the dresser.

'Here's Emmy, Phil.'

'There's a letter for you, Baines.'

'Emmy,' Baines said, 'it's from her.' But he wouldn't open it. 'You bet she's coming back.'

'We'll have supper, anyway,' Emmy said. 'She can't harm that.'

'You don't know her,' Baines said. 'Nothing's safe. Damn it,' he said, 'I was a man once,' and he opened the letter.

'Can I start?' Philip asked, but Baines didn't hear; he presented in his stillness an example of the importance grown-up people attached to the written word: you had to write your thanks, not wait and speak them, as if letters couldn't lie. But Philip knew better than that, sprawling his thanks across a page to Aunt Alice who had given him a teddy bear he was too old for. Letters could lie all right, but they made the lie permanent. They lay as evidence against you: they made you meaner than the spoken word.

'She's not coming back till tomorrow night,' Baines said. He opened the bottles, he pulled up the chairs, he kissed Emmy again against the dresser.

'You oughtn't to,' Emmy said, 'with the boy here.'

'He's got to learn,' Baines said, 'like the rest of us,' and he helped Philip to three sausages. He only took one himself; he said he wasn't hungry, but when Emmy said she wasn't hungry either he stood over her and made her eat. He was timid and rough with her and made her drink the harvest burgundy because he said she needed building up; he wouldn't take no for an answer, but when he touched her his hands were light and clumsy too, as if he was afraid to damage something delicate and didn't know how to handle anything so light.

'This is better than milk and biscuits, eh?'

'Yes,' Philip said, but he was scared, scared for Baines as much as for himself. He couldn't help wondering at every bite, at every draught of the ginger pop, what Mrs Baines would say if she ever learnt of this meal; he couldn't imagine it, there was a depth of bitterness and rage in Mrs Baines you couldn't sound. He said, 'She won't be coming back tonight?' but you could tell by the way they immediately understood him that she wasn't really away at all; she was there in the basement with them, driving them to longer drinks and louder talk, biding her time for the right cutting word. Baines wasn't really happy; he was only watching happiness from close to instead of from far away.

'No,' he said, 'she'll not be back till late tomorrow.' He couldn't keep his eyes off happiness. He'd played around as much as other men; he kept on reverting to the Coast as if to excuse himself for his innocence. He wouldn't have been so innocent if he'd lived his life in London, so innocent when it came to tenderness. 'If it was you, Emmy,' he said, looking at the white dresser, the scrubbed chairs, 'this'd be like a home.' Already the room was not quite so harsh; there was a little dust in corners, the silver needed a final polish, the morning's paper lay untidily on a chair. 'You'd better go to bed, Phil; it's been a long day.'

They didn't leave him to find his own way up through the dark shrouded house; they went with him, turning on lights, touching each other's fingers on the switches. Floor after floor they drove the night back. They spoke softly among the covered chairs. They watched him undress, they didn't make him wash or clean his teeth, they saw him into bed and lit his night-light and left his door ajar. He could hear their voices on the stairs, friendly like the guests he heard at dinner-parties when they moved down the hall, saying good night. They belonged; wherever they were they made a home. He heard a door open and a clock strike, he heard their voices for a long while, so. that he felt they were not far away and he was safe. The voices didn't dwindle, they simply went out, and he could be sure that they were still somewhere not far from him, silent together in one of the many empty rooms, growing sleepy together as he grew sleepy after the long day.

He just had time to sigh faintly with satisfaction, because this too perhaps had been life, before he slept and the inevitable terrors of sleep came round him: a man with a tricolour hat beat at the door on His Majesty's service, a bleeding head lay on the kitchen table in a basket, and the Siberian wolves crept closer. He was bound hand and foot and couldn't move; they leapt round him breathing heavily; he opened his eyes and Mrs Baines was there, her grey untidy hair in threads over his face, her black hat askew. A loose hairpin fell on the pillow and one musty thread brushed his mouth. 'Where are they?' she whispered. 'Where are they?'

4

Philip watched her in terror. Mrs Baines was out of breath as if she had been searching all the empty rooms, looking under loose covers.

With her untidy grey hair and her black dress buttoned to her throat, her gloves of black cotton, she was so like the witches of his dreams that he didn't dare to speak. There was a stale smell in her breath.

'She's here,' Mrs Baines said, 'you can't deny she's here.' Her face was simultaneously marked with cruelty and misery; she wanted to 'do things' to people, but she suffered all the time. It would have done her good to scream, but she daren't do that: it would warn them. She came ingratiatingly back to the bed where Philip lay rigid on his back and whispered, 'I haven't forgotten the Meccano set. You shall have it tomorrow, Master Philip. We've got secrets together, haven't we? Just tell me where they are.'

He couldn't speak. Fear held him as firmly as any nightmare. She said, 'Tell Mrs Baines, Master Philip. You love your Mrs Baines, don't you?' That was too much; he couldn't speak, but he could move his mouth in terrified denial, wince away from her dusty image.

She whispered, coming closer to him, 'Such deceit. I'll tell your father. I'll settle with you myself when I've found them. You'll smart; I'll see you smart.' Then immediately she was still, listening. A board had creaked on the floor below, and a moment later, while she stooped listening above his bed, there came the whispers of two people who were happy and sleepy together after a long day. The night-light stood beside the mirror and Mrs Baines could see there her own reflection, misery and cruelty wavering in the glass, age and dust and nothing to hope for. She sobbed without tears, a dry, breathless sound, but her cruelty was a kind of pride which kept her going; it was her best quality, she would have been merely pitiable without it. She went out of the door on tiptoe, feeling her way across the landing, going so softly down the stairs that no one behind a shut door could hear her. Then there was complete silence again; Philip could move; he raised his knees; he sat up in bed; he wanted to die. It wasn't fair, the walls were down again between his world and theirs, but this time it was something worse than merriment that the grown people made him share; a passion moved in the house he recognized but could not understand.

It wasn't fair, but he owed Baines everything: the Zoo, the ginger pop, the bus ride home. Even the supper called to his loyalty. But he was frightened; he was touching something he touched in dreams; the bleeding head, the wolves, the knock, knock, knock. Life fell on him with savagery, and you couldn't blame him if he never faced it again in sixty years. He got out of bed. Carefully from habit he put on his bedroom slippers and tiptoed to the door: it wasn't quite dark on the landing below because the curtains had been taken down for the cleaners and the light from the street washed in through the tall windows. Mrs Baines had her hand on the glass door-knob; she was very carefully turning it; he screamed: 'Baines, Baines.'

Mrs Baines turned and saw him cowering in his pyjamas by the banisters; he was helpless, more helpless even than Baines, and cruelty grew at the sight of him and drove her up the stairs. The nightmare was on him again and he couldn't move; he hadn't any more courage left, he couldn't even scream.

But the first cry brought Baines out of the best spare bedroom and he moved quicker than Mrs Baines. She hadn't reached the top of the stairs before he'd caught her round the waist. She drove her black cotton gloves at his face and he bit her hand. He hadn't time to think, he fought her like a stranger, but she fought back with knowledgeable hate. She was going to teach them all and it didn't really matter whom she began with; they had all deceived her; but the old image in the glass was by her side, telling her she must be dignified, she wasn't young enough to yield her dignity; she could beat his face, but she mustn't bite; she could push, but she mustn't kick.

Age and dust and nothing to hope for were her handicaps. She went over the banisters in a flurry of black clothes and fell into the hall; she lay before the front door like a sack of coals which should have gone down the area into the basement. Philip saw; Emmy saw; she sat down suddenly in the doorway of the best spare bedroom with her eyes open as if she were too tired to stand any longer. Baines went slowly down into the hall.

It wasn't hard for Philip to escape; they'd forgotten him completely. He went down the back, the servants' stairs, because Mrs Baines was in the hall. He didn't understand what she was doing lying there; like the pictures in a book no one had read to him, the things he didn't understand terrified him. The whole house had been turned over to the grown-up world; he wasn't safe in the night nursery; their passions had flooded in. The only thing he could do was to get away, by the back stairs, and up through the area, and never come back. He didn't think of the cold, of the need for food and sleep; for an hour it would seem quite possible to escape from people for ever.

He was wearing pyjamas and bedroom slippers when he came up into the square, but there was no one to see him. It was that hour of the evening in a residential district when everyone is at the theatre or at home. He climbed over the iron railings into the little garden: the plane-trees spread their large pale palms between him and the sky. It might have been an illimitable forest into which he had escaped. He crouched behind a trunk and the wolves retreated; it seemed to him between the little iron seat and the tree-trunk that no one would ever find him again. A kind of embittered happiness and self-pity made him cry; he was lost; there wouldn't be any more secrets to keep; he surrendered responsibility once and for all. Let grown-up people keep to their world and he would keep to his, safe in the small garden between the plane-trees.

Presently the door of 48 opened and Baines looked this way and that; then he signalled with his hand and Emmy came; it was as if they were only just in time for a train, they hadn't a chance of saying good-bye. She went quickly by like a face at a window swept past the platform, pale and unhappy and not wanting to go. Baines went in again and shut the door; the light was lit in the basement, and a policeman walked round the square, looking into the areas. You could tell how many families were at home by the lights behind the first-floor curtains.

Philip explored the garden: it didn't take long: a twenty-yard square of bushes and plane-trees, two iron seats and a gravel path, a padlocked gate at either end, a scuffle of old leaves. But he couldn't stay: something stirred in the bushes and two illuminated eyes peered out at him like a Serbian wolf, and he thought how terrible it would be if Mrs Baines found him there. He'd have no time to climb the railings; she'd seize him from behind.

He left the square at the unfashionable end and was immediately among the fish-and-chip shops, the little stationers selling *Bagatelle*, among the accommodation addresses and the dingy hotels with open doors. There were few people about because the pubs were open, but a blowsy woman carrying a parcel called out to him across the street and the commissionaire outside a cinema would have stopped him if he hadn't crossed the road. He went deeper: you could go farther and lose yourself more completely here than among the plane-trees. On the fringe of the square he was in danger of being stopped and taken back: it was obvious where he belonged; but as he went deeper he lost the marks of his origin. It was a warm night: any child in those free-living parts might be expected to play truant from bed. He found a kind of camaraderie even among grown-up people; he might have been a neighbour's child as he went quickly by, but they weren't going to tell on him, they'd been young once themselves. He picked up a protective coating of dust from the pavements, of smuts from the trains which passed along the backs in a spray of fire. Once he was caught in a knot of children running away from something or somebody, laughing as they ran; he was whirled with them round a turning and abandoned, with a sticky fruit-drop in his hand.

He couldn't have been more lost, but he hadn't the stamina to keep on. At first he feared that someone would stop him; after an hour he hoped that someone would. He couldn't find his way back, and in any case he was afraid of arriving home alone; he was afraid of Mrs Baines, more afraid than he had ever been. Baines was his friend, but something had happened which gave Mrs Baines all the power. He began to loiter on purpose to be noticed, but no one noticed him. Families were having a last breather on the doorsteps, the refuse bins had been put out and bits of cabbage stalks soiled his slippers. The air was full of voices, but he was cut off; these people were strangers and would always now be strangers; they were marked by Mrs Baines and he shied away from them into a deep class-consciousness. He had been afraid of policemen, but now he wanted one to take him home; even Mrs Baines could do nothing against a policeman. He sidled past a constable who was directing traffic, but he was too busy to pay him any attention. Philip sat down against a wall and cried.

It hadn't occurred to him that that was the easiest way, that all you had to do was to surrender, to show you were beaten and accept kindness . . . It was lavished on him at once by two women and a pawnbroker. Another policeman appeared, a young man with a sharp incredulous face. He looked as if he noted everything he saw in pocket-books and drew conclusions. A woman offered to see Philip home, but he didn't trust her: she wasn't a match for Mrs Baines immobile in the hall. He wouldn't give his address; he said he was afraid to go home. He had his way; he got his protection. 'I'll take him to the station,' the policeman said, and holding him awkwardly by the hand (he wasn't married; he had his career to make) he led him round the corner, up the stone stairs into the little bare over-heated room where Justice lived.

5

Justice waited behind a wooden counter on a high stool; it wore a heavy moustache; it was kindly and had six children ('three of them nippers like yourself'); it wasn't really interested in Philip, but it pretended to be, it wrote the address down and sent a constable to fetch a glass of milk. But the young constable was interested; he had a nose for things.

'Your home's on the telephone, I suppose,' Justice said. 'We'll ring them up and say you are safe. They'll fetch you very soon. What's your name, sonny?'

'Philip.'

'Your other name?'

'I haven't got another name.' He didn't want to be fetched; he wanted to be taken home by someone who would impress even Mrs Baines. The constable watched him, watched the way he drank the milk, watched him when he winced away from questions.

'What made you run away? Playing truant, eh?'

'I don't know.'

'You oughtn't to do it, young fellow. Think how anxious your father and mother will be.'

'They are away.'

'Well, your nurse.'

'I haven't got one.'

'Who looks after you, then?' The question went home. Philip saw Mrs Baines coming up the stairs at him, the heap of black cotton in the hall. He began to cry.

'Now, now, now,' the sergeant said. He didn't know what to do; he wished his wife were with him; even a policewoman might have been useful.

'Don't you think it's funny,' the constable said, 'that there hasn't been an inquiry?'

'They think he's tucked up in bed.'

'You are scared, aren't you?' the constable said. 'What scared you?'

'I don't know.'

'Somebody hurt you?'

'No.'

'He's had bad dreams,' the sergeant said. 'Thought the house was on fire, I expect. I've brought up six of them. Rose is due back. She'll take him home.'

'I want to go home with you,' Philip said; he tried to smile at the constable, but the deceit was immature and unsuccessful.

'I'd better go,' the constable said. 'There may be something wrong.'

'Nonsense,' the sergeant said. 'It's a woman's job. Tact is what you need. Here's Rose. Pull up your stockings, Rose. You're a disgrace to the Force. I've got a job of work for you.' Rose shambled in: black cotton stockings drooping over her boots, a gawky Girl Guide manner, a hoarse hostile voice. 'More tarts, I suppose.'

'No, you've got to see this young man home.' She looked at him owlishly.

'I won't go with her,' Philip said. He began to cry again. 'I don't like her.'

'More of that womanly charm, Rose,' the sergeant said. The telephone rang on his desk. He lifted the receiver. 'What? What's that?' he said. 'Number 48? You've got a doctor?' He put his hand over the telephone mouth. 'No wonder this nipper wasn't reported,' he said. 'They've been too busy. An accident. Woman slipped on the stairs.'

'Serious?' the constable asked. The sergeant mouthed at him; you didn't mention the word death before a child (didn't he know? he had six of them), you made noises in the throat, you grimaced, a complicated shorthand for a word of only five letters anyway.

'You'd better go, after all,' he said, 'and make a report. The doctor's there.'

Rose shambled from the stove; pink apply-dapply cheeks, loose stockings. She stuck her hands behind her. Her large morgue-like mouth was full of blackened teeth. 'You told me to take him and now just because something interesting . . . I don't expect justice from a man . . .'

'Who's at the house?' the constable asked.

'The butler.'

'You don't think,' the constable said, 'he saw . . .'

'Trust me,' the sergeant said. 'I've brought up six. I know 'em through and through. You can't teach me anything about children.'

'He seemed scared about something.'

'Dreams,' the sergeant said.

'What name?'

'Baines.'

'This Mr Baines,' the constable said to Philip, 'you like him, eh? He's good to you?' They were trying to get something out of him; he was suspicious of the whole roomful of them; he said 'yes' without conviction because he was afraid at any moment of more responsibilities, more secrets.

'And Mrs Baines?'

'Yes.'

They consulted together by the desk. Rose was hoarsely aggrieved; she was like a female impersonator, she bore her womanhood with an unnatural emphasis even while she scorned it in her creased stockings and her weather-exposed face. The charcoal shifted in the stove; the room was over-heated in the mild late summer evening. A notice on the wall described a body found in the Thames, or rather the body's clothes: wool vest, wool pants, wool shirt with blue stripes, size ten boots, blue serge suit worn at the elbows, fifteen and a half celluloid collar. They couldn't find anything to say about the body, except its measurements, it was just an ordinary body.

'Come along,' the constable said. He was interested, he was glad to be going, but he couldn't help being embarrassed by his company, a small boy in pyjamas. His nose smelt something, he didn't know what, but he smarted at the sight of the amusement they caused: the pubs had closed and the streets were full again of men making as long a day of it as they could. He hurried through the less frequented streets, chose the darker pavements, wouldn't loiter, and Philip wanted more and more to loiter, pulling at his hand, dragging with his feet. He dreaded the sight of Mrs Baines waiting in the hall: he knew now that she was dead. The sergeant's mouthing had conveyed that; but she wasn't buried, she wasn't out of sight: he was going to see a dead person in the hall when the door opened.

The light was on in the basement, and to his relief the constable made for the area steps. Perhaps he wouldn't have to see Mrs Baines at all. The constable knocked on the door because it was too dark to see the bell, and Baines answered. He stood there in the doorway of the neat bright basement room and you could see the sad complacent plausible sentence he had prepared wither at the sight of Philip; he hadn't expected Philip to return like that in the policeman's company. He had to begin thinking all over again; he wasn't a deceptive man. If it hadn't been for Emmy he would have been quite ready to let the truth lead him where it would.

'Mr Baines?' the constable asked.

He nodded; he hadn't found the right words; he was daunted by the shrewd knowing face, the sudden appearance of Philip there.

'This little boy from here?'

'Yes,' Baines said. Philip could tell that there was a message he was trying to convey, but he shut his mind to it. He loved Baines, but Baines had involved him in secrets, in fears he didn't understand. That was what happened when you loved – you got involved; and Philip extricated himself from life, from love, from Baines.

'The doctor's here,' Baines said. He nodded at the door, moistened his mouth, kept his eyes on Philip, begging for something like a dog you can't understand, 'There's nothing to be done. She slipped on these stone basement stairs. I was in here. I heard her fall.' He wouldn't look at the notebook, at the constable's spidery writing which got a terrible lot on one page.

'Did the boy see anything?'

'He can't have done. I thought he was in bed. Hadn't he better go up? It's a shocking thing. O,' Baines said, losing control, 'it's a shocking thing for a child.'

'She's through there?' the constable asked.

'I haven't moved her an inch,' Baines said.

'He'd better then—'

'Go up the area and through the hall,' Baines said, and again he begged dumbly like a dog: one more secret, keep this secret, do this for old Baines, he won't ask another.

'Come along,' the constable said. 'I'll see you up to bed. You're a gentleman. You must come in the proper way through the front door like the master should. Or will you go along with him, Mr Baines, while I see the doctor?'

'Yes,' Baines said, 'I'll go.' He came across the room to Philip, begging, begging, all the way with his old soft stupid expression: this is Baines, the old Coaster; what about a palm-oil chop, eh?; a man's life; forty niggers; never used a gun; I tell you I couldn't help loving them; it wasn't what we call love, nothing we could understand. The messages flickered out from the last posts at the border, imploring, beseeching, reminding: this is your old friend Baines; what about an elevenses; a glass of ginger pop won't do you any harm; sausages; a long day. But the wires were cut, the messages just faded out into the vacancy of the scrubbed room in which there had never been a place where a man could hide his secrets.

'Come along, Phil, it's bedtime. We'll just go up the steps . . .'

Tap, tap, tap, at the telegraph; you may get through, you can't tell, somebody may mend the right wire. 'And in at the front door.'

'No,' Philip said, 'no. I won't go. You can't make me go. I'll fight. I won't see her.'

The constable turned on them quickly. 'What's that? Why won't you go?'

'She's in the hall,' Philip said. 'I know she's in the hall. And she's dead. I won't see her.'

'You moved her then?' the constable said to Baines. 'All the way down here? You've been lying, eh? That means you had to tidy up . . . Were you alone?'

'Emmy,' Philip said, 'Emmy.' He wasn't going to keep any more secrets: he was going to finish once and for all with everything, with Baines and Mrs Baines and the grown-up life beyond him. 'It was all Emmy's fault,' he protested with a quaver which reminded Baines that after all he was only a child; it had been hopeless to expect help there; he was a child; he didn't understand what it all meant; he couldn't read this shorthand of terror; he'd had a long day and he was tired out. You could see him dropping asleep where he stood against the dresser, dropping back into the comfortable nursery peace. You couldn't blame him. When he woke in the morning, he'd hardly remember a thing.

'Out with it,' the constable said, addressing Baines with professional ferocity, 'who is she?' just as the old man sixty years later startled his secretary, his only watcher, asking, 'Who is she? Who is she?' dropping lower and lower to death, passing on the way perhaps the image of Baines: Baines hopeless, Baines letting his head drop, Baines 'coming clean'.

A Day Saved

I had stuck closely to him, as people say like a shadow. But that's absurd. I'm no shadow. You can feel me, touch me, hear me, smell me. I'm Robinson. But I had sat at the next table, followed twenty yards behind down every street, when he went upstairs I waited at the bottom, and when he came down I passed out before him and paused at the first corner. In that way I was really like a shadow, for sometimes I was in front of him and sometimes I was behind him.

Who was he? I never knew his name. He was short and ordinary in appearance and he carried an umbrella; his hat was a bowler, and he wore brown gloves. But this was his importance to me: he carried something I dearly, despairingly wanted. It was beneath his clothes, perhaps in a pouch, a purse, perhaps dangling next to his skin. Who knows how cunning the most ordinary man can be? Surgeons can make clever insertions. He may have carried it even closer to his heart than the outer skin.

What was it? I never knew. I can only guess, as I might guess at his name, calling him Jones or Douglas, Wales, Canby, Fotheringay. Once in a restaurant I said 'Fotheringay' softly to my soup and I thought he looked up and round about him. I don't know. This is the horror I cannot escape: knowing nothing, his name, what it was he carried, why I wanted it so, why I followed him.

Presently we came to a railway bridge and underneath it he met a friend. I am using words again very inexactly. Bear with me. I try to be exact. I pray to be exact. All I want in the world is to know. So when I say he met a friend, I do not know that it was a friend, I know only that it was someone he greeted with apparent affection. The friend said to him, 'When do you leave?' He said, 'At two from Dover.' You may be sure I felt my pocket to make sure the ticket was there.

Then his friend said, 'If you fly you will save a day.'

He nodded, he agreed, he would sacrifice his ticket, he would save a day.

I ask you, what does a day saved matter to him or to you? A day saved from what? for what? Instead of spending the day travelling, you will see your friend a day earlier, but you cannot stay indefinitely, you will travel home twenty-four hours sooner, that is all. But you will fly home and again save a day? Save it from what, for what? You will begin work a day earlier, but you cannot work on indefinitely. It only means that you will cease work a day earlier. And then, what? You cannot die a day earlier. So you will realize perhaps how rash it was of you to save a day, when you discover how you cannot escape those twenty-four hours you have so carefully preserved; you may push them forward and push them forward, but some time they must be spent, and then you may wish you had spent them as innocently as in the train from Ostend.

But this thought never occurred to him. He said, 'Yes, that's true. It would save a day. I'll fly.' I nearly spoke to him then. The selfishness of the man. For that day which he thought he was saving might be his despair years later, but it was my despair at the instant. For I had been looking forward to the long train journey in the same compartment. It was winter, and the train would be nearly empty, and with the least luck we should be alone together. I had planned everything. I was going to talk to him. Because I knew nothing about him, I should begin in the usual way by asking whether he minded the window being raised a little or a little lowered. That would show him that we spoke the same language and he would probably be only too ready to talk, feeling himself in a foreign country; he would be grateful for any help I might be able to give him, translating this or that word.

Of course I never believed that talk would be enough. I should learn a great deal about him, but I believed that I should have to kill him before I knew all. I should have killed him, I think, at night, between the two stations which are the farthest parted, after the customs had examined our luggage and our passports had been stamped at the frontier, and we had pulled down the blinds and turned out the light. I had even planned what to do with his body, with the bowler hat and the umbrella and the brown gloves, but only if it became necessary, only if in no other way he would yield what I wanted. I am a gentle creature, not easily roused.

But now he had chosen to go by aeroplane and there was nothing that I could do. I followed him, of course, sat in the seat behind, watched his tremulousness at his first flight, how he avoided for a long while the sight of the sea below, how he kept his bowler hat upon his knees, how he gasped a little when the grey wing tilted up like the arm of a windmill to the sky and the houses were set on edge. There were times, I believe, when he regretted having saved a day.

We got out of the aeroplane together and he had a small trouble with the customs. I translated for him. He looked at me curiously and said, 'Thank you.' He was – again I suggest that I know when all I mean is I assume by his manner and his conversation – stupid and good-natured, but I believe for a moment he suspected me, thought he had seen me somewhere, in a tube, in a bus, in a public baths, below the railway bridge, on how many stairways. I asked him the time. He said, 'We put our clocks back an hour here,' and beamed with an absurd pleasure because he had saved an hour as well as a day.

I had a drink with him, several drinks with him. He was absurdly grateful for my help. I had beer with him at one place, gin at another, and at a third he insisted on my sharing a bottle of wine. We became for the time being friends. I felt more warmly towards him than towards any other man I have known, for, like love between a man and a woman, my affection was partly curiosity. I told him that I was Robinson; he meant to give me a card, but while he was looking for one he drank another glass of wine and forgot about it. We were both a little drunk. Presently I began to call him Fotheringay. He never contradicted me and it may have been his name, but I seem to remember also calling him Douglas, Wales and Canby without correction. He was very generous and I found it easy to talk with him; the stupid are often companionable. I told him that I was desperate and he offered me money. He could not understand what I wanted.

I said, 'You've saved a day. You can afford to come with me tonight to a place I know.'

He said, 'I have to take a train tonight.' He told me the name of the town, and he was not surprised when I told him that I was coming too.

We drank together all that evening and went to the station together. I was planning, if it became necessary, to kill him. I thought in all friendliness that perhaps after all I might save him from having saved a day. But it was a small local train; it crept from station to station, and at every station people got out of the train and other people got into the train. He insisted on travelling third class and the carriage was never empty. He could not speak a word of the language and he simply curled up in his corner and slept; it was I who remained awake and had to listen to the weary painful gossip, a servant speaking of her mistress, a peasant woman of the day's market, a soldier of the Church, and a man who, I believe, was a tailor of adultery, wire-worms and the harvest of three years ago.

It was two o'clock in the morning when we reached the end of our journey. I walked with him to the house where his friends lived. It was quite close to the station and I had no time to plan or carry out any plan. The garden gate was open and he asked me in. I said no. I would go to the hotel. He said his friends would be pleased to put me up for the remainder of the night, but I said no. The lights were on in a downstairs room and the curtains were not drawn. A man was asleep in a chair by a great stove and there were glasses on a tray, a decanter of whisky, two bottles of beer and a long thin bottle of Rhine wine. I stepped back and he went in and almost immediately the room was full of people. I could see his welcome in their eyes and in their gestures. There was a woman in a dressing-gown and a girl who sat with thin knees drawn up to her chin and three men, two of them old. They did not draw the curtains, though he must surely have guessed that I was watching them. The garden was cold; the winter beds were furred with weeds. I laid my hand on some prickly bush. It was as if they gave a deliberate display of their unity and companionship. My friend – I call him my friend, but he was really no more than an acquaintance and was my friend only for so long as we both were drunk – sat in the middle of them all, and I could tell from the way his lips were moving that he was telling them many things which he had never told me. Once I thought I could detect from his lip movements, 'I have saved a day.' He looked stupid and good-natured and happy. I could not bear the sight for long. It was an impertinence to display himself like that to me. I have never ceased to pray from that moment that the day he saved may be retarded and retarded until eventually he suffers its eighty-six thousand four hundred seconds when he has the most desperate need, when he is following another as I followed him, closely as people say like a shadow, so that he has to stop, as I have had to stop, to reassure himself: you can smell me, you can touch me, you can hear me, I am not a shadow: I am Fotheringay, Wales, Canby, I am Robinson.

Across the Bridge

A Drive in the Country

Across the Bridge

'They say he's worth a million,' Lucia said. He sat there in the little hot damp Mexican square, a dog at his feet, with an air of immense and forlorn patience. The dog attracted your attention at once; for it was very nearly an English setter, only something had gone wrong with the tail and the feathering. Palms wilted over his head, it was all shade and stuffiness round the bandstand, radios talked loudly in Spanish from the little wooden sheds where they changed your pesos into dollars at a loss. I could tell he didn't understand a word from the way he read his newspaper — as I did myself picking out the words which were like English ones. 'He's been here a month,' Lucia said, 'they turned him out of Guatemala and Honduras.'

You couldn't keep any secrets for five hours in this border town. Lucia had only been twenty-four hours in the place, but she knew all about Mr Joseph Calloway. The only reason I didn't know about him (and I'd been in the place two weeks) was because I couldn't talk the language any more than Mr Calloway could. There wasn't another soul in the place who didn't know the story — the whole story of Hailing Investment Trust and the proceedings for extradition. Any man doing dusty business in any of the wooden booths in the town is better fitted by long observation to tell Mr Calloway's tale than I am, except that I was in — literally — at the finish. They all watched the drama proceed with immense interest, sympathy and respect. For, after all, he had a million.

Every once in a while through the long steamy day, a boy came and cleaned Mr Calloway's shoes: he hadn't the right words to resist them – they pretended not to know his English. He must have had his shoes cleaned the day Lucia and I watched him at least half a dozen times. At midday he took a stroll across the square to the Antonio Bar and had a bottle of beer, the setter sticking to heel as if they were out for a country walk in England (he had, you may remember, one of the biggest estates in Norfolk). After his bottle of beer, he would walk down between the money-changers' huts to the Rio Grande and look across the bridge into the United States: people came and went constantly in cars. Then back to the square till lunch-time. He was staying in the best hotel, but you don't get good hotels in this border town: nobody stays in them more than a night. The good hotels were on the other side of the bridge: you could see their electric signs twenty storeys high from the little square at night, like lighthouses marking the United States.

You may ask what I'd been doing in so drab a spot for a fortnight. There was no interest in the place for anyone; it was just damp and dust and poverty, a kind of shabby replica of the town across the river. Both had squares in the same spots; both had the same number of cinemas. One was cleaner than the other, that was all, and more expensive, much more expensive. I'd stayed across there a couple of nights waiting for a man a tourist bureau said was driving down from Detroit to Yucatan and would sell a place in his car for some fantastically small figure – twenty dollars, I think it was. I don't know if he existed or was invented by the optimistic half-caste in the agency; anyway, he never turned up and so I waited, not much caring, on the cheap side of the river. It didn't much matter; I was living. One day I meant to give up the man from Detroit and go home or go south, but it was easier not to decide anything in a hurry. Lucia was just waiting for a car the other way, but she didn't have to wait so long. We waited together and watched Mr Calloway waiting – for God knows what.

I don't know how to treat this story – it was a tragedy for Mr Calloway, it was poetic retribution, I suppose, in the eyes of the shareholders whom he'd ruined with his bogus transactions, and to Lucia and me, at this stage, it was comedy – except when he kicked the dog. I'm not a sentimentalist about dogs, I prefer people to be cruel to animals rather than to human beings, but I couldn't help being revolted at the way he'd kick that animal – with a hint of cold-blooded venom, not in anger but as if he were getting even for some trick it had played him a long while ago. That generally happened when he returned from the bridge: it was the only sign of anything resembling emotion he showed. Otherwise he looked a small, set, gentle creature with silver hair and a silver moustache and gold-rimmed glasses, and one gold tooth like a flaw in character.

Lucia hadn't been accurate when she said he'd been turned out of Guatemala and Honduras; he'd left voluntarily when the extradition proceedings seemed likely to go through and moved north. Mexico is still not a very centralized state, and it is possible to get round governors as you can't get round cabinet ministers or judges. And so he waited there on the border for the next move. That earlier part of the story was, I suppose, dramatic, but I didn't watch it and I can't invent what I haven't seen – the long waiting in ante-rooms, the bribes taken and refused, and growing fear of arrest, and then the flight – in gold-rimmed glasses – covering his tracks as well as he could, but this wasn't finance and he was an amateur at escape. And so he'd washed up here, under my eyes and Lucia's eyes, sitting all day under the bandstand, nothing to read but a Mexican paper, nothing to do but look across the river at the United States, quite unaware, I suppose, that everyone knew everything about him, once a day kicking his dog. Perhaps in its semi-setter way it reminded him too much of the Norfolk estate – though that, too, I suppose, was the reason he kept it.

And the next act again was pure comedy. I hesitate to think what this man worth a million was costing his country as they edged him out from this land and that. Perhaps somebody was getting tired of the business, and careless; anyway, they sent across two detectives with an old photograph. He'd grown his silvery moustache since that had been taken, and he'd aged a lot, and they couldn't catch sight of him. They hadn't been across the bridge two hours when everybody knew that there were two foreign detectives in town looking for Mr Calloway – everybody knew, that is to say, except Mr Calloway, who couldn't talk Spanish. There were plenty of people who could have told him in English, but they didn't. It wasn't cruelty, it was a sort of awe and respect: like a bull, he was on show, sitting there mournfully in the plaza with his dog, a magnificent spectacle for which we all had ring-side seats.

I ran into one of the policemen in the Bar Antonio. He was disgusted; he had had some idea that when he crossed the bridge life was going to be different, so much more colour and sun, and – I suspect – love, and all he found were wide mud streets where the nocturnal rain lay in pools, and mangy dogs, smells and cockroaches in his bedroom, and the nearest to love, the open door of the Academia Comercial, where pretty mestizo girls sat all morning learning to typewrite. Tip-tap-tip-tap-tip – perhaps they had a dream too – jobs on the other side of the bridge, where life was going to be so much more luxurious, refined and amusing.

We got into conversation; he seemed surprised that I knew who they both were and what they wanted. He said, 'We've got information this man Calloway's in town.'

'He's knocking around somewhere,' I said.

'Could you point him out?'

'Oh, I don't know him by sight,' I said.

He drank his beer and thought a while. 'I'll go out and sit in the plaza. He's sure to pass sometime.'

I finished my beer and went quickly off and found Lucia. I said, 'Hurry, we're going to see an arrest.' We didn't care a thing about Mr Calloway, he was just an elderly man who kicked his dog and swindled the poor, and deserved anything he got. So we made for the plaza; we knew Calloway would be there, but it had never occurred to either of us that the detectives wouldn't recognize him. There was quite a surge of people round the place; all the fruit-sellers and boot-blacks in town seemed to have arrived together; we had to force our way through, and there in the little green stuffy centre of the place, sitting on adjoining seats, were the two plain-clothes men and Mr Calloway. I've never known the place so silent; everybody was on tiptoe, and the plain-clothes men were staring at the crowd for Mr Calloway, and Mr Calloway sat on his usual seat staring out over the money-changing booths at the United States.

'It can't go on. It just can't,' Lucia said. But it did. It got more fantastic still. Somebody ought to write a play about it. We sat as close as we dared. We were afraid all the time we were going to laugh. The semi-setter scratched for fleas and Mr Calloway watched the USA. The two detectives watched the crowd, and the crowd watched the show with solemn satisfaction. Then one of the detectives got up and went over to Mr Calloway. That's the end, I thought. But it wasn't, it was the beginning. For some reason they had eliminated him from their list of suspects. I shall never know why. The man said:

'You speak English?'

'I *am* English,' Mr Calloway said.

Even that didn't tear it, and the strangest thing of all was the way Mr Calloway came alive. I don't think anybody had spoken to him like that for weeks. The Mexicans were too respectful – he was a man with a million – and it had never occurred to Lucia and me to treat him casually like a human being; even in our eyes he had been magnified by the colossal theft and the worldwide pursuit.

He said, 'This is rather a dreadful place, don't you think?'

'It is,' the policeman said.

'I can't think what brings anybody across the bridge.'

'Duty,' the policeman said gloomily. 'I suppose you are passing through.'

'Yes,' Mr Calloway said.

'I'd have expected over here there'd have been – you know what I mean – life. You read things about Mexico.'

'Oh, life,' Mr Calloway said. He spoke firmly and precisely, as if to a committee of shareholders. 'That begins on the other side.'

'You don't appreciate your own country until you leave it.'

'That's very true,' Mr Calloway said. 'Very true.'

At first it was difficult not to laugh, and then after a while there didn't seem to be much to laugh at: an old man imagining all the fine things going on beyond the international bridge. I think he thought of the town opposite as a combination of London and Norfolk – theatres and cocktail bars, a little shooting and a walk round the field at evening with the dog – that miserable imitation of a setter – poking the ditches. He'd never been across, he couldn't know it was just the same thing over again – even the same layout; only the streets were paved and the hotels had ten more storeys, and life was more expensive, and everything was a little bit cleaner. There wasn't anything Mr Calloway would have called living – no galleries, no bookshops, just *Film Fun* and the local paper, and *Click* and *Focus* and the tabloids.

'Well,' said Mr Calloway, 'I think I'll take a stroll before lunch. You need an appetite to swallow the food here. I generally go down and look at the bridge about now. Care to come, too?'

The detective shook his head. 'No,' he said, 'I'm on duty. I'm looking for a fellow.' And that, of course, gave *him* away. As far as Mr Calloway could understand, there was only one 'fellow' in the world anyone was looking for – his brain had eliminated friends who were seeking their friends, husbands who might be waiting for their wives, all objectives of any search but just the one. The power of elimination was what had made him a financier – he could forget the people behind the shares.

That was the last we saw of him for a while. We didn't see him going into the Botica Paris to get his aspirin, or walking back from the bridge with his dog. He simply disappeared, and when he disappeared, people began to talk and the detectives heard the talk. They looked silly enough, and they got busy after the very man they'd been sitting next to in the garden. Then they, too, disappeared. They, as well as Mr Calloway, had gone to the state capital to see the Governor and the Chief of Police, and it must have been an amusing sight there, too, as they bumped into Mr Calloway and sat with him in the waiting-rooms. I suspect Mr Calloway was generally shown in first, for everyone knew he was worth a million. Only in Europe is it possible for a man to be a criminal as well as a rich man.

Anyway, after about a week the whole pack of them returned by the same train. Mr Calloway travelled Pullman, and the two policemen travelled in the day coach. It was evident that they hadn't got their extradition order.

Lucia had left by that time. The car came and went across the bridge. I stood in Mexico and watched her get out at the United States Customs. She wasn't anything in particular, but she looked beautiful at a distance as she gave me a wave out of the United States and got back into the car. And I suddenly felt sympathy for Mr Calloway, as if there were something over there which you couldn't find here, and turning round I saw him back on his old beat, with the dog at his heels.

I said, 'Good afternoon,' as if it had been all along our habit to greet each other. He looked tired and ill and dusty, and I felt sorry for him – to think of the kind of victory he'd been winning, with so much expenditure of cash and care – the prize this dirty and dreary town, the booths of the money-changers, the awful little beauty parlours with their wicker chairs and sofas looking like the reception rooms of brothels, that hot and stuffy garden by the bandstand.

He replied gloomily, 'Good afternoon,' and the dog started to sniff at some ordure and he turned and kicked it with fury, with depression, with despair.

And at that moment a taxi with the two policemen in it passed us on its way to the bridge. They must have seen that kick; perhaps they were cleverer than I had given them credit for, perhaps they were just sentimental about animals, and thought they'd do a good deed, and the rest happened by accident. But the fact remains – those two pillars of the law set about the stealing of Mr Calloway's dog.

He watched them go by. Then he said, 'Why don't you go across?'

'It's cheaper here,' I said.

'I mean just for an evening. Have a meal at that place we can see at night in the sky. Go to the theatre.'

'There isn't one.'

He said angrily, sucking his gold tooth, 'Well, anyway, get away from here.' He stared down the hill and up the other side. He couldn't see that the street climbing up from the bridge contained only the same money-changers' booths as this one.

I said, 'Why don't *you* go?'

He said evasively, 'Oh – business.'

I said, 'It's only a question of money. You don't *have* to pass by the bridge.'

He said with faint interest, 'I don't talk Spanish.'

'There isn't a soul here,' I said, 'who doesn't talk English.'

He looked at me with surprise. 'Is that so?' he said. 'Is that so?'

It's as I have said; he'd never tried to talk to anyone, and they respected him too much to talk to him – he was worth a million. I don't know whether I'm glad or sorry that I told him that. If I hadn't, he might be there now, sitting by the bandstand having his shoes cleaned – alive and suffering.

Three days later his dog disappeared. I found him looking for it calling softly and shamefacedly between the palms of the garden. He looked embarrassed. He said in a low angry voice, 'I *hate* that dog. The beastly mongrel,' and called 'Rover, Rover' in a voice which didn't carry five yards. He said, 'I bred setters once. I'd have shot a dog like that.' It reminded him, I *was* right, of Norfolk, and he lived in the memory, and he hated it for its imperfection. He was a man without a family and without friends, and his only enemy was that dog. You couldn't call the law an enemy; you have to be intimate with an enemy.

Late that afternoon someone told him they'd seen the dog walking across the bridge. It wasn't true, of course, but we didn't know that then – they paid a Mexican five pesos to smuggle it across. So all that afternoon and the next Mr Calloway sat in the garden having his shoes cleaned over and over again, and thinking how a dog could just walk across like that, and a human being, an immortal soul, was bound here in the awful routine of the little walk and the unspeakable meals and the aspirin at the botica. That dog was seeing things he couldn't see – that hateful dog. It made him mad – I think literally mad. You must remember the man had been going on for months. He had a million and he was living on two pounds a week, with nothing to spend his money on. He sat there and brooded on the hideous injustice of it. I think he'd have crossed over one day in any case, but the dog was the last straw.

Next day when he wasn't to be seen, I guessed he'd gone across and I went too. The American town is as small as the Mexican. I knew I couldn't miss him if he was there, and I was still curious. A little sorry for him, but not too much.

I caught sight of him first in the only drug-store, having a Coca-Cola, and then once outside a cinema looking at the posters; he had dressed with extreme neatness, as if for a party, but there was no party. On my third time round, I came on the detectives – they were having Coca-Colas in the drug-store, and they must have missed Mr Calloway by inches. I went in and sat down at the bar.

'Hello,' I said, 'you still about.' I suddenly felt anxious for Mr Calloway. I didn't want them to meet.

One of them said, 'Where's Calloway?'

'Oh,' I said, 'he's hanging on.'

'But not his dog,' he said and laughed. The other looked a little shocked, he didn't like anyone to *talk* cynically about a dog. Then they got up – they had a car outside.

'Have another?' I said.

'No thanks. We've got to keep going.'

The men bent close and confided to me, 'Calloway's on this side.'

'No!' I said.

'And his dog.'

'He's looking for it,' the other said.

'I'm damned if he is,' I said, and again one of them looked a little shocked, as if I'd insulted the dog.

I don't think Mr Calloway was looking for his dog, but his dog certainly found him. There was a sudden hilarious yapping from the car and out plunged the semi-setter and gambolled furiously down the street. One of the detectives – the sentimental one – was into the car before we got to the door and was off after the dog. Near the bottom of the long road to the bridge was Mr Calloway – I do believe he'd come down to look at the Mexican side when he found there was nothing but the drug-store and the cinemas and the paper shops on the American. He saw the dog coming and yelled at it to go home – 'home, home, home,' as if they were in Norfolk – it took no notice at all, pelting towards him. Then he saw the police car coming, and ran. After that, everything happened too quickly, but I think the order of events was this – the dog started across the road right in front of the car, and Mr Calloway yelled, at the dog or the car, I don't know which. Anyway, the detective swerved – he said later, weakly, at the inquiry, that he couldn't run over a dog, and down went Mr Calloway, in a mess of broken glass and gold rims and silver hair, and blood. The dog was on to him before any of us could reach him, licking and whimpering and licking. I saw Mr Calloway put up his hand, and down it went across the dog's neck and the whimper rose to a stupid bark of triumph, but Mr Calloway was dead – shock and a weak heart.

'Poor old geezer,' the detective said, 'I bet he really loved that dog,' and it's true that the attitude in which he lay looked more like a caress than a blow. I thought it was meant to be a blow, but the detective may have been right. It all seemed to me a little too touching to be true as the old crook lay there with his arm over the dog's neck, dead with his million between the money-changers' huts, but it's as well to be humble in the face of human nature. He had come across the river for something, and it may, after all, have been the dog he was looking for. It sat there, baying its stupid and mongrel triumph across his body, like a piece of sentimental statuary: the nearest he could get to the fields, the ditches, the horizon of his home. It was comic and it was pitiable, but it wasn't less comic because the man was dead. Death doesn't change comedy to tragedy, and if that last gesture was one of affection, I suppose it was only one more indication of a human being's capacity for self-deception, our baseless optimism that is so much more appalling than our despair.

A Drive in the Country

As every other night she listened to her father going round the house, locking the doors and windows. He was head clerk at Bergson's Export Agency, and lying in bed she would think with dislike that his home was like his office, run on the same lines, its safety preserved with the same meticulous care, so that he could present a faithful steward's account to the managing-director. Regularly every Sunday he presented the account, accompanied by his wife and two daughters, in the little neo-Gothic church in Park Road. They always had the same pew, they were always five minutes early, and her father sang loudly with no sense of tune, holding an outsize prayer book on the level of his eyes. 'Singing songs of exultation' – he was presenting the week's account (one household duly safeguarded) – 'marching to the Promised Land.' When they came out of church, she looked carefully away from the corner by the 'Bricklayers' Arms' where Fred always stood, a little lit because the Arms had been open for half an hour, with his air of unbalanced exultation.

She listened: the back door closed, she could hear the catch of the kitchen window click, and the restless pad of his feet going back to try the front door. It wasn't only the outside doors he locked: he locked the empty rooms, the bathroom, the lavatory. He was locking something out, but obviously it was something capable of penetrating his first defences. He raised his second line all the way up to bed.

She laid her ear against the thin wall of the jerry-built villa and could hear the faint voices from the neighbouring room; as she listened they came clearer as though she were turning the knob of a wireless set. Her mother said '... margarine in the cooking ...' and her father said '... much easier in fifteen years.' Then the bed creaked and there were dim sounds of tenderness and comfort between the two middle-aged strangers in the next room. In fifteen years, she thought unhappily, the house will be his; he had paid twenty-five pounds down and the rest he was paying month by month as rent. 'Of course,' he was in the habit of saying after a good meal, 'I've improved the property,' and he expected at least one of them to follow him into his study. 'I've wired this room for power,' he padded back past the little downstairs lavatory, 'this radiator', the final stroke of satisfaction, 'the garden', and if it was a fine evening he would fling the french window of the dining-room open on the little carpet of grass as carefully kept as a college lawn. 'A pile of bricks,' he'd say, 'that's all it was.' Five years of Saturday afternoons and fine Sundays had gone into the patch of turf, the surrounding flower-bed, the one apple-tree which regularly produced one crimson tasteless apple more each year.

'Yes,' he said, 'I've improved the property,' looking round for a nail to drive in, a weed to be uprooted. 'If we had to sell now, we should get back more than I've paid from the society.' It was more than a sense of property, it was a sense of honesty. Some people who bought their houses through the society let them go to rack and ruin and then cleared out.

She stood with her ear against the wall, a small, furious, immature figure. There was no more to be heard from the other room, but in her inner ear she still heard the chorus of a property owner, the tap-tap of a hammer, the scrape of a spade, the whistle of radiator steam, a key turning, a bolt pushed home, the little trivial sounds of men building barricades. She stood planning her treachery.

It was a quarter past ten; she had an hour in which to leave the house, but it did not take so long. There was really nothing to fear. They had played their usual rubber of three-handed bridge while her sister altered a dress for the local 'hop' next night; after the rubber she had boiled a kettle and brought in a pot of tea; then she had filled the hot-water bottles and put them in the beds while her father locked up. He had no idea whatever that she was an enemy.

She put on a scarf and a heavy coat because it was still cold at night; the spring was late that year, as her father commented, watching for the buds on the apple-tree. She didn't pack a suitcase; that would have reminded her too much of week-ends at the sea, a family expedition to Ostend from all of which one returned; she wanted to match the odd reckless quality of Fred's mind. This time she wasn't going to return. She went softly downstairs into the little crowded hall, unlocked the door. All was quiet upstairs, and she closed the door behind her.

She was touched by a faint feeling of guilt because she couldn't lock it from the outside. But her guilt vanished by the time she reached the end of the crazy-paved path and turned to the left down the road which after five years was still half made, past the gaps between the villas where the wounded fields remained grimly alive in the form of thin grass and heaps of clay and dandelions.

She walked fast, passing a long line of little garages like the graves in a Latin cemetery where the coffin lies below the fading photograph of its occupant. The cold night air touched her with exhilaration. She was ready for anything, as she turned by the Belisha beacon into the shuttered shopping street; she was like a recruit in the first months of a war. The choice made she could surrender her will to the strange, the exhilarating, the gigantic event.

Fred, as he had promised, was at the corner where the road turned down towards the church; she could taste the spirit on his lips as they kissed, and she was satisfied that no one else could have so adequately matched the occasion; his face was bright and reckless in the lamp-light, he was as exciting and strange to her as the adventure. He took her arm and ran her into a blind unlighted alley, then left her for a moment until two headlamps beamed softly at her out of the cavern. She cried with astonishment, 'You've got a car?' and felt the jerk of his nervous hand urging her towards it. 'Yes,' he said, 'do you like it?' grinding into second gear, changing clumsily into top as they came out between the shuttered windows.

She said, 'It's lovely. Let's drive a long way.'

'We will,' he said, watching the speedometer needle go quivering to fifty-five.

'Does it mean you've got a job?'

'There are no jobs,' he said, 'they don't exist any more than the Dodo. Did you see that bird?' he asked sharply, turning his headlights full on as they passed the turning to the housing estate and quite suddenly came out into the country between a café ('Draw in here'), a boot-shop ('Buy the shoes worn by your favourite film star'), and an undertaker's with a large white angel lit by a neon light.

'I didn't see any bird.'

'Not flying at the windscreen?'

'No.'

'I nearly hit it,' he said. 'It would have made a mess. Bad as those fellows who run someone down and don't stop. Should *we* stop?' he asked, turning out his switchboard light so that they couldn't see the needle vibrate to sixty.

'Whatever you say,' she said, sitting deep in a reckless dream.

'You going to love me tonight?'

'Of course I am.'

'Never going back there?'

'No,' she said, abjuring the tap of hammer, the click of latch, the pad of slippered feet making the rounds.

'Want to know where we are going?'

'No.' A little flat cardboard copse ran forward into the green light and darkly by. A rabbit turned its scut and vanished into a hedge. He said, 'Have you any money?'

'Half a crown.'

'Do you love me?' For a long time she expended on his lips all she had patiently had to keep in reserve, looking the other way on Sunday mornings, saying nothing when his name came up at meals with disapproval. She expended herself against dry unresponsive lips as the car leapt ahead and his foot trod down on the accelerator. He said, 'It's the hell of a life.'

She echoed him, 'The hell of a life.'

He said, 'There's a bottle in my pocket. Have a drink.'

'I don't want one.'

'Give me one then. It has a screw top,' and with one hand on her and one on the wheel he tipped his head, so that she could pour a little whisky into his mouth out of the quarter bottle. 'Do you mind?' he said.

'Of course I don't mind.'

'You can't save,' he said, 'on ten shillings a week pocket-money. I lay it out the best I can. It needs a hell of a lot of thought. To give variety. Half a crown on Weights. Three and six on whisky. A shilling on the pictures. That leaves three shillings for beer. I take my fun once a week and get it over.'

The whisky had dribbled on to his tie and the smell filled the small coupé. It pleased her. It was *his* smell. He said, 'They grudge it me. They think I ought to get a job. When you're that age you don't realize there aren't any jobs for some of us – any more for ever.'

'I know,' she said. 'They are old.'

'How's your sister?' he asked abruptly; the bright glare swept the road ahead of them clean of small scurrying birds and animals.

'She's going to the hop tomorrow. I wonder where we shall be.'

He wouldn't be drawn; he had his own idea and kept it to himself.

'I'm loving this.'

He said, 'There's a club out this way. At a road-house. Mick made me a member. Do you know Mick?'

'No.'

'Mick's all right. If they know you, they'll serve you drinks till midnight. We'll look in there. Say hullo to Mick. And then in the morning – we'll decide that later when we've had a few drinks.'

'Have you the money?' A small village, a village fast asleep already behind closed doors and windows, sailed down the hill towards them as if it was being carried smoothly by a landslide into the scarred plain from which they'd come. A low grey Norman church, an inn without a sign, a clock striking eleven. He said, 'Look in the back. There's a suitcase there.'

'It's locked.'

'I forgot the key,' he said.

'What's in it?'

'A few things,' he said vaguely. 'We could pop them for drinks.'

'What about a bed?'

'There's the car. You are not scared, are you?'

'No,' she said. 'I'm not scared. This is—' but she hadn't words for the damp cold wind, the darkness, the strangeness, the smell of whisky and the rushing car. 'It moves,' she said. 'We must have gone a long way already. This is real country,' seeing an owl sweep low on furry wings over a ploughed field.

'You've got to go farther than this for real country,' he said. 'You won't find it yet on *this* road. We'll be at the road-house soon.'

She discovered in herself a nostalgia for their dark windy

solitary progress. She said, 'Need we go to the club? Can't we go farther into the country?'

He looked sideways at her; he had always been open to *any* suggestion: like some meteorological instrument, he was made for the winds to blow through. 'Of course,' he said, 'anything you like.' He didn't give the club a second thought; they swept past it a moment later, a long lit Tudor bungalow, a crash of voices, a bathing-pool filled for some reason with hay. It was immediately behind them, a patch of light whipping round a corner out of sight.

He said, 'I suppose this is country now. They none of them get farther than the club. We're quite alone now. We could lie in these fields till doomsday as far as *they* are concerned, though I suppose a ploughman . . . if they do plough here.' He raised his foot from the accelerator and let the car's speed gradually diminish. Somebody had left a wooden gate open into a field and he turned the car in; they jolted a long way down the field beside the hedge and came to a standstill. He turned out the headlamps and they sat in the tiny glow of the switchboard light. 'Peaceful,' he said uneasily; and they heard a screech owl hunting overhead and a small rustle in the hedge where something went into hiding. They belonged to the city; they hadn't a name for anything round them; the tiny buds breaking in the bushes were nameless. He nodded at a group of dark trees at the hedge ends. 'Oaks?'

'Elms?' she asked, and their mouths went together in a mutual ignorance. The touch excited her; she was ready for the most reckless act; but from his mouth, the dry spiritous lips, she gained a sense that he was less excited than he had hoped to be.

She said, to reassure herself, 'It's good to be here – miles away from anyone we know.'

'I dare say Mick's there. Down the road.'

'Does he know?'

'Nobody knows.'

She said, 'That's how I wanted it. How did you get this car?'

He grinned at her with unbalanced amusement. 'I saved from the ten shillings.'

'No but how? Did someone lend it you?'

'Yes,' he said. He suddenly pushed the door open and said, 'Let's take a walk.'

'We've never walked in the country before.' She took his arm, and she could feel the tense nerves responding to her touch. It was what she liked; she couldn't tell what he would do next. She said, 'My father calls you crazy. I like you crazy. What's all this stuff?' kicking at the ground.

'Clover,' he said, 'isn't it? I don't know.' It was like being in a foreign city where you can't understand the names on shops, the traffic signs: nothing to catch hold of, to hold you down to this and that, adrift together in a dark vacuum. 'Shouldn't you turn on the headlamps?' she said. 'It won't be so easy finding our way back. There's not much moon.' Already they seemed to have gone a long way from the car; she couldn't see it clearly any longer.

'We'll find our way,' he said. 'Somehow. Don't worry.' At the hedge end they came to the trees. He pulled a twig down and felt the sticky buds. 'What is it? Beech?'

'I don't know.'

He said, 'If it had been warmer, we could have slept out here. You'd think we might have had that much luck, tonight of all nights. But it's cold and it's going to rain.'

'Let's come in the summer,' but he didn't answer. Some other wind had blown, she could tell it, and already he had lost interest in her. There was something hard in his pocket; it hurt her side; she put her hand in. The metal chamber had absorbed all the cold there had been in the windy ride. She whispered fearfully, 'Why are you carrying that?' She had always before drawn a line round his recklessness. When her father had said he was crazy she had secretly and possessively smiled because she thought she knew the extent of his craziness. Now, while she waited for him to answer her, she could feel his craziness go on and on, out of her reach, out of her sight; she couldn't see where it ended; it had no end, she couldn't possess it any more than she could possess a darkness or a desert.

'Don't be scared,' he said. 'I didn't mean you to find that tonight.' He suddenly became more tender than he had ever been; he put his hand on her breast; it came from his fingers, a great soft meaningless flood of tenderness. He said, 'Don't you see? Life's hell. There's nothing we can do.' He spoke very gently, but she had never been more aware of his recklessness: he was open to every wind, but the wind now seemed to have set from the east: it blew like sleet through his words. 'I haven't a penny,' he said. 'We can't live on nothing. It's no good hoping that I'll get a job.' He repeated, 'There aren't any more jobs any more. And every year, you know, there's less chance, because there are more people younger than I am.'

'But why,' she said, 'have we come—?'

He became softly and tenderly lucid. 'We do love each other, don't we? We can't live without each other. It's no good hanging around, is it, waiting for our luck to change. We don't even get a fine night,' he said, feeling for rain with his hand. 'We can have a good time tonight — in the car — and then in the morning—'

'No, no,' she said. She tried to get away from him. 'I couldn't. It's horrible. I never said—'

'You wouldn't know anything,' he said gently and inexorably. Her words, she could realize now, had never made any real impression; he was swayed by them but no more than he was swayed by anything: now that the wind had set, it was like throwing scraps of paper towards the sky to speak at all, or to argue. He said, 'Of course we neither of us believe in God, but there may be a chance, and it's company, going together like that.' He added with pleasure, 'It's a gamble,' and she remembered more occasions than she could count when their last coppers had gone ringing down in fruit machines.

He pulled her closer and said with complete assurance, 'We love each other. It's the only way, you know. You can trust me.' He was like a skilled logician; he knew all the stages of the argument. She despaired of catching him out on any point but the premise: we love each other. *That* she doubted for the first time, faced by the mercilessness of his egotism. He repeated, 'It will be company.'

She said, 'There must be some way . . .'

'Why *must?*'

'Otherwise, people would be doing it all the time – everywhere!'

'They are,' he said triumphantly, as if it were more important for him to find his argument flawless than to find – well, a way, a way to go on living. 'You've only got to read the papers,' he said. He whispered gently, endearingly, as if he thought the very sound of the words tender enough to dispel all fear. 'They call it a suicide pact. It's happening all the time.'

'I couldn't. I haven't the nerve.'

'You needn't do anything,' he said. 'I'll do it all.'

His calmness horrified her. 'You mean – you'd kill me?'

He said, 'I love you enough for that, I promise it won't hurt you.' He might have been persuading her to play some trivial and uncongenial game. 'We shall be together always.' He added rationally, 'Of course, if there *is* an always,' and suddenly she saw his love as a mere flicker of gas flame playing on the marshy depth of his irresponsibility, but now she realized that it was without any limit at all; it closed over the head. She pleaded, 'There are things we can sell. That suitcase.'

She knew that he was watching her with amusement, that he

had rehearsed all her arguments and had an answer; he was only pretending to take her seriously. 'We might get fifteen shillings,' he said. 'We could live a day on that – but we shouldn't have much fun.'

'The things inside it?'

'Ah, that's another gamble. They might be worth thirty shillings. Three days, that would give us – with economy.'

'We might get a job.'

'I've been trying for a good many years now.'

'Isn't there the dole?'

'I'm not an insured worker. I'm one of the ruling class.'

'Your people, they'd give us something.'

'But we've got our pride, haven't we?' he said with remorseless conceit.

'The man who lent you the car?'

He said, 'You remember Cortez, the fellow who burnt his boats? I've burned mine. I've *got* to kill myself. You see, I stole that car. We'd be stopped in the next town. It's too late even to go back.' He laughed; he had reached the climax of his argument and there was nothing more to dispute about. She could tell that he was perfectly satisfied and perfectly happy. It infuriated her. '*You've* got to, maybe. But I haven't. Why should I kill myself? What right have you—?' She dragged herself away from him and felt against her back the rough massive trunk of the living tree.

'Oh,' he said in an irritated tone, 'of course if you like to go on without me.' She had admired his conceit; he had always carried his unemployment with a manner. Now you could no longer call it conceit: it was a complete lack of any values. 'You can go home,' he said, 'though I don't quite know how – I can't drive you back because I'm staying here. You'll be able to go to the hop tomorrow night. And there's a whist-drive, isn't there, in the church hall? My dear, I wish you joy of home.'

There was a savagery in his manner. He took security, peace, order in his teeth and worried them so that she couldn't help feeling a little pity for what they had joined in despising: a hammer tapped at her heart, driving in a nail here and a nail there. She tried to think of a bitter retort, for after all there was something to be said for the negative virtues of doing no injury, of simply going on, as her father was going on for another fifteen years. But the next moment she felt no anger. They had trapped each other. He had always wanted this: the dark field, the weapon in his pocket, the escape and the gamble; but she less honestly had wanted a little of both worlds: irresponsibility and a safe love, danger and a secure heart.

He said, 'I'm going now. Are you coming?'

'No,' she said. He hesitated; the recklessness for a moment wavered; a sense of something lost and bewildered came to her through the dark. She wanted to say: Don't be a fool. Leave the car where it is. Walk back with me, and we'll get a lift home, but she knew any thought of hers had occurred to him and been answered already: ten shillings a week, no job, getting older. Endurance was a virtue of one's fathers.

He suddenly began to walk fast down the hedge; he couldn't see where he was going; he stumbled on a root and she heard him swear. 'Damnation' – the little commonplace sound in the darkness overwhelmed her with pain and horror. She cried out, 'Fred. Fred. Don't do it,' and began to run in the opposite direction. She couldn't stop him and she wanted to be out of hearing. A twig broke under her foot like a shot, and the owl screamed across the ploughed field beyond the hedge. It was like a rehearsal with sound effects. But when the real shot came, it was quite different: a thud like a gloved hand striking a door and no cry at all. She didn't notice it at first and afterwards she thought that she had never been conscious of the exact moment when her lover ceased to exist.

She bruised herself against the car, running blindly; a blue-spotted Woolworth handkerchief lay on the seat in the light of the switchboard bulb. She nearly took it, but no, she thought, no one must know that I have been here. She turned out the light and picked her way as quietly as she could across the clover. She could begin to be sorry when she was safe. She wanted to close a door behind her, thrust a bolt down, hear the catch grip.

It wasn't ten minutes walk down the deserted lane to the roadhouse. Tipsy voices spoke a foreign language, though it was the language Fred had spoken. She could hear the clink of coins in fruit machines, the hiss of soda; she listened to these sounds like an enemy, planning her escape. They frightened her like something mindless: there was no appeal one could make to that egotism. It was simply a Want to be satisfied; it gaped at her like a mouth. A man was trying to wind up his car; the self-starter wouldn't work. He said, 'I'm a Bolshie. Of course I'm a Bolshie. I believe—'

A thin girl with red hair sat on the step and watched him. 'You're all wrong,' she said.

'I'm a Liberal Conservative.'

'You *can't* be a liberal Conservative.'

'Do you love me?'

'I love Joe.'

'You *can't* love Joe.'

'Let's go home, Mike.'

The man tried to wind up the car again, and she came up to them as if she'd come out of the club and said, 'Give me a lift?'

'Course. Delighted. Get in.'

'Won't the car go?'

'No.'

'Have you flooded—?'

'That's an idea.' He lifted the bonnet and she pressed the self-starter. It began to rain slowly and heavily and drenchingly, the kind of rain you always expect to fall on graves, and her thoughts went down the lane towards the field, the hedge, the trees – oak, beech, elm? She imagined the rain on his face, the pool collecting in each eye-socket and streaming down on either side the nose. But she could feel nothing but gladness because she had escaped from him.

'Where are you going?' she said.

'Devizes.'

'I thought you might be going to London.'

'Where do you want to go to?'

'Golding's Park.'

'Let's go to Golding's Park.'

The red-haired girl said, 'I am going in, Mike. It's raining.'

'Aren't you coming?'

'I'm going to find Joe.'

'All right.' He smashed his way out of the little car-park, bending his mudguard on a wooden post, scraping the paint of another car.

'That's the wrong way,' she said.

'We'll turn.' He backed the car into a ditch and out again. 'Was a good party,' he said. The rain came down harder; it blinded the windscreen and the electric wiper wouldn't work, but her companion didn't care. He drove straight on at forty miles an hour; it was an old car, it wouldn't do any more; the rain leaked through the hood. He said, 'Twis' that knob. Have a tune,' and when she turned it and the dance music came through, he said, 'That's Harry Roy. Know him anywhere,' driving into the thick wet night carrying the hot music with them. Presently, he said, 'A friend of mine, one of the best, you'd know him, Peter Weatherall. You know him.'

'No.'

'You must know Peter. Haven't seen him about lately. Goes off on the drink for weeks. They sent out an SOS for Peter once in the middle of the dance music. "Missing from Home". We were in the car. We had a laugh about that.'

She said, 'Is that what people do – when people are missing?'

'Know this tune,' he said. 'This isn't Harry Roy. This is Alf Cohen.'

She said suddenly, 'You're Mike, aren't you? Wouldn't *you* lend—'

He sobered up. 'Stony broke,' he said. 'Comrades in misfortune. Try Peter. Why do you want to go to Golding's Park?'

'My home.'

'You mean you live there?'

'Yes.' She said, 'Be careful. There's a speed limit here.' He was perfectly obedient. He raised his foot and let the car crawl at fifteen miles an hour. The lamp standards marched unsteadily to meet them and lit his face: he was quite old, forty if a day, ten years older than Fred. He wore a striped tie and she could see his sleeve was frayed. He had more than ten shillings a week, but perhaps not so very much more. His hair was going thin.

'You can drop me here,' she said. He stopped the car and she got out and the rain went on. He followed her on to the road. 'Let me come in?' he asked. She shook her head; the rain wetted them through; behind her was the pillar-box, the Belisha beacon, the road through the housing estate. 'Hell of a life,' he said politely, holding her hand, while the rain drummed on the hood of the cheap car and ran down his face, across his collar and the school tie. But she felt no pity, no attraction, only a faint horror and repulsion. A kind of dim recklessness gleamed in his wet eye, as the hot music of Alf Cohen's band streamed from the car, a faded irresponsibility. 'Le's go back,' he said, 'le's go somewhere. Le's go for a ride in the country. Le's go to Maidenhead,' holding her hand limply.

She pulled it away, he didn't resist, and walked down the half-made road to No. 64. The crazy paving in the front garden seemed to hold her feet firmly up. She opened the door and heard through the dark and the rain a car grind into second gear and drone away – certainly not towards Maidenhead or Devizes or the country. Another wind must have blown.

Her father called down from the first landing: 'Who's there?'

'It's me,' she said. She explained, 'I had a feeling you'd left the door unbolted.'

'And had I?'

'No,' she said gently, 'it's bolted all right,' driving the bolt softly and firmly home. She waited till his door closed. She touched the radiator to warm her fingers – he had put it in himself, he had improved the property; in fifteen years, she thought, it will be ours. She was quite free from pain, listening to the rain on the roof; he had been over the whole roof that winter inch by inch, there was nowhere for the rain to enter. It was kept outside, drumming on the shabby hood, pitting the clover field. She stood by the door, feeling only the faint repulsion she always had for things weak and crippled, thinking, 'It isn't tragic at all,' and looking down with an emotion like tenderness at the flimsy bolt from a sixpenny store any man could have broken, but which a Man had put in, the head clerk of Bergson's.

The Innocent

The Destructors

The Innocent

It was a mistake to take Lola there. I knew it the moment we alighted from the train at the small country station. On an autumn evening one remembers more of childhood than at any other time of year, and her bright veneered face, the small bag which hardly pretended to contain our things for the night, simply didn't go with the old grain warehouses across the small canal, the few lights up the hill, the posters of an ancient film. But she said, 'Let's go into the country,' and Bishop's Hendron was, of course, the first name which came into my head. Nobody would know me there now, and it hadn't occurred to me that it would be I who remembered.

Even the old porter touched a chord. I said, 'There'll be a four-wheeler at the entrance,' and there was, though at first I didn't notice it, seeing the two taxis and thinking; 'The old place is coming on.' It was very dark, and the thin autumn mist, the smell of wet leaves and canal water were deeply familiar.

Lola said, 'But why did you choose this place? It's grim.' It was no use explaining to her why it wasn't grim to me, that that sand heap by the canal had always been there (when I was three I remember thinking it was what other people meant by the seaside). I took the bag (I've said it was light; it was simply a forged passport of respectability) and said we'd walk. We came up over the little humpbacked bridge and passed the alms-houses. When I was five I saw a middle-aged man run into one to commit suicide; he carried a knife and all the neighbours pursued him up the stairs. She said, 'I never thought the country was like *this*.' They were ugly alms-houses, little grey stone boxes, but I knew them as I knew nothing else. It was like listening to music, all that walk.

But I had to say something to Lola. It wasn't her fault that she didn't belong here. We passed the school, the church, and came round into the old wide High Street and the sense of the first twelve years of life. If I hadn't come, I shouldn't have known that sense would be so strong, because those years hadn't been particularly happy or particularly miserable; they had been ordinary years, but now with the smell of wood fires, of the cold striking up from the dark damp paving stones, I thought I knew what it was that held me. It was the smell of innocence.

I said to Lola, 'It's a good inn, and there'll be nothing here, you'll see, to keep us up. We'll have dinner and drinks and go to bed.' But the worst of it was that I couldn't help wishing that I were alone. I hadn't been back all these years; I hadn't realized how well I remembered the place. Things I'd quite forgotten, like that sand heap, were coming back with an effect of pathos and nostalgia. I could have been very happy that night in a melancholy autumnal way, wandering about the little town, picking up clues to that time of life when, however miserable we are, we have expectations. It wouldn't be the same if I came back again, for then there would be the memories of Lola, and Lola meant just nothing at all. We had happened to pick each other up at a bar the day before and liked each other. Lola was all right, there was no one I would rather spend the night with, but she didn't fit in with *these* memories. We ought to have gone to Maidenhead. That's country too.

The inn was not quite where I remembered it. There was the Town Hall, but they had built a new cinema with a Moorish dome and a café, and there was a garage which hadn't existed in my time. I had forgotten too the turning to the left up a steep villaed hill.

'I don't believe that road was there in my day,' I said.

'Your day?' Lola asked.

'Didn't I tell you? I was born here.'

'You must get a kick out of bringing me here,' Lola said. 'I suppose you used to think of nights like this when you were a boy.'

'Yes,' I said, because it wasn't her fault. She was all right. I liked her scent. She used a good shade of lipstick. It was costing me a lot, a fiver for Lola and then all the bills and fares and drinks, but I'd have thought it money well spent anywhere else in the world.

I lingered at the bottom of that road. Something was stirring in the mind, but I don't think I should have remembered what, if a crowd of children hadn't come down the hill at that moment into the frosty lamplight, their voices sharp and shrill, their breath fuming as they passed under the lamps. They all carried linen bags, and some of the bags were embroidered with initials. They were in their best clothes and a little self-conscious. The small girls kept to themselves in a kind of compact beleaguered group, and one thought of hair ribbons and shining shoes and the sedate tinkle of a piano. It all came back to me: they had been to a dancing lesson, just as I used to go, to a small square house with a drive of rhododendrons half-way up the hill. More than ever I wished that Lola were not with me, less than ever did she fit, as I thought 'something's missing from the picture,' and a sense of pain glowed dully at the bottom of my brain.

We had several drinks at the bar, but there was half an hour before they would agree to serve dinner. I said to Lola, 'You don't want to drag round this town. If you don't mind, I'll just slip out for ten minutes and look at a place I used to know.' She didn't mind. There was a local man, perhaps a schoolmaster, at the bar simply longing to stand her a drink. I could see how he envied me, coming down with her like this from town just for a night.

I walked up the hill. The first houses were all new. I resented them. They hid such things as fields and gates I might have remembered. It was like a map which had got wet in the pocket and pieces had stuck together; when you opened it there were whole patches hidden. But half-way up, there the house really was, the drive; perhaps the same old lady was giving lessons. Children exaggerate age. She may not in those days have been more than thirty-five. I could hear the piano. She was following the same routine. Children under eight, 6–7 p.m. Children eight to thirteen, 7–8. I opened the gate and went in a little way. I was trying to remember.

I don't know what brought it back. I think it was simply the autumn, the cold, the wet frosting leaves, rather than the piano, which had played different tunes in those days. I remembered the small girl as well as one remembers anyone without a photograph to refer to. She was a year older than I was: she must have been just on the point of eight. I loved her with an intensity I have never felt since, I believe, for anyone. At least I have never made the mistake of laughing at children's love. It has a terrible inevitability of separation because there *can* be no satisfaction. Of course one invents tales of houses on fire, of war and forlorn charges which prove one's courage in her eyes, but never of marriage. One knows without being told that that can't happen, but the knowledge doesn't mean that one suffers less. I remembered all the games of blind-man's buff at birthday parties when I vainly hoped to catch her, so that I might have the excuse to touch and hold her, but I never caught her; she always kept out of my way.

But once a week for two winters I had my chance: I danced with her. That made it worse (it was cutting off our only contact) when she told me during one of the last lessons of the winter that next year she would join the older class. She liked me too, I knew it, but we had no way of expressing it. I used to go to her birthday parties and she would come to mine, but we never even ran home together after the dancing class. It would have seemed odd; I don't think it occurred to us. I had to join my own boisterous teasing male companions, and she the besieged, the hustled, the shrilly indignant sex on the way down the hill.

I shivered there in the mist and turned my coat collar up. The piano was playing a dance from an old C. B. Cochran revue. It seemed a long journey to have taken to find only Lola at the end of it. There *is* something about innocence one is never quite resigned to lose. Now when I am unhappy about a girl, I can simply go and buy another one. Then the best I could think of was to write some passionate message and slip it into a hole (it was extraordinary how I began to remember everything) in the wood-work of the gate. I had once told her about the hole, and sooner or later I was sure she would put in her fingers and find the message. I wondered what the message could have been. One wasn't able to express much, I thought, in those days; but because the expression was inadequate, it didn't mean that the pain was shallower than what one sometimes suffered now. I remembered how for days I had felt in the hole and always found the message there. Then the dancing lessons stopped. Probably by the next winter I had forgotten.

As I went out of the gate I looked to see if the hole existed. It was there. I put in my finger, and, in its safe shelter from the seasons and the years, the scrap of paper rested yet. I pulled it out and opened it. Then I struck a match, a tiny glow of heat in the mist and dark. It was a shock to see by its diminutive flame a picture of crude obscenity. There could be no mistake; there were my initials below the childish inaccurate sketch of a man and woman. But it woke fewer memories than the fume of breath, the linen bags, a damp leaf, or the pile of sand. I didn't recognize it; it might have been drawn by a dirty-minded stranger on a lavatory wall. All I could remember was the purity, the intensity, the pain of that passion.

I felt at first as if I had been betrayed. 'After all,' I told myself, 'Lola's not so much out of place here.' But later that night, when Lola turned away from me and fell asleep, I began to realize the deep innocence of that drawing. I had believed I was drawing something with a meaning and beautiful; it was only now after thirty years of life that the picture seemed obscene.

The Destructors

1

It was on the eve of August Bank Holiday that the latest recruit became the leader of the Wormsley Common Gang. No one was surprised except Mike, but Mike at the age of nine was surprised by everything. 'If you don't shut your mouth,' somebody once said to him, 'you'll get a frog down it.' After that Mike kept his teeth tightly clamped except when the surprise was too great.

The new recruit had been with the gang since the beginning of the summer holidays, and there were possibilities about his brooding silence that all recognized. He never wasted a word even to tell his name until that was required of him by the rules. When he said 'Trevor' it was a statement of fact, not as it would have been with the others a statement of shame or defiance. Nor did anyone laugh except Mike, who finding himself without support and meeting the dark gaze of the newcomer opened his mouth and was quiet again. There was every reason why T, as he was afterwards referred to, should have been an object of mockery – there was his name (and they substituted the initial because otherwise they had no excuse not to laugh at it), the fact that his father, a former architect and present clerk, had 'come down in the world' and that his mother considered herself better than the neighbours. What but an odd quality of danger, of the unpredictable, established him in the gang without any ignoble ceremony of initiation?

The gang met every morning in an impromptu car-park,

the site of the last bomb of the first blitz. The leader, who was known as Blackie, claimed to have heard it fall, and no one was precise enough in his dates to point out that he would have been one year old and fast asleep on the down platform of Wormsley Common Underground Station. On one side of the car-park leant the first occupied house, No. 3, of the shattered Northwood Terrace – literally leant, for it had suffered from the blast of the bomb and the side walls were supported on wooden struts. A smaller bomb and incendiaries had fallen beyond, so that the house stuck up like a jagged tooth and carried on the further wall relics of its neighbour, a dado, the remains of a fireplace. T, whose words were almost confined to voting 'Yes' or 'No' to the plan of operations proposed each day by Blackie, once startled the whole gang by saying broodingly, 'Wren built that house, father says.'

'Who's Wren?'

'The man who built St Paul's.'

'Who cares?' Blackie said. 'It's only Old Misery's.'

Old Misery – whose real name was Thomas – had once been a builder and decorator. He lived alone in the crippled house, doing for himself: once a week you could see him coming back across the common with bread and vegetables, and once as the boys played in the car-park he put his head over the smashed wall of his garden and looked at them.

'Been to the lav,' one of the boys said, for it was common knowledge that since the bombs fell something had gone wrong with the pipes of the house and Old Misery was too mean to spend money on the property. He could do the redecorating himself at cost price, but he had never learnt plumbing. The lav was a wooden shed at the bottom of the narrow garden with a star-shaped hole in the door: it had escaped the blast which had smashed the house next door and sucked out the window-frames of No. 3.

The next time the gang became aware of Mr Thomas was more surprising. Blackie, Mike and a thin yellow boy, who for some reason was called by his surname Summers, met him on the common coming back from the market. Mr Thomas stopped them. He said glumly, 'You belong to the lot that play in the car-park?'

Mike was about to answer when Blackie stopped him. As the leader he had responsibilities. 'Suppose we are?' he said ambiguously.

'I got some chocolates,' Mr Thomas said. 'Don't like 'em my self. Here you are. Not enough to go round, I don't suppose. There never is,' he added with sombre conviction. He handed over three packets of Smarties.

The gang was puzzled and perturbed by this action and tried to explain it away. 'Bet someone dropped them and he picked 'em up,' somebody suggested.

'Pinched 'em and then got in a bleeding funk,' another thought aloud.

'It's a bribe,' Summers said. 'He wants us to stop bouncing balls on his wall.'

'We'll show him we don't take bribes,' Blackie said, and they sacrificed the whole morning to the game of bouncing that only Mike was young enough to enjoy. There was no sign from Mr Thomas.

Next day T astonished them all. He was late at the rendezvous, and the voting for that day's exploit took place without him. At Blackie's suggestion the gang was to disperse in pairs, take buses at random and see how many free rides could be snatched from unwary conductors (the operation was to be carried out in pairs to avoid cheating). They were drawing lots for their companions when T arrived.

'Where you been, T?' Blackie asked. 'You can't vote now. You know the rules.'

'I've been *there*,' T said. He looked at the ground, as though he had thoughts to hide.

'Where?'

'At Old Misery's.' Mike's mouth opened and then hurriedly closed again with a click. He had remembered the frog.

'At Old Misery's?' Blackie said. There was nothing in the rules against it, but he had a sensation that T was treading on dangerous ground. He asked hopefully, 'Did you break in?'

'No. I rang the bell.'

'And what did you say?'

'I said I wanted to see his house.'

'What did he do?'

'He showed it me.'

'Pinch anything?'

'No.'

'What did you do it for then?'

The gang had gathered round: it was as though an impromptu court were about to form and try some case of deviation. T said, 'It's a beautiful house,' and still watching the ground, meeting no one's eyes, he licked his lips first one way, then the other.

'What do you mean, a beautiful house?' Blackie asked with scorn.

'It's got a staircase two hundred years old like a corkscrew. Nothing holds it up.'

'What do you mean, nothing holds it up. Does it float?'

'It's to do with opposite forces, Old Misery said.'

'What else?'

'There's panelling.'

'Like in the Blue Boar?'

'Two hundred years old.'

'Is Old Misery two hundred years old?'

Mike laughed suddenly and then was quiet again. The meeting was in a serious mood. For the first time since T had strolled into the car-park on the first day of the holidays his position was in danger. It only needed a single use of his real name and the gang would be at his heels.

'What did you do it for?' Blackie asked. He was just, he had no jealousy, he was anxious to retain T in the gang if he could. It was the word 'beautiful' that worried him – that belonged to a class world that you could still see parodied at the Wormsley Common Empire by a man wearing a top hat and a monocle, with a haw-haw accent. He was tempted to say, 'My dear Trevor, old chap,' and unleash his hell hounds. 'If you'd broken in,' he said sadly – that indeed would have been an exploit worthy of the gang.

'This was better,' T said. 'I found out things.' He continued to stare at his feet, not meeting anybody's eye, as though he were absorbed in some dream he was unwilling – or ashamed – to share.

'What things?'

'Old Misery's going to be away all tomorrow and Bank Holiday.'

Blackie said with relief, 'You mean we could break in?'

'And pinch things?' somebody asked.

Blackie said, 'Nobody's going to pinch things. Breaking in – that's good enough, isn't it? We don't want any court stuff.'

'I don't want to pinch anything,' T said. 'I've got a better idea.'

'What is it?'

T raised eyes, as grey and disturbed as the drab August day. 'We'll pull it down,' he said. 'We'll destroy it.'

Blackie gave a single hoot of laughter and then, like Mike, fell quiet, daunted by the serious implacable gaze. 'What'd the police be doing all the time?' he said.

'They'd never know. We'd do it from inside. I've found a way in.' He said with a sort of intensity, 'We'd be like worms, don't you see, in an apple. When we came out again there'd be nothing there, no staircase, no panels, nothing but just walls, and then we'd make the walls fall down – somehow.'

'We'd go to jug,' Blackie said.

'Who's to prove? and anyway we wouldn't have pinched anything.' He added without the smallest flicker of glee, 'There wouldn't be anything to pinch after we'd finished.'

'I've never heard of going to prison for breaking things,' Summers said.

'There wouldn't be time,' Blackie said. 'I've seen housebreakers at work.'

'There are twelve of us,' T said. 'We'd organize.'

'None of us know how . . .'

'I know,' T said. He looked across at Blackie. 'Have you got a better plan?'

'Today,' Mike said tactlessly, 'we're pinching free rides . . .'

'Free rides,' T said. 'Kid stuff. You can stand down, Blackie, if you'd rather . . .'

'The gang's got to vote.'

'Put it up then.'

Blackie said uneasily, 'It's proposed that tomorrow and Monday we destroy Old Misery's house.'

'Here, here,' said a fat boy called Joe.

'Who's in favour?'

T said, 'It's carried.'

'How do we start?' Summers asked.

'He'll tell you,' Blackie said. It was the end of his leadership. He went away to the back of the car-park and began to kick a stone, dribbling it this way and that. There was only one old Morris in the park, for few cars were left there except lorries: without an attendant there was no safety. He took a flying kick at the car and scraped a little paint off the rear mudguard. Beyond, paying no more attention to him than to a stranger, the gang had gathered round T; Blackie was dimly aware of the fickleness of favour. He thought of going home, of never returning, of letting them all discover the hollowness of T's leadership, but suppose after all what T proposed was possible — nothing like it had ever been done before. The fame of the Wormsley Common car-park gang would surely reach around London. There would be headlines in the papers. Even the grown-up gangs who ran the betting at the all-in wrestling and the barrow-boys would hear with respect of how Old Misery's house had been destroyed. Driven by the pure, simple and altruistic ambition of fame for the gang, Blackie came back to where T stood in the shadow of Old Misery's wall.

T was giving his orders with decision: it was as though this plan had been with him all his life, pondered through the seasons, now in his fifteenth year crystallized with the pain of puberty. 'You,' he said to Mike, 'bring some big nails, the biggest you can find, and a hammer. Anybody who can, better bring a hammer and a screwdriver. We'll need plenty of them. Chisels too. We can't have too many chisels. Can anybody bring a saw?'

'I can,' Mike said.

'Not a child's saw,' T said. 'A real saw.'

Blackie realized he had raised his hand like any ordinary member of the gang.

'Right, you bring one, Blackie. But now there's a difficulty. We want a hacksaw.'

'What's a hacksaw?' someone asked.

'You can get 'em at Woolworth's,' Summers said.

The fat boy called Joe said gloomily, 'I knew it would end in a collection.'

'I'll get one myself,' T said. 'I don't want your money. But I can't buy a sledge-hammer.'

Blackie said, 'They are working on No. 15. I know where they'll leave their stuff for Bank Holiday.'

'Then that's all,' T said. 'We meet here at nine sharp.'
'I've got to go to church,' Mike said.
'Come over the wall and whistle. We'll let you in.'

2

On Sunday morning all were punctual except Blackie, even Mike. Mike had a stroke of luck. His mother felt ill, his father was tired after Saturday night, and he was told to go to church alone with many warnings of what would happen if he strayed. Blackie had difficulty in smuggling out the saw, and then in finding the sledgehammer at the back of No. 15. He approached the house from a lane at the rear of the garden, for fear of the policeman's beat along the main road. The tired evergreens kept off a stormy sun: another wet Bank Holiday was being prepared over the Atlantic, beginning in swirls of dust under the trees. Blackie climbed the wall into Misery's garden.

There was no sign of anybody anywhere. The lav stood like a tomb in a neglected graveyard. The curtains were drawn. The house slept. Blackie lumbered nearer with the saw and the sledgehammer. Perhaps after all nobody had turned up: the plan had been a wild invention: they had woken wiser. But when he came close to the back door he could hear a confusion of sound hardly louder than a hive in swarm: a clickety-clack, a bang bang, a scraping, a creaking, a sudden painful crack. He thought: it's true, and whistled.

They opened the back door to him and he came in. He had at once the impression of organization, very different from the old happy-go-lucky ways under his leadership. For a while he wandered up and down stairs looking for T. Nobody addressed him: he had a sense of great urgency, and already he could begin to see the plan. The interior of the house was being carefully demolished without touching the walls. Summers with hammer and chisel was ripping out the skirting-boards in the ground-floor dining-room: he had already smashed the panels of the door. In the same room Joe was heaving up the parquet blocks, exposing the soft wood floorboards over the cellar. Coils of wire came out of the damaged skirting and Mike sat happily on the floor clipping the wires.

On the curved stairs two of the gang were working hard with an inadequate child's saw on the banisters – when they saw Blackie's big saw they signalled for it wordlessly. When he next saw them a quarter of the banisters had been dropped into the hall. He found T at last in the bathroom – he sat moodily in the least cared-for room in the house, listening to the sounds coming up from below.

'You've really done it,' Blackie said with awe. 'What's going to happen?'

'We've only just begun,' T said. He looked at the sledgehammer and gave his instructions. 'You stay here and break the bath and the wash-basin. Don't bother about the pipes. They come later.'

Mike appeared at the door. 'I've finished the wires, T,' he said.

'Good. You've just got to go wandering round now. The kitchen's in the basement. Smash all the china and glass and bottles you can lay hold of. Don't turn on the taps – we don't want a flood – yet. Then go into all the rooms and turn out the drawers. If they are locked get one of the others to break them open. Tear up any papers you find and smash all the ornaments. Better take a carving knife with you from the kitchen. The bedroom's opposite here. Open the pillows and tear up the sheets. That's enough for the moment. And you, Blackie, when you've finished in here crack the plaster in the passage up with your sledge-hammer.'

'What are you going to do?' Blackie asked.

'I'm looking for something special,' T said.

It was nearly lunch-time before Blackie had finished and went in search of T. Chaos had advanced. The kitchen was a shambles of broken glass and china. The dining-room was stripped of parquet, the skirting was up, the door had been taken off its hinges, and the destroyers had moved up a floor. Streaks of light came in through the closed shutters where they worked with the seriousness of creators – and destruction after all is a form of creation. A kind of imagination had seen this house as it had now become.

Mike said, 'I've got to go home for dinner.'

'Who else?' T asked, but all the others on one excuse or another had brought provisions with them.

They squatted in the ruins of the room and swapped unwanted sandwiches. Half an hour for lunch and they were at work again. By the time Mike returned they were on the top floor, and by six the superficial damage was completed. The doors were all off, all the skirtings raised, the furniture pillaged and ripped and smashed – no one could have slept in the house except on a bed of broken plaster. T gave his orders – eight o'clock next morning, and to escape notice they climbed singly over the garden wall, into the car-park. Only Blackie and T were left: the light had nearly gone, and when they touched a switch, nothing worked – Mike had done his job thoroughly.

'Did you find anything special?' Blackie asked.

T nodded. 'Come over here,' he said, 'and look.' Out of both pockets he drew bundles of pound notes. 'Old Misery's savings,' he said. 'Mike ripped out the mattress, but he missed them.'

'What are you going to do? Share them?'

'We aren't thieves,' T said. 'Nobody's going to steal anything from this house. I kept these for you and me – a celebration.' He knelt down on the floor and counted them out – there were seventy in all. 'We'll burn them,' he said, 'one by one,' and taking it in turns they held a note upwards and lit the top corner, so that the flame burnt slowly towards their fingers. The grey ash floated above them and fell on their heads like age. 'I'd like to see Old Misery's face when we are through,' T said.

'You hate him a lot?' Blackie asked.

'Of course I don't hate him,' T said. 'There'd be no fun if I hated him.' The last burning note illuminated his brooding face. 'All this hate and love,' he said, 'it's soft, it's hooey. There's only things, Blackie,' and he looked round the room crowded with the unfamiliar shadows of half things, broken things, former things. 'I'll race you home, Blackie,' he said.

3

Next morning the serious destruction started. Two were missing – Mike and another boy whose parents were off to Southend and Brighton in spite of the slow warm drops that had begun to fall and the rumble of thunder in the estuary like the first guns of the old blitz. 'We've got to hurry,' T said.

Summers was restive. 'Haven't we done enough?' he asked. 'I've been given a bob for slot machines. This is like work.'

'We've hardly started,' T said. 'Why, there's all the floors left, and the stairs. We haven't taken out a single window. You voted like the others. We are going to *destroy* this house. There won't be anything left when we've finished.'

They began again on the first floor picking up the top floorboards next the outer wall, leaving the joists exposed. Then they sawed through the joists and retreated into the hall, as what was left of the floor heeled and sank. They had learnt with practice, and the second floor collapsed more easily. By the evening an odd exhilaration seized them as they looked down the great hollow of the house. They ran risks and made mistakes: when they thought of the windows it was too late to reach them. 'Cor,' Joe said, and dropped a penny down into the dry rubble-filled well. It cracked and span amongst the broken glass.

'Why did we start this?' Summers asked with astonishment; T was already on the ground, digging at the rubble, clearing a space along the outer wall. 'Turn on the taps,' he said. 'It's too dark for anyone to see now, and in the morning it won't matter.' The water overtook them on the stairs and fell through the floorless rooms.

It was then they heard Mike's whistle at the back. 'Something's wrong,' Blackie said. They could hear his urgent breathing as they unlocked the door.

'The bogies?' Summers asked.

'Old Misery,' Mike said. 'He's on his way,' he said with pride.

'But why?' T said. 'He told me . . .' He protested with the fury of the child he had never been, 'It isn't fair.'

'He was down at Southend,' Mike said, 'and he was on the train coming back. Said it was too cold and wet.' He paused and gazed at the water. 'My, you've had a storm here. Is the roof leaking?'

'How long will he be?'

'Five minutes. I gave Ma the slip and ran.'

'We better clear,' Summers said. 'We've done enough, anyway.'

'Oh no, we haven't. Anybody could do this –' 'this' was the shattered hollowed house with nothing left but the walls. Yet walls could be preserved. Façades were valuable. They could build inside again more beautifully than before. This could again be a home. He said angrily, 'We've got to finish. Don't move. Let me think.'

'There's no time,' a boy said.

'There's got to be a way,' T said. 'We couldn't have got this far . . .'

'We've done a lot,' Blackie said.

'No. No, we haven't. Somebody watch the front.'

'We can't do any more.'

'He may come in at the back.'

'Watch the back too.' T began to plead. 'Just give me a minute and I'll fix it. I swear I'll fix it.' But his authority had gone with his ambiguity. He was only one of the gang. 'Please,' he said.

'Please,' Summers mimicked him, and then suddenly struck home with the fatal name. 'Run along home, Trevor.'

T stood with his back to the rubble like a boxer knocked groggy against the ropes. He had no words as his dreams shook and slid. Then Blackie acted before the gang had time to laugh, pushing Summers backward. 'I'll watch the front, T,' he said, and cautiously he opened the shutters of the hall. The grey wet common stretched ahead, and the lamps gleamed in the puddles. 'Someone's coming, T. No, it's not him. What's your plan, T?'

'Tell Mike to go out to the lav and hide close beside it. When he hears me whistle he's got to count ten and start to shout.'

'Shout what?'

'Oh, "Help", anything.'

'You hear, Mike,' Blackie said. He was the leader again. He took a quick look between the shutters. 'He's coming, T.'

'Quick, Mike. The lav. Stay here, Blackie, all of you, till I yell.'

'Where are you going, T?'

'Don't worry. I'll see to this. I said I would, didn't I?'

Old Misery came limping off the common. He had mud on his shoes and he stopped to scrape them on the pavement's edge. He didn't want to soil his house, which stood jagged and dark between the bomb-sites, saved so narrowly, as he believed, from destruction. Even the fan-light had been left unbroken by the bomb's blast. Somewhere somebody whistled. Old Misery looked sharply round. He didn't trust whistles. A child was shouting: it seemed to come from his own garden. Then a boy ran into the road from the car-park. 'Mr Thomas,' he called, 'Mr Thomas.'

'What is it?'

'I'm terribly sorry, Mr Thomas. One of us got taken short, and we thought you wouldn't mind, and now he can't get out.'

'What do you mean, boy?'

'He's got stuck in your lav.'

'He'd no business . . . Haven't I seen you before?'

'You showed me your house.'

'So I did. So I did. That doesn't give you the right to . . .'

'Do hurry, Mr Thomas. He'll suffocate.'

'Nonsense. He can't suffocate. Wait till I put my bag in.'

'I'll carry your bag.'

'Oh no, you don't. I carry my own.'

'This way, Mr Thomas.'

'I can't get in the garden that way. I've got to go through the house.'

'But you *can* get in the garden this way, Mr Thomas. We often do.'

'You often do?' He followed the boy with a scandalized fascination. 'When? What right . . . ?'

'Do you see . . . ? the wall's low.'

'I'm not going to climb walls into my own garden. It's absurd.'

'This is how we do it. One foot here, one foot there, and over.' The boy's face peered down, an arm shot out, and Mr Thomas found his bag taken and deposited on the other side of the wall.

'Give me back my bag,' Mr Thomas said. From the loo a boy yelled and yelled. 'I'll call the police.'

'Your bag's all right, Mr Thomas. Look. One foot there. On your right. Now just above. To your left.' Mr Thomas climbed over his own garden wall. 'Here's your bag, Mr Thomas.'

'I'll have the wall built up,' Mr Thomas said, 'I'll not have you boys coming over here, using my loo.' He stumbled on the path, but the boy caught his elbow and supported him. 'Thank you, thank you, my boy,' he murmured automatically. Somebody shouted again through the dark. 'I'm coming, I'm coming,' Mr Thomas called. He said to the boy beside him, 'I'm not unreasonable. Been a boy myself. As long as things are done regular. I don't mind you playing round the place Saturday mornings. Sometimes I like company. Only it's got to be regular. One of you asks leave and I say Yes. Sometimes I'll say No. Won't feel like it. And you come in at the front door and out at the back. No garden walls.'

'Do get him out, Mr Thomas.'

'He won't come to any harm in my loo,' Mr Thomas said, stumbling slowly down the garden. 'Oh, my rheumatics,' he said. 'Always get 'em on Bank Holiday. I've got to be careful. There's loose stones here. Give me your hand. Do you know what my horoscope said yesterday? "Abstain from any dealings in first half of week. Danger of serious crash." That might be on this path,' Mr Thomas said. 'They speak in parables and double meanings.' He paused at the door of the loo. 'What's the matter in there?' he called. There was no reply.

'Perhaps he's fainted,' the boy said.

'Not in my loo. Here, you, come out,' Mr Thomas said, and giving a great jerk at the door he nearly fell on his back when it swung easily open. A hand first supported him and then pushed him hard. His head hit the opposite wall and he sat heavily down. His bag hit his feet. A hand whipped the key out of the lock and the door slammed. 'Let me out,' he called, and heard the key turn in the lock. 'A serious crash,' he thought, and felt dithery and confused and old.

A voice spoke to him softly through the star-shaped hole in the door. 'Don't worry, Mr Thomas,' it said, 'we won't hurt you, not if you stay quiet.'

Mr Thomas put his head between his hands and pondered. He had noticed that there was only one lorry in the car-park, and he felt certain that the driver would not come for it before the morning. Nobody could hear him from the road in front, and the lane at the back was seldom used. Anyone who passed there would be hurrying home and would not pause for what they would certainly take to be drunken cries. And if he did call 'Help,' who, on a lonely Bank Holiday evening, would have the courage to investigate? Mr Thomas sat on the loo and pondered with the wisdom of age.

After a while it seemed to him that there were sounds in the silence – they were faint and came from the direction of his house. He stood up and peered through the ventilation-hole – between the cracks in one of the shutters he saw a light, not the light of a lamp, but the wavering light that a candle might give. Then he thought he heard the sound of hammering and scraping and chipping. He thought of burglars – perhaps they had employed the boy as a scout, but why should burglars engage in what sounded more and more like a stealthy form of carpentry? Mr Thomas let out an experimental yell, but nobody answered. The noise could not even have reached his enemies.

4

Mike had gone home to bed, but the rest stayed. The question of leadership no longer concerned the gang. With nails, chisels, screwdrivers, anything that was sharp and penetrating, they moved around the inner walls worrying at the mortar between the bricks. They started too high, and it was Blackie who hit on the damp course and realized the work could be halved if they weakened the joints immediately above. It was a long, tiring, un-amusing job, but at last it was finished. The gutted house stood there balanced on a few inches of mortar between the damp course and the bricks.

There remained the most dangerous task of all, out in the open at the edge of the bomb-site. Summers was sent to watch the road for passers-by, and Mr Thomas, sitting on the loo, heard clearly now the sound of sawing. It no longer came from the house, and that a little reassured him. He felt less concerned. Perhaps the other noises too had no significance.

A voice spoke to him through the hole. 'Mr Thomas.'

'Let me out,' Mr Thomas said sternly.

'Here's a blanket,' the voice said, and a long grey sausage was worked through the hole and fell in swathes over Mr Thomas's head.

'There's nothing personal,' the voice said. 'We want you to be comfortable tonight.'

'Tonight,' Mr Thomas repeated incredulously.

'Catch,' the voice said. 'Penny buns – we've buttered them, and sausage-rolls. We don't want you to starve, Mr Thomas.'

Mr Thomas pleaded desperately. 'A joke's a joke, boy. Let me out and I won't say a thing. I've got rheumatics. I got to sleep comfortable.'

'You wouldn't be comfortable, not in your house, you wouldn't. Not now.'

'What do you mean, boy?' But the footsteps receded. There was only the silence of night: no sound of sawing. Mr Thomas tried one more yell, but he was daunted and rebuked by the silence – a long way off an owl hooted and made away again on its muffled flight through the soundless world.

At seven next morning the driver came to fetch his lorry. He climbed into the seat and tried to start the engine. He was vaguely aware of a voice shouting, but it didn't concern him. At last the engine responded and he backed the lorry until it touched the great wooden shore that supported Mr Thomas's house. That way he could drive right out and down the street without reversing. The lorry moved forward, was momentarily checked as though something were pulling it from behind, and then went on to the sound of a long rumbling crash. The driver was astonished to see bricks bouncing ahead of him, while stones hit the roof of his cab. He put on his brakes. When he climbed out the whole landscape had suddenly altered. There was no house beside the car-park, only a hill of rubble. He went round and examined the back of his lorry for damage, and found a rope tied there that was still twisted at the other end round part of a wooden strut.

The driver again became aware of somebody shouting. It came from the wooden erection which was the nearest thing to a house in that desolation of broken brick. The driver climbed the smashed wall and unlocked the door. Mr Thomas came out of the loo. He was wearing a grey blanket to which flakes of pastry adhered. He gave a sobbing cry. 'My house,' he said. 'Where's my house?'

'Search me,' the driver said. His eye lit on the remains of a bath and what had once been a dresser and he began to laugh. There wasn't anything left anywhere.

'How dare you laugh,' Mr Thomas said. 'It was my house. My house.'

'I'm sorry,' the driver said, making heroic efforts, but when he remembered the sudden check of his lorry, the crash of bricks falling, he became convulsed again. One moment the house had stood there with such dignity between the bomb-sites like a man in a top hat, and then, bang, crash, there wasn't anything left – not anything. He said, 'I'm sorry. I can't help it, Mr Thomas. There's nothing personal, but you got to admit it's funny.'

Men at Work

*A Little Place
Off the
Edgware Road*

Men at Work

Richard Skate had taken a couple of hours away from the Ministry to see whether his house was still standing after the previous night's raid. He was a thin, pale, hungry-looking man of early middle age. All his life had been spent in keeping his nose above water, lecturing at night-schools and acting as temporary English master at some of the smaller public schools and in the process he had acquired a small house, a wife and one child – a rather precocious girl with a talent for painting who despised him. They lived in the country, his house was cut off from him by the immeasurable distance of bombed London – he visited it hurriedly twice a week, and his whole world was now the Ministry, the high heartless building with complicated lifts and long passages like those of a liner and lavatories where the water never ran hot and the nail-brushes were chained like Bibles. Central heating gave it a stuffy smell of mid-Atlantic except in the passages where the windows were always open for fear of blast and the cold winds whistled in. One expected to see people wrapped in rugs lying in deckchairs and the messengers carried round minutes like soup. Skate slept downstairs in the basement on a camp-bed, emerging at about ten o'clock for breakfast, and these imprisoned weeks were beginning to give him the appearance of a pit-pony – a purblind air as of something that lived underground. The Establishments branch of the Ministry of Information thought it wise to send a minute to the staff advising them to spend an hour or two a day in the open air, and some members did indeed reach the King's Arms at the corner. But Skate didn't drink.

And yet in spite of everything he was happy. Showing his pass at the outer gate, nodding to the Home Guard who was a specialist in early Icelandic customs, he was happy. For his nose was now well above water: he had a permanent job, he was a Civil Servant. His ambition had been to be a playwright (one Sunday performance in St John's Wood had enabled him to register as a dramatist in the Central Register), and now that the London theatres were most of them closed, he was no longer taunted by the sight of other men's success.

He opened the door of his dark room. It had been built of plywood in a passage, for as the huge staff of the Ministry accumulated like a kind of fungoid life – old divisions sprouting daily new sections which then broke away and became divisions and spawned in turn – the five hundred rooms of the great university block became inadequate: corners of passages were turned into rooms, and corridors disappeared overnight.

'All well?' his assistant asked: the large-breasted young woman who mothered him, bringing him cups of coffee when he looked peaky and guarding the telephone.

'Oh, yes, thanks. It's still there. A pane of glass gone, that's all.'

'A Mr Savage rang up.'

'Oh, did he? What did he want?'

'He said he'd joined the Air Force and wanted to show you his uniform.'

'Old Savage,' Skate said. 'He always was a bit wild.'

The telephone rang, and Miss Manners grasped it like an enemy.

'Yes,' she said, 'yes, RS is back. It's HG,' she explained to Skate. All the junior staff called people by initials: it was a sort of social compromise, between a Christian name and a Mr. It made telephone conversations as obscure as a cable in code.

'Hello, Graves. Yes, it's still standing. Will you be at the Book

Committee? I simply haven't got any agenda. Can't you invent something?' He said to Miss Manners, 'Graves wants to know who'll be at the Committee.'

Miss Manners recited quickly down the phone, 'RK, DH, FL, and BL says he'll be late. All right, I'll tell RS. Goodbye.' She said to Skate, 'HG asks why you don't just put Report on Progress down on the agenda.'

'He will have his little joke,' Skate said miserably. 'As if there could be any progress.'

'You want your tea,' Miss Manners said. She unlocked a drawer and took out Skate's teaspoon. No teaspoons had been supplied in the Ministry after the initial loss of 6,000 in the opening months of the war, and indeed it was becoming more and more necessary to lock everything portable up. Even the blankets disappeared from the ARP shelters. Like the wreck of a German plane the place seemed to be the prey of the relic-hunters, so that one could foresee the day when only the heavy Portland stone would remain, stripped bare, scorched by incendiaries and pitted with bullet-holes where the Home Guard unloaded their rifles.

'Oh dear, oh dear,' Skate said, 'I must get this agenda done.' His worry was only skin deep: it was all a game played in a corner under the gigantic shadow. Propaganda was a means of passing the time: work was not done for its usefulness but for its own sake – simply as an occupation. He wrote wearily down 'The Problem of India' on the agenda.

Leaving his room Skate stood aside for an odd little procession of old men in robes, led by a mace-bearer. They passed – one of them sneezing – towards the Chancellor's Hall, like humble ghosts still carrying out the ritual of another age. They had once been kings in this palace, the gigantic building had been built to house them, and now the civil servants passed up and down through their procession as though it had no more consistency than smoke. Long before he reached the room where the Book Committee sat he heard a familiar voice saying, 'What we want is a really colossal campaign . . .' It was King, of course, putting his shoulder to the war-effort: these outbreaks occurred periodically like desire. King had been an advertising man, and the need to sell something would regularly overcome him. Memories of Ovaltine and Halitosis and the Mustard Club sought an outlet all the time, until suddenly, overwhelmingly, he would begin to sell the war. The Treasury and the Stationery Office always saw to it that his great schemes came to nothing: only once, because somebody was on holiday, a King campaign really got under way. It was when the meat ration went down to a shilling; the hoardings all over London carried a curt King message. 'DON'T GROUSE ABOUT MUTTON. WHAT'S WRONG WITH YOUR GREENS?' A ribald Labour member asked a question in Parliament, the posters were withdrawn at a cost of twenty thousand pounds, the Permanent Secretary resigned, the Prime Minister stood by the Minister who stood by his staff ('I consider we are one of the fighting services'), and King, after being asked to resign, was instead put in charge of the Books Division of the Ministry at a higher salary. Here it was felt he could do no harm.

Skate slid in and handed round copies of the agenda unobtrusively like a maid laying napkins. He didn't bother to listen to King: something about a series of pamphlets to be distributed free to six million people really explaining what we were fighting for. 'Tell 'em what freedom means,' King said. 'Democracy. Don't use long words.'

Hill said, 'I don't think the Stationery Office . . .' Hill's thin voice was always the voice of reason. He was said to be the author of the official explanation and defence of the Ministry's existence: 'A negative action may have positive results.'

On Skate's agenda was written:

1. Arising from the Minutes.
2. Pamphlet in Welsh on German labour conditions.
3. Facilities for Wilkinson to visit the ATS.
4. Objections to proposed Bone pamphlet.
5. Suggestion for a leaflet from Meat Marketing Board.
6. The Problem of India.

The list, Skate thought, looked quite impressive.

'Of course,' King went on, 'the details need working out. We've got to get the right authors. Priestley and people like him. I feel there won't be any difficulty about money if we can present a really clear case. Would you look into it, Skate, and report back?'

Skate agreed. He didn't know what it was all about, but that didn't matter. A few minutes would be passed to and fro, and King's blood would cool in the process. To send a minute to anybody else in the great building and to receive a reply took at least twenty-four hours; on an urgent matter an exchange of three minutes might be got through in a week. Time outside the Ministry went at quite a different pace. Skate remembered how the minutes on who should write a 'suggested' pamphlet about the French war-effort were still circulating indecisively while Germany broke the line, passed the Somme, occupied Paris and received the delegates at Compiègne.

The committee as usual lasted an hour – it was always, to Skate, an agreeable meeting with men from other divisions, the Religions Division, the Empire Division and so on. Sometimes they co-opted another man they thought was nice. It gave an opportunity for all sorts of interesting discussions – on books and authors and artists and plays and films. The agenda didn't really matter: it was quite easy to invent one at the last moment.

Today everybody was in a good temper; there hadn't been

any bad news for a week, and as the policy of the latest Permanent Secretary was that the Ministry should not do anything to attract attention, there was no reason to fear a purge in the immediate future. The decision, too, eased everybody's work. And there was quite a breath of the larger life in the matter of Wilkinson. Wilkinson was a very popular novelist who wanted to sound a clarion-note to women, and he had asked permission to make a special study of the ATS. Now the military authorities refused permission – nobody knew why. Speculation continued for ten minutes. Skate said he thought Wilkinson was a bad writer and King disagreed – that led to a general literary discussion. Lewis from the Empire Division, who had fought in Gallipoli during the last war, dozed uneasily.

He woke up when they got on to the Bone pamphlet. Bone had been asked to write a pamphlet about the British Empire: it was to be distributed, fifty thousand copies of it, free at public meetings. But now that it was in type, all sorts of tactless phrases were discovered by the experts. India objected to a reference to Canadian dairy herds, and Australia objected to a phrase about Botany Bay. The Canadian authority was certain that mention of Wolfe would antagonize the French-Canadians, and the New Zealand authority felt that undue emphasis had been laid on the Australian fruit-farms. Meanwhile the public meetings had all been held, so that there was no means of distributing the pamphlet. Somebody suggested that it might be sent to America for the New York World Fair, but the American Division then demanded certain cuts in the references to the War of Independence, and by the time those had been made the World Fair had closed. Now Bone had written objecting to his own pamphlet which he said was unrecognizable.

'We could get somebody else to sign it,' Skate suggested – but that meant paying another fee, and the Treasury, Hill said, would never sanction that.

'Look here, Skate,' King said, 'you're a literary man. You write to Bone and sort of smooth things over.'

Lowndes came in hurriedly, smelling a little of wine. He said, 'Sorry to be late. Had to lunch a man on business. Seen the news?'

'No.'

'Daylight raids again. Fifty Nazi planes shot down. They are turning on the heat. Fifteen of ours lost.'

'We must really get Bone's pamphlet out,' Hill said.

Skate suddenly, to his surprise, said savagely, 'That'll show them,' and then sat down in humble collapse as though he had been caught out in treachery.

'Well,' Hill said, 'we mustn't get rattled, Skate. Remember what the Minister said: It's our duty just to carry on our work whatever happens.'

'Yes, I didn't mean anything.'

Without reaching a decision on the Bone pamphlet they passed on to the Meat Marketing Leaflet. Nobody was interested in this, so the matter was left in Skate's hands to report back. 'You talk to 'em, Skate,' King said. 'Good idea. You know about these things. Might ask Priestley,' he vaguely added, and then frowned thoughtfully at that old-timer on the minutes, 'The Problem of India'. 'Need we really discuss it this week?' he said. 'There's nobody here who knows about India. Let's get in Lawrence next week.'

'Good chap, Lawrence,' Lowndes said. 'Wrote a naughty novel once called *Parson's Pleasure*.'

'We'll co-opt him,' King said.

The Book Committee was over for another week, and since the room would be empty now until morning, Skate opened the big windows against the night's blast. Far up in the pale enormous sky little white lines, like the phosphorescent spoor of snails, showed where men were going home after work.

A Little Place Off the Edgware Road

Craven came up past the Achilles statue in the thin summer rain. It was only just after lighting-up time, but already the cars were lined up all the way to the Marble Arch, and the sharp acquisitive faces peered out ready for a good time with anything possible which came along. Craven went bitterly by with the collar of his mackintosh tight round his throat: it was one of his bad days.

All the way up the park he was reminded of passion, but you needed money for love. All that a poor man could get was lust. Love needed a good suit, a car, a flat somewhere, or a good hotel. It needed to be wrapped in cellophane. He was aware all the time of the stringy tie beneath the mackintosh, and the frayed sleeves: he carried his body about with him like something he hated. (There were moments of happiness in the British Museum reading-room, but the body called him back.) He bore, as his only sentiment, the memory of ugly deeds committed on park chairs. People talked as if the body died too soon – that wasn't the trouble, to Craven, at all. The body kept alive – and through the glittering tinselly rain, on his way to a rostrum, he passed a little man in a black suit carrying a banner, 'The Body shall rise again.' He remembered a dream from which three times he had woken trembling: he had been alone in the huge dark cavernous burying ground of all the world. Every grave was connected to another under the ground: the globe was honeycombed for the sake of the dead, and on each occasion of dreaming he had discovered anew the horrifying fact that the body doesn't decay. There are no worms and dissolution. Under the ground the world was littered with masses of dead flesh ready to rise again with their warts and boils and eruptions. He had lain in bed and remembered — as 'tidings of great joy' — that the body after all was corrupt.

He came up into the Edgware Road walking fast — the Guardsmen were out in couples, great languid elongated beasts — the bodies like worms in their tight trousers. He hated them, and hated his hatred because he knew what it was, envy. He was aware that every one of them had a better body than himself: indigestion creased his stomach: he felt sure that his breath was foul — but who could he ask? Sometimes he secretly touched himself here and there with scent: it was one of his ugliest secrets. Why should he be asked to believe in the resurrection of this body he wanted to forget? Sometimes he prayed at night (a hint of religious belief was lodged in his breast like a worm in a nut) that *his* body at any rate should never rise again.

He knew all the side streets round the Edgware Road only too well: when a mood was on, he simply walked until he tired, squinting at his own image in the windows of Salmon & Gluckstein and the ABCs. So he noticed at once the posters outside the disused theatre in Culpar Road. They were not unusual, for sometimes Barclays Bank Dramatic Society would hire the place for an evening — or an obscure film would be trade-shown there. The theatre had been built in 1920 by an optimist who thought the cheapness of the site would more than counter-balance its disadvantage of lying a mile outside the conventional theatre zone. But no play had ever succeeded, and it was soon left to gather rat-holes and spider-webs. The covering of the seats was never renewed, and all that ever happened to the place was the temporary false life of an amateur play or a trade show.

Craven stopped and read — there were still optimists it appeared, even in 1939, for nobody but the blindest optimist could hope to make money out of the place as 'The Home of the Silent Film'. The first season of 'primitives' was announced (a highbrow phrase): there would never be a second. Well, the seats were cheap, and it was perhaps worth a shilling to him, now that he was tired, to get in somewhere out of the rain. Craven bought a ticket and went in to the darkness of the stalls.

In the dead darkness a piano tinkled something monotonous recalling Mendelssohn: he sat down in a gangway seat, and could immediately feel the emptiness all round him. No, there would never be another season. On the screen a large woman in a kind of toga wrung her hands, then wobbled with curious jerky movements towards a couch. There she sat and stared out like a sheepdog distractedly through her loose and black and stringy hair. Sometimes she seemed to dissolve altogether into dots and flashes and wiggly lines. A sub-title said, 'Pompilia betrayed by her beloved Augustus seeks an end to her troubles.'

Craven began at last to see – a dim waste of stalls. There were not twenty people in the place – a few couples whispering with their heads touching, and a number of lonely men like himself, wearing the same uniform of the cheap mackintosh. They lay about at intervals like corpses – and again Craven's obsession returned: the tooth-ache of horror. He thought miserably – I am going mad: other people don't feel like this. Even a disused theatre reminded him of those interminable caverns where the bodies were waiting for resurrection.

'A slave to his passion Augustus calls for yet more wine.'

A gross middle-aged Teutonic actor lay on an elbow with his arm round a large woman in a shift. The Spring Song tinkled ineptly on, and the screen flickered like indigestion. Somebody felt his way through the darkness, scrabbling past Craven's knees – a small man: Craven experienced the unpleasant feeling of a large beard brushing his mouth. Then there was a long sigh as the newcomer found the next chair, and on the screen events had moved with such rapidity that Pompilia had already stabbed herself – or so Craven supposed – and lay still and buxom among her weeping slaves.

A low breathless voice sighed out close to Craven's ear, 'What's happened? Is she asleep?'

'No. Dead.'

'Murdered?' the voice asked with a keen interest.

'I don't think so. Stabbed herself.'

Nobody said 'Hush': nobody was enough interested to object to a voice. They drooped among the empty chairs in attitudes of weary inattention.

The film wasn't nearly over yet: there were children somehow to be considered: was it all going on to a second generation? But the small bearded man in the next seat seemed to be interested only in Pompilia's death. The fact that he had come in at that moment apparently fascinated him. Craven heard the word 'coincidence' twice, and he went on talking to himself about it in low out-of-breath tones. 'Absurd when you come to think of it,' and then 'no blood at all'. Craven didn't listen: he sat with his hands clasped between his knees, facing the fact as he had faced it so often before, that he was in danger of going mad. He had to pull himself up, take a holiday, see a doctor (God knew what infection moved in his veins). He became aware that his bearded neighbour had addressed him directly. 'What?' he asked impatiently, 'what did you say?'

'There would be more blood than you can imagine.'

'What are you talking about?'

When the man spoke to him, he sprayed him with damp breath. There was a little bubble in his speech like an impediment. He said, 'When you murder a man . . .'

'This was a woman,' Craven said impatiently.

'That wouldn't make any difference.'

'And it's got nothing to do with murder anyway.'

'That doesn't signify.' They seemed to have got into an absurd and meaningless wrangle in the dark.

'I know, you see,' the little bearded man said in a tone of enormous conceit.

'Know what?'

'About such things,' he said with guarded ambiguity.

Craven turned and tried to see him clearly. Was he mad? Was this a warning of what he might become – babbling incomprehensibly to strangers in cinemas? He thought, By God, no, trying to see: I'll be sane yet. I *will* be sane. He could make out nothing but a small black hump of body. The man was talking to himself again. He said, 'Talk. Such talk. They'll say it was all for fifty pounds. But that's a lie. Reasons and reasons. They always take the first reason. Never look behind. Thirty years of reasons. Such simpletons,' he added again in that tone of breathlessness and unbounded conceit. So this was madness. So long as he could realize that, he must be sane himself – relatively speaking. Not so sane perhaps as the seekers in the park or the Guardsmen in the Edgware Road, but saner than this. It was like a message of encouragement as the piano tinkled on.

Then again the little man turned and sprayed him. 'Killed herself, you say? But who's to know that? It's not a mere question of what hand holds the knife.' He laid a hand suddenly and confidingly on Craven's: it was damp and sticky: Craven said with horror as a possible meaning came to him, 'What are you talking about?'

'I know,' the little man said. 'A man in my position gets to know almost everything.'

'What is your position?' Craven asked, feeling the sticky hand on his, trying to make up his mind whether he was being hysterical or not – after all, there were a dozen explanations – it might be treacle.

'A pretty desperate one *you'd* say.' Sometimes the voice almost died in the throat altogether. Something incomprehensible had happened on the screen – take your eyes from these early pictures for a moment and the plot had proceeded on at such a pace ... Only the actors moved slowly and jerkily. A young woman in a night-dress seemed to be weeping in the arms of a Roman centurion: Craven hadn't seen either of them before. '*I am not afraid of death, Lucius – in your arms.*'

The little man began to titter – knowingly. He was talking to himself again. It would have been easy to ignore him altogether if it had not been for those sticky hands which he now removed: he seemed to be fumbling at the seat in front of him. His head had a habit of lolling sideways – like an idiot child's. He said distinctly and irrelevantly: 'Bayswater Tragedy.'

'What was that?' Craven said. He had seen those words on a poster before he entered the park.

'What?'

'About the tragedy.'

'To think they call Cullen Mews Bayswater.' Suddenly the little man began to cough – turning his face towards Craven and coughing right at him: it was like vindictiveness. The voice said, 'Let me see. My umbrella.' He was getting up.

'You didn't have an umbrella.'

'My umbrella,' he repeated. 'My—' and seemed to lose the word altogether. He went scrabbling out past Craven's knees.

Craven let him go, but before he had reached the billowy dusty curtains of the Exit the screen went blank and bright – the film had broken, and somebody immediately turned up one dirt-choked chandelier above the circle. It shone down just enough for Craven to see the smear on his hands. This wasn't hysteria: this was a fact. He wasn't mad: he had sat next to a madman who in some mews – what was the name, Colon, Collin ... Craven jumped up and made his own way out: the black curtain flapped in his mouth. But he was too late: the man had gone and there were three turnings to choose from. He chose instead a telephone-box and dialled with a sense odd for him of sanity and decision 999.

It didn't take two minutes to get the right department. They were interested and very kind. Yes, there had been a murder in a mews – Cullen Mews. A man's neck had been cut from ear to ear with a bread knife – a horrid crime. He began to tell them how he had sat next the murderer in a cinema: it couldn't be anyone else: there was blood on his hands – and he remembered with repulsion as he spoke the damp beard. There must have been a terrible lot of blood. But the voice from the Yard interrupted him. 'Oh no,' it was saying, 'we have the murderer – no doubt of it at all. It's the body that's disappeared.'

Craven put down the receiver. He said to himself aloud, 'Why should this happen to *me?* Why to *me?*' He was back in the horror of his dream – the squalid darkening street outside was only one of the innumerable tunnels connecting grave to grave where the imperishable bodies lay. He said, 'It was a dream, a dream,' and leaning forward he saw in the mirror above the telephone his own face sprinkled by tiny drops of blood like dew from a scent-spray. He began to scream, 'I won't go mad. I won't go mad. I'm sane. I won't go mad.' Presently a little crowd began to collect, and soon a policeman came.

A Visit to Morin

The Hint of an Explanation

A Visit to Morin

1

Le Diable au Ciel – there it was on a shelf in the Colmar bookshop causing a memory to reach out to me from the past of twenty years ago. One didn't often, in the 1950s, see Pierre Morin's novels on display, and yet here were two copies of his once famous book, and looking along the rows of paper-bindings I discovered others, as though there existed in Alsace a secret *cave*, like those hidden cellars where wines were once preserved from the enemy for the days when peace would return.

I had admired Pierre Morin when I was a boy, but I had almost forgotten him. He was even then an older writer on the point of abandonment by his public, but the language-class in an English public school is always a long way behind the Paris fashions. We happened at Collingworth to have a Roman Catholic master who belonged to the generation which Morin had pleased or offended. He had offended the orthodox Catholics in his own country and pleased the liberal Catholics abroad; he had pleased, too, the French Protestants who believed in God with the same intensity he seemed to show, and he found enthusiastic readers among non-Christians who, when once they had accepted imaginatively his premises, perhaps detected in his work the freedom of speculation which put his fellow Catholics on their guard. How fresh and exciting his work had appeared to my schoolmaster's generation; and to me, brought up in a lower form on *Les Misérables* and the poems of Lamartine, he was a revolutionary writer. But it is the fate of revolutionaries that the world accepts them. The excitement has gone from Morin's pages. Only the orthodox read him now, when the whole world seems prepared to believe in a god, except strangely enough – but I will not anticipate the point of my small anecdote which may yet provide a footnote to the literary history of Morin's day. When I publish it no harm can be done. Morin will be dead in the flesh as well as being dead as a writer, and he has left, so far as I am aware, no descendants and no disciples.

I yet recall with pleasure those French classes presided over by a Mr Strangeways from Chile; his swarthy complexion was said by his enemies to indicate Spanish blood (it was the period of the Spanish Civil War when anything Spanish and Roman was regarded as Fascist) and by his friends, of whom I was one, a dash of Indian. In dull fact his father was an engineer from Wolverhampton and his mother came from Louisiana and was only Latin after three removes. At these senior classes we no longer studied syntax – at which Mr Strangeways was in any case weak. Mr Strangeways read aloud to us and we read aloud to him, but after five minutes we would launch into literary criticism, pulling to pieces with youthful daring – Mr Strangeways like so many schoolmasters remained always youthful – the great established names and building up with exaggerated appreciation those who had not yet 'arrived'. Of course Morin had arrived years before, but of that we were unaware in our brick prison five hundred miles from the Seine – he hadn't reached the school text-books; he hadn't yet been mummified by Messrs Hachette et Cie. Where we didn't understand his meaning, there were no editor's notes to kill speculation.

'Can he really believe that?' I remember exclaiming to Mr Strangeways when a character in *Le Diable au Ciel* made some dark and horrifying statement on the Atonement or the Redemption, and I remember Mr Strangeways' blunt reply, flapping the sleeves of his short black gown, 'But I believe it too, Dunlop.'

He did not leave it at that or allow himself to get involved in a theological debate, which might have imperilled his post in my Protestant school. He went on to indicate that we were unconcerned with what the author believed. The author had chosen as his viewpoint the character of an orthodox Catholic – all his thoughts therefore must be affected, as they would be in life, by his orthodoxy. Morin's technique forbade him to play a part in the story himself; even to show irony would be to cheat, though perhaps we might detect something of Morin's view from the fact that the orthodoxy of Durobier was extended to the furthest possible limits, so that at the close of the book we had the impression of a man stranded on a long strip of sand from which there was no possibility of advance, and to retreat towards the shore would be to surrender. 'Is this true or is it not true?' His whole creed was concerned in the answer.

'You mean,' I asked Mr Strangeways, 'that perhaps Morin does not believe?'

'I mean nothing of the kind. No one has seriously questioned his Catholicism, only his prudence. Anyway that's not true criticism. A novel is made up of words and characters. Are the words well chosen and do the characters live? All the rest belongs to literary gossip. You are not in this class to learn how to be gossip-writers.'

And yet in those days I would have liked to know. Sometimes Mr Strangeways, recognizing my interest in Morin, would lend me Roman Catholic literary periodicals which contained notices of the novelist's work that often offended his principle of leaving the author's views out of account. I found Morin was sometimes accused of Jansenism – whatever that might be: others called him an Augustinian – a name which meant as little to me – and in the better-printed and bulkier reviews I thought I detected a note of grievance. He believed all the right things, they could find no specific fault, and yet . . . it was as though some of his characters accepted a dogma so wholeheartedly that they drew out its implications to the verge of absurdity, while others examined a dogma as though they were constitutional lawyers determined on confining it to a kind of legal minimum. Durobier, I am sure, would have staked his life on a literal Assumption: at some point in history, somewhere in the latter years of the first century AD, the body of the Virgin had floated skywards, leaving an empty tomb. On the other hand there was a character called Sagrin, in one of the minor novels, perhaps *Le Bien Pensant*, who believed that the holy body had rotted in the grave like other bodies. The strange thing was that both views seemed to possess irritating qualities to Catholic reviewers, and yet both proved to be equally in accordance with the dogmatic pronouncement when it came. One could assert therefore that they were orthodox; yet the orthodox critics seemed to scent heresy like a rat dead somewhere under the boards, at a spot they could not locate.

These, of course, were ancient criticisms, fished out of Mr Strangeways' cupboard, full of old French magazines dating back to his long-lost sojourn in Paris some time during the late 'twenties, when he had attended lectures at the Sorbonne and drunk beer at the Dôme. The word 'paradox' was frequently used with an air of disapproval. Perhaps after all the orthodox were proved right, for I certainly was to discover just how far Morin carried in his own life the sense of paradox.

2

I am not one of those who revisit their old school, or what a disappointment I would have proved to Mr Strangeways, who must by now be on the point of retirement. I think he had pictured me in the future as a distinguished writer for the weeklies on the subject of French literature – perhaps even as the author of a scholarly biography of Corneille. In fact, after an undistinguished war-record, I obtained a post, with the help of influential connections, in a firm of wine-merchants. My French syntax, so neglected by Mr Strangeways, had been improved by the war and proved useful to the firm, and I suppose I had a certain literary flair which enabled me to improve on the rather old-fashioned style of the catalogues. The directors had been content for too long with the jargon of the Wine and Food Society – 'An unimportant but highly sympathetic wine for light occasions among friends'. I introduced a more realistic note and substituted knowledge for knowingness. 'This wine comes from a small vineyard on the western slopes of the Mont Soleil range. The soil in this region has Jurassic elements, as the vineyard is on the edge of the great Jurassic fissure which extends across Europe from the Urals, and this encourages the cultivation of a small, strong, dark grape with a high sugar-content, less vulnerable than more famous wines to the chances of weather.' Of course it was the same 'unimportant' wine, but my description gave the host material for his vanity.

Business had brought me to Colmar – we had found it necessary to change our agent there, and as I am a single man and find the lonely Christmases of London sad and regretful, I had chosen to combine my visit with the Christmas holiday. One does not feel alone abroad; I imagined drinking my way through the festival itself in some *bierhaus* decorated with holly, myself invisible behind the fume of cigars. A German Christmas is Christmas *par excellence:* singing, sentiment, gluttony.

I said to the shop assistant, 'You seem to have a good supply of M. Morin's books.'

'He is very popular,' she said.

'I got the impression that in Paris he is no longer much read.'

'We are Catholics here,' she said with a note of reproof.

'Besides, he lives near Colmar, and we are very proud he chose to settle in our neighbourhood.'

'How long has he been here?'

'He came immediately after the war. We consider him almost one of us. We have all his books in German also – you will see them over there. Some of us feel he is even finer in German than in French. German,' she said, scrutinizing me with contempt as I picked up a French edition of *Le Diable au Ciel*, 'has a better vocabulary for the profundities.'

I told her I had admired M. Morin's novels since my schooldays. She softened towards me then, and I left the shop with M. Morin's address – a village fifteen miles from Colmar. I was uncertain all the same whether I would call on him. What really had I to say to him to excuse the vulgarity of my curiosity? Writing is the most private of all the arts, and yet few of us hesitate to invade the writer's home. We have all heard of that one caller from Porlock, but hundreds of callers every day are ringing doorbells, lifting receivers, thrusting themselves into the secret room where a writer works and lives.

I doubt whether I should have ventured to ring M. Morin's bell, but I caught sight of him two days later at the Midnight Mass in a village outside Colmar; it was not the village where I had been told he lived, and I wondered why he had come such a distance alone. Midnight Mass is a service which even a non-believer like myself finds inexplicably moving. Perhaps there is some memory of childhood which makes the journey through the darkness, the lighted windows and the frosty night, the slow gathering of silent strangers from the four quarters of the countryside moving and significant. There was a crib to the left of the door as I came in – the plaster-baby sprawled in the plaster-lap, and the cows, the sheep and the shepherd cast long shadows in the candlelight. Among the kneeling women was an old man whose face I seemed to remember: a round head like a peasant's, the skin wrinkled like a stale apple, with the hair gone from the crown. He knelt, bowed his head, and rose again. There had just been time, I suppose, for a formal prayer, but it must have been a short one. His chin was stubbled white like the field ouside, and there was so little about him to suggest a member of the French Academy that I might have taken him for the peasant he appeared to be, in his suit of respectable and shiny black and his black tie like a bootlace, if I had not been attracted by the eyes. The eyes gave him away: they seemed to know too much and to have seen further than the season and the fields. Of a very clear pale blue, they continually shifted focus, looking close and looking away, observant, sad and curious like those of a man caught in some great catastrophe which it is his duty to record, but which he cannot bear to contemplate for any length of time. It was not, of course, during his short prayer before the crib that I had time to watch Morin so closely; but when the congregation was shuffling up towards the altar for Communion, Morin and I found ourselves alone among the empty chairs. It was then I recognized him – perhaps from memories of old photographs in Mr Strangeways' reviews. I do not know, yet I was convinced of his identity, and I wondered what it was that kept this old distinguished Catholic from going up with the others, at this Mass of all Masses in the year, to receive the Sacrament. Had he perhaps inadvertently broken his fast, or was he a man who suffered from scruples and did he believe that he had been guilty of some act of uncharity or greed? There could not be many serious temptations, I thought, for a man who must be approaching his eightieth year. And yet I would not have believed him scrupulous; it was from his own novels I had learnt of the existence of this malady of the religious, and I would never have supposed the creator of Durobier to have suffered from the same disease as his character. However, a novelist may sometimes write most objectively of his own failings.

We sat there alone at the back of the church. The air was as cold and still as a frozen tree and the candles burned straight on the altar and God, so they believed, passed along the altar-rail. This was the birth of Christianity: outside in the dark was old savage Judea, but in here the world was only a few minutes old. It was the Year One again, and I felt the old sentimental longing to believe as those, I suppose, believed who came back one by one from the rail, with lips set like closed doors around the dissolving wafer and with crossed hands. If I had said to one of them, 'Teach me why you believe,' what would the answer have been? I thought perhaps I knew, for once in the war – driven by fear and disgust at the sight of the dead – I had spoken to a Catholic chaplain in just that way. He didn't belong to my unit, he was a busy man – it isn't the job of a chaplain in the line to instruct or convert and he was not to blame that he could convey nothing of his faith to an outsider like myself. He lent me two books – one a penny-catechism with its catalogue of preposterous questions and answers, smug and explanatory – mystery like a butterfly killed by cyanide, stiffened and laid out with pins and paper-strips; the other a sober enough study of gospel dates. I lost them both in a few days, with three bottles of whisky, my jeep and the corporal whose name I had not had time to learn before he was killed, while I was peeing in the green canal close by. I don't suppose I'd have kept the books much longer anyway. They were not the kind of help I needed, nor was the chaplain the man to give it me. I remember asking him if he had read Morin's novels. 'I haven't time to waste with him,' he said abruptly.

'They were the first books,' I said, 'to interest me in your faith.'

'You'd have done much better to read Chesterton,' he said.

So it was odd to find myself there at the back of the church with Morin himself. He was the first to leave and I followed him out. I was glad to go, for the sentimental attraction of a Midnight Mass was lost in the long *ennui* of the communions.

'M. Morin,' I said in that low voice we assume in a church or hospital.

He looked quickly, and I thought defensively, up.

I said, 'Forgive my speaking to you like this, M. Morin, but your books have given me such great pleasure.' Had the man from Porlock employed the same banal phrases?

'You are English?' he asked.

'Yes.'

He spoke to me then in English. 'You write yourself? Forgive my asking, but I do not know your name.'

'Dunlop. But I don't write. I buy and sell wine.'

'A profession more worthy of respect,' M. Morin said. 'If you would care to drive with me – I live only ten kilometres from here – I think I could show you a wine you may not have encountered.'

'Surely, it's rather late, M. Morin. And I have a driver . . .'

'Send him home. After Midnight Mass I find it difficult to sleep. You would be doing me a kindness.' When I hesitated he said, 'As for tomorrow, that is just any day of the year, and I don't like visitors.'

I tried to make a joke of it. 'You mean it's my only chance?' and he replied 'Yes' with seriousness. The doors of the church swung open and the congregation came slowly out into the frosty glitter, pecking at the holy water stoup with their forefingers, chatting cheerfully again as the mystery receded, greeting neighbours. A wailing child marked the lateness of the hour like a clock. M. Morin strode away and I followed him.

3

M. Morin drove with clumsy violence, wrenching at his gears, scraping the right-hand hedgerows as though the car were a new invention and he a courageous pioneer in its use. 'So you have read some of my books?' he asked.

'A great many, when I was a schoolboy . . .'

'You mean they are fit only for children?'

'I mean nothing of the sort.'

'What can a child find in them?'

'I was sixteen when I began to read them. That's not a child.'

'Oh well, now they are only read by the old – and the pious. Are you pious, Mr Dunlop?'

'I'm not a Catholic.'

'I'm glad to hear that. Then I shan't offend you.'

'Once I thought of becoming one.'

'Second thoughts are best.'

'I think it was your books that made me curious.'

'I will not take responsibility,' he said. 'I am not a theologian.' We bumped over a little branch railway-track without altering speed and swerved right through a gateway much in need of repair. A light hanging in a porch shone on an open door.

'Don't you lock up,' I asked him, 'in these parts?'

He said, 'Ten years ago – times were bad then – a hungry man was frozen to death near here on Christmas morning. He could find no one to open a door: there was a blizzard, but they were all at church. Come in,' he said angrily from the porch; 'are you looking round, making notes of how I live? Have you deceived me? Are you a journalist?'

If I had had my own car with me I would have driven away. 'M. Morin,' I said, 'there are different kinds of hunger. You seem only to cater for one kind.' He went ahead of me into a small study – a desk, a table, two comfortable chairs, and some bookshelves oddly bare – I could see no sign of his own books. There was a bottle of brandy on the table, ready perhaps for the stranger and the blizzard that would never again come together in this place.

'Sit down,' he said, 'sit down. You must forgive me if I was discourteous. I am unused to company. I will go and find the wine I spoke of. Make yourself at home.' I had never seen a man less at home himself. It was as if he were camping in a house that belonged to another.

While he was away, I looked more closely at his bookshelves. He had not re-bound any of his paper-backs and his shelves had the appearance of bankrupt stock: small tears and dust and the discoloration of sunlight. There was a great deal of theology, some poetry, very few novels. He came back with the wine and a plate of salami. When he had tasted the wine himself, he poured me a glass. 'It will do,' he said.

'It's excellent. Remarkable.'

'A small vineyard twenty miles away. I will give you the address before you go. For me, on a night like this, I prefer brandy.' So perhaps it was really for himself and not for the stranger, I thought, that the bottle stood ready.

'It's certainly cold.'

'It was not the weather I meant.'

'I have been looking at your library. You read a lot of theology?'

'Not now.'

'I wonder if you would recommend . . .' But I had even less success with him than with the chaplain.

'No. Not if you want to believe. If you are foolish enough to want that you must avoid theology.'

'I don't understand.'

He said, 'A man can accept anything to do with God until scholars begin to go into the details and the implications. A man can accept the Trinity, but the arguments that follow . . .' He gave a gesture of rejection. 'I would never try to determine some point in differential calculus with a two-times-two table. You end by disbelieving the calculus.' He poured out two more glasses and drank his own as though it were vodka. 'I used to believe in revelation, but I never believed in the capacity of the human mind.'

'You used to believe?'

'Yes, Mr Dunlop – was that the name? – *used*. If you are one of those who come seeking belief, go away. You won't find it here.'

'But from your books . . .'

'You will find none of them,' he said, 'on my shelves.'

'I noticed you have some theology.'

'Even disbelief,' he said, with his eye on the brandy bottle, 'needs bolstering.' I noticed that the brandy affected him very quickly, not only his readiness to communicate with me, but even the physical appearance of his eyeballs. It was as if the little blood-cells had been waiting under the white membrane to burst at once like buds with the third glass. He said, 'Can you find anything more inadequate than the scholastic arguments for the existence of God?'

'I'm afraid I don't know them.'

'The arguments from an agent, from a cause?'

'No.'

'They tell you that in all change there are two elements, that which is changed and that which changes it. Each agent of change is itself determined by some higher agent. Can this go on *ad infinitum*? Oh no, they say, that would not give the finality that thought demands. But does thought demand it? Why shouldn't the chain go on for ever? Man has invented the idea of infinity. In any case how trivial any argument based on what human thought demands must be. The thoughts of you and me and Monsieur Dupont. I would prefer the thoughts of an ape. Its instincts are less corrupted. Show me a gorilla praying and I might believe again.'

'But surely there are other arguments?'

'Four. Each more inadequate than the other. It needs a child to say to these theologians, Why? Why not? Why not an infinite series of causes? Why should the existence of a good and a better imply the existence of a best? This is playing with words. We invent the words and make arguments from them. The better is not a fact: it is only a word and a human judgement.'

'You are arguing,' I said, 'against someone who can't answer you back. You see, M. Morin, I don't believe either. I'm curious, that's all.'

'Ah,' he said, 'you've said that before – curious. Curiosity is a great trap. They used to come here in their dozens to see me. I used to get letters saying how I had converted them by this book or that. Long after I ceased to believe myself I was a carrier of belief, like a man can be a carrier of disease without being sick. Women especially.' He added with disgust, 'I had only to sleep with a woman to make a convert.' He turned his red eyes towards me and really seemed to require an answer when he said, 'What sort of Rasputin life was that?' The brandy by now had really taken a hold; I wondered how many years he had been waiting for some stranger without faith to whom he could speak with frankness.

'Did you never tell this to a priest? I always imagined in your faith . . .'

'There were always too many priests,' he said, 'around me. The priests swarmed like flies. Near me and any woman I knew. First I was an exhibit for their faith. I was useful to them, a sign that even an intelligent man could believe. That was the period of the Dominicans, who liked the literary atmosphere and good wine. Then afterwards when the books stopped, and they smelt something – gamey – in my religion, it was the turn of the Jesuits, who never despair of what they call a man's soul.'

'And why did the books stop?'

'Who knows? Did you never write verses for some girl when you were a boy?'

'Of course.'

'But you didn't marry the girl, did you? The unprofessional poet writes of his feelings and when the poem is finished he finds his love dead on the page. Perhaps I wrote away my belief like the young man writes away his love. Only it took longer – twenty years and fifteen books.' He held up the wine. 'Another glass?'

'I would rather have some of your brandy.' Unlike the wine it was a crude and common mark, and I thought again, For a beggar's sake or his own? I said, 'All the same you go to Mass.'

'I go to Midnight Mass on Christmas Eve,' he said. 'The worst of Catholics goes then – even those who do not go at Easter. It is the Mass of our childhood. And of mercy. What would they think if I were not there? I don't want to give scandal. You must realize I wouldn't speak to any one of my neighbours as I have spoken to you. I am their Catholic author, you see. Their Academician. I never wanted to help anyone believe, but God knows I wouldn't take a hand in robbing them . . .'

'I was surprised at one thing when I saw you there, M. Morin.'

'Yes?'

I said rashly, 'You and I were the only ones who didn't take Communion.'

'That is why I don't go to the church in my own village. That too would be noticed and cause scandal.'

'Yes, I can see that.' I stumbled heavily on (perhaps the brandy had affected me too). 'Forgive me, M. Morin, but I wondered at your age what kept you from Communion. Of course now I know the reason.'

'Do you?' Morin said. 'Young man, I doubt it.' He looked at me across his glass with impersonal enmity. He said, 'You don't understand a thing I have been saying to you. What a story you would make of this if you were a journalist and yet there wouldn't be a word of truth . . .'

I said stiffly, 'I thought you made it perfectly clear that you had lost your faith.'

'Do you think that would keep anyone from the Confessional? You are a long way from understanding the Church or the human mind, Mr Dunlop. Why, it is one of the most common confessions of all for a priest to hear – almost as common as adultery. "Father, I have lost my faith." The priest, you may be sure, makes it himself often enough at the altar before he receives the Host.'

I said – I was angry in return now, 'Then what keeps you away? Pride? One of your Rasputin women?'

'As you so rightly thought,' he said, 'women are no longer a problem at my age.' He looked at his watch. 'Two-thirty. Perhaps I ought to drive you back.'

'No,' I said, 'I don't want to part from you like this. It's the drink that makes us irritable. Your books are still important to me. I know I am ignorant. I am not a Catholic and never shall be, but in the old days your books made me understand that at least it might be possible to believe. You never closed the door in my face as you are doing now. Nor did your characters, Durobier, Sagrin.' I indicated the brandy bottle. 'I told you just now – people are not only hungry and thirsty in that way. Because you've lost *your* faith . . .'

He interrupted me ferociously. 'I never told you that.'

'Then what have you been talking about all this time?'

'I told you I had lost my belief. That's quite a different thing. But how are you to understand?'

'You don't give me a chance.'

He was obviously striving to be patient. He said, 'I will put it this way. If a doctor prescribed you a drug and told you to take it every day for the rest of your life and you stopped obeying him and drank no more, and your health decayed, would you not have faith in your doctor all the more?'

'Perhaps. But I still don't understand you.'

'For twenty years,' Morin said, 'I excommunicated myself voluntarily. I never went to Confession. I loved a woman too much to pretend to myself that I would ever leave her. You know the condition of absolution? A firm purpose of amendment. I had no such purpose. Five years ago my mistress died and my sex died with her.'

'Then why couldn't you go back?'

'I was afraid. I am still afraid.'

'Of what the priest would say?'

'What a strange idea you have of the Church. No, not of what the priest would say. He would say nothing. I dare say there is no greater gift you can give a priest in the confessional, Mr Dunlop, than to return to it after many years. He feels of use again. But can't you understand? I can tell myself now that my lack of belief is a final proof that the Church is right and the faith is true. I had cut myself off for twenty years from grace and my belief withered as the priests said it would. I don't believe in God and His Son and His angels and His saints, but I know the reason why I don't believe and the reason is – the Church is true and what she taught me is true. For twenty years I have been without the sacraments and I can see the effect. The wafer must be more than wafer.'

'But if you went back . . .'

'If I went back and belief did not return? That is what I fear, Mr Dunlop. As long as I keep away from the sacraments, my lack of belief is an argument for the Church. But if I returned and they failed me, then I would really be a man without faith, who had better hide himself quickly in the grave so as not to discourage others.' He laughed uneasily. 'Paradoxical, Mr Dunlop?'

'That is what they said of your books.'

'I know.'

'Your characters carried their ideas to extreme lengths. So your critics said.'

'And you think I do too?'

'Yes, M. Morin.'

His eyes wouldn't meet mine. He grimaced beyond me. 'At least I am not a carrier of disease any longer. You have escaped infection.' He added, 'Time for bed, Mr Dunlop. Time for bed. The young need more sleep.'

'I am not as young as that.'

'To me you seem very young.'

He drove me back to my hotel and we hardly spoke. I was thinking of the strange faith which held him even now after he had ceased to believe. I had felt very little curiosity since that moment of the war when I had spoken to the chaplain, but now I began to wonder again. M. Morin considered he had ceased to be a carrier, and I couldn't help hoping that he was right. He had forgotten to give me the address of the vineyard, but I had forgotten to ask him for it when I said good night.

The Hint of an Explanation

A long train journey on a late December evening, in this new version of peace, is a dreary experience. I suppose that my fellow traveller and I could consider ourselves lucky to have a compartment to ourselves, even though the heating apparatus was not working, even though the lights went out entirely in the frequent Pennine tunnels and were too dim anyway for us to read our books without straining the eyes, and though there was no restaurant car to give at least a change of scene. It was when we were trying simultaneously to chew the same kind of dry bun bought at the same station buffet that my companion and I came together. Before that we had sat at opposite ends of the carriage, both muffled to the chin in overcoats, both bent low over type we could barely make out, but as I threw the remains of my cake under the seat our eyes met, and he laid his book down.

By the time we were half-way to Bedwell Junction we had found an enormous range of subjects for discussion; starting with buns and the weather, we had gone on to politics, the Government, foreign affairs, the atom bomb, and by an inevitable progression, God. We had not, however, become either shrill or acid. My companion, who now sat opposite me, leaning a little forward, so that our knees nearly touched, gave such an impression of serenity that it would have been impossible to quarrel with him, however much our views differed, and differ they did profoundly.

I had soon realized I was speaking to a Roman Catholic – to someone who believed – how do they put it? – in an omnipotent and omniscient Deity, while I am what is loosely called an agnostic. I have a certain intuition (which I do not trust, founded as it may well be on childish experiences and needs) that a God exists, and I am surprised occasionally into belief by the extraordinary coincidences that beset our path like the traps set for leopards in the jungle, but intellectually I am revolted at the whole notion of such a God who can so abandon his creatures to the enormities of Free Will. I found myself expressing this view to my companion who listened quietly and with respect. He made no attempt to interrupt – he showed none of the impatience or the intellectual arrogance I have grown to expect from Catholics; when the lights of a wayside station flashed across his face which had escaped hitherto the rays of the one globe working in the compartment, I caught a glimpse suddenly of – what? I stopped speaking, so strong was the impression. I was carried back ten years, to the other side of the great useless conflict, to a small town, Gisors in Normandy. I was again, for a moment, walking on the ancient battlements and looking down across the grey roofs, until my eyes for some reason lit on one stony 'back' out of the many, where the face of a middle-aged man was pressed against a window pane (I suppose that face has ceased to exist now, just as perhaps the whole town with its medieval memories has been reduced to rubble). I remembered saying to myself with astonishment, 'That man is happy – completely happy.' I looked across the compartment at my fellow traveller, but his face was already again in shadow. I said weakly, 'When you think what God – if there is a God – allows. It's not merely the physical agonies, but think of the corruption, even of children . . .'

He said, 'Our view is so limited,' and I was disappointed at the conventionality of his reply. He must have been aware of my disappointment (it was as though our thoughts were huddled as closely as ourselves for warmth), for he went on, 'Of course there is no answer here. We catch hints . . .' and then the train roared into another tunnel and the lights again went out. It was the longest tunnel yet; we went rocking down it and the cold seemed to become more intense with the darkness, like an icy fog (when one sense – of sight – is robbed, the others grow more acute). When we emerged into the mere grey of night and the globe lit up once more, I could see that my companion was leaning back on his seat.

I repeated his last word as a question, 'Hints?'

'Oh, they mean very little in cold print – or cold speech,' he said, shivering in his overcoat. 'And they mean nothing at all to another human being than the man who catches them. They are not scientific evidence – or evidence at all for that matter. Events that don't, somehow, turn out as they were intended – by the human actors, I mean, or by the thing behind the human actors.'

'The thing?'

'The word Satan is so anthropomorphic.' I had to lean forward now: I wanted to hear what he had to say. I am – I really am, God knows – open to conviction. He said, 'One's words are so crude, but I sometimes feel pity for that thing. It is so continually finding the right weapon to use against its Enemy and the weapon breaks in its own breast. It sometimes seems to me so – powerless. You said something just now about the corruption of children. It reminded me of something in my own childhood. You are the first person – except for one – that I have thought of telling it to, perhaps because you are anonymous. It's not a very long story, and in a way it's relevant.'

I said, 'I'd like to hear it.'

'You mustn't expect too much meaning. But to me there seems to be a hint. That's all. A hint.'

He went slowly on turning his face to the pane, though he could have seen nothing in the whirling world outside except an occasional signal lamp, a light in a window, a small country station torn backwards by our rush, picking his words with precision. He said, 'When I was a child they taught me to serve at Mass. The church was a small one, for there were very few Catholics where I lived. It was a market town in East Anglia, surrounded by flat chalky fields and ditches – so many ditches. I don't suppose there were fifty Catholics all told, and for some reason there was a tradition of hostility to us. Perhaps it went back to the burning of a Protestant martyr in the sixteenth century – there was a stone marking the place near where the meat stalls stood on Wednesdays. I was only half aware of the enmity, though I knew that my school nickname of Popey Martin had something to do with my religion and I had heard that my father was very nearly excluded from the Constitutional Club when he first came to the town.

'Every Sunday I had to dress up in my surplice and serve Mass. I hated it – I have always hated dressing up in any way (which is funny when you come to think of it), and I never ceased to be afraid of losing my place in the service and doing something which would put me to ridicule. Our services were at a different hour from the Anglican, and as our small, far-from-select band trudged out of the hideous chapel the whole of the townsfolk seemed to be on the way past to the proper church – I always thought of it as the proper church. We had to pass the parade of their eyes, indifferent, supercilious, mocking; you can't imagine how seriously religion can be taken in a small town – if only for social reasons.

'There was one man in particular; he was one of the two bakers in the town, the one my family did not patronize. I don't think any of the Catholics patronized him because he was called a free-thinker – an odd title, for, poor man, no one's thoughts were less free than his. He was hemmed in by his hatred – his hatred of us. He was very ugly to look at, with one wall-eye and a head the shape of a turnip, with the hair gone on the crown, and he was unmarried. He had no interests, apparently, but his baking and his hatred, though now that I am older I begin to see other sides of his nature – it did contain, perhaps, a certain furtive love. One would come across him suddenly, sometimes, on a country walk, especially if one was alone and it was Sunday. It was as though he rose from the ditches and the chalk smear on his clothes reminded one of the flour on his working overalls. He would have a stick in his hand and stab at the hedges, and if his mood were very black he would call out after you strange, abrupt words that were like a foreign tongue – I know the meaning of those words, of course, now. Once the police went to his house because of what a boy said he had seen, but nothing came of it except that the hate shackled him closer. His name was Blacker, and he terrified me.

'I think he had a particular hatred of my father – I don't know why. My father was manager of the Midland Bank, and it's possible that at some time Blacker may have had unsatisfactory dealings with the bank – my father was a very cautious man who suffered all his life from anxiety about money – his own and other people's. If I try to picture Blacker now I see him walking along a narrowing path between high windowless walls, and at the end of the path stands a small boy of ten – me. I don't know whether it's a symbolic picture or the memory of one of our encounters – our encounters somehow got more and more frequent. You talked just now about the corruption of children. That poor man was preparing to revenge himself on everything he hated – my father, the Catholics, the God whom people persisted in crediting – by corrupting me. He had evolved a horrible and ingenious plan.

'I remember the first time I had a friendly word from him. I was passing his shop as rapidly as I could when I heard his voice call out with a kind of sly subservience as though he were an under-servant. "Master David," he called, "Master David," and I hurried on. But the next time I passed that way he was at his door (he must have seen me coming) with one of those curly cakes in his hand that we called Chelsea buns. I didn't want to take it, but he made me, and then I couldn't be other than polite when he asked me to come into his parlour behind the shop and see something very special.

'It was a small electric railway – a rare sight in those days, and he insisted on showing me how it worked. He made me turn the switches and stop and start it, and he told me that I could come in any morning and have a game with it. He used the word "game" as though it were something secret, and it's true that I never told my family of this invitation and of how, perhaps twice a week those holidays, the desire to control that little railway became overpowering, and looking up and down the street to see if I were observed, I would dive into the shop.'

Our larger, dirtier, adult train drove into a tunnel and the light went out. We sat in darkness and silence, with the noise of the train blocking our ears like wax. When we were through we didn't speak at once and I had to prick him into continuing.

'An elaborate seduction,' I said.

'Don't think his plans were as simple as that,' my companion said, 'or as crude. There was much more hate than love, poor man, in his make-up. Can you hate something you don't believe in? And yet he called himself a free-thinker. What an impossible paradox, to be free and to be so obsessed. Day by day all through those holidays his obsession must have grown, but he kept a grip; he bided his time. Perhaps that thing I spoke of gave him the strength and the wisdom. It was only a week from the end of the holidays that he spoke to me of what concerned him so deeply.

'I heard him behind me as I knelt on the floor, coupling two coaches. He said, "You won't be able to do this, Master David, when school starts." It wasn't a sentence that needed any comment from me any more than the one that followed, "You ought to have it for your own, you ought," but how skilfully and un-emphatically he had sowed the longing, the idea of a possibility . . . I was coming to his parlour every day now; you see I had to cram every opportunity in before the hated term started again, and I suppose I was becoming accustomed to Blacker, to that wall-eye, that turnip head, that nauseating subservience. The Pope, you know, describes himself as "The servant of the servants of God", and Blacker – I sometimes think, that Blacker was "the servant of the servants of . . ." well, let it be.

'The very next day, standing in the doorway watching me play, he began to talk to me about religion. He said, with what untruth even I recognized, how much he admired the Catholics; he wished he could believe like that, but how could a baker believe? He accented "a baker" as one might say a biologist, and the tiny train spun round the gauge-O track. He said, "I can bake the things you eat just as well as any Catholic can," and disappeared into his shop. I hadn't the faintest idea what he meant. Presently he emerged again, holding in his hand a little wafer. "Here," he said, "eat that and tell me . . ." When I put it in my mouth I could tell that it was made in the same way as our wafers for communion – he had got the shape a little wrong, that was all, and I felt guilty and irrationally scared. "Tell me," he said, "what's the difference?"

' "Difference?" I asked.

' "Isn't that just the same as you eat in church?"

'I said smugly, "It hasn't been consecrated."

'He said, "Do you think if I put the two of them under a microscope, you could tell the difference?" But even at ten I had the answer to that question. "No," I said, "the – accidents don't change," stumbling a little on the word "accidents" which had suddenly conveyed to me the idea of death and wounds.

'Blacker said with sudden intensity, "How I'd like to get one of yours in my mouth – just to see . . ."

'It may seem odd to you, but this was the first time that the idea of transubstantiation really lodged in my mind. I had learnt it all by rote; I had grown up with the idea. The Mass was as lifeless to me as the sentences in *De Bello Gallico*, communion a routine like drill in the school-yard, but here suddenly I was in the presence of a man who took it seriously, as seriously as the priest whom naturally one didn't count – it was his job. I felt more scared than ever.

'He said, "It's all nonsense, but I'd just like to have it in my mouth."

'"You could if you were a Catholic," I said naïvely. He gazed at me with his one good eye like a Cyclops. He said, "You serve at Mass, don't you? It would be easy for you to get at one of those things. I tell you what I'd do – I'd swap this electric train set for one of your wafers – consecrated, mind. It's got to be consecrated."

'"I could get you one out of the box," I said. I think I still imagined that his interest was a baker's interest – to see how they were made.

'"Oh, no," he said. "I want to see what your God tastes like."

'"I couldn't do that."

'"Not for a whole electric train, just for yourself? You wouldn't have any trouble at home. I'd pack it up and put a label inside that your Dad could see – 'For my bank manager's little boy from a grateful client.' He'd be pleased as Punch with that."

'Now that we are grown men it seems a trivial temptation, doesn't it? But try to think back to your own childhood. There was a whole circuit of rails on the floor at our feet, straight rails and curved rails, and a little station with porters and passengers, a tunnel, a foot-bridge, a level crossing, two signals, buffers, of course — and above all, a turntable. The tears of longing came into my eyes when I looked at the turntable. It was my favourite piece — it looked so ugly and practical and true. I said weakly, "I wouldn't know how."

'How carefully he had been studying the ground. He must have slipped several times into Mass at the back of the church. It would have been no good, you understand, in a little town like that, presenting himself for communion. Everybody there knew him for what he was. He said to me, "When you've been given communion you could just put it under your tongue a moment. He serves you and the other boy first, and I saw you once go out behind the curtain straight afterwards. You'd forgotten one of those little bottles."

'"The cruet," I said.

'"Pepper and salt." He grinned at me jovially, and I — well, I looked at the little railway which I could no longer come and play with when term started. I said, "You'd just swallow it, wouldn't you?"

'"Oh, yes," he said, "I'd just swallow it."

'Somehow I didn't want to play with the train any more that day. I got up and made for the door, but he detained me, gripping my lapel. He said, "This will be a secret between you and me. Tomorrow's Sunday. You come along here in the afternoon. Put it in an envelope and post it in. Monday morning the train will be delivered bright and early."

'"Not tomorrow," I implored him.

'"I'm not interested in any other Sunday," he said. "It's your only chance." He shook me gently backwards and forwards. "It will always have to be a secret between you and me," he said. "Why, if anyone knew they'd take away the train and there'd be me to reckon with. I'd bleed you something awful. You know how I'm always about on Sunday walks. You can't avoid a man like me. I crop up. You wouldn't even be safe in your own house. I know ways to get into houses when people are asleep." He pulled me into the shop after him and opened a drawer. In the drawer was an odd-looking key and a cut-throat razor. He said, "That's a master key that opens all locks and that – that's what I bleed people with." Then he patted my cheek with his plump floury fingers and said, "Forget it. You and me are friends."

'That Sunday Mass stays in my head, every detail of it, as though it had happened only a week ago. From the moment of the Confession to the moment of Consecration it had a terrible importance; only one other Mass has ever been so important to me – perhaps not even one, for this was a solitary Mass which could never happen again. It seemed as final as the last Sacrament, when the priest bent down and put the wafer in my mouth where I knelt before the altar with my fellow server.

'I suppose I had made up my mind to commit this awful act – for, you know, to us it must always seem an awful act – from the moment when I saw Blacker watching from the back of the church. He had put on his best Sunday clothes, and as though he could never quite escape the smear of his profession, he had a dab of dried talcum on his cheek, which he had presumably applied after using that cut-throat of his. He was watching me closely all the time, and I think it was fear – fear of that terrible undefined thing called bleeding – as much as covetousness that drove me to carry out my instructions.

'My fellow server got briskly up and taking the communion plate preceded Father Carey to the altar rail where the other Communicants knelt. I had the Host lodged under my tongue: it felt like a blister. I got up and made for the curtain to get the cruet that I had purposely left in the sacristy. When I was there I looked quickly round for a hiding-place and saw an old copy of the *Universe* lying on a chair. I took the Host from my mouth and inserted it between two sheets – a little damp mess of pulp.

Then I thought: perhaps Father Carey has put the paper out for a particular purpose and he will find the Host before I have time to remove it, and the enormity of my act began to come home to me when I tried to imagine what punishment I should incur. Murder is sufficiently trivial to have its appropriate punishment, but for this act the mind boggled at the thought of any retribution at all. I tried to remove the Host, but it had stuck clammily between the pages and in desperation I tore out a piece of the newspaper and, screwing the whole thing up, stuck it in my trouser pocket. When I came back through the curtain carrying the cruet my eyes met Blacker's. He gave me a grin of encouragement and unhappiness – yes, I am sure, unhappiness. Was it perhaps that the poor man was all the time seeking something incorruptible?

'I can remember little more of that day. I think my mind was shocked and stunned and I was caught up too in the family bustle of Sunday. Sunday in a provincial town is the day for relations. All the family are at home and unfamiliar cousins and uncles are apt to arrive packed in the back seats of other people's cars. I remember that some crowd of that kind descended on us and pushed Blacker temporarily out of the foreground of my mind. There was somebody called Aunt Lucy with a loud hollow laugh that filled the house with mechanical merriment like the sound of recorded laughter from inside a hall of mirrors, and I had no opportunity to go out alone even if I had wished to. When six o'clock came and Aunt Lucy and the cousins departed and peace returned, it was too late to go to Blacker's and at eight it was my own bed-time.

'I think I had half forgotten what I had in my pocket. As I emptied my pocket the little screw of newspaper brought quickly back the Mass, the priest bending over me, Blacker's grin. I laid the packet on the chair by my bed and tried to go to sleep, but I was haunted by the shadows on the wall where the curtains blew, the squeak of furniture, the rustle in the chimney, haunted by the presence of God there on the chair. The Host had always been to me – well, the Host. I knew theoretically, as I have said, what I had to believe, but suddenly, as someone whistled in the road outside, whistled secretively, knowingly, to me, I knew that this which I had beside my bed was something of infinite value – something a man would pay for with his whole peace of mind, something that was so hated one could love it as one loves an outcast or a bullied child. These are adult words and it was a child of ten who lay scared in bed, listening to the whistle from the road, Blacker's whistle, but I think he felt fairly clearly what I am describing now. That is what I meant when I said this Thing, whatever it is, that seizes every possible weapon against God, is always, everywhere, disappointed at the moment of success. It must have felt as certain of me as Blacker did. It must have felt certain, too, of Blacker. But I wonder, if one knew what happened later to that poor man, whether one would not find again that the weapon had been turned against its own breast.

'At last I couldn't bear that whistle any more and got out of bed. I opened the curtains a little way, and there right under my window, the moonlight on his face, was Blacker. If I had stretched my hand down, his fingers reaching up could almost have touched mine. He looked up at me, flashing the one good eye, with hunger – I realize now that near-success must have developed his obsession almost to the point of madness. Desperation had driven him to the house. He whispered up at me, "David, where is it?"

'I jerked my head back at the room. "Give it me," he said, "quick. You shall have the train in the morning."

'I shook my head. He said, "I've got the bleeder here, and the key. You'd better toss it down."

' "Go away," I said, but I could hardly speak with fear.

' "I'll bleed you first and then I'll have it just the same."

' "Oh no, you won't," I said. I went to the chair and picked it – Him – up. There was only one place where He was safe. I couldn't separate the Host from the paper, so I swallowed both. The newsprint stuck like a prune to the back of my throat, but I rinsed it down with water from the ewer. Then I went back to the window and looked down at Blacker. He began to wheedle me. "What have you done with it, David? What's the fuss? It's only a bit of bread," looking so longingly and pleadingly up at me that even as a child I wondered whether he could really think that, and yet desire it so much.

' "I swallowed it," I said.

' "Swallowed it?"

' "Yes," I said. "Go away." Then something happened which seems to me now more terrible than his desire to corrupt or my thoughtless act: he began to weep – the tears ran lopsidedly out of the one good eye and his shoulders shook. I only saw his face for a moment before he bent his head and strode off, the bald turnip head shaking, into the dark. When I think of it now, it's almost as if I had seen that Thing weeping for its inevitable defeat. It had tried to use me as a weapon and now I had broken in its hands and it wept its hopeless tears through one of Blacker's eyes.'

The black furnaces of Bedwell Junction gathered around the line. The points switched and we were tossed from one set of rails to another. A spray of sparks, a signal light changed to red, tall chimneys jetting into the grey night sky, the fumes of steam from stationary engines – half the cold journey was over and now remained the long wait for the slow cross-country train. I said, 'It's an interesting story. I think I should have given Blacker what he wanted. I wonder what he would have done with it.'

'I really believe,' my companion said, 'that he would first of all have put it under his microscope – before he did all the other things I expect he had planned.'

'And the hint?' I said. 'I don't quite see what you mean by that.'

'Oh, well,' he said vaguely, 'you know for me it was an odd beginning, that affair, when you come to think of it,' but I should never have known what he meant had not his coat, when he rose to take his bag from the rack, come open and disclosed the collar of a priest.

I said, 'I suppose you think you owe a lot to Blacker.'

'Yes,' he said. 'You see, I am a very happy man.'

Cheap in August

The Moment of Truth

Cheap in August

1

It was cheap in August: the essential sun, the coral reefs, the bamboo bar and the calypsos – they were all of them at cut prices, like the slightly soiled slips in a bargain-sale. Groups arrived periodically from Philadelphia in the manner of school-treats and departed with less *bruit*, after an exact exhausting week, when the picnic was over. Perhaps for twenty-four hours the swimming-pool and the bar were almost deserted, and then another school-treat would arrive, this time from St Louis. Everyone knew everyone else; they had bussed together to an airport, they had flown together, together they had faced an alien customs; they would separate during the day and greet each other noisily and happily after dark, exchanging impressions of 'shooting the rapids', the botanic gardens, the Spanish fort. 'We are doing that tomorrow.'

Mary Watson wrote to her husband in Europe, 'I had to get away for a bit and it's so cheap in August.' They had been married ten years and they had only been separated three times. He wrote to her every day and the letters arrived twice a week in little bundles. She arranged them like newspapers by the date and read them in the correct order. They were tender and precise; what with his research, with preparing lectures and writing letters, he had little time to *see* Europe – he insisted on calling it 'your Europe' as though to assure her that he had not forgotten the sacrifice which she must have made by marrying an American professor from New England, but sometimes little criticisms of 'her Europe' escaped him: the food was too rich, cigarettes too expensive, wine too often served and milk very difficult to obtain at lunchtime – which might indicate that, after all, she ought not to exaggerate her sacrifice. Perhaps it would have been a good thing if James Thomson, who was his special study at the moment, had written *The Seasons* in America – an American fall, she had to admit, was more beautiful than an English autumn.

Mary Watson wrote to him every other day, but sometimes a postcard only, and she was apt to forget if she had repeated the postcard. She wrote in the shade of the bamboo bar where she could see everyone who passed on the way to the swimming-pool. She wrote truthfully, 'It's so cheap in August; the hotel is not half full, and the heat and the humidity are very tiring. But, of course, it's a change.' She had no wish to appear extravagant; the salary, which to her European eyes had seemed astronomically large for a professor of literature, had long dwindled to its proper proportions, relative to the price of steaks and salads – she must justify with a little enthusiasm the money she was spending in his absence. So she wrote also about the flowers in the botanic gardens – she had ventured that far on one occasion – and with less truth of the beneficial changes wrought by the sun and the lazy life on her friend Margaret who from 'her England' had written and demanded her company: a Margaret, she admitted frankly to herself, who was not visible to any eye but the eye of faith. But then Charlie had complete faith. Even good qualities become with the erosion of time a reproach. After ten years of being happily married, she thought, one undervalues security and tranquillity.

She read Charlie's letters with great attention. She longed to find in them one ambiguity, one evasion, one time-gap which he had ill-explained. Even an unusually strong expression of love would have pleased her, for its strength might have been there to counterweigh a sense of guilt. But she couldn't deceive herself that there was any sense of guilt in Charlie's facile flowing informative script. She calculated that if he had been one of the poets he was now so closely studying, he would have completed already a standard-sized epic during his first two months in 'her Europe', and the letters, after all, were only a spare-time occupation. They filled up the vacant hours, and certainly they could have left no room for any other occupation. 'It is ten o'clock at night, it is raining outside and the temperature is rather cool for August, not above fifty-six degrees. When I have said goodnight to you, my dear one, I shall go happily to bed with the thought of you. I have a long day tomorrow at the museum and dinner in the evening with the Henry Wilkinsons who are passing through on their way from Athens – you remember the Henry Wilkinsons, don't you?' (Didn't she just?) She had wondered whether, when Charlie returned, she might perhaps detect some small unfamiliar note in his love-making which would indicate that a stranger had passed that way. Now she disbelieved in the possibility, and anyway the evidence would arrive too late – it was no good to her now that she might be justified later. She wanted her justification immediately, a justification not alas! for any act that she had committed but only for an intention, for the intention of betraying Charlie, of having, like so many of her friends, a holiday affair (the idea had come to her immediately the dean's wife had said, 'It's so cheap in Jamaica in August').

The trouble was that, after three weeks of calypsos in the humid evenings, the rum punches (for which she could no longer disguise from herself a repugnance), the warm Martinis, the interminable red snappers, and tomatoes with everything, there had been no affair, not even the hint of one. She had discovered with disappointment the essential morality of a holiday resort in the cheap season; there were no opportunities for infidelity, only for writing postcards – with great brilliant blue skies and seas – to Charlie. Once a woman from St Louis had taken too obvious pity on her, when she sat alone in the bar writing postcards, and invited her to join their party which was about to visit the botanic gardens – 'We are an awfully jolly bunch,' she had said with a big turnip smile. Mary exaggerated her English accent to repel her better and said that she didn't much care for flowers. It had shocked the woman as deeply as if she had said she did not care for television. From the motion of the heads at the other end of the bar, the agitated clinking of the Coca-Cola glasses, she could tell that her words were being repeated from one to another. Afterwards, until the jolly bunch had taken the airport limousine on the way back to St Louis, she was aware of averted heads. She was English, she had taken a superior attitude to flowers, and as she preferred even warm Martinis to Coca-Cola, she was probably in their eyes an alcoholic.

It was a feature common to most of these jolly bunches that they contained no male attachment, and perhaps that was why the attempt to look attractive was completely abandoned. Huge buttocks were exposed in their full horror in tight large-patterned Bermuda shorts. Heads were bound in scarves to cover rollers which were not removed even by lunchtime – they stuck out like small mole-hills. Daily she watched the bums lurch by like hippos on the way to the water. Only in the evening would the women change from the monstrous shorts into monstrous cotton frocks, covered with mauve or scarlet flowers, in order to take dinner on the terrace where formality was demanded in the book of rules, and the few men who appeared were forced to wear jackets and ties though the thermometer stood at close on eighty degrees after sunset. The market in femininity being such, how could one hope to see any male foragers? Only old and broken husbands were sometimes to be seen towed towards an Issa store advertising freeport prices.

She had been encouraged during the first week by the sight of three men with crew-cuts who went past the bar towards the swimming-pool wearing male bikinis. They were far too young for her, but in her present mood she would have welcomed altruistically the sight of another's romance. Romance is said to be contagious, and if in the candle-lit evenings the 'informal' coffee-tavern had contained a few young amorous couples, who could say what men of maturer years might not eventually arrive to catch the infection? But her hopes dwindled. The young men came and went without a glance at the Bermuda shorts or the pinned hair. Why should they stay? They were certainly more beautiful than any girl there and they knew it.

By nine o'clock most evenings Mary Watson was on her way to bed. A few evenings of calypsos, of quaint false impromptus and the hideous jangle of rattles, had been enough. Outside the closed windows of the hotel annexe the boxes of the air-conditioners made a continuous rumble in the starred and palmy night like over-fed hotel guests. Her room was full of dried air which bore no more resemblance to fresh air than the dried figs to the newly picked fruit. When she looked in the glass to brush her hair she often regretted her lack of charity to the jolly bunch from St Louis. It was true she did not wear Bermuda shorts nor coil her hair in rollers, but her hair was streaky nonetheless with heat and the mirror reflected more plainly than it seemed to do at home her thirty-nine years. If she had not paid in advance for a four-weeks *pension* on her individual round-trip tour, with tickets exchangeable for a variety of excursions, she would have turned tail and returned to the campus. Next year, she thought, when I am forty, I must feel grateful that I have preserved the love of a good man.

She was a woman given to self-analysis, and perhaps because it is a great deal easier to direct questions to a particular face rather than to a void (one has the right to expect some kind of a response even from eyes one sees many times a day in a compact), she posed the questions to herself with a belligerent direct stare into the looking-glass. She was an honest woman, and for that reason the questions were all the cruder. She would say to herself, I have slept with no one other than Charlie (she wouldn't admit as sexual experiences the small exciting half-way points that she had reached before marriage); why am I now seeking to find a strange body, which will probably give me less pleasure than the body I already know? It had been more than a month before Charlie brought her real pleasure. Pleasure, she learnt, grew with habit, so that if it were not really pleasure that she now looked for, what was it? The answer could only be the unfamiliar. She had friends, even on the respectable campus, who had admitted to her, in the frank admirable American way, their adventures. These had usually been in Europe — a momentary marital absence had given the opportunity for a momentary excitement, and then with what a sigh of relief they had found themselves safely at home. All the same they felt afterwards that they had enlarged their experience; they understood something that their husbands did not really understand — the real character of a Frenchman, an Italian, even — there were such cases — of an Englishman.

Mary Watson was painfully aware, as an Englishwoman, that her experience was confined to one American. They all, on the campus, believed her to be European, but all she knew was confined to one man and he was a citizen of Boston who had no curiosity for the great Western regions. In a sense she was more American by choice than he was by birth. Perhaps she was less European even than the wife of the Professor of Romance Languages, who had confided to her that once — overwhelmingly — in Antibes . . . it had happened only once because the sabbatical year was over . . . her husband was up in Paris checking manuscripts before they flew home . . .

Had she herself, Mary Watson sometimes wondered, been just such a European adventure which Charlie mistakenly had domesticated? (She couldn't pretend to be a tigress in a cage, but they kept smaller creatures in cages, white mice, lovebirds.) And, to be fair, Charlie too was her adventure, her American adventure, the kind of man whom at twenty-seven she had not before encountered in frowsy London. Henry James had described the type, and at that moment in her history she had been reading a great deal of Henry James: 'A man of intellect whose body was not much to him and its senses and appetites not importunate.' All the same for a while she had made the appetites importunate.

That was her private conquest of the American continent, and when the Professor's wife had spoken of the dancer of Antibes (no, that was a Roman inscription – the man had been a *marchand de vin*) she had thought, The lover I know and admire is American and I am proud of it. But afterwards came the thought: American or New England? Yet to know a country must one know every region sexually?

It was absurd at thirty-nine not to be content. She had her man. The book on James Thomson would be published by the University Press, and Charlie had the intention afterwards of making a revolutionary break from the romantic poetry of the eighteenth century into a study of the American image in European literature – it was to be called *The Double Reflection*: the effect of Fenimore Cooper on the European scene: the image of America presented by Mrs Trollope – the details were not yet worked out. The study might possibly end with the first arrival of Dylan Thomas on the shores of America – at the Cunard quay or at Idlewild? That was a point for later research. She examined herself again closely in the glass – the new decade of the forties stared frankly back at her – an Englander who had become a New Englander. After all she hadn't travelled very far – Kent to Connecticut. This was not just the physical restlessness of middle age, she argued; it was the universal desire to see a little bit further, before one surrendered to old age and the blank certitude of death.

2

Next day she picked up her courage and went as far as the swimming-pool. A strong wind blew and whipped up the waves in the almost land-girt harbour – the hurricane season would soon be here. All the world creaked around her: the wooden struts of the shabby harbour, the jalousies of the small hopeless houses which looked as though they had been knocked together from a make-it-yourself kit, the branches of the palms – a long, weary, worn-out creaking. Even the water of the swimming-pool imitated in miniature the waves of the harbour.

She was glad that she was alone in the swimming-pool, at least for all practical purposes alone, for the old man splashing water over himself, like an elephant, in the shallow end hardly counted. He was a solitary elephant and not one of the hippo band. They would have called her with merry cries to join them – and it's difficult to be stand-offish in a swimming-pool which is common to all as a table is not. They might even in their resentment have ducked her – pretending like schoolchildren that it was all a merry game; there was nothing she put beyond those thick thighs, whether they were encased in bikinis or Bermuda shorts. As she floated in the pool her ears were alert for their approach. At the first sound she would get well away from the water, but today they were probably making an excursion to Tower Isle on the other side of the island, or had they done that yesterday? Only the old man watched her, pouring water over his head to keep away sunstroke. She was safely alone, which was the next best thing to the adventure she had come here to find. All the same, as she sat on the rim of the pool, and let the sun and wind dry her, she realized the extent of her solitude. She had spoken to no one but black waiters and Syrian receptionists for more than two weeks. Soon, she thought, I shall even begin to miss Charlie – it would be an ignoble finish to what she had intended to be an adventure.

A voice from the water said to her, 'My name's Hickslaughter – Henry Hickslaughter.' She couldn't have sworn to the name in court, but that was how it had sounded at the time and he never repeated it. She looked down at a polished mahogany crown surrounded by white hair; perhaps he resembled Neptune more than an elephant. Neptune was always outsize, and as he had pulled himself a little out of the water to speak, she could see the rolls of fat folding over the blue bathing-slip, with tough hair lying like weeds along the ditches. She replied with amusement, 'My name is Watson. Mary Watson.'

'You're English?'

'My husband's American,' she said in extenuation.

'I haven't seen him around, have I?'

'He's in England,' she said with a small sigh, for the geographical and national situation seemed too complicated for casual explanation.

'You like it here?' he asked and lifting a hand-cup of water he distributed it over his bald head.

'So so.'

'Got the time on you?'

She looked in her bag and told him, 'Eleven fifteen.'

'I've had my half hour,' he said and trod heavily away towards the ladder at the shallow end.

An hour later, staring at her lukewarm Martini with its great green unappetizing olive, she saw him looming down at her from the other end of the bamboo bar. He wore an ordinary shirt open at the neck and a brown leather belt; his type of shoes in her childhood had been known as co-respondent, but one seldom saw them today. She wondered what Charlie would think of her pick-up; unquestionably she had landed him, rather as an angler struggling with a heavy catch finds that he has hooked nothing better than an old boot. She was no angler; she didn't know whether a boot would put an ordinary hook out of action altogether, but she knew that *her* hook could be irremediably damaged. No one would approach her if she were in his company. She drained the Martini in one gulp and even attacked the olive so as to have no excuse to linger in the bar.

'Would you do me the honour,' Mr Hickslaughter asked, 'of having a drink with me?' His manner was completely changed; on dry land he seemed unsure of himself and spoke with an old-fashioned propriety.

'I'm afraid I've only just finished one. I have to be off.' Inside the gross form she thought she saw a tousled child with disappointed eyes. 'I'm having lunch early today.' She got up and added rather stupidly, for the bar was quite empty, 'You can have my table.'

'I don't need a drink that much,' he said solemnly. 'I was just after company.' She knew that he was watching her as she moved to the adjoining coffee tavern, and she thought with guilt, at least I've got the old boot off the hook. She refused the shrimp cocktail with tomato ketchup and fell back as was usual with her on a grapefruit, with grilled trout to follow. 'Please no tomato with the trout,' she implored, but the black waiter obviously didn't understand her. While she waited she began with amusement to picture a scene between Charlie and Mr Hickslaughter, who happened for the purpose of her story to be crossing the campus. 'This is Henry Hickslaughter, Charlie. We used to go bathing together when I was in Jamaica.' Charlie, who always wore English clothes, was very tall, very thin, very concave. It was a satisfaction to know that he would never lose his figure – his nerves would see to that and his extreme sensibility. He hated anything gross; there was no grossness in *The Seasons*, not even in the lines on spring.

She heard slow footsteps coming up behind her and panicked. 'May I share your table?' Mr Hickslaughter asked. He had recovered his terrestrial politeness, but only so far as speech was concerned, for he sat firmly down without waiting for her reply. The chair was too small for him; his thighs overlapped like a double mattress on a single bed. He began to study the menu.

'They copy American food; it's worse than the reality,' Mary Watson said.

'You don't like American food?'

'Tomatoes even with the trout!'

'Tomatoes? Oh, you mean tomatoes,' he said, correcting her accent. 'I'm very fond of tomatoes myself.'

'And fresh pineapple in the salad.'

'There's a lot of vitamins in fresh pineapple.' Almost as if he wished to emphasize their disagreement, he ordered shrimp cocktail, grilled trout and a sweet salad. Of course, when her trout arrived, the tomatoes were there. 'You can have mine if you want to,' she said and he accepted with pleasure. 'You are very kind. You are really very kind.' He held out his plate like Oliver Twist.

She began to feel oddly at ease with the old man. She would have been less at ease, she was certain, with a possible adventure: she would have been wondering about her effect on him, while now she could be sure that she gave him pleasure – with the tomatoes. He was perhaps less the old anonymous boot than an old shoe comfortable to wear. And curiously enough, in spite of his first approach and in spite of his correcting her over the pronunciation of tomatoes, it was not really an old American shoe of which she was reminded. Charlie wore English clothes over his English figure, he studied English eighteenth-century literature, his book would be published in England by the Cambridge University Press who would buy sheets, but she had the impression that he was far more fashioned as an American shoe than Hick-slaughter. Even Charlie, whose manners were perfect, if they had met for the first time today at the swimming-pool, would have interrogated her more closely. Interrogation had always seemed to her a principal part of American social life – an inheritance perhaps from the Indian smoke-fires: 'Where are you from? Do you know the so and so's? Have you been to the botanic gardens?' It came over her that Mr Hickslaughter, if that were really his name, was perhaps an American reject – not necessarily more flawed than the pottery rejects of famous firms you find in bargain-basements.

She found herself questioning *him*, with circumlocutions, while he savoured the tomatoes. 'I was born in London. I couldn't have been born more than six hundred miles from there without drowning, could I? But you belong to a continent thousands of miles wide and long. Where were you born?' (She remembered a character in a Western movie directed by John Ford who asked, 'Where do you hail from, stranger?' The question was more frankly put than hers.)

He said, 'St Louis.'

'Oh, then there are lots of your people here – you are not alone.' She felt a slight disappointment that he might belong to the jolly bunch.

'I'm alone,' he said. 'Room 63.' It was in her own corridor on the third floor of the annexe. He spoke firmly as though he were imparting information for future use. 'Five doors down from you.'

'Oh.'

'I saw you come out your first day.'

'I never noticed you.'

'I keep to myself unless I see someone I like.'

'Didn't you see anyone you liked from St Louis?'

'I'm not all that fond of St Louis, and St Louis can do without me. I'm not a favourite son.'

'Do you come here often?'

'In August. It's cheap in August.' He kept on surprising her. First there was his lack of local patriotism, and now his frankness about money or rather about the lack of it, a frankness that could almost be classed as an un-American activity.

'Yes.'

'I have to go where it's reasonable,' he said, as though he were exposing his bad hand to a partner at gin.

'You've retired?'

'Well – I've been retired.' He added, 'You ought to take salad . . . It's good for you.'

'I feel quite well without it.'

'You could do with more weight.' He added appraisingly, 'A couple of pounds.' She was tempted to tell him that he could do with less. They had both seen each other exposed.

'Were you in business?' She was being driven to interrogate. He hadn't asked her a personal question since his first at the pool.

'In a way,' he said. She had a sense that he was supremely uninterested in his own doings; she was certainly discovering an America which she had not known existed.

She said, 'Well, if you'll excuse me . . .'

'Aren't you taking any dessert?'

'No, I'm a light luncher.'

'It's all included in the price. You ought to eat some fruit.' He was looking at her under his white eyebrows with an air of disappointment which touched her.

'I don't care much for fruit and I want a nap. I always have a nap in the afternoon.'

Perhaps, after all, she thought, as she moved away through the formal dining-room, he is disappointed only because I'm not taking full advantage of the cheap rate.

She passed his room going to her own: the door was open and a big white-haired mammy was making the bed. The room was exactly like her own; the same pair of double beds, the same wardrobe, the same dressing-table in the same position, the same heavy breathing of the air-conditioner. In her own room she looked in vain for the thermos of iced water; then she rang the bell and waited for several minutes. You couldn't expect good service in August. She went down the passage; Mr Hickslaughter's door was still open and she went in to find the maid. The door of the bathroom was open too and a wet cloth lay on the tiles.

How bare the bedroom was. At least she had taken the trouble to add a few flowers, a photograph and half a dozen books on a bedside table which gave her room a lived-in air. Beside his bed there was only a literary digest lying open and face down; she turned it over to see what he was reading – as she might have expected it was something to do with calories and proteins. He had begun writing a letter at his dressing-table and with the simple unscrupulousness of an intellectual she began to read it with her ears cocked for any sound in the passage.

'Dear Joe,' she read, 'the draft was two weeks late last month and I was in real difficulties. I had to borrow from a Syrian who runs a tourist junk-shop in Curaçao and pay him interest. You owe me a hundred dollars for the interest. It's your own fault. Mum never gave us lessons on how to live with an empty stomach. Please add it to the next draft and be sure to do that, you wouldn't want me coming back to collect. I'll be here till the end of August. It's cheap in August, and a man gets tired of nothing but Dutch, Dutch, Dutch. Give my love to Sis.'

The letter broke off unfinished. Anyway she would have had no opportunity to read more because someone was approaching down the passage. She went to the door in time to see Mr Hickslaughter on the threshold. He said, 'You looking for me?'

'I was looking for the maid. She was in here a minute ago.'

'Come in and sit down.'

He looked through the bathroom door and then at the room in general. Perhaps it was only an uneasy conscience which made her think that his eyes strayed a moment to the unfinished letter.

'She's forgotten my iced water.'

'You can have mine if it's filled.' He shook his thermos and handed it to her.

'Thanks a lot.'

'When you've had your sleep . . .' he began and looked away from her. Was he looking at the letter?

'Yes?'

'We might have a drink.'

She was, in a sense, trapped. She said, 'Yes.'

'Give me a ring when you wake up.'

'Yes.' She said nervously, 'Have a good sleep yourself.'

'Oh, I don't sleep.' He didn't wait for her to leave the room before turning away, swinging that great elephantine backside of his towards her. She had walked into a trap baited with a flask of iced water, and in her room she drank the water gingerly as though it might have a flavour different from hers.

3

She found it difficult to sleep: the old fat man had become an individual now that she had read his letter. She couldn't help comparing his style with Charlie's. 'When I have said goodnight to you, my dear one, I shall go happily to bed with the thought of you.' In Mr Hickslaughter's there was an ambiguity, a hint of menace. Was it possible that the old man could be dangerous?

At half past five she rang up room 63. It was not the kind of adventure she had planned, but it was an adventure nonetheless. 'I'm awake,' she said.

'You coming for a drink?' he asked.

'I'll meet you in the bar.'

'Not the bar,' he said. 'Not at the prices they charge for bourbon. I've got all we need here.' She felt as though she were being brought back to the scene of a crime, and she needed a little courage to knock on the door.

He had everything prepared: a bottle of Old Walker, a bucket of ice, two bottles of soda. Like books, drinks can make a room inhabited. She saw him as a man fighting in his own fashion against the sense of solitude.

'Siddown,' he said, 'make yourself comfortable,' like a character in a movie. He began to pour out two highballs.

She said, 'I've got an awful sense of guilt. I did come in here for iced water, but I was curious too. I read your letter.'

'I knew someone had touched it,' he said.

'I'm sorry.'

'Who cares? It was only to my brother.'

'I had no business . . .'

'Look,' he said, 'if I came into your room and found a letter open I'd read it, wouldn't I? Only your letter would be more interesting.'

'Why?'

'I don't write love letters. Never did and I'm too old now.' He sat down on a bed – she had the only easy chair. His belly hung in heavy folds under his sports-shirt, and his flies were a little open. Why was it always fat men who left them unbuttoned? He said, 'This is good bourbon,' taking a drain of it. 'What does your husband do?' he asked – it was his first personal question since the pool and it took her by surprise.

'He writes about literature. Eighteenth-century poetry,' she added, rather inanely under the circumstances.

'Oh.'

'What did you do? I mean when you worked.'

'This and that.'

'And now?'

'I watch what goes on. Sometimes I talk to someone like you. Well, no, I don't suppose I've ever talked to anyone like you before.' It might have seemed a compliment if he had not added, 'A professor's wife.'

'And you read the *Digest*?'

'Ye-eh. They make books too long – I haven't the patience. Eighteenth-century poetry. So they wrote poetry back in those days, did they?'

She said, 'Yes,' not sure whether or not he was mocking her.

'There was a poem I liked at school. The only one that ever stuck in my head. By Longfellow, I think. You ever read Longfellow?'

'Not really. They don't read him much in school any longer.'

'Something about "Spanish sailors with bearded lips and the something and mystery of the ships and the something of the sea." It hasn't stuck at all that well, after all, but I suppose I learned it sixty years ago and even more. Those were the days.'

'The 1900s?'

'No, no. I meant pirates, Kidd and Bluebeard and those fellows. This was their stamping ground, wasn't it? The Caribbean. It makes you kind of sick to see those women going around in their shorts here.' His tongue had been tingled into activity by the bourbon.

It occurred to her that she had never really been curious

about another human being; she had been in love with Charlie, but he hadn't aroused her curiosity except sexually, and she had satisfied that only too quickly. She asked him, 'Do you love your sister?'

'Yes, of course, why? How do you know I've got a sister?'

'And Joe?'

'You certainly read my letter. Oh, he's OK.'

'OK?'

'Well, you know how it is with brothers. I'm the eldest in my family. There was one that died. My sister's twenty years younger than I am. Joe's got the means. He looks after her.'

'You haven't got the means?'

'I had the means. I wasn't good at managing them though. We aren't here to talk about myself.'

'I'm curious. That's why I read your letter.'

'You? Curious about me?'

'It could be, couldn't it?'

She had confused him, and now that she had the upper hand, she felt that she was out of the trap; she was free, she could come and go as she pleased, and if she chose to stay a little longer, it was her own choice.

'Have another bourbon?' he said. 'But you're English. Maybe you'd prefer Scotch?'

'Better not mix.'

'No.' He poured her another glass. He said, 'I was wondering – sometimes I want to get away from this joint for a little. What about having dinner down the road?'

'It would be stupid,' she said. 'We've both paid our *pension* here, haven't we? And it would be the same dinner in the end. Red snapper. Tomatoes.'

'I don't know what you have against tomatoes.' But he did not deny the good sense of her economic reasoning: he was the first unsuccessful American she had ever had a drink with. One must have seen them in the street . . . But even the young men who came to the house were not yet unsuccessful. The Professor of Romance Languages had perhaps hoped to be head of a university – success is relative, but it remains success.

He poured out another glass. She said, 'I'm drinking all your bourbon.'

'It's in a good cause.'

She was a little drunk by now and things – which only *seemed* relevant – came to her mind. She said, 'That thing of Longfellow's. It went on – something about "the thoughts of youth are long, long thoughts". I must have read it somewhere. That was the refrain, wasn't it?'

'Maybe. I don't remember.'

'Did you want to be a pirate when you were a boy?'

He gave an almost happy grin. He said, 'I succeeded. That's what Joe called me once – "pirate".'

'But you haven't any buried treasure?'

He said, 'He knows me well enough not to send me a hundred dollars. But if he feels scared enough that I'll come back – he might send fifty. And the interest was only twenty-five. He's not mean, but he's stupid.'

'How?'

'He ought to know I wouldn't go back. I wouldn't do one thing to hurt Sis.'

'Would it be any good if I asked you to have dinner with me?'

'No. It wouldn't be right.' In some ways he was obviously very conservative. 'It's as you said – you don't want to go throwing money about.' When the bottle of Old Walker was half empty, he said, 'You'd better have some food even if it is red snapper and tomatoes.'

'Is your name really Hickslaughter?'

'Something like that.'

They went downstairs, following rather carefully in each

other's footsteps like ducks. In the formal restaurant open to all the heat of the evening, the men sat and sweated in their jackets and ties. They passed, the two of them, through the bamboo bar into the coffee tavern, which was lit by candles that increased the heat. Two young men with crew-cuts sat at the next table – they weren't the same young men she had seen before, but they came out of the same series. One of them said, 'I'm not denying that he has a certain style, but even if you *adore* Tennessee Williams...'

'Why did he call you a pirate?'

'It was just one of those things.'

When it came to the decision there seemed nothing to choose except red snapper and tomatoes, and again she offered him her tomatoes; perhaps he had grown to expect it and already she was chained by custom. He was an old man, he had made no pass which she could reasonably reject – how could a man of his age make a pass to a woman of hers? – and yet all the same she had a sense that she had landed on a conveyor belt... The future was not in her hands, and she was a little scared. She would have been more frightened if it had not been for her unusual consumption of bourbon.

'It was good bourbon,' she commented for something to say, and immediately regretted it. It gave him an opening.

'We'll have another glass before bed.'

'I think I've drunk enough.'

'A good bourbon won't hurt you. You'll sleep well.'

'I always sleep well.' It was a lie – the kind of unimportant lie one tells a husband or a lover in order to keep some privacy. The young man who had been talking about Tennessee Williams rose from his table. He was very tall and thin and he wore a skin-tight black sweater; his small elegant buttocks were outlined in skintight trousers. It was easy to imagine him a degree more naked. Would he have looked at her, she wondered, with interest if she had not been sitting there in the company of a fat old man so horribly clothed? It was unlikely; his body was not designed for a woman's caress.

'I don't.'

'You don't what?'

'I don't sleep well.' The unexpected self-disclosure after all his reticences came as a shock. It was as though he had put out one of his square brick-like hands and pulled her to him. He had been aloof, he had evaded her personal questions, he had lulled her into a sense of security, but now every time she opened her mouth, she seemed doomed to commit an error, to invite him nearer. Even her harmless remark about the bourbon . . . She said stupidly, 'Perhaps it's the change of climate.'

'What change of climate?'

'Between here and . . . and . . .'

'Curaçao? I guess there's no great difference. I don't sleep there either.'

'I've got some very good pills . . .' she said rashly.

'I thought you said you slept well.'

'Oh, there are always times. It's sometimes just a question of digestion.'

'Yes, digestion. You're right there. A bourbon will be good for that. If you've finished dinner . . .'

She looked across the coffee tavern to the bamboo bar, where the young man stood *déhanche*, holding a glass of crème-de-menthe between his face and his companion's like an exotically coloured monocle.

Mr Hickslaughter said in a shocked voice, 'You don't care for that type, do you?'

'They're often good conversationalists.'

'Oh, conversation . . . If that's what you want.' It was as though she had expressed an un-American liking for snails or frogs' legs.

'Shall we have our bourbon in the bar? It's a little cooler tonight.'

'And pay and listen to their chatter? No, we'll go upstairs.'

He swung back again in the direction of old-fashioned courtesy and came behind her to pull her chair – even Charlie was not so polite, but was it politeness or the determination to block her way of escape to the bar?

They entered the lift together. The black attendant had a radio turned on, and from the small brown box came the voice of a preacher talking about the Blood of the Lamb. Perhaps it was a Sunday, and that would explain the temporary void around them – between one jolly bunch and another. They stepped out into the empty corridor like undesirables marooned. The boy followed them out and sat down upon a chair beside the elevator to wait for another signal, while the voice continued to talk about the Blood of the Lamb. What was she afraid of? Mr Hickslaughter began to unlock his door. He was much older than her father would have been if he had been still alive; he could be her grandfather – the excuse, 'What will the boy think?' was inadmissible – it was even shocking, for his manner had never ceased to be correct. He might be old, but what right had she to think of him as 'dirty'?

'Damn the hotel key . . .' he said. 'It won't open.'

She turned the handle for him. 'The door wasn't locked.'

'I can sure do with a bourbon after those nancies . . .'

But now she had her excuse ready on the lips. 'I've had one too many already, I'm afraid. I've got to sleep it off.' She put her hand on his arm. 'Thank you so much . . . It was a lovely evening.' She was aware how insulting her English accent sounded as she walked quickly down the corridor leaving it behind her like a mocking presence, mocking all the things she liked best in him: his ambiguous character, his memory of Longfellow, his having to make ends meet.

She looked back when she reached her room: he was standing in the passage as though he couldn't make up his mind to go in. She was reminded of an old man whom she had passed one day on the campus leaning on his broom among the unswept autumn leaves.

4

In her room she picked up a book and tried to read. It was Thomson's *Seasons*. She had carried it with her, so that she could understand any reference to his work that Charlie might make in a letter. This was the first time she had opened it, and she was not held:

> And now the mounting Sun dispels the Fog:
> The rigid Hoar-Frost melts! before his Beam;
> And hung on every Spray, on every Blade
> Of Grass, the myriad Dew-Drops twinkle round.

If she could be so cowardly, she thought, with a harmless old man like that, how could she have faced the real decisiveness of an adventure? One was not, at her age, 'swept off the feet'. Charlie had been proved just as sadly right to trust her as she was right to trust Charlie. Now with the difference in time he would be leaving the Museum, or rather, if this were a Sunday as the Blood of the Lamb seemed to indicate, he would probably have just quit writing in his hotel room. After a successful day's work he always resembled an advertisement for a new shaving-cream: a kind of glow . . . She found it irritating, like living with a halo. Even his voice had a different timbre and he would call her 'old girl' and pat her bottom patronizingly. She preferred him when he was touchy with failure: only temporary failure, of course, the failure of an idea which hadn't worked out, the touchiness of a child's disappointment at a party which has not come up to his expectations, not the failure of the old man – the rusted framework of a ship transfixed once and for all upon the rock where it had struck.

She felt ignoble. What earthly risk could the old man represent to justify refusing him half an hour's companionship? He could no more assault her than the boat could detach itself from the rock and steam out to sea for the Fortunate Islands. She pictured him sitting alone with his half-empty bottle of bourbon seeking unconsciousness. Or was he perhaps finishing the crude blackmailing letter to his brother? What a story she would make of it one day, she thought with self-disgust as she took off her dress, her evening with a blackmailer and 'pirate'.

There was one thing she could do for him: she could give him her bottle of pills. She put on her dressing-gown and retrod the corridor, room by room, until she arrived at 63. His voice told her to come in. She opened the door and in the light of the bedside lamp saw him sitting on the edge of the bed wearing a crumpled pair of cotton pyjamas with broad mauve stripes. She began, 'I've brought you . . .' and then she saw to her amazement that he had been crying. His eyes were red and the evening darkness of his cheeks sparkled with points like dew. She had only once before seen a man cry – Charlie, when the University Press had decided against his first volume of literary essays.

'I thought you were the maid,' he said. 'I rang for her.'

'What did you want?'

'I thought she might take a glass of bourbon,' he said.

'Did you want so much . . . ? I'll take a glass.' The bottle was still on the dressing-table where they had left it and the two glasses – she identified hers by the smear of lipstick. 'Here you are,' she said, 'drink it up. It will make you sleep.'

He said, 'I'm not an alcoholic.'

'Of course you aren't.'

She sat on the bed beside him and took his left hand in hers. It was cracked and dry, and she wanted to clean back the cuticle until she remembered that was something she did for Charlie.

'I wanted company,' he said.

'I'm here.'

'You'd better turn off the bell-light or the maid will come.'

'She'll never know what she missed in the way of Old Walker.'

When she returned from the door he was lying back against the pillows in an odd twisted position, and she thought again of the ship broken-backed upon the rocks. She tried to pick up his feet to lay them on the bed, but they were like heavy stones at the bottom of a quarry.

'Lie down,' she said, 'you'll never be sleepy that way. What do you do for company in Curaçao?'

'I manage,' he said.

'You've finished the bourbon. Let me put out the lights.'

'It's no good pretending to you,' he said.

'Pretending?'

'I'm afraid of the dark.'

She thought, I'll smile later when I think of who it was I feared. She said, 'Do the old pirates you fought come back to haunt you?'

'I've done some bad things,' he said, 'in my time.'

'Haven't we all?'

'Nothing extraditable,' he explained as though that were an extenuation.

'If you take one of my pills . . .'

'You won't go – not yet?'

'No, no. I'll stay till you're sleepy.'

'I've been wanting to talk to you for days.'

'I'm glad you did.'

'Would you believe it – I hadn't got the nerve.' If she had shut her eyes it might have been a very young man speaking. 'I don't know your sort.'

'Don't you have my sort in Curaçao?'

'No.'

'You haven't taken the pill yet.'

'I'm afraid of not waking up.'

'Have you so much to do tomorrow?'

'I mean ever.' He put out his hand and touched her knee, searchingly, without sensuality, as if he needed support from the bone. 'I'll tell you what's wrong. You're a stranger, so I can tell you. I'm afraid of dying, with nobody around, in the dark.'

'Are you ill?'

'I wouldn't know. I don't see doctors. I don't like doctors.'

'But why should you think . . . ?'

'I'm over seventy. The Bible age. It could happen any day now.'

'You'll live to a hundred,' she said with an odd conviction.

'Then I'll have to live with fear the hell of a long time.'

'Was that why you were crying?'

'No. I thought you were going to stay awhile, and then suddenly you went. I guess I was disappointed.'

'Are you never alone in Curaçao?'

'I pay not to be alone.'

'As you'd have paid the maid?'

'Ye-eh. Sort of.'

It was as though she were discovering for the first time the interior of the enormous continent on which she had elected to live. America had been Charlie, it had been New England; through books and movies she had been aware of the wonders of nature like some great cineramic film with Lowell Thomas cheapening the Painted Desert and the Grand Canyon with his clichés. There had been no mystery anywhere from Miami to Niagara Falls, from Cape Cod to the Pacific Palisades; tomatoes were served on every plate and Coca-Cola in every glass.

Nobody anywhere admitted failure or fear; they were like sins 'hushed up' – worse perhaps than sins, for sins have glamour – they were bad taste. But here stretched on the bed, dressed in striped pyjamas which Brooks Brothers would have disowned, failure and fear talked to her without shame, and in an American accent. It was as though she were living in the remote future, after God knew what catastrophe.

She said, 'I wasn't for sale? There was only the Old Walker to tempt *me*.'

He raised his antique Neptune head a little way from the pillow and said, 'I'm not afraid of death. Not sudden death. Believe me, I've looked for it here and there. It's the certain-sure business, closing in on you, like tax-inspectors . . .'

She said, 'Sleep now.'

'I can't.'

'Yes, you can.'

'If you'd stay with me awhile . . .'

'I'll stay with you. Relax.' She lay down on the bed beside him on the outside of the sheet. In a few minutes he was deeply asleep and she turned off the light. He grunted several times and spoke only once, when he said, 'You've got me wrong,' and after that he became for a little while like a dead man in his immobility and his silence, so that during that period she fell asleep. When she woke she was aware from his breathing that he was awake too. He was lying away from her so that their bodies wouldn't touch. She put out her hand and felt no repulsion at all at his excitement. It was as though she had spent many nights beside him in the one bed, and when he made love to her, silently and abruptly in the darkness, she gave a sigh of satisfaction. There was no guilt; she would be going back in a few days, resigned and tender, to Charlie and Charlie's loving skill, and she wept a little, but not seriously, at the temporary nature of this meeting.

'What's wrong?' he asked.

'Nothing. Nothing. I wish I could stay.'

'Stay a little longer. Stay till it's light.' That would not be very long. Already they could distinguish the grey masses of the furniture standing around them like Caribbean tombs.

'Oh yes, I'll stay till it's light. That wasn't what I meant.' His body began to slip out of her, and it was as though he were carrying away her unknown child, away in the direction of Curaçao, and she tried to hold him back, the fat old frightened man whom she almost loved.

He said, 'I never had this in mind.'

'I know. Don't say it. I understand.'

'I guess after all we've got a lot in common,' he said, and she agreed in order to quieten him. He was fast asleep by the time the light came back, so she got off the bed without waking him and went to her room. She locked the door and began with resolution to pack her bag: it was time for her to leave, it was time for term to start again. She wondered afterwards, when she thought of him, what it was they could have had in common, except the fact, of course, that for both of them Jamaica was cheap in August.

The Moment of Truth

The near approach of death is like a crime which one is ashamed to confess to friends or fellow workers, and yet there remains a longing to confide in someone – perhaps a stranger in the street. Arthur Burton carried his secret to and fro to the kitchen and back, just as he carried the plates and the orders of the clients, as he had done for years in the Kensington restaurant which was called Chez Auguste. There was nothing French about it except the name and the menu, where the English dishes were given French names, explained at length in English under each title.

Twice in one week an American couple had booked the same table, a small one in a corner under a window, a man of about sixty years and a woman in her late forties – a very happy couple.

There are clients whom one likes at the first encounter and these were among them. They asked Arthur Burton's advice before they ordered and later they expressed their appreciation of his choice. They trusted him even over the wine, and on their second visit, they asked him little questions about himself as though he were a fellow guest whom they were anxious to know better.

'Been here long?' Mr Hogminster asked. (Arthur Burton had learnt his curious name when he telephoned for his reservation.)

'About twenty years,' Burton replied. 'It was a different restaurant when I came called The Queen's.'

'Better in those days?'

Arthur Burton tried to be loyal. 'I wouldn't say better. Simpler. Tastes change.'

'Is he French – your boss?'

'No, sir, but he's been to France a lot, I think.'

'We're happy to have your help. We don't know all these French words in the menu.'

'But it's put in English, sir.'

'I guess we don't understand that sort of English either. Anyway we'll be along again tomorrow. If you let us have the same table – Arthur, isn't it? I think I heard the boss call you Arthur?'

'That's right, sir. I'll see that you have this table.'

'And your help, Arthur,' Mrs Hogminster said.

He was touched by the use of his first name and the smile of real friendship which he received from Mrs Hogminster. In all his years as a waiter, he had known nothing like it before.

Arthur Burton was in the habit of observing the customers superficially, if only to keep an interest in his job which it was too late to change. He was alone in life, so there was no initiative for a change and now he was well aware that it was too late. The crime of death had touched him.

Often when he went home at night – if a bed-sitting-room with a shared shower could be called a home – he would remember certain customers: married customers who seemed to lunch together without interest, watching those who came in with a certain envy if the newcomers had words to say to each other: obvious new lovers who paid attention to no one else: sometimes a married young woman (he always looked at the left hand) with a look of anxiety, accompanied by a much older man. She lowered her voice or even ceased to talk when neighbours took the next table and Arthur Burton wished that he could have left it empty, so that they would be free to solve their problem.

When he got home that night, he thought of Mr and Mrs Hogminster. He wished he had spoken more to them. He felt that he could trust them, like strangers in the street. He might at least have hinted at the crime which separated him from the manager, the cook, the other waiters, the washers-up — only hinted of course, he wouldn't like them to be distressed.

They were half an hour late the next day for their reservation, and the manager wanted him to give up the table to other guests who asked for it. 'They won't be coming,' the manager argued, 'and anyway, there are three other tables to choose from.'

'But they like this table,' Arthur Burton said, 'and I promised they would have it.' He added, 'They are kind good people,' but he probably would have been forced to give way if they had not at that moment arrived.

'Oh, I'm so sorry, Arthur, we are terribly late.' He was touched that she had remembered his name. 'It was the Sales, Arthur. We got involved.'

'*She* got involved,' Mr Hogminster said.

'Oh, it will be your turn tomorrow.'

Arthur told them, 'There are restaurants closer to the men's shops. I can recommend one near Jermyn Street.'

'Oh, but it's Chez Augustine that we love.'

'Chez Auguste,' Mr Hogminster corrected her.

'And Arthur. He chooses so well for us. We don't have to think.'

A man with a secret is a very lonely man, and it was relief to Arthur Burton when he could uncover even a small corner of his secret. He said, 'I'm sorry, ma'am, but tomorrow I won't be here. But I'm sure the manager . . .'

'Not here? *Quelle désastre!* Why?'

'I have to go to hospital.'

'Oh, Arthur, I'm so sorry. What for? Is it serious?'

'A check-up, ma'am.'

'Very wise,' Mr Hogminster said. 'I believe in check-ups.'

'He's had four or is it six.' Mrs Hogminster added, 'I think he enjoys them, but it always worries me. What are they checking you for?'

'They've already done the check-up. Now they have to tell me the result.'

'Oh, I'm sure it will be all right, Arthur.'

'I'm happy you've enjoyed yourselves here, ma'am.'

'We have. All thanks to you.'

Arthur Burton said with truth, 'I'm sorry that we have to say goodbye.'

'Oh no – not yet. We'll be here again on Thursday. Tomorrow, we'll take your advice and eat near the men's shops, but we'll be back the day after to have our last meal at Chez Augustine.'

'Chez Auguste,' Mr Hogminster corrected her again, but she ignored him.

'We are flying to New York on Friday, but we'll certainly see you on Thursday and hear your good news, Arthur. I'm sure it will be good news. I'll be thinking of you and crossing my fingers, but I'm sure, quite sure.'

'I have a check-up every six months,' Mr Hogminster said. 'Always satisfactory.'

'Is there anything special you would like on Thursday, ma'am? I can ask the cook . . .'

'No, no. We'll take what you recommend. Until then – and good luck, Arthur.'

Arthur Burton knew that no good luck awaited him. He had known it even before the check-up by the evasiveness of his doctor. He wondered whether a man in the dock could tell the jury's verdict even before they retired from the court in the days when there was still a death sentence: an emanation of shame at what they were going to pronounce. Yet he had a sense of relief because he had at least confessed half his crime to her and she had not rejected him. If, as he believed, the verdict was death, however they wrapped it up in medical phrases of hope, might she be the stranger in the street to whom he could confess the whole? They would never see each other again. She was leaving for New York on Friday. They had no friends in common to whom she could spread the news of his crime. He felt an odd tenderness for her.

That night Arthur Burton dreamt of her. It was not an erotic dream, nor a love dream, a very commonplace dream in which she played an unimportant part and yet he woke with a sense of relaxation he had not known for many months. It was as though he had spoken to her and somehow she had given him words of sympathy which lent him courage to face his enemies, who were about to disclose the shameful truth.

He had taken a day off his work, though his appointment with the surgeon was not until the evening at five, and then he was kept waiting for nearly an hour. The surgeon asked him to sit down in a tone of such grave sympathy that he was able to guess accurately enough the report which followed. 'An operation urgently required . . . yes, cancer, but you mustn't be frightened by the sound of a word . . . I have known cases as bad as yours . . . taken in time there's always a good hope . . .'

'When do you want to operate?'

'I would like you to come into hospital tomorrow morning, and I'll operate the next day.'

'If I could come in the afternoon. You see – they are expecting me to be back at work tomorrow morning.' It was not of work he was thinking, but of Mrs Hogminster. She would be expecting news from him.

'I would much rather you had a quiet day in bed. However . . . I will be coming to see you with the anaesthetist at six.'

As he lay in bed that night, Arthur Burton thought: doctors and surgeons are not necessarily good psychologists; perhaps, because their interests are so concentrated on the body that they forget the mind, they don't realize how much a tone of voice reveals to the patient. They say 'there's always a good hope', but what the patient hears is 'there is very little hope if any'.

It was not that he was frightened of death. No one could avoid that universal fate, and yet the population of the world was not dominated by fear. All Arthur Burton wanted was to share his knowledge and his secret with a stranger who would not be seriously affected like a wife or a child – he possessed neither – but might with a word of kindly interest share with him this criminal secret – 'I am condemned'. Mrs Hogminster was just such a woman. He had read it in her eyes. Somehow the next day he would find a way of conveying to her the truth, when she asked for the result of the check-up, without words which might involve her husband in his crime. She would ask him: 'What did the doctor say, Arthur?' And his answer? No, no words, a small shrug of the shoulders would be enough to convey, 'It's all up. Thank you for thinking of me,' and the glance that she gave him back would just as discreetly tell him she shared his secret.

He would not go alone into the future.

'You needn't keep that table,' the manager said. 'Those Americans were in yesterday and I found them one they liked much better.'

'They were in yesterday?'

'Yes, they do seem to like this place.'

'I thought they were going to the men's Sales.'

'I wouldn't know about that. I think you talk too much to the customers, Arthur. Often they want to feel alone.'

He left hurriedly to meet Mr and Mrs Hogminster at the door. Mrs Hogminster nodded and smiled at Arthur as they went by to a little table isolated in a corner of the restaurant. They had no view now of the street outside, but perhaps, as the manager had suggested, they preferred privacy, and perhaps too they preferred to be served by the manager himself.

It was only at the end of their meal after they had paid their bill that Mrs Hogminster called to him as he passed to the kitchen. 'Arthur, do come and have a word with us.'

He went willingly with a lightening of the heart.

'Arthur, we missed you, but the manager was so kind and we didn't want to hurt his feelings.'

'I hope you enjoyed your lunch, ma'am.'

'Oh, but we always do at Chez Augustine.'

'Chez Auguste,' Mr Hogminster said.

'With the Sales you were so right to send us to Jermyn Street. My husband bought two pairs of pyjamas and can you believe it, three – three – shirts!'

'She chose them of course,' Mr Hogminster said.

Arthur Burton excused himself and went on into the kitchen. The problem which he had so feared had not arisen, but the thought gave him no relief from the depression of his secret. He was going to say nothing to the manager: the next day he would simply not turn up. The hospital could inform them in due course if he were dead or alive.

He spent as little time as he could in the restaurant, though it pained him to see another waiter looking after the Hogminsters and exchanging words with them.

Half an hour later the manager came into the kitchen and spoke to him. He carried a letter in his hand. He said, 'Mrs Hogminster asked me to give you this. They've left for the airport.'

Arthur Burton put the envelope in his pocket. He felt an immense relief. Of course Mrs Hogminster had done the right thing. They couldn't have talked about his secret in the restaurant for others to hear. Now he would be able to carry with him to the hospital her sympathetic question about his secret and read it again next day immediately before the anaesthetist arrived. He felt alone no longer. He would be holding the hand of a stranger in the street. She could never receive the answer to her question, 'What did the doctor tell you?' but she had asked it in her letter and it was that which counted.

Before putting out the light above his hospital bed, he opened the envelope. He was surprised when three one-pound notes came out first.

Mrs Hogminster wrote: 'Dear Arthur, I felt I must write you a word of thanks before we catch our plane. We have so enjoyed our visits to Chez Augustine and shall certainly return one day. And the Sales, we got such wonderful bargains – you were so right about Jermyn Street.'

The letter was signed Dolly Hogminster.

*The Root of
All Evil*

*A Branch of the
Service*

The Root of All Evil

This story was told me by my father who heard it directly from his father, the brother of one of the participants; otherwise I doubt whether I would have credited it. But my father was a man of absolute rectitude, and I have no reason to believe that this virtue did not then run in the family.

The events happened in 189–, as they say in old Russian novels, in the small market town of B——. My father was German, and when he settled in England he was the first of the family to go further than a few kilometres from the home commune, province, canton or whatever it was called in those parts. He was a Protestant who believed in his faith, and no one has a greater ability to believe, without doubt or scruple, than a Protestant of that type. He would not even allow my mother to read us fairy-stories, and he walked three miles to church rather than go to one with pews. 'We've nothing to hide,' he said. 'If I sleep I sleep, and let the world know the weakness of my flesh. Why,' he added, and the thought touched my imagination strongly and perhaps had some influence on my future, 'they could play cards in those pews and no one the wiser.'

That phrase is linked in my mind with the fashion in which he would begin this story. 'Original sin gave man a tilt towards secrecy,' he would say. 'An open sin is only half a sin, and a secret innocence is only half innocent. When you have secrets, there, sooner or later, you'll have sin. I wouldn't let a Freemason cross my threshold. Where I come from secret societies were illegal, and the government had reason. Innocent though they might be at the start, like that club of Schmidt's.'

It appears that among the old people of the town where my father lived were a couple whom I shall continue to call Schmidt, being a little uncertain of the nature of the laws of libel and how limitations and the like affect the dead. Herr Schmidt was a big man and a heavy drinker, but most of his drinking he preferred to do at his own board to the discomfort of his wife, who never touched a drop of alcohol herself. Not that she wished to interfere with her husband's potations; she had a proper idea of a wife's duty, but she had reached an age (she was over sixty and he well past seventy) when she had a great yearning to sit quietly with another woman knitting something or other for her grandchildren and talking about their latest maladies. You can't do that at ease with a man continually on the go to the cellar for another litre. There is a man's atmosphere and a woman's atmosphere, and they don't mix except in the proper place, under the sheets. Many a time Frau Schmidt in her gentle way had tried to persuade him to go out of an evening to the inn. 'What and pay more for every glass?' he would say. Then she tried to persuade him that he had need of men's company and men's conversation. 'Not when I'm tasting a good wine,' he said.

So last of all she took her trouble to Frau Muller who suffered in just the same manner as herself. Frau Muller was a stronger type of woman and she set out to build an organization. She found four other women starved of female company and female interests, and they arranged to forgather once a week with their sewing and take their evening coffee together. Between them they could summon up more than two dozen grandchildren, so you can imagine they were never short of subjects to talk about. When one child had finished with the chicken-pox, at least two would have started the measles. There were all the varying treatments to compare, and there was one school of thought which took the motto 'starve a cold' to mean 'if you starve a cold you will feed a fever' and another school which took the more traditional view. But their debates were never heated like those they had with their husbands, and they took it in turn to act hostess and make the cakes.

But what was happening all this time to the husbands? You might think they would be content to go on drinking alone, but not a bit of it. Drinking's like reading a 'romance' (my father used the term with contempt, he had never turned the pages of a novel in his life); you don't need talk, but you need company, otherwise it begins to feel like work. Frau Muller had thought of that and she suggested to her husband – very gently, so that he hardly noticed – that, when the women were meeting elsewhere, he should ask the other husbands in with their own drinks (no need to spend extra money at the bar) and they could sit as silent as they wished with their glasses till bedtime. Not, of course, that they would be silent all the time. Now and then no doubt one of them would remark on the wet or the fine day, and another would mention the prospects for the harvest, and a third would say that they'd never had so warm a summer as the summer of 188–. Men's talk, which, in the absence of women, would never become heated.

But there was one snag in this arrangement and it was the one which caused the disaster. Frau Muller roped in a seventh woman, who had been widowed by something other than drink, by her husband's curiosity. Frau Puckler had a husband whom none of them could abide, and, before they could settle down to their friendly evenings, they had to decide what to do about him. He was a little vinegary man with a squint and a completely bald head who would empty any bar when he came into it. His eyes, coming together like that, had the effect of a gimlet, and he would stay in conversation with one man for ten minutes on end with his eyes fixed on the other's forehead until you expected sawdust to come out. Unfortunately Frau Puckler was highly respected. It was essential to keep from her any idea that her husband was unwelcome, so for some weeks they had to reject Frau Muller's proposal. They were quite happy, they said, sitting alone at home with a glass when what they really meant was that even loneliness was preferable to the company of Herr Puckler. But they got so miserable all this time that often, when their wives returned home, they would find their husbands tucked up in bed and asleep.

It was then Herr Schmidt broke his customary silence. He called round at Herr Muller's door, one evening when the wives were away, with a four-litre jug of wine, and he hadn't got through more than two litres when he broke silence. This lonely drinking, he said, must come to an end – he had had more sleep the last few weeks than he had had in six months and it was sapping his strength. 'The grave yawns for us,' he said, yawning himself from habit.

'But Puckler?' Herr Muller objected. 'He's worse than the grave.'

'We shall have to meet in secret,' Herr Schmidt said. 'Braun has a fine big cellar,' and that was how the secret began; and from secrecy, my father would moralize, you can grow every sin in the calendar. I pictured secrecy like the dark mould in the cellar where we cultivated our mushrooms, but the mushrooms were good to eat, so that their secret growth . . . I always found an ambivalence in my father's moral teaching.

It appears that for a time all went well. The men were happy drinking together – in the absence, of course, of Herr Puckler, and so were the women, even Frau Puckler, for she always found her husband in bed at night ready for domesticities. He was far too proud to tell her of his ramblings in search of company between the strokes of the town-clock. Every night he would try a different house and every night he found only the closed door and the darkened window. Once in Herr Braun's cellar the husbands heard the knocker hammering overhead. At the Gasthof too he would look regularly in – and sometimes irregularly, as though he hoped that he might catch them off their guard. The street-lamp shone on his bald head, and often some late drinker going home would be confronted by those gimlet-eyes which believed nothing you said. 'Have you seen Herr Muller tonight?' or 'Herr Schmidt, is he at home?' he would demand of another reveller. He sought them here, he sought them there – he had been content enough aforetime drinking in his own home and sending his wife down to the cellar for a refill, but he knew only too well, now he was alone, that there was no pleasure possible for a solitary drinker. If Herr Schmidt and Herr Muller were not at home, where were they? And the other four with whom he had never been well acquainted, where were they? Frau Puckler was the very reverse of her husband, she had no curiosity, and Frau Muller and Frau Schmidt had mouths which clinked shut like the clasp of a well-made handbag.

Inevitably after a certain time Herr Puckler went to the police. He refused to speak to anyone lower than the Superintendent. His gimlet-eyes bored like a migraine into the Superintendent's forehead. While the eyes rested on the one spot, his words wandered ambiguously. There had been an anarchist outrage at Schloss – I can't remember the name; there were rumours of an attempt on a Grand Duke. The Superintendent shifted a little this way and a little that way on his seat, for these were big affairs which did not concern him, while the squinting eyes bored continuously at the sensitive spot above his nose where his migraine always began. Then the Superintendent blew loudly and said, 'The times are evil,' a phrase which he had remembered from the service on Sunday.

'You know the law about secret societies,' Herr Puckler said.
'Naturally.'
'And yet here, under the nose of the police,' and the squint-eyes bored deeper, 'there exists just such a society.'

'If you would be a little more explicit . . .'

So Herr Puckler gave him the whole row of names, beginning with Herr Schmidt. 'They meet in secret,' he said. 'None of them stays at home.'

'They are not the kind of men I would suspect of plotting.'

'All the more dangerous for that.'

'Perhaps they are just friends.'

'Then why don't they meet in public?'

'I'll put a policeman on the case,' the Superintendent said half-heartedly, so now at night there were two men looking around to find where the six had their meeting-place. The policeman was a simple man who began by asking direct questions, but he had been seen several times in the company of Puckler, so the six assumed quickly enough that he was trying to track them down on Puckler's behalf and they became more careful than ever to avoid discovery. They stocked up Herr Braun's cellar with wine, and they took elaborate precautions not to be seen entering – each one sacrificed a night's drinking in order to lead Herr Puckler and the policeman astray. Nor could they confide in their wives for fear that it might come to the ears of Frau Puckler, so they pretended the scheme had not worked and it was every man for himself again now in drinking. That meant they had to tell a lot of lies if they failed to be the first home – and so, my father said, sin began to enter in.

One night too, Herr Schmidt, who happened to be the decoy, led Herr Puckler on a long walk into the suburbs, and then seeing an open door and a light burning in the window with a comforting red glow and being by that time very dry in the mouth, he mistook the house in his distress for a quiet inn and walked inside. He was warmly welcomed by a stout lady and shown into a parlour, where he expected to be served with wine. Three young ladies sat on a sofa in various stages of undress and greeted Herr Schmidt with giggles and warm words. Herr Schmidt was afraid to leave the house at once, in case Puckler was lurking outside, and while he hesitated the stout lady entered with a bottle of champagne on ice and a number of glasses. So for the sake of the drink (though champagne was not his preference – he would have liked the local wine) he stayed, and thus out of secrecy, my father said, came the second sin. But it didn't end there with lies and fornication.

When the time came to go, if he were not to overstay his welcome, Herr Schmidt took a look out of the window, and there, in place of Puckler, was the policeman walking up and down the pavement. He must have followed Puckler at a distance, and then taken on his watch while Puckler went rabbiting after the others. What to do? It was growing late; soon the wives would be drinking their last cup and closing the file on the last grandchild. Herr Schmidt appealed to the kind stout lady; he asked her whether she hadn't a back-door so that he might avoid the man he knew in the street outside. She had no back-door, but she was a woman of great resource, and in no time she had decked Herr Schmidt out in a great cartwheel of a skirt, like peasant-women in those days wore at market, a pair of white stockings, a blouse ample enough and a floppy hat. The girls hadn't enjoyed themselves so much for a long time, and they amused themselves decking his face with rouge, eye-shadow and lipstick. When he came out of the door, the policeman was so astonished by the sight that he stood rooted to the spot long enough for Herr Schmidt to billow round the corner, take to his heels down a sidestreet and arrive safely home in time to scour his face before his wife came in.

If it had stopped there all might have been well, but the policeman had not been deceived, and now he reported to the Superintendent that members of the secret society dressed themselves as women and in that guise frequented the gay houses of the town. 'But why dress as women to do that?' the Superintendent asked, and Puckler hinted at orgies which went beyond the natural order of things. 'Anarchy,' he said, 'is out to upset everything, even the proper relationship of man and woman.'

'Can't you be more explicit?' the Superintendent asked him for the second time; it was a phrase of which he was pathetically fond, but Puckler left the details shrouded in mystery.

It was then that Puckler's fanaticism took a morbid turn; he suspected every large woman he saw in the street at night of being a man in disguise. Once he actually pulled off the wig of a certain Frau Hackenfurth (no one till that day, not even her husband, knew that she wore a wig), and presently he sallied out into the streets himself dressed as a woman with the belief that one transvestite would recognize another and that sooner or later he would find himself enlisted in the secret orgies. He was a small man and he played the part better than Herr Schmidt had done – only his gimlet-eyes would have betrayed him to an acquaintance in daylight.

The men had been meeting happily enough now for two weeks in Herr Braun's cellar, the policeman had tired of his search, the Superintendent was in hopes that all had blown over, when a disastrous decision was taken. Frau Schmidt and Frau Muller in the old days had the habit of cooking pasties for their husbands to go with the wine, and the two men began to miss this treat which they described to their fellow drinkers, their mouths wet with the relish of the memory. Herr Braun suggested that they should bring in a woman to cook for them – it would mean only a small contribution from each, for no one would charge very much for a few hours' work at the end of the evening. Her duty would be to bring in fresh warm pasties every half an hour or so as long as their wine-session lasted. He advertised the position openly enough in the local paper, and Puckler, taking a long chance – the advertisement had referred to a men's club – applied, dressed up in his wife's best Sunday blacks. He was accepted by Herr Braun, who was the only one who did not know Herr Puckler except by repute, and so Puckler found himself installed at the very heart of the mystery, with a grand opportunity to hear all their talk. The only trouble was that he had little skill at cooking and often with his ears to the cellar-door he allowed the pasties to burn. On the second evening Herr Braun told him that, unless the pasties improved, he would find another woman.

However Puckler was not worried by that because he had all the information he required for the Superintendent, and it was a real pleasure to make his report in the presence of the policeman, who contributed nothing at all to the inquiry.

Puckler had written down the dialogue as he had heard it, leaving out only the long pauses, the gurgle of the wine-jugs, and the occasional rude tribute that wind makes to the virtue of young wine. His report read as follows:

> Inquiry into the Secret Meetings held in the Cellar of Herr Braun's House at 27—strasse. The following dialogue was overheard by the investigator.
>
> MULLER: If the rain keeps off another month, the wine harvest will be better than last year.
> UNIDENTIFIED VOICE: Ugh.
> SCHMIDT: They say the postman nearly broke his ankle last week. Slipped on a step.
> BRAUN: I remember sixty-one vintages.
> DOBEL: Time for a pasty.
> UNIDENTIFIED VOICE: Ugh.
> MULLER: Call in that cow.
>   The investigator was summoned and left a tray of pasties.
> BRAUN: Careful. They are hot.
> SCHMIDT: This one's burnt to a cinder.
> DOBEL: Uneatable.

KASTNER: Better sack her before worse happens.
BRAUN: She's paid till the end of the week. We'll give her till then.
MULLER: It was fourteen degrees at midday.
DOBEL: The town-hall clock's fast.
SCHMIDT: Do you remember that dog the mayor had with black spots?
UNIDENTIFIED VOICE: Ugh.
KASTNER: No, why?
SCHMIDT: I can't remember.
MULLER: When I was a boy we had plum-duff they never make now.
DOBEL: It was the summer of '87.
UNIDENTIFIED VOICE: What was?
MULLER: The year Mayor Kalnitz died.
SCHMIDT: '88.
MULLER: There was a hard frost.
DOBEL: Not as hard as '86.
BRAUN: That was a shocking year for wine.

So it went on for twelve pages. 'What's it all about?' the Superintendent asked.

'If we knew that, we'd know all.'

'It sounds harmless.'

'Then why do they meet in secret?'

The policeman said 'Ugh' like the unidentified voice.

'My feeling is,' Puckler said, 'a pattern will emerge. Look at all those dates. They need to be checked.'

'There was a bomb thrown in '86,' the Superintendent said doubtfully. 'It killed the Grand Duke's best grey.'

'A shocking year for wine,' Puckler said. 'They missed. No wine. No royal blood.'

'The attempt was mistimed,' the Superintendent remembered.

'The town-hall clock's fast,' Puckler quoted.

'I can't believe it all the same.'

'A code. To break a code we have need of more material.'

The Superintendent agreed with some reluctance that the report should continue, but then there was the difficulty of the pasties. 'We need a good assistant-cook for the pasties,' Puckler said, 'and then I can listen without interruption. They won't object if I tell them that it will cost no more.'

The Superintendent said to the policeman, 'Those were good pasties I had in your house.'

'I cooked them myself,' the policeman said gloomily.

'Then that's no help.'

'Why no help?' Puckler demanded. 'If I can dress up as a woman, so can he.'

'His moustache?'

'A good blade and a good lather will see to that.'

'It's an unusual thing to demand of a man.'

'In the service of the law.'

So it was decided, though the policeman was not at all happy about the affair. Puckler, being a small man, was able to dress in his wife's clothes, but the policeman had no wife. In the end Puckler was forced to agree to buy the clothes himself; he did it late in the evening, when the assistants were in a hurry to leave and were unlikely to recognize his gimlet-eyes, as they judged the size of the skirt, blouse, knickers. There had been lies, fornication: I don't know in what further category my father placed the strange shopping expedition, which didn't, as it happened, go entirely unnoticed. Scandal – perhaps that was the third offence which secrecy produced, for a late customer coming into the shop did in fact recognize Puckler, just as he was holding up the bloomers to see if the seat seemed large enough. You can imagine how quickly that story got around, to every woman except Frau Puckler, and she felt at the next sewing-party an odd – well, it might have been deference or it might have been compassion. Everyone stopped to listen when she spoke; no one contradicted or argued with her, and she was not allowed to carry a tray or pour a cup. She began to feel so like an invalid that she developed a headache and decided to go home early. She could see them all nodding at each other as though they knew what was the matter better than she did, and Frau Muller volunteered to see her home.

Of course she hurried straight back to tell them about it. 'When we arrived,' she said, 'Herr Puckler was not at home. Of course the poor woman pretended not to know where he could be. She got in quite a state about it. She said he was always there to welcome her when she came in. She had half a mind to go round to the police-station and report him missing, but I dissuaded her. I almost began to believe that she didn't know what he was up to. She muttered about the strange goings-on in town, anarchists and the like, and would you believe it, she said that Herr Puckler told her a policeman had seen Herr Schmidt dressed up in women's clothes.'

'The little swine,' Frau Schmidt said, naturally referring to Puckler, for Herr Schmidt had the figure of one of his own wine-barrels. 'Can you imagine such a thing?'

'Distracting attention,' Frau Muller said, 'from his own vices. For look what happened next. We come to the bedroom, and Frau Puckler finds her wardrobe door wide open, and she looks inside, and what does she find – her black Sunday dress missing. "There's truth in the story after all," she said, "and I'm going to look for Herr Schmidt," but I pointed out to her that it would have to be a very small man indeed to wear her dress.'

'Did she blush?'

'I really believe she knows nothing about it.'

'Poor, poor woman,' Frau Dobel said. 'And what do you think he does when he's all dressed up?' and they began to speculate. So thus it was, my father would say, that foul talk was added to the other sins of lies, fornication, scandal. Yet there still remained the most serious sin of all.

That night Puckler and the policeman turned up at Herr Braun's door, but little did they know that the story of Puckler had already reached the ears of the drinkers, for Frau Muller had reported the strange events to Herr Muller, and at once he remembered the gimlet-eyes of the cook Anna peering at him out of the shadows. When the men met, Herr Braun reported that the cook was to bring an assistant to help her with the pasties and as she had asked for no extra money he had consented. You can imagine the babble of voices that broke out from these silent men when Herr Muller told his story. What was Puckler's motive? It was a bad one or it would not have been Puckler. One theory was that he was planning with the help of an assistant to poison them with the pasties in revenge for being excluded. 'It's not beyond Puckler,' Herr Dobel said. They had good reason to be suspicious, so my father, who was a just man, did not include unworthy suspicion among the sins of which the secret society was the cause. They began to prepare a reception for Puckler.

Puckler knocked on the door and the policeman stood just behind him, enormous in his great black skirt with his white stockings crinkling over his boots because Puckler had forgotten to buy him suspenders. After the second knock the bombardment began from the upper windows. Puckler and the policeman were drenched with unmentionable liquids, they were struck with logs of wood. Their eyes were endangered from falling forks. The policeman was the first to take to his heels, and it was a strange sight to see so huge a woman go beating down the street. The blouse had come out of the waistband and flapped like a sail as its owner tacked to avoid the flying objects – which now included a toilet-roll, a broken teapot and a portrait of the Grand Duke.

Puckler, who had been hit on the shoulder with a rolling-pin, did not at first run away. He had his moment of courage or bewilderment. But when the frying-pan he had used for pasties struck him, he turned too late to follow the policeman. It was then that he was struck on the head with a chamber-pot and lay in the street with the pot fitting over his head like a vizor. They had to break it with a hammer to get it off, and by that time he was dead, whether from the blow on the head or the fall or from fear or from being stifled by the chamber-pot nobody knew, though suffocation was the general opinion. Of course there was an inquiry which went on for many months into the existence of an anarchist plot, and before the end of it the Superintendent had become secretly affianced to Frau Puckler, for which nobody blamed her, for she was a popular woman – except my father who resented the secrecy of it all. (He suspected that the Superintendent's love for Frau Puckler had extended the inquiry, since he pretended to believe her husband's accusations.)

Technically, of course, it was murder – death arising from an illegal assault – but the courts after about six months absolved the six men. 'But there's a greater court,' my father would always end his story, 'and in that court the sin of murder never goes unrequited. You begin with a secret,' and he would look at me as though he knew my pockets were stuffed with them, as indeed they were, including the note I intended to pass the next day at school to the yellow-haired girl in the second row, 'and you end with every sin in the calendar.' He began to recount them over again for my benefit. 'Lies, drunkenness, fornication, scandal-bearing, murder, the subornation of authority.'

'Subornation of authority?'

'Yes,' he said and fixed me with his glittering eye. I think he had Frau Puckler and the Superintendent in mind. He rose towards his climax. 'Men in women's clothes – the terrible sin of Sodom.'

'And what's that?' I asked with excited expectation.

'At your age,' my father said, 'some things must remain secret.'

A Branch of the Service

1

I have been forced reluctantly to retire from a profession which I found of great interest and on a few occasions even dangerous because I have lost my appetite for food. Nowadays I can eat only in order to drink a little – before my meal a glass or two of vodka, and then a half bottle of wine: I find it quite impossible to face a menu, leave alone the heavy three- or even four-course meals in restaurants which my profession demanded.

I owed it to my father that I got the job I am now leaving, though he died before I was, as we call it, recruited. My earliest memories are the smells of a kitchen – they are happy memories even though I now find it a burden to eat. The kitchen was not one in my home: it was, as it were, an abstract kitchen which represented all the kitchens in which my father cooked – kitchens in England, Switzerland, Germany, Italy, and once I believe for a short while in Russia. He was a great chef – but he was never officially recognized. He moved from country to country. He was never out of a job, but he never kept a job long because he always knew better than his employer when it was time for him to leave.

Of my mother I remember nothing – I think she must always have been left behind on our travels. How I enjoyed eating in those days, yet I never learnt how to cook. That was my father's pride and secret. What I learnt were languages – never very well but a smattering of many. I could understand better than I spoke. The man who later recruited me understood that. I remember him saying, 'To understand is the only important thing. We don't want you to talk.'

You may wonder why it was necessary for me to eat large meals in order to keep my job. Even in a good restaurant one does not feel bound to eat more than two courses and one may always linger a long time over the wine. Yes, but I was supposed to be judging the food not the wine, even awarding stars to the food in the fashion of Michelin, but of course stars differently designed. I even had to inspect the lavatories.

In my father's eyes I would never have made a first-class cook, and he didn't wish me to spend my life as a kitchen help. Through an admirer of his English cooking in a little restaurant in St Albans where he worked for a year before quarrelling with his employer, he introduced me to a new organization which called itself International Reliable Restaurants Association, but before I had finished my first six months' training they changed the name. IRRA was a little putting off because of the Irish difficulties, and so they became instead the International Guide to Good Restaurants or the IGGR.

Their advertisements and their reputation rose together; at any rate for English customers, for they soon outbid Michelin. Michelin was too nationalist. Michelin awarded to Paris in those days five stars to eight restaurants, while to London they gave no five stars and only two four stars. The IGGR was far more generous, and that proved an advantage.

I had been an inspector for the IGGR for two years before I was recruited for special duties.

As I learnt during my training in these so-called duties we were not really interested in the number of stars or even in the cleanness of the lavatories. The people with whom we were concerned were unlikely to be found in very expensive restaurants, for costly eating can make the eater conspicuous.

'Rich eaters are not the main interest of this section,' my

instructor told me, 'here we look out for an ordinary customer. Especially those who are more than usually ordinary – they are the likely ones.'

I found his lessons at first a little obscure, until he told me a story which explained one of my puzzling memories of Paris. He said, 'Of course in this section we are not concerned with police work, but all the same we have taken a hint from the French police. Do you remember the lottery sellers who used to come into the bistros and the small restaurants in France?'

'Yes. You never see them now.'

'And yet lottery selling is not illegal. They are gone because they had outlived their usefulness.'

'What was their usefulness?'

'The police showed them the photographs of wanted men – small fry, thieves and the like, and they would go from table to table looking at the faces. This gave us an idea for a rather more important work, a work which involves our ears more than our eyes.'

He made a long pause; he meant I think to arouse our curiosity, and curious we certainly were at having been taken away from tasting food and inspecting lavatories. But we were wrong. There was a gleam of amusement in our speaker's eyes. 'The lavatories are of particular importance,' he said.

'From the point of view of cleanness of course?' a novice (not me) asked.

I still had no idea what our instructor was talking about. 'No, no,' he said. 'Cleanness isn't our concern, but the lavatory is a private place if you want to exchange a word or a packet with a friend. Unless of course your friend is a woman, but we'll come to that possibility later.'

A lot of other possibilities came later.

'There are phrases in conversation that you hear in a restaurant which are worth attention. *Pas de problème* is less interesting in France where it is in such common use, but if one of your neighbours in a small unfashionable restaurant in Manchester (a restaurant which hasn't got even one star) says, "There's no problem" it's worth paying attention.'

I think that he felt among the novices a certain scepticism. He went on, 'A hundred chances to one, of course, nothing of interest – of obvious interest – will follow – but make a note. There remains the one chance. The lavatory too – though perhaps the chances there are a little greater. For example two men peeing beside each other and talking. Our organization fills a gap – an important gap in security. A house is watched – but that again is not our job. The telephone is tapped. Not our job. Even street meetings are in other hands. But restaurants – we are doing a great service to the state.'

A question came to my mind. 'But when once we have given a star to a restaurant we have no excuse to go on eating there?'

'You are wrong. Two stars might be gained for the next edition – or a star could be lost. A certain blackmail is sometimes necessary. You will always be welcome and given the best food.'

The best food – yes, that was my problem. A career of eating. Of course it didn't worry me at the beginning, and what attracted me was not so much being of service to the state as the hint of mystery about the whole affair. The phrase 'no problem' stayed like a tune in my ears.

2

Of course, when first sent on duty one made serious mistakes, but unlike other professions one was excused – even sometimes praised – for a mistake because it might have added a little to one's experience. My first bad mistake – which in any other profession would have ruined my career – happened to be concerned with a lavatory. But I would prefer to speak of my first lucky success which far outweighed my lavatory error, although that success too concerned a lavatory. The occasion took place in a three-starred restaurant, a smart one, but not too smart like the Ritz. In my first three years I was only told to take a watch in the Ritz once, the expense was too great and the chances too small. Waiters there were apt to notice strangers. I had been shown a photograph, but a very bad one, of a suspect who apparently had been seen at this restaurant more than once and was believed to be a foreigner. In his case they had already paid three experienced watchers – one a day – and they were almost ready to give up. His companion at table was always different.

Quite by chance – in our profession nearly everything is a chance – I happened to be sitting at the next table to a solitary man. Some instinct had made me choose the table next to him for I could see little resemblance to photographs I had been shown. However there was a foreign look about him, and perhaps (I might have imagined it) a look of impatience or anxiety, and his table was laid for two. He had ordered a glass of port (not a usual aperitif for an Englishman) and he lingered over it. I lingered too over my very dry Martini, trying to outlinger him.

At last the friend he was awaiting arrived – a woman. I write 'friend', but the greeting which he gave her struck me as very odd – 'Pleased to meet you', that very antiquated English phrase, was spoken in a distinctly foreign accent.

For the rest of my meal there could no longer be any malingering. In my training I had been taught that I must always finish my meal and pay my bill while those whom I had chosen to watch were still eating. Of course I could spend quite a lot of time, after paying, with a coffee, but I must be prepared to leave my table a little before those I watched or a very little after. I had to keep in touch, at all costs, but avoid the suspicion of keeping them under observation.

This early experience of mine in the Royalty restaurant was a physically very painful one, for the pair whom I had chosen to watch had a large meal and I have always, as I have said, had a very small appetite. First they chose a mixed salad, then roast beef, then cheese and then to my horror, they ordered a dessert – this too was a foreign touch for in England we finish with cheese. It confirmed for me that the two were of different nationalities, and that 'pleased to meet you' had been an agreed signal. A momentary disagreement over cheese before dessert confirmed me in thinking that the man was French and the woman English.

Their conversation was mainly on the subject of Flaubert about whom the woman was writing a book. Of course it occurred to me that Flaubert might be the pseudonym of a third agent and Madame Bovary of yet another. They made no attempt to lower their voices.

'It's very good of you to see me,' the woman told him. 'I have used your great work on Flaubert a good deal, and it's very kind of you to allow me to quote from it.'

I knew little of Flaubert's life, but I began to learn quite a lot, and there really seemed nothing wrong with the couple.

'I'd have liked to see you once again and show you my text before it goes to the publisher, but I know how busy you are,' the woman said.

'Yes, I would like to see it, but I'm afraid I'm off by an early plane tomorrow. At 9.30.'

I made a mental note to check the time and destination, but I had really lost all suspicion and I would have called it a wasted day if it had not been for the cigarettes. After the meat course, when they were waiting for the cheese trolley, she offered him a cigarette.

He hesitated, and I thought he glanced at me.

'A Benson and Hedges Extra Mild,' she told him.

'Yes, I do like one of those, but do you mind – I only smoke one after I have finished eating. It's a habit.' However she took a cigarette and laid it by his plate.

'You don't mind if I smoke?' she asked.

'Of course not.'

He lit her cigarette and the cheese trolley arrived. She chose a Stilton and he chose a Brie. I chose the smallest bit of Gruyère that I could persuade the waiter to cut and shuddered at the thought of the dessert which was yet to come. I took an ice and after the apple tarts which they picked the woman took a coffee. I did the same. He seemed to have forgotten her cigarette, for he left it still unlit beside his plate. Perhaps a Benson and Hedges, I thought, was too mild for his taste. They continued to talk about Flaubert, but what they said was quite beyond me. At last the man asked for his bill and I quickly did the same, but theirs came first and I had no time to wait for it before I followed them from the restaurant. The man still carried his cigarette. Perhaps he had no intention of smoking it, but didn't wish to offend his companion by throwing it away.

At the door he said goodbye to her. She said, 'We haven't spoken at all of *Education Sentimentale*. If you could manage another meeting . . .'

'I'll certainly do my best,' he said. 'It has been a great pleasure meeting you.' When she had left he turned away towards the lavatory still carrying his cigarette. A tidy man, I thought, he's going to throw it into the toilet, but all the same a reasonless curiosity had settled in my brain. There was another reason too. I wanted to practise my new profession. A good cook progresses through his errors. A short pause and then I followed him walking as quietly as I could.

He was washing his hands when I entered and he had laid the cigarette to one side out of the way of the water – that eternal unsmoked cigarette. I snatched it and before he had time to turn I was out of the lavatory. There was no shout from behind me – only the sound of pursuing feet. At the hotel entrance I pushed the porter to one side and ran into the street. Luck was with me. A taxi had just deposited a customer. As I drove away I saw the customer rushing after me into the street followed by the waiter who was waving my unpaid bill. Poor man. I paid it later indirectly with interest by recommending the restaurant for a fourth star, which it certainly did not deserve.

In the taxi I looked more closely at the cigarette. There was an odd feeling in the centre – a kind of hardening of the tobacco, and at one end a kind of roughening in the packing of the cigarette. I was careful not to finger it more. It had already passed through three hands and was a little damp from its lavatory lodging – there seemed reason enough for all this. All the same I had learnt in my training to hand over any object however trivial belonging to a suspect, and this I did as soon as I reached the office of the International Guide to Good Restaurants. Then I sat down to write my report, and my instinct made me enclose with it the untidy cigarette.

3

I hadn't given in my report long when the telephone sounded. 'Scramble,' my chief's voice said, and I touched the button which would make our conversation unintelligible to anyone who might be tapping our line.

'The woman I feel pretty sure was English and the man French, I think, but they spoke to each other in English although they were both experts on Flaubert.'

'I think they wanted you to listen. They were proving, you might say, their innocence.'

'But are they guilty?'

'Guilty as hell. You've done a first-rate job. Come along in an hour and see me.'

When I went to him the cigarette lay torn in half on his desk in a small litter of flakes. 'Benson and Hedges Special Mild,' he said with a smile of satisfaction. 'Low in tar content, but certainly not low in valuable information.' He showed a little bit of wrinkled paper. 'A good way to conceal it,' he said, 'in the middle of a cigarette.'

'What's on it?' I asked.

'We'll soon know. Microdots and a code of course. You've done a good job. It was very acute of you to take the cigarette.'

Such a good job indeed that they forgave me several months later for a very bad mistake which also involved a lavatory.

4

The cigarette had led us to a new suspect for our file, a doctor who had connections with the chemical industry. He was now placed under continuous surveillance; a whole team of us was employed night and day. His open practice was in a small country town not far from the factory which used him as a consultant when one of the employees went sick. He had been very thoroughly vetted by MI5, but our relations were closer to MI6 and there was a good deal of rivalry and even jealousy between the two establishments. The foundation of the international food guide was regarded by MI5 as an intrusion into their territory, and it was true that we had not passed on to them the information contained in the cigarette. Counter-espionage abroad certainly belonged to MI6, but our food guide was international and it would be inefficient to split the English section from the foreign. No watcher was employed more than once in two weeks and always at different mealtimes in order that the suspect would never become aware of a familiar face. Unfortunately for me the doctor was a man of inordinate appetite and after two months my turn came at the hour of dinner – the hour when his appetite was greatest. Unfortunately too I had suffered from a succession of heavy meals earlier. To award a star even to breakfasts had to be considered, and it was extraordinary how many people still preserved a pre-war appetite for what is still called an English breakfast as distinct from a continental one – eggs and bacon, or even worse sausages and bacon, sometimes even preceded by a helping of haddock.

I took over from his watcher outside a quite simple inn which was called the Star and Garter only half a mile from his own house. We were the only diners and I sat down at a table well away from his. I noticed he looked quite often at his watch, but he was obviously not expecting a friend for he had already chosen his meal. To my horror when I looked at the menu I found a set menu at a very reasonable price and he had ordered the first course which was an onion soup and my stomach cannot abide onions. If I left out the soup I would find myself well in advance of him and I would be out of touch with him when I finished the last course. Another watcher was stationed in sight of the door who would take over when he left, but I had to remain till then in sight of the doctor in case he was contacted during his meal. A doctor was always of course liable to a phone call when he was away from home, but the Star and Garter telephone would have been tapped as soon as we knew where he was in the habit of dining.

I allowed myself a glance at him every now and then when he lowered his eyes to the obnoxious soup. To me he looked a thoroughly honest man. Why would an honest man be mixed up with the man of the cigarette? Then I remembered he was a doctor. A doctor doesn't judge his patients. If he had attended the deathbed of a murderer that wouldn't have made him a murderer. If a priest appeared on our microdot file would he be reasonably a guilty man? The doctor finished his soup and ordered roast beef. Reluctantly I did the same. I had to keep in step, though I could already feel the effect of the onion soup. He was a slow eater and read a newspaper between bites. I was glad that he showed no interest in me. It confirmed my impression of his honesty. It was a cold night and I felt sorry for the watcher outside keeping his unnecessary vigil.

To my distress the doctor ordered an apple tart to follow. The only alternative on the little restaurant's menu was an ice-cream, but an ice-cream needs to be eaten with some speed before it melts, so I was forced to order the tart. My trouble was I suffer from acidity, and when the doctor followed the tart with a piece of cheese, I had to leave the table, for I felt the approach of diarrhoea. The lavatory was upstairs and as I left I ordered my bill, so as to be ready to leave on my return if the doctor didn't wait for coffee. If I found him with coffee I could spin out the time with a little difficulty over change and when he left my colleague would take over. 'And see him safely home to bed,' I thought with irritation at this unnecessary routine watch.

I won't go into the unsavoury details of my diarrhoea – it was a severe one and more than five minutes had passed before I went downstairs to the restaurant. I found that the doctor had gone, and I thought with relief, 'My job is over.' I would take something to ease my stomach when I got home.

As I paid my bill I remarked to the waiter, an elderly man, who, I found, was also the landlord, 'Not much custom tonight.'

'At night,' he told me, 'the bar trade's better. And we do more at lunchtime – passing motorists, but the doctor's a good regular and he likes simple food.'

I felt it my duty to inquire a little more about our suspect.

'Doesn't he ever dine at home?'

'No, he's a single man.'

'Not much custom for a doctor in a place this size?'

'There's always the flu. And babies. But of course his main work is up at the chemical factory. Two hundred men. Plenty of patients there. I hope you enjoyed your food, sir, and that we'll see you again. It's a small place but my own, and I keep a sharp eye on the kitchen.'

'I can tell that. Here is my card.'

'International Good Food Guide! My goodness! I never expected to see one of your fellows in my little place. So that's why you went to the lavatory?'

'Yes. We always inspect those. And I looked in on the kitchen on my way,' I lied. 'I could tell at a glance . . .'

'What?'

'Clean. Which I already knew from the food it would be.'

'It's very kind of you, sir. I do hope you'll come again.'

'Not for a year. In the meanwhile we'll give you a mention in the guide.'

'I'm very honoured, sir. Perhaps some of the big shots from the factory will read it.'

'What I advise you in the meantime is to have at least two menus. Perhaps then we could promote you to a star.'

'Never did I dream . . . When I tell the missus . . .'

'By the way what do they do in the factory?'

'All sorts of medicines, sir. Even cures for the hiccups they say. Me, I am content with a bit of Eno's. It serves most purposes.'

I bade him a warm goodbye and gave him a copy of the guide in which his restaurant would appear in the next edition. I was glad to be off because my stomach was still queasy and I had no further duties that day. I would go home and perhaps as the man had reminded me take a glass of Eno's.

I went outside and to my astonishment saw my fellow watcher pretending interest in a shop window across the road. He turned and saw me with equal astonishment.

'What the hell have you come out for?'

'What are you doing here?'

'Waiting for the doctor of course.'

'But the doctor's gone.'

'He hasn't passed that door.'

'Oh the hell. There must be a back door.'

'But why didn't you signal me as soon as you lost touch?'

'I had to go to the loo. I was only gone a few minutes and he wasn't there when I came down. He came in this way and I thought he'd gone out the same way and you'd be following him.'

'He must have had suspicions.'

'I took him for an honest man whatever the damned microdots said.'

'We've certainly messed things up this time.'

5

That was exactly what my boss said when I reported to him. 'You've badly messed things. You should never have left the restaurant before him. Even for a minute.'

'It was the onion soup and the tomatoes.'

'Onion soup and tomatoes! Is that what I have to tell the big chief?'

'I had diarrhoea. I couldn't stay and shit in my trousers.'

'You know I would have sacked you like a shot, if you hadn't made that splendid coup with the cigarette.'

'You needn't sack me. I resign. But I'd swear – microdot or not – that man was honest. He was no traitor.'

'Traitor is a silly word that journalists use. A traitor can be as honest as you or me. That chemical factory has connection with chemical warfare. A man can feel that chemical warfare is a betrayal of the world we have to live in. He could be fighting for something greater than his country. An honest spy is the most dangerous. He is not spying for money, he's spying for a cause. Look, that cigarette is more important than this mistake. One learns from mistakes, and you are a good learner. You have given me a good idea of how to use your mistake. He may have been suspicious of you. Or it may have been his regular drill. To go in by the front and go out by the back.'

I said, 'I can't go on. I'm sorry. I can't go on.'

'But why? This mistake of yours will be forgiven and forgotten.'

'But the onion soup. Tomatoes. And all the meat I have to eat. Garlic with the lamb. Cheese as well as dessert. Why do all these suspects have such a good appetite?'

'Perhaps it gives them time to observe the people around them.'

'But *they* never seem to get diarrhoea.'

'About your diarrhoea. I have an idea.' He paused and played with his pencil. 'Suppose we gave you a week's holiday.'

'I don't need a holiday except from onion soup, and tomatoes etc.'

'But I see a way of using them. Suppose you stayed a week at that little hotel and had all your meals there. The doctor would begin to accept you as a regular. You would consult him about your stomach. He might give you a treatment. Of course you would take nothing he gave you, for if he remained suspicious he might try to poison you. Any prescription he gave you would send on to us and we would have it examined. If there was anything dangerous about it our suspicions would be confirmed and we would close in on him.'

'And if they weren't?'

'We'd give him more time. He would need to have *his* suspicions confirmed too if he's a man with scruples. We would think of some way. A warning from somewhere would reach him. Or one of your own reports perhaps. We would watch his reactions very closely. All you would need to do is . . .'

'To eat,' I said. 'No. I've made up my mind. I can't make a career out of eating. No more onion soup, no more tomatoes, no more garlic. I resign.'

So it was that I abandoned the International Guide to Good Restaurants. Sometimes from curiosity I buy a copy of the latest number. At least I have done one good deed in my life. The little country restaurant remains as a 'mention' in the guide, though it has never received a star.

*Two Gentle
People*

*Church
Militant*

Two Gentle People

They sat on a bench in the Parc Monceau for a long time without speaking to one another. It was a hopeful day of early summer with a spray of white clouds lapping across the sky in front of a small breeze: at any moment the wind might drop and the sky become empty and entirely blue, but it was too late now – the sun would have set first.

In younger people it might have been a day for a chance encounter – secret behind the long barrier of perambulators with only babies and nurses in sight. But they were both of them middle-aged, and neither was inclined to cherish an illusion of possessing a lost youth, though he was better looking than he believed, with his silky old-world moustache like a badge of good behaviour, and she was prettier than the looking-glass ever told her. Modesty and disillusion gave them something in common; though they were separated by five feet of green metal they could have been a married couple who had grown to resemble each other. Pigeons like old grey tennis balls rolled unnoticed around their feet. They each occasionally looked at a watch, though never at one another. For both of them this period of solitude and peace was limited.

The man was tall and thin. He had what are called sensitive features, and the cliché fitted him; his face was comfortably, though handsomely, banal – there would be no ugly surprises when he spoke, for a man may be sensitive without imagination. He had carried with him an umbrella which suggested caution. In her case one noticed first the long and lovely legs as unsensual as those in a society portrait. From her expression she found the summer day sad, yet she was reluctant to obey the command of her watch and go – somewhere – inside.

They would never have spoken to each other if two teen-aged louts had not passed by, one with a blaring radio slung over his shoulder, the other kicking out at the pre-occupied pigeons. One of his kicks found a random mark, and on they went in a din of pop, leaving the pigeon lurching on the path.

The man rose, grasping his umbrella like a riding-whip. 'Infernal young scoundrels,' he exclaimed, and the phrase sounded more Edwardian because of the faint American intonation – Henry James might surely have employed it.

'The poor bird,' the woman said. The bird struggled upon the gravel, scattering little stones. One wing hung slack and a leg must have been broken too, for the pigeon swivelled round in circles unable to rise. The other pigeons moved away, with disinterest, searching the gravel for crumbs.

'If you would look away for just a minute,' the man said. He laid his umbrella down again and walked rapidly to the bird where it thrashed around; then he picked it up, and quickly and expertly he wrung its neck – it was a kind of skill anyone of breeding ought to possess. He looked round for a refuse bin in which he tidily deposited the body.

'There was nothing else to do,' he remarked apologetically when he returned.

'I could not myself have done it,' the woman said, carefully grammatical in a foreign tongue.

'Taking life is *our* privilege,' he replied with irony rather than pride.

When he sat down the distance between them had narrowed; they were able to speak freely about the weather and the first real day of summer. The last week had been unseasonably cold, and even today . . . He admired the way in which she spoke English and apologized for his own lack of French, but she reassured him: it was no ingrained talent. She had been 'finished' at an English school at Margate.

'That's a seaside resort, isn't it?'

'The sea always seemed very grey,' she told him, and for a while they lapsed into separate silences. Then perhaps thinking of the dead pigeon she asked him if he had been in the army. 'No, I was over forty when the war came,' he said. 'I served on a government mission, in India. I became very fond of India.' He began to describe to her Agra, Lucknow, the old city of Delhi, his eyes alight with memories. The new Delhi he did not like, built by a Britisher – Lut-Lut-Lut? No matter. It reminded him of Washington.

'Then you do not like Washington?'

'To tell you the truth,' he said, 'I am not very happy in my own country. You see, I like old things. I found myself more at home – can you believe it? – in India, even with the British. And now in France, I find it's the same. My grandfather was British Consul in Nice.'

'The Promenade des Anglais was very new then,' she said.

'Yes, but it aged. What we Americans build never ages beautifully. The Chrysler Building, Hilton hotels . . .'

'Are you married?' she asked. He hesitated a moment before replying, 'Yes,' as though he wished to be quite, quite accurate. He put out his hand and felt for his umbrella – it gave him confidence in this surprising situation of talking so openly to a stranger.

'I ought not to have asked you,' she said, still careful with her grammar.

'Why not?' He excused her awkwardly.

'I was interested in what you said.' She gave him a little smile. 'The question came. It was *imprévu*.'

'Are *you* married?' he asked, but only to put her at her ease, for he could see her ring.

'Yes.'

By this time they seemed to know a great deal about each other, and he felt it was churlish not to surrender his identity. He said, 'My name is Greaves, Henry C. Greaves.'

'Mine is Marie-Claire. Marie-Claire Duval.'

'What a lovely afternoon it has been,' the man called Greaves said.

'But it gets a little cold when the sun sinks.' They escaped from each other again with regret.

'A beautiful umbrella you have,' she said, and it was quite true – the gold band was distinguished, and even from a few feet away one could see there was a monogram engraved there – an H certainly, entwined perhaps with a C or a G.

'A present,' he said without pleasure.

'I admired so much the way you acted with the pigeon. As for me I am *lâche*.'

'That I am quite sure is not true,' he said kindly.

'Oh, it is. It is.'

'Only in the sense that we are all cowards about something.'

'You are not,' she said, remembering the pigeon with gratitude.

'Oh yes, I am,' he replied, 'in one whole area of life.' He seemed on the brink of a personal revelation, and she clung to his coat-tail to pull him back; she literally clung to it, for lifting the edge of his jacket she exclaimed, 'You have been touching some wet paint.' The ruse succeeded; he became solicitous about her dress, but examining the bench they both agreed the source was not there. 'They have been painting on my staircase,' he said.

'You have a house here?'

'No, an apartment on the fourth floor.'

'With an *ascenseur*?'

'Unfortunately not,' he said sadly. 'It's a very old house in the *dix-septième*.'

The door of his unknown life had opened a crack, and she wanted to give something of her own life in return, but not too much. A 'brink' would give her vertigo. She said, 'My apartment is only too depressingly new. In the *huitième*. The door opens electrically without being touched. Like in an airport.'

A strong current of revelation carried them along. He learned how she always bought her cheeses in the Place de la Madeleine – it was quite an expedition from her side of the *huitième*, near the Avenue George V, and once she had been rewarded by finding Tante Yvonne, the General's wife, at her elbow choosing a Brie. He on the other hand bought his cheeses in the Rue de Tocqueville, only round the corner from his apartment.

'You yourself?'

'Yes, I do the marketing,' he said in a voice suddenly abrupt. She said, 'It is a little cold now. I think we should go.'

'Do you come to the Parc often?'

'It is the first time.'

'What a strange coincidence,' he said. 'It's the first time for me too. Even though I live close by.'

'And I live quite far away.'

They looked at one another with a certain awe, aware of the mysteries of providence. He said, 'I don't suppose you would be free to have a little dinner with me.'

Excitement made her lapse into French. '*Je suis libre, mais vous . . . votre femme . . . ?*'

'She is dining elsewhere,' he said. 'And your husband?'

'He will not be back before eleven.'

He suggested the Brasserie Lorraine, which was only a few minutes' walk away, and she was glad that he had not chosen something more chic or more flamboyant. The heavy bourgeois atmosphere of the *brasserie* gave her confidence, and, though she had small appetite herself, she was glad to watch the comfortable military progress down the ranks of the sauerkraut trolley. The menu too was long enough to give them time to readjust to the startling intimacy of dining together. When the order had been given, they both began to speak at once. 'I never expected . . .'

'It's funny the way things happen,' he added, laying unintentionally a heavy inscribed monument over that conversation.

'Tell me about your grandfather, the consul.'

'I never knew him,' he said. It was much more difficult to talk on a restaurant sofa than on a park bench.

'Why did your father go to America?'

'The spirit of adventure perhaps,' he said. 'And I suppose it was the spirit of adventure which brought me back to live in Europe. America didn't mean Coca-Cola and *Time-Life* when my father was young.'

'And have you found adventure? How stupid of me to ask. Of course you married here?'

'I brought my wife with me,' he said. 'Poor Patience.'

'Poor?'

'She is fond of Coca-Cola.'

'You can get it here,' she said, this time with intentional stupidity.

'Yes.'

The wine-waiter came and he ordered a Sancerre. 'If that will suit you?'

'I know so little about wine,' she said.

'I thought all French people . . .'

'We leave it to our husbands,' she said, and in his turn he felt an obscure hurt. The sofa was shared by a husband now as well as a wife, and for a while the *sole meunière* gave them an excuse not to talk. And yet silence was not a genuine escape. In the silence the two ghosts would have become more firmly planted, if the woman had not found the courage to speak.

'Have you any children?' she asked.

'No. Have you?'

'No.'

'Are you sorry?'

She said, 'I suppose one is always sorry to have missed something.'

'I'm glad at least I did not miss the Parc Monceau today.'

'Yes, I am glad too.'

The silence after that was a comfortable silence: the two ghosts went away and left them alone. Once their fingers touched over the sugar-castor (they had chosen strawberries). Neither of them had any desire for further questions; they seemed to know each other more completely than they knew anyone else. It was like a happy marriage; the stage of discovery was over – they had passed the test of jealousy, and now they were tranquil in their middle age. Time and death remained the only enemies, and coffee was like the warning of old age. After that it was necessary to hold sadness at bay with a brandy, though not successfully. It was as though they had experienced a lifetime, which was measured as with butterflies in hours.

He remarked of the passing head waiter, 'He looks like an undertaker.'

'Yes,' she said. So he paid the bill and they went outside. It was a death-agony they were too gentle to resist for long. He asked, 'Can I see you home?'

'I would rather not. Really not. You live so close.'

'We could have another drink on the *terrasse*?' he suggested with half a sad heart.

'It would do nothing more for us,' she said. 'The evening was perfect. *Tu es vraiment gentil.*' She noticed too late that she had used 'tu' and she hoped his French was bad enough for him not to have noticed. They did not exchange addresses or telephone numbers, for neither of them dared to suggest it: the hour had come too late in both their lives. He found her a taxi and she drove away towards the great illuminated Arc, and he walked home by the Rue Jouffroy, slowly. What is cowardice in the young is wisdom in the old, but all the same one can be ashamed of wisdom.

Marie-Claire walked through the self-opening doors and thought, as she always did, of airports and escapes. On the sixth floor she let herself into the flat. An abstract painting in cruel tones of scarlet and yellow faced the door and treated her like a stranger.

She went straight to her room, as softly as possible, locked the door and sat down on her single bed. Through the wall she could hear her husband's voice and laugh. She wondered who was with him tonight – Toni or François. François had painted the abstract picture, and Toni, who danced in ballet, always claimed, especially before strangers, to have modelled for the little stone phallus with painted eyes that had a place of honour in the living-room. She began to undress. While the voice next door spun its web, images of the bench in the Parc Monceau returned and of the sauerkraut trolley in the Brasserie Lorraine. If he had heard her come in, her husband would soon proceed to action: it excited him to know that she was a witness. The voice said, 'Pierre, Pierre,' reproachfully. Pierre was a new name to her. She spread her fingers on the dressing-table to take off her rings and she thought of the sugar-castor for the strawberries, but at the sound of the little yelps and giggles from next door the sugar-castor turned into the phallus with painted eyes. She lay down and screwed beads of wax into her ears, and she shut her eyes and thought how different things might have been if fifteen years ago she had sat on a bench in the Parc Monceau, watching a man with pity killing a pigeon.

'I can smell a woman on you,' Patience Greaves said with pleasure, sitting up against two pillows. The top pillow was punctured with brown cigarette burns.

'Oh no, you can't. It's your imagination, dear.'

'You said you would be home by ten.'

'It's only twenty past now.'

'You've been up in the Rue de Douai, haven't you, in one of those bars, looking for a *fille*.'

'I sat in the Parc Monceau and then I had dinner at the Brasserie Lorraine. Can I give you your drops?'

'You want me to sleep so that I won't expect anything. That's it, isn't it, you're too old now to do it twice.'

He mixed the drops from the carafe of water on the table between the twin beds. Anything he might say would be wrong when Patience was in a mood like this. Poor Patience, he thought, holding out the drops towards the face crowned with red curls, how she misses America – she will never believe that the Coca-Cola tastes the same here. Luckily this would not be one of their worst nights, for she drank from the glass without further argument, while he sat beside her and remembered the street outside the *brasserie* and how – by accident he was sure – he had been called '*tu*'.

'What are you thinking?' Patience asked. 'Are you still in the Rue de Douai?'

'I was thinking that things might have been different,' he said.

It was the biggest protest he had ever allowed himself to make against the condition of life.

Church Militant

As we drove out of the reservation in Father Donnell's old tinpot of a jeep we passed the Archbishop in his Cadillac. It came to rest a few yards off, between the rows of coffee plants. 'If we hadn't stopped at your friend's after lunch,' Father Donnell complained, putting on his brakes, 'we'd have missed him altogether.' He got unwillingly out and went over to the Archbishop who sat at the wheel. The back of the car was full of women in strange, grey clothes on which were sewn grey linen crosses.

Father Donnell came thoughtfully back. He said, 'We can go on, but he wants us to meet him at the Niguru Mission for a chat at teatime. He's going up to my place now. I hope to God there's someone at home besides Patsy One-Eye.'

'Who were those women?' I asked.

Father Donnell replied gloomily and ambiguously, 'I fear the worst.'

That afternoon we called on some women settlers who were living alone very courageously on the edge of the Kikuyu reserve. The shotguns in the hall, the revolvers on their laps, the big Boxer dogs couched protectively by the wire fences called to my mind what life must have been like in the early days of American colonization. Father Donnell was preoccupied. When one of the women mentioned the attack on his mission a few weeks gone, he hadn't the heart to tell a good story. 'Oh, the poor fellows,' he said, 'they didn't know any better.'

'If you hadn't had twenty yards start to the forest—'

'They've been misled,' he said.

The Niguru Mission was quite a different spot from Father Donnell's tin hut on the top of a hill. Outside the reserve, on land owned by Europeans, it had been built in less troublesome times and built to last. I was reminded a little of a military barracks designed by Lutyens. The very sight of it in the distance aroused Father Donnell; he became as mischievous as a small boy from a poor home taken to see a rich and pompous relative.

'We'll pull Father Schmidt's leg,' he said. 'Poor man, living there with all those holy nuns, year in, year out.'

'Have they had any trouble?' I asked.

'Trouble!' Father Donnell exclaimed in his house-proud accent. 'They've got fifty Home Guards stuck around the place and if a dog so much as barks, away goes a rocket and they have the Devons shooting up the drive. What chance have the Mau Mau, poor devils, with a place like that?'

We parked the car as silently as Father Donnell's gears would permit round a corner of the Italianate chapel and went to look for Father Schmidt. In the great square of the place a nun went bustling by and Father Donnell called out to her, 'Hi, sister!'

'How are you, father?'

'Trying to avoid me, are you? Think I've come begging for eggs, eh?'

'I just didn't see you, father.'

'Well, I've some bad news for all of you, sister.'

'Bad news? Is it General Kimathi?'

'What, that poor ignorant fellow? No, sister. The Archbishop's descending on you all, in next to no time! In his brand new Cadillac.'

'But what's he doing this way?'

'I have my fears,' Father Donnell said, moving on.

We found Father Schmidt in his room. He was fast asleep on a couple of chairs, with the shutters drawn to keep the sun out; a very old man with snow-white hair, very close to the last sleep of all. I wouldn't have woken him, but Father Donnell had no such scruples. 'Father Schmidt, Father Schmidt!' he called.

Father Schmidt raised one thick white eyebrow. 'Oh it's you,' he said, and prepared to sleep again.

'Wake up, father. It's serious trouble we have.'

Father Schmidt reluctantly put his feet on the floor. 'Have they attacked you again? I heard no shots last night.'

'They've done worse, Father Schmidt. They've driven away the cows and killed the chickens and we've come to beg for some of your home-made wine.'

'I suppose I can give you a few bottles, perhaps, but what has wine got to do with your cows?'

'Oh, they poisoned our well too. We've nothing to drink, father. And we'll need six of your labourers to carry the things.'

'What is wrong with your car?'

'They burnt that.'

'Then how did you come here?'

'We walked all the way.'

The old man shambled to his feet and made for the cupboard. The bottom shelf was full of bottles.

'We're starving, father. We'll need all those bottles.'

'They have not been filled yet. We will have to take them to the barrel.'

'And bread, father. We've used up all our bread.'

Grumbling gutturally old Father Schmidt produced two loaves and half a pound of butter. 'It is all I have, Father Donnell.'

'And eggs.'

He took three eggs out of a china dish.

'And a side of beef, father.'

'What reason would I have for keeping a side of beef? You know very well I do not eat meat. For that you must go to the sister-in-charge. I have some biscuits. You had better sit down and eat.'

I wondered how far Father Donnell would let the joke go, for there were only a very few sweet biscuits left in the tin and Father Schmidt turned away his face to hide a grimace when Father Donnell dipped a finger towards the tin.

'Look at his face,' Father Donnell said. 'The sweetest tooth this side of the Indian Ocean. Don't be afraid, father. It was a little jest we were having.'

Father Schmidt looked down at his big black boots and said, 'Will you ever grow up, Father Donnell?'

'Ah, don't be angry, father. I'll be as old as you one day. But I've real news for you. The Archbishop's due here any minute with a cargo of ladies.'

'Ladies?'

'The Little Sisters of Charles de Foucauld.'

'Haven't I got enough women in the place?'

'They don't want to have anything to do with you, father. They want a plot in the reserve.'

'Who's going to pay for them?'

'They want to live like African women, build their own huts . . . till the ground . . . I told them I wanted nurses for a hospital, but they'll have none of that they say, except the emptying of the slops. "Perhaps you'll teach in my school?" I said. Oh, no. They'll sweep the floors, they won't teach. I said, "There's no room for you in my small mission," and they said they'd take a bit of ground outside it. "We only want half an hectare," they said. "It belongs to the Kikuyu," I said, "with all this trouble, how can we ask them for land?" "If the Lord wants us here, the Lord will give us half a hectare," they said. What's a hectare and what can you do with women like that?'

'It's not right,' Father Schmidt said. 'They ought to stay in Europe.'

'There's a lot of them in the north.'

'The north is different. There's plenty of room for madness in the desert.'

'Here's the Archbishop,' Father Donnell said, as the Cadillac bumped softly in.

Father Schmidt went to greet him and Father Donnell whispered to me, 'A saint if ever there was one.'

'The Archbishop?'

'Of course not. Oh, he's a good man in his way, but . . .'

The Archbishop entered. His big cross lay at a slight angle over his stomach.

'How are you? How are you?' he said. 'I'm very glad to meet you. It's a beautiful day for a ride if it wasn't for the state of the roads. I like to get out of the city, and the sisters were a good excuse. No, I won't have a cup of tea, thank you. Just one of those sweet biscuits, thank you, thank you. The sisters are looking after my ladies and showing them the chapel and then we must be off. I like to get back before it's very late in these dangerous days. Oh, thank you, thank you, but I seem to be eating them all up, when I really just wanted to explain about my ladies. They're French, father, like you.'

'I'm no more French,' Father Schmidt said, 'than you're English.'

'Ah, touché, touché,' the Archbishop said with a genial laugh. His bonhomie was continuous. I was reminded of a cheer-leader at a baseball match.

'What do they want here?' Father Schmidt asked.

'Well, you know how it is with the Sisters of Charles de Foucauld. They want a bit of land to work like the natives.'

'These parts are unsuitable for women,' Father Schmidt said.

'That's why they want to be here. It's their vocation.' The Archbishop brushed some crumbs off his waistcoat and said, 'I've given them one plot in the city at Moragumbi.'

'But that is a terrible place,' Father Schmidt said. 'That was where they dug up those strangled bodies. Their throats will all be cut,' he added accusingly.

'It's their vocation, father, it's their vocation. You are too materialist. We all of us have our vocations. You and me and Father Donnell. One mustn't interfere with a vocation.'

'Fifty-five years ago I remember a novice master who didn't believe in encouraging a vocation.'

'I'm not dealing with novices, father. It's as I said, you are too materialist, living here comfortably with all these sisters to look after you.'

'They will not stay alive a month. Who will look after *them*?'

'They'll look after themselves, father.'

'They are women,' Father Schmidt said sadly and wistfully.

The Archbishop took Father Donnell out into the shadowy square 'to meet the ladies properly'. He walked jauntily, like a leader: there was no question about his vocation either.

Father Schmidt sat silent over his empty tin of sweet biscuits. Once he shook his head at his own thoughts.

I wondered how I could cheer him up. I was an outsider, a visiting journalist. I said, 'These empty bottles in your cupboard . . .'

He raised his old eyes.

I said, 'If we loaded half a dozen in the back of Father Donnell's jeep, then when he drives off where'll be such a clatter . . . I don't know what the Archbishop will think.'

Father Schmidt rose. 'It is a very good idea.' He stumped in his big boots towards the cupboard. The Archbishop was talking earnestly to Father Donnell. Neither of them saw us laden with the bottles. Father Schmidt took up a position between me and them, straddling with his legs, making a curtain of his soutane, while I laid the bottles in the bottom of the jeep. Then we went back to where the Archbishop, surrounded by the non-comprehending French faces of his ladies, was having his last word with Father Donnell.

'At a time like this,' Father Donnell said, 'we can't ask the poor creatures for even half an acre.'

'It's to help a vocation.'

'How can you expect the Kikuyu to understand that? They'll think we are stealing the land. And aren't we stealing it?'

'For God, father.'

'I thought God owned the land already. Without us.' He got angrily into his jeep and I followed him. 'Goodbye, your Grace.'

'Goodbye, father. Just think about it. I'm sure you'll come round to my opinion.'

'Goodbye, Father Schmidt.'

'Goodbye, Father Donnell.'

He drove off and the bottles merrily clinked and clanked, but looking back I could see no sign that the Archbishop had heard, nor had Father Donnell. He bumped onwards into the reserve lost in thought. I had to turn on the lights myself. The noise of our progress made me uneasy in the growing darkness. I said, 'Don't you think . . . these bottles . . .'

'Bottles?'

'They are so noisy. If the Mau Mau—' I tried nervously to suggest.

'Poor fellows,' Father Donnell said. 'How could we ever make them understand . . . ?'

The Other Side of the Border

Under the Garden

The Other Side of the Border

Note

I suppose most novelists' careers are littered with abandoned novels: some may be abandoned because the novelist has lost interest in the story or his characters: some because a more imperative demand-to-be-written pushes out the earlier mood. The other day, looking through a drawer, I came on the MS. of just such a novel, and as I read it the characters, the scene and the half-unfolded story seemed to me to have more interest than many tales of mine that had appeared fully dressed between covers. Why shouldn't this book too, I felt, have its chance? I could identify the year when I began to write it as probably 1936, after I had returned from a journey in Liberia: at any rate, if it has no other merit, the book seems to me stamped unmistakably with the atmosphere of the middle thirties – Hitler is still quite new, dictatorship is only a tang on the breeze blowing from Europe: in England is depression and a kind of Metroland culture.

An odd thing is that though I remember the characters in the book well – Hands, young Morrow, Billings – I can't remember what was going to happen to them. Why did I abandon the book? I think for two main reasons – because another book, *Brighton Rock*, was more insistent to be written, and because I realized that I had already dealt with the main character in a story called *England Made Me*. Hands, I realized, had the same origin as Anthony Farrent in that novel.

Another point interested me: since those days I have been back to the West African port described in Part Two and I realize now that this picture of the place, its whole atmosphere, couldn't be more 'wrong'. I spent a week there in 1936 before this novel was begun, but now I know the port from a year's residence. It is every bit as seedy, depressed and drab as I have described it, but in a totally different way. Denton of Part One on the other hand, which is the town in the Home Counties where I was born and brought up, seems to me right. Between the two lies the whole difference between the passport photograph and the family snapshot.

Part One: The Map

1

The first thing young Morrow noticed in the waiting-room was the Map. There it hung where you would naturally expect it in the new offices of the New Syndicate, representing the coast, the rivers running in parallel black threads from the interior, the mountains feathered on the northern border and the forest a splash of green over everything – representing too to Morrow a whole obscure state of mind, a mystery from which he felt he had at last escaped. He was home now. He could understand what went on. Movies were clear. He had a sudden feeling of sentiment for the word 'home', for words like 'the pictures', 'school', 'bus'. There was no obscurity about this varnished and glittering room, the pile of technical magazines upon the table full of advertisements for drills and ore crushers; he could hear the tugs hooting on the Mersey. His young face wore such expressions as 'Cheerio', 'Glad to be back'. A woman opened the door and said, 'Mr Danvers can see you now.' She was, Morrow supposed, the General Manager's secretary, but she had much more the manner of a nurse – her voice was gentle, friendly and determined, and she gave him a kind of clinical glare as he passed her. Morrow went in.

Mr Danvers rose behind his desk and held out his hand. He hadn't changed at all in two years – time didn't move at home in the same way: he gripped with the same grip he had given Morrow the day he sailed; the signet ring made the same painful impression. And he was just as forthright as he had always been – there were lines Morrow had learnt at school about 'the good grey head that all men loved', which always came to mind. Mr Danvers said, 'Well, young Morrow, I'm glad to see you, very glad. Take a chair. Help yourself to a cigarette.' He wore hospitality like a flower in the buttonhole: you felt he was going to ask you to smell it. He said, 'Don't think you've been forgotten these last two years. I've had reports of your work – very favourable reports – from Hands.'

It was as if that particular name had been dropped between them too soon; it fell with an effect of embarrassment, like a cup at a tea-party. They were both silent, and then Mr Danvers edged as it were away from the awkward sound. 'The Board have decided to raise your salary.'

'Didn't you get my letter?' Morrow asked.

'I discounted that,' Mr Danvers said gently.

'But I *have* resigned.'

'Forgive me,' Mr Danvers said, 'if I talk to you a little like a father. After all – I knew him. I sat under him.' He sketched in his tone of voice – full of dim respect and gentle memory and kindly amusement – the parsonage house which lay next door to his own rarely visited acres. He said, 'If you leave us, what can you do?'

'I shall find something,' Morrow said and shivered a little: it had been cold on the tug coming off in the early morning over the grey blowy Irish Sea.

'You've been ill,' Mr Danvers said. 'That's the truth of the matter.' He tried to slip the name through less obtrusively this time. '*He* wrote to us,' and then went quickly on, 'you've only to look in that glass.'

He *could* look in the glass: it hung there behind Mr Danvers' desk and attracted his gaze. He saw his own face – it looked the same to him as it had always done – because he'd lived with it. If it had changed, it had changed so gradually that he had never noticed, shaving in the lid of the biscuit tin when his glass had been broken, deliberately, by Hands. He was unhappy when he thought that he hadn't shed a continent from his face.

'You're quite yellow with fever,' Mr Danvers said. 'A skeleton. That attack of dysentery must have got you badly down. I really think it would be a good thing if you went and saw someone at the Hospital for Tropical Diseases. Have a blood test. And then,' he sketched vaguely in the air, 'the fleshpots, you know. Fatten up.'

The secretary – she seemed after that advice more than ever like a nurse – put her head in at the door. 'Sir Frederick,' she announced softly.

'Ask him to wait just two minutes.' Mr Danvers went on, rising from his chair, coming round to the front of his desk, holding out his threatening hand, 'The Board likes to look after its servants.'

'But there are things I've simply got to tell you,' Morrow said. 'The whole business – it's fantastic. The gold – and Hands himself – so many deaths – Colley – and then there's Billings.'

'Billings?'

'He must have written you about Billings. He picked him up on the English side of the border. The most appalling . . .'

'Oh, Billings. Of course I remember Billings. You must understand,' Mr Danvers said in a voice of reproof, 'I trust Hands' judgment – absolutely.'

'That's why I've resigned. You mustn't trust it too far. You've got to know – the Board have got to know—' He was taken with the attack of ague he'd been expecting all the morning. His teeth clicked like billiard balls. The secretary had left the door ajar and the draught had set him going.

'There, you see,' Mr Danvers justified himself. He rang the bell and told the secretary, 'My car will take Mr Morrow to his hotel.' He came and laid his hand on Morrow's shoulder. 'Such dreams,' he said. 'We'll talk about it all when you're better.'

'At least,' Morrow said, 'you'll let me write a report?'

'Of course. If you wish,' Mr Danvers said. 'We are always interested . . .' The secretary stayed behind a moment, and Morrow in the waiting-room allowed himself to be drawn, with a feeling of obscure distress, towards the map. He had believed that back here everything would be very simple: he had resigned: he had his duty to do, and his young yellowed face was like an old intaglio of duty, cut symbolically for a signet ring. Loyalty and duty – they were the only qualities he had to live by, and now that he had resigned he owed no loyalty to Hands. Hands was there – on the map: they had drawn a little ring round Hands in red ink: a little to the left of Zigita, up beyond Nicaboozu.

2

Hands wiped the soot and steam from the pane and peered out at Willesden Junction. It was safe, if they punched your ticket at Euston, to travel first, but you could never be quite sure. He had a sense of daring, gazing across at the gritty refreshment room – the sense of too many failures slipped from his shoulders: there were limitless possibilities for a man of his experience – experience in Africa, Central America, on the London Midland

& Scottish. He felt for a while, all by himself in the first class, that he hadn't failed, he'd been experimenting, seeing life.

A ticket collector passed and for a moment Hands' face seemed to slide – the mouth weakened, the handsome too boyish face turned sullen, he aged perceptibly in seconds, you could see the lines coming out. Then the train began to move and all was well again. He took out his cigarette-case and lit up, as history slid by along the London Midland & Scottish line – an ancient castlework, a canal bridge built for a Jubilee, a pre-war Municipal building estate.

The whole line down to Denton was familiar to him – it was in a way his life, travelling up to the dentist, the pantomime, the oculist, to school: travelling up to catch this boat and that: travelling down it to home. The lights came out in the workmen's cottages: a man on a bicycle paused to light up: an old horse pushed jingling back into the dark dragging a barge, and the idea came to him. Ideas often came to him like that – out of the sooty air, in his bath, shaving. They were like a saint's voices – only they didn't as a rule lead to action good or bad. He didn't really hope for anything from this one – it was just a way of putting things to his father – 'I've been getting into touch with various companies' – a hint of mystery and importance: not in his wildest dreams did it involve anyone like Morrow or Danvers or Billings or the hundred blacks whom Morrow calculated had died between 1936 and 1938.

He came breezily out at Denton with his third-class ticket: a cheery word to everyone, the ticket collector, the two porters, the man in the luggage room: he liked to imagine a kind of feudal atmosphere – 'Master Hands comes home': he regretted that his father was not somebody other than a retired bank manager. He called 'Good evening' to the single taxi-driver, and then thought – why not blow a shilling on a cab? It didn't look well to have to walk home every evening.

His father was at dinner in the little dark dining-room — the rissoles which always followed the day after the joint — but he must have heard the taxi draw up, for he looked questioningly up. Hands could read on his face a kind of incredulous hope. He was not a man to take a taxi except on great occasions. He said, 'You've had a good day? You've found something?' The room was all carved mahogany and gilt frames and pale water colours: rhododendrons pressed up towards the window, and you could see over the low garden wall the leaning graves of an old cemetery. Nobody was buried there now: only dim inscriptions spoke of falling asleep and peace and hope of resurrection. A cat sat on a flat stone looking in.

'I've made contacts,' Hands said, sitting down and looking distastefully at the rissoles. 'Some big companies. It's a long story.'

'Are they interested — I mean have they any vacancies?'

'This isn't going to be a job of that kind,' Hands said. 'This is going to be more—' The dream grew as he talked. '—more of an administrative job, men under me. It's what I've always wanted, you know—'

But Mr Hands wasn't listening: he was eating a rissole: his old tired grey face had peculiar nobility. For nearly seventy years he had been believing in human nature, against every evidence — it hadn't been good for his promotion in the bank. He was a Liberal, he thought men could govern themselves if they were left alone to it, that wealth did not corrupt and that statesmen loved their country. All that had marked his face until it was a kind of image of what he believed the world to be. But it was breaking up now, since his wife had died and his son had begun to come — regularly — home with his excuses and breezy anecdotes and unjustified contempt. If he lived long enough his face might become more probable, more like the other people's world. He said wearily, 'You've had a tiring day. Shall I get out a little burgundy?'

'Oh, no,' Hands said. 'I'm in training.'

'Harvest burgundy won't hurt you.'

'No, really. I'm not drinking.' He sighed at the cabbage and a very faint smell of whisky percolated through the room. He smelt it himself: it infuriated him. How could a fellow succeed with such a father? Smelling his breath, grudging the taxi, disbelieving. He said stubbornly, 'You know – what I've always needed is – well, to show I can lead men.'

'Can you?' Mr Hands said.

The clock over a black carved mahogany mantel began to strike. 'You wait and see,' Hands said. He remembered the old childish saying that you keep the face you make when a clock strikes – for ever. He tightened his mouth.

'Well,' Mr Hands said hopelessly, 'leaders seem cheap these days.' He began to finish his cabbage: he hadn't troubled to ask about the idea: 'The *Manchester Guardian* today . . .' possibilities of hate moved behind the nobility as he said, 'the Fascists . . .'

'It's no good being a Liberal in these times,' Hands said. He began to lecture his father. 'You don't realize here in Denton. I've been about the world . . .'

Mr Hands said nothing. He pushed his plate a little on one side and rang the bell: he didn't look at Hands: at the other end of the room where his gaze could unobtrusively rest hung an enlarged tinted photograph of his wife – a high whalebone collar, grey dress, long hair, cheeks stained a wax-like pink and brown spaniel too-devoted eyes – devoted but not to Mr Hands. Mr Hands knew to whom that devotion went. He said absent-mindedly to Hands, 'You think there may be a vacancy?'

Hands got furiously up. He said, 'I'm going out.'

'Aren't you going to wait for the blancmange?'

'No. I want to think. I want some air.' A man needed encouragement: he had never, he told himself, had encouragement since his mother died. 'I'm going to take a walk.'

He walked out past the rhododendrons and the forgotten graves into Metroland. Denton sprawled in red villas up the hillside, but there remained in the long High Street, between the estate agents, the cafés and the two super-cinemas, dwindling signs of the old market town – there was a crusader's helmet in the church. People are made by places and this town had formed Hands: he called it 'home', dim sentiment moved in the summer evening among the red brick villas, but it had no real hold on anyone. You bought a season ticket and stayed away. Smoke moved into the sky behind the photographer's roof and showed the 8:52 was in. He would write those letters ... you never knew ... and after all the stuff existed, or so he understood. You couldn't live in a place like this: it was somewhere to which you returned for sleep and rissoles by the 7:50 or the 8:52: people had lived here once and died with their feet crossed to show they had been on a crusade, but now ... He stared into the photographer's window: yellowing photographs peered out of the diamonded Elizabethan pane – a genuine pane, but you couldn't believe it because of the Tudor Café across the street. He saw a face he knew in a wedding group, but it had been taken five years ago: there was something passé about the waistcoat: with a train every hour to town there was no need to be photographed at home these days – except of course for passports in a hurry. He couldn't count how many passport photographs old Millet had made of him.

He pushed the door open (Millet never locked up) and the bell jingled. There was a smell of chemicals, and in the dim bare light an antique pillar of plaster with a velvet top to rest the elbow on. Something hooded stood in a corner, and a metal clamp to fix the neck in. It wasn't up to date, the studio, but old Millet had had a flair for character in his day. As much as the crusader he was a relic of the time when Denton was a place in which to live. He came out now from an inner room, thin and courtly in pince-nez, wearing a velvet jacket – he used to represent the arts in Denton. His grey hair was very smooth and fine and he walked with a stoop – a scholar of the night-school and the institute.

He said, 'Ah, Mr Hands, another passport photograph?'

'Well not exactly, not yet. I came in for a chat, you know.'

'Sit down,' Millet said, 'sit down.' But there was nothing to sit on but a photographic chair, a stiff carved regal seat. The photographer leant on the pillar and said, 'Are you off again?' The door into the inner room was open. He said, 'Mr Hands is a great wanderer. You ought to write a book about all those places you've been in,' and then explained, 'My niece in there. She can't come out. She's sprained her ankle. Now where is it to be, Mr Hands?' He listened hungry for experience.

'Africa,' Hands said. 'The West Coast.'

'And when are you off?'

'It's not fixed definitely.'

'Those will be wild parts?'

'Oh,' Hands said, 'there's ivory, of course. And diamonds. Gold – You have to have men with you you can trust – in an emergency.' He seemed to brood on actual fact – 'Old Colley.' He had an audience at last: in the inner room he could just see the girl's face listening. It wasn't a pretty face, and it wasn't very young. He would have liked something a bit better, but it was an audience. 'There are chances in those parts for a man who knows the niggers.'

'They – take handling, I suppose?' Millet said.

'You've got to let them know who's master. I remember once,' he said, and as he started on the long fake tale he felt happy and ready for anything because no one here knew of the last jobs and the borrowed money and the accumulated failures. The whole world was at his feet while the photographer leant on the plaster pillar and under the reading-lamp in the inner room the woman raised her compliant and patient face, the kind of face you feel has known too much unimportant pain, the sprained ankle, the disappointment at the local hop, the varicose veins, a series of small humiliations uncomplainingly borne. 'It was up in the mountains,' Hands said, 'beyond Tapi,' and like Othello he sat there on the hard nobbly throne speaking of pigmies and poisoned arrows, the wild elephant and the leopard and the hidden treasures in the rocks, to old Millet and to Desdemona. He held them fast, he could feel their attention like praise, while the feet of the season ticket-holders went by on the pavement, and the moon swam up above the flinty church and the Tudor Café.

3

The answers came regularly in by the morning and evening post – or else didn't come in at all. The names on the envelopes created a good impression. With so much correspondence nobody could accuse him of not seeking work. They all contained roughly speaking the same reply: the company thanked Mr Hands for his interest, but was unwilling at the moment to increase its commitments. It did not feel any useful purpose could be served by an interview. Hands had borrowed a typewriter when he sent off his original letter and sometimes, for the sake of appearance, he would put in twenty minutes at the machine rap-tapping imaginary replies. 'Hands,' he would tap, 'Hands. Hands. Hands.' Line after line of it, and sometimes the date. 'March 2. March 2. March two. March Two.' Then he came down to lunch with ruffled hair and accepted a glass of harvest burgundy.

The chief companies never replied to his letter: Hands respected them for it. Later he didn't trouble to open all the envelopes marked this and that company or trust. He tore them into little bits in the quiet of his room and went out for a walk past the municipal housing estate, the Norman castle (a tiny piece of ruined wall scheduled as an ancient monument), the watercress beds. He walked by himself and dreamed enormous dreams. Sometimes Millet's niece figured like Cophetua's beggar maid and received his love humbly, sometimes plunging heroically to his death he came out on the other side where his mother waited for him with approval. They looked down together from the region of glory at old Mr Hands – or the Prime Minister – putting up a monument. He was like an adolescent struck suddenly with the curse of physical age: the ignobility of the years weakened his mouth while he dreamed.

He very nearly tore up the letter from the New Syndicate unread, but his fingers had got accustomed to a certain size, and this letter seemed a larger one than usual. In fact, it wasn't: the paper was thicker that was all; and again he nearly tore it up, seeing the usual three or four lines of type. And then he wished he had, reading, 'We shall be pleased to discuss further the subject of your letter of February 12 ult. if you will call at this office between 2 and 5 on Wednesday, March 5 prox . . .'

It was like having a bluff called at cards. Somebody had taken his suggestion seriously, somebody would demand details, samples, geological facts. His face flushed with his future humiliation. He was frightened. If Mr Hands had not come into breakfast and seen the letter he might have torn it up. But in any case it would have spoiled the dreams: with that letter ignored he couldn't have gone on telling himself – oh, magnificent things, sitting among the gorse bushes on the heath watching the cars go by like common life on the road at the bottom of the hill. He went to the public library and read up all he could: it wasn't much: 'The Geological Formation of Sierra Leone': a book about the Leopard Society in French Guinea: *A White Woman Among Cannibals* by Maisie Whitfield: nothing at all on that obscure republic of which he claimed expert knowledge. He looked at a map of Africa – it didn't mean a thing: he was up against truth. He felt hatred of Mr Danvers who had signed the letter: he read sarcasm into the reply. 'By God,' he thought without conviction, 'I'll make them pay my fare.'

Liverpool looked grey and middle-aged (it could never look old): the wind blew from the Mersey and you couldn't get away from the hooting of the steamers under the low and stormy sky. Rain blew round shabby street corners and suddenly ceased and a pale heartless sun, like a paper streamer flung by a stranger, shone on a tug and a toss of leaden water. Then the thin rain blew again. Nobody knew where the Syndicate offices were. Everybody said, 'I'm a stranger here myself': it was a city of strangers who caught tugs and trains and got away again as quickly as they could. Streets led nowhere: it was like a small town which just went on and on instead of stopping, growing away from the Mersey like a natural formation, a coral reef. In a small news-agent's yard he caught sight of two apple trees, bare and bleak and sooty and barren.

He ran the Syndicate to earth at last – up a side street near the docks, a red brick building with stained glass windows on the lowest floor, a date in chiselled brick over the door, 1873, and a yellow stone close by: 'This foundation stone was laid by Jonas E. Wallbrook, Lord Mayor of Liverpool on Feb. 14, 1873'. There was an insurance office on the ground floor, and on the second floor a philatelic agency, and between the two the New Syndicate. The lift was very small and was worked by a rope.

Hands wore his best suit and an old Mill Hill tie. A little whisky loosened his tongue. 'Not very good weather,' he said to the liftman. They ground laboriously upward.

'It's Liverpool weather,' the man said.

His stomach failed him on the landing: it began to rumble – he had had no appetite for lunch and the liquor and soda water rolled like a barrel inside him. 'I beg your pardon,' he said to the woman who opened the frosted door.

'Have you an appointment with Mr Danvers?'

'Oh, yes, yes. My name is Hands.' He smiled confidentially, he had a way with women – but again his stomach rumbled and his face sullenly set.

The waiting-room was tiny: a small French-polished table, two hard chairs, a copy of *The Ironworker*, *Punch*, and the *Tatler* for January 1932. He opened it at random and came on a picture of deck-chairs and umbrellas, three men in bathing-slips and a girl. 'Mr "Jimmy" Danvers,' he read, 'the popular managing director of the recently formed New Reef Syndicate disporting himself at Juan les Pins' – a baldish head, a high light on a stomach . . . It had been treasured a long while – everyone was grinning in the sunlight, four years younger, full of all kinds of hopes. The Syndicate apparently had not progressed. Hands went to the window and looked out: a tram went by, sparking slowly: between two warehouses you could see a few grey inches of water moving from left to right: smoke blew backwards and forwards and the soot fell on the Mersey, on the Royal Adelphi Hotel, on apple trees in a back yard.

'Mr Danvers will see you now.'

Hands exchanged greetings with a four-year-old photograph: Mr Danvers hadn't changed at all. He said, 'It's good of you to come all this way . . .' He took out a box of cigars. 'We were very interested.' Hands watched him, waiting for the awkward question and the afternoon deepened and it never came. The word 'gold' wasn't even mentioned: Mr Danvers called it 'it'.

'I've got just the man to send with you,' he said. 'A very trustworthy boy. I want to do him a good turn. His name's Morrow. You'll need someone else too.' The lights came out all over Liverpool: they said Booth's for the Teeth and Codling's Cough Cure: a gull fell out of the sky past a huge glass of harvest burgundy, rose and turned and made for the Mersey. A siren wailed and wailed and Hands said with a touch of bewilderment, loneliness and horror, 'There's a man called Colley. We know each other . . . I'd like to take him too.' There were things he couldn't understand: everything had gone too easily: he might have been selling a gold brick in the Strand to an Australian. He said with bewilderment, 'I thought you'd need to see . . .'

'We've already had samples of it,' Mr Danvers said, 'from another source. A Dutchman. Poor fellow he died – of yellow fever. That's why your letter seemed so timely. We want – the torch handed on.'

'Yellow fever,' Hands said.

'All the best things in life are dangerous,' Mr Danvers said. He opened the drawer of a desk and took out a cardboard box which had once held Egyptian cigarettes. Out of it he picked a small lump of greyish rock. 'You notice the signs,' he said. 'It's there, all right: no doubt of it. Take it. Look at it. The stratification.'

The small grey lump lay in Hands' palm and he thought – he's got me now: I've got to go on, and with a lightening of the heart – It was damned clever: to deceive a man like Danvers who's in the business: it won't be hard after this to deceive him awhile longer, and when he finds out – well – I'll have had my salary for a few weeks at least.

He fingered the stone – was this gold? He had no idea.

4

Colley, standing in the great steel coach station, felt the familiar sadness and unrest of departure. A modern clock-face without numerals, a chromium milk-bar, a faint smell of petrol: they took him back nevertheless to the stone quays and the slap of water, the oil and the seagulls of his usual loneliness. He was only going a few hundred miles north, but that's how new places, new people, always made him feel. It was no good hanging about for half an hour. The grinding of the gears as the buses drew in and out of their lines got on his nerves. Light glittered back from the steel sides, people sat deep down in seats, like expensive theatre stalls, and peered out at him; sometimes they munched chocolate; they looked warm and sleepy and content as if they were definitely going to some place, into the smoke and dust and night outside Victoria; it seemed just as important as when a liner leaves the dock.

It was too familiar. He wanted a drink. There was no one he had to kiss and grin at through the glass. It had been just the same when he was seventeen and went off to Brazil to take the place of a clerk who had died of yellow fever. All the good-byes were always said in Surrey (they became on each occasion more perfunctory), and even that first time he had found his way to the mail-boat's bar while everyone else was throwing paper ribbons. And it was the same the time he went to Africa, except that then the bar had not been open; he'd lain down on his bunk with a comic paper, without the heart to turn the leaf so that now the one dreadful joke was impressed for ever on his mind: a man hunting thrown in a ditch and a yokel bending over a hedge and a piece of dialogue he couldn't even yet understand. You'd think you'd get used to new jobs and going away from the places you know, but the loneliness repeats itself every time.

He went into a bar in the Wilton Road and had a b. and s. He couldn't stand Scotch any more; it had nearly rotted him in Africa, that and the iced crème de menthe the swells all served after every meal. It was one of those big bogus panelled bars you find near railway stations; there was a different tartan on every panel, and people kept coming in and out in a hurry because they had trains to catch: young City men with rolled umbrellas and double-breasted waistcoats on their way to Oxted or Hayward's Heath. When he had drunk two brandies he felt better; he said 'Good evening' to a pair of them, but they just looked him over and went on talking about an interim dividend Dunlop's had declared.

He had another brandy. It seemed to him that he knew them better than anyone else in the world, that he had lived with them all his life, from seventeen to thirty-three, first fellow-novices in strange employments, then senior clerks and eventually in their steady influential progress, the managers who got rid of him. They were bright and bonhomous with each other, they came from the same school, they'd seen the same show the week before at the Prince of Wales, their wives were on the best of terms, and they would no more have trusted each other in business than they would have trusted him. And to him they wouldn't even speak: that was the difference. He knew what was wrong; you can always disguise a frayed sleeve; no one can see much of your socks and your shirt's well out of sight; it's the shoes which give you away. That's why strange women always look at your shoes.

Well, he thought, I'd better be getting on. The bus left at 8:30 and was due in Liverpool some time in the early morning. He couldn't afford another brandy and he wouldn't sleep if he had one. Three brandies were enough to give him the courage of good-bye. It was not that he had been particularly happy in London, but you couldn't help making certain contacts if it was only with a particular table in an A.B.C.; you couldn't even help, perennially at this time of year, wandering back and forth from the Achilles statue to the Marble Arch, feeling certain hopes; they sprang, like the hardy daffodil, regularly to life, the hope of a human relationship based on something which wasn't lust and wasn't interest.

He hated the world – that was the permanent, the first article of his creed – you couldn't help drinking, you couldn't help moving on, but the emotion which made every departure a sad one suggested that somewhere – something – he had no terms for it – there existed... He pushed his coins across the counter and went out into the cool and grimy winter night. The sky paled, like vapour, above Battersea Power Station. Somebody was selling flowers outside the coach station, and a bus pushed its way out into the night.

Flower scent and petrol and the smoke from Pimlico chimneys, the vague spring air, forcing its way with the defenceless persistence of self-seeded grasses between concrete setts, combined to touch his brain with hope. All the jobs he had held up and down the seedy margins of strange continents had left impressions which came up at this time of year into his sour consciousness with an effect of sadness and for some reason beauty: the face of a stoker on a mail boat in '31 and of a dago child; they had mounted for a breath of air on to the steerage deck; he saw their patient lamp-lit faces as they sat side by side on a coil of rope and panted in the heavy night; a one-armed boy in Sierra Leone kneeling at Benediction in a tin church, who had cut his own arm off with a knife when he had broken it gathering palm nuts; a small African village where everyone had died of yellow fever and lay, horribly disfigured but with an air of extreme fidelity, each with his own family, in his own hut. A man in a bowler hat ran by with a suitcase calling out to someone behind, 'We'll be late. We'll be late.'

He too apparently was going north, an elderly man bound (he wanted to show it in his manner) on important business to do with Diesel engines, but not quite important enough to pay his fare by train. None of them in the coach was of *that* importance; a priest sat in the very front seat where he would see nothing but night pressing up against the windscreen: he was a stout young-old man with a little black bag in the rack and an umbrella: he was prepared to sit quiet all the night long reading in a book of devotion; the important man sat with a thin shabby clerk-like companion and talked in a loud voice about the Diesel engines.

Colley picked his way down the centre of the coach to the only empty pair of seats. An elderly woman with a basket of sandwiches and bananas explained to a younger one, 'You got to be prepared for trouble when Ted knows.' A pack of young men (perhaps they were a football team) had filled the back seats with suitcases and paper bags: they blocked the door bellowing with laughter. They were being seen off by two men with grey moustaches and tweed caps who kept on repeating, 'You boys remember—': and the young men slapped them on the back and tried to punch them in the ribs and said, 'You bet.' They had been drinking a little; when a whistle blew and they turned back into the gangway the coach was scented with their stale beery breath. Nobody else could get at the door: a young man outside pressed a pale miserable face to the glass, scrabbling with his fingernails, trying to convey some sense of tenderness and assurance to a girl in black who had been crying. She couldn't get the window down to speak to him; she looked towards the door, but 'You boys remember—' the men outside said, and something about 'Keep on the ball.' Colley leant across a schoolboy and pulled down her window. She didn't thank him, nor did the young man, the whistle had blown, they had no time, they leant towards each other with urgent messages they hadn't time to speak as the bus ground out between the white lines, swung round past the milk-bar and the fruit machines. 'What ho, she bumps,' the young men shouted, coming up the gangway. You could tell that they too were not important enough for the railway fare. They weren't a League team.

It was just like any other sailing at night: the lamps slipping away from you, the turned faces, swinging round by the high stone palace wall in Grosvenor Gardens like a dockside, out into the churn of small tugs and tramps by Hyde Park Corner. Even the young men at the back were momentarily silent as London dragged slowly backward, a kind of summary of London: the Achilles statue, the queue outside the Regal, a policeman, a coffee stall, a Guardsman, and a man in evening dress making tentative passes at a girl in a taxi and then the long wounded length of the Finchley Road, villas and flats and beyond Hendon a patch of grass and a pile of potato peelings, and more villas and a bigger patch of grass, a hole in a field full of old bicycle wheels and parts of car bodies, the country.

The girl sat with her eyes closed and her mouth tight shut as if she were repeating to herself, 'I am asleep. I am asleep.' The schoolboy ate chocolate. A voice from near the front said sharply, importantly, reprovingly, 'Fifty horse-power.' England was like a magnet which had lost its power. There was nothing any longer to hold you to it. It shook you off. Colley thought: I've stuck it long enough for a good reference, and now I may as well shoot it abroad again. But this time he didn't even know what kind of a job it was: except that old Hands had written, 'It might suit you.'

He had a pair of seats to himself. He was the only one who had. He wondered whether there was something in his appearance which kept people away (his shoes were hidden: and in any case these other people's shoes were not so good themselves), but soon he realized the reason. He was seated over the wheel. He was jarred by every unevenness on the Great North Road. They had all been more knowledgeable than he. Like the first time at anything, the novice was 'done'; the time he went to Brazil, he remembered, he had been left the worst place on the whole deck for his canvas chair. Now he was always first at that: the sunniest or the most sheltered corner was his before people had finished saying good-bye. If you had to compete even for your smallest comfort, compete he would with the quickest of them. 'I said oil-burning,' the elderly man screamed above the din of bottom gear as the coach dragged up a long Chiltern hill. The priest whispered softly his devotions, his plump lips hardly moving, vibrating gently on his seat with the engine. The spring night blossomed under the headlamps, a twig of budding beech scraped the windows from a chalky bank, and Colley thought with misery and a kind of thwarted murderous love in his heart, 'Competition. I'll give them competition. Every man for himself'; as if he hadn't already been beaten at *that* game in Brazil, in Africa.

5

'I could recognize at once,' Mr Danvers told the reporter, 'that Hands was a man of extraordinary character. Take a cigar. That's right. And put one in your pocket. What was I saying? Yes. He's an adventurer of the old school. A bit of Sir Walter Raleigh.'

'But Raleigh didn't find gold,' the reporter said.

'Ah,' Mr Danvers countered him quickly, 'but he didn't have proper support. You can take my word for it, the gold is there – you don't imagine we haven't seen satisfactory specimens.'

'And how did Hands come to approach you?'

'I'm going to be frank,' Mr Danvers said. 'I'm not going to let discretion spoil a romantic story. I said, didn't I, that Hands was an adventurer – in the best sense of the word, of course.'

'Like Raleigh,' the reporter said.

'You should hear the stories he has to tell. A rolling stone, you know, and he hasn't gathered any moss – except, of course, the best kind of all, friendships. Worked for others. Threw up the job when he got the wanderlust, moved on. Seeing the world. Learning to deal with all kinds of men. He quelled a strike once – single-handed. Well, he's been home a month or two – and he got restless. A man who hates inaction. And so he thought he'd capitalize his experience. He brought to mind the time he tumbled on this gold in West Africa – the government wasn't doing anything about it – it's a half-caste government, you know. Medieval conditions. Only a few Dutch prospectors were snooping around. There was a big chance for a concession. And so he wrote to a number of companies offering his services. He knows the country, knows the natives, he used to work just over the border in British territory, he's even had contact with members of the government. God knows what he was doing down there. Above all he can handle niggers. In a country like that, it's all-important. Undeveloped. No roads. Everything has to begin from scratch. It's a case of men, not machinery. When you cross over from British Territory, you go back a hundred years. To the time of Stanley, Livingstone,' Mr Danvers said, inaccurately, squinting at his notes.

'What about the other companies?'

'I'm going to be frank again,' Mr Danvers said. 'They didn't believe in him. But then they didn't even grant him an interview. I was sceptical myself till I talked to him. He told me he had had only two other replies, and they were formal notes saying the companies were not considering extending their activities.'

'Of course – to finance this—'

'A new issue of two hundred thousand Ordinary shares. We've taken a page in your paper tomorrow – as I imagine you know.'

'And Hands is going out himself?'

'Of course. This isn't ordinary mining work, young man. It's pioneering: it's adventure. That's the point I want you to make in the paper. Will you take a whisky and soda?'

'I don't drink,' the reporter said.

'Candidly,' Mr Danvers said, 'I want – a Legend. I've spoken to your advertisement manager and you'll be given space. I want Hands – made a figure. It's not only a question of selling shares – I don't want you to think that – it's a question of politics. These niggers need to be impressed. In a way, you know, the man who leads this expedition is an ambassador – the ambassador of Europe, of civilization.'

'Has he technical knowledge of mining?'

'That won't be his main job. His work is to lead the way, handle the men, cut forests, make roads. What an adventure,' Mr Danvers exclaimed; 'if I was a young man I'd go myself.'

'He'll be accompanied by experts?'

'They'll follow, as it were, on his heels.'

'Could I see a map?'

Mr Danvers spread out across his desk the big white sheet – more blank space than anything else.

'There are no reliable maps,' he said, 'yet. We'll have to make our own.' The map was marked 'United States War Department.' The reporter leant over it, pad in hand making notes – it didn't mean a thing to him: it was a paragraph to fill a column. He saw a white space somewhere to the right marked Cannibals, a few strange names like Mendi and Boozie which would sound well on paper, he saw the bottom of a column and a crosshead.

Mr Danvers leant beside him with a possessive smile and bent a double-jointed thumb on a mountain range. 'Up there,' he said, 'we'll get the gold. The problem,' he smeared his thumb towards the sea, 'is whether to bring it down here or take it across the border into British territory. And up here,' the thumb moved north, 'is French territory.' He fell silent, while the reporter made notes: a map is like a crystal in which men see many different things – success and failure, suicide in a second-rate hotel and a government contract, perverse loves and strange homes, a snake in a lavatory. Mr Danvers saw an office building and Doric columns, inlaid furniture, electric clocks and six floors: he saw two hundred thousand Ordinary shares at a premium: he saw no gold.

6

Mr Hands said, 'A moment while I get the encyclopaedia.'

He opened the map of West Africa with an immense desire to understand. The country was very small: 250 miles perhaps from the French border to the sea, 300 miles of seaboard, and the scale was 200 miles to an inch. There was no separate map. Only six towns were marked. He thought of Latvia, Luxembourg, the League of Nations, a picture postcard of Brussels Town Hall. He had no conception whatever of heat, dryness, desolation.

Hands said, 'Of course they treat their own people like dirt.'

Mr Hands thought of suffering minorities everywhere, and the Treaty of Versailles, and looking down at the map he thought, It's a job, he's got a job again, this time perhaps everything will go well, he'll stay and make money, I shall be proud of him, I shall say, 'My son who is the manager . . . writes . . .' and he felt a little shame at the jubilation which moved in his heart.

Hands himself hardly bothered to look. He knew what he would see – that rough rectangular shape was a bluff which hadn't been called, the jackpot if he had the courage to hold his hand, it was success. The world was going to hear of Hands, he was smart, my God how smart, my God. He was afraid. He said, 'I think I'll go and have a word with old Millet,' and with an uncertain swagger, he moved down the Metroland High Street, past the Moorish super-cinema, the dead Crusader and the Tudor Café towards his only listeners.

Part Two: The Expedition

Billings wore black in the blinding West African heat: it wasn't respect for the dead minister; it was – paradoxically – because he didn't want to be noticed. Billings trod through the world like an Indian hunter – but the twigs always broke under his feet. In England this suit was really inconspicuous: he was so used to it that he felt on the ship to Africa people would look at him if he changed and wore white, would observe more closely the pigeon breast, the dry and spotty skin, the bloodshot eyes. And then, when he landed in his dusty black and people looked, passing by in their Palm Beach suits, pride wouldn't allow him to change. 'The damned outsider,' he imagined them saying, 'he didn't know beforehand what a white man wears, but he's copying us now.'

He stood there in the tin-roofed church and looked round – the small bare crossless altar, the yellow pitch-pine benches, the big tin tank for total immersion. It was a kind of home. Here he had had authority, holding out the money bag to the blacks. Midday struck outside from the fake Norman church, and the sun weighed down on the tin roof: somewhere outside a steamer wailed. The hymns were still up for the minister's funeral: he changed the numbers ready for Sunday – it was like a gesture to England – Billings had taken over. He dipped his hand in the tank: it hadn't been emptied since the last baptism because of drought: the water was warm and dusty.

Then he went out into the vertical sun, into the shabby street of tin-roofed stores. Nobody was about: the hammocks droned in inner rooms, and the birds of prey squatted like domestic pigeons on the roofs, turning their little moron heads this way and that, spying for carrion. One rose, flapping the midday air with serrated dusty wings, and made across the roofs for the butcher's yard where a dozen of its fellows rooted like turkeys: the others looked down at Billings – black clothes, black ministerial hat – walking with the obsequious pomp of a priest at a funeral. He looked up and met the appraising gaze: they might have been saying as they leant their heads together for confidences, 'He'll do in a few more years. But too much skin and bone.' He thought of death under the awful sun and Mr Baines who had petered out last week while he prayed impromptu by the bed. It was three days now since he had cabled home. He thought defiantly of the emptiness of that death: the consolation of religion – the harmonium in the sitting-room for socials, himself sticking half-way through a prayer. It was a good death, no mummery about it.

He side-stepped away from the fake Norman cathedral. The cross above the door was like an evil eye to Billings: he hated the too eloquent symbols of religion: they seemed to mock him like a Palm Beach suit with lack of breeding – a 'gentleman's religion'. God was a bare room. God was pitch-pine and an undraped table and a piece of dry bread. Between bread and wafer a great gulf was fixed – the bread stuck in the throat for salvation, the wafer melted easily for damnation. The bishop came out of the cathedral and said 'Good morning' pleasantly to Billings, and Billings grunted back. You wait, he thought, you wait: within another thirty years they would both 'see', and he quivered in the secret pride of his own salvation, while the sweat gathered and dripped under the black cloth.

He went into the post office: the big Negro behind the counter watched him insolently: he too belonged to the gentlemen's religion.

Billings said, 'I'm expecting a cable.'

The black wore a clean white suit: he looked Billings up and down – he always did. 'What name?' he asked though he knew it as well as his own, and leaning arrogantly back in his swivel chair, he handed a penny through a window to a small girl outside. 'Three oranges,' he said. 'You can keep the change.'

'Billings.'

'Nothing,' the black said, but as Billings turned, he called after him, 'Hi, wait a moment. There may be something.'

He knew very well there was – the cable from England. He even knew the contents – there was a sneer and a satisfaction in his manner that broke the news. Billings took the envelope in his hand and went out. He had cabled back to the mission centre announcing the minister's death and suggesting, on account of his knowledge of the congregation, that he himself should take the dead man's place: he had spent a great deal on that cable – there was so much to be conveyed – a proper grief and ambition to serve.

He made his way through the siesta-empty street towards his home, but it was less a home than the chapel – the functional rectangular dwelling of God. The sun beat on the black hat and the expected misery.

His hut was raised a foot from the ground because of rats and ants. Outside hung an old photographic sign, a bathing beauty spotted by heat and damp. He could develop films but few people came to Billings for that purpose. No tourists spent much time in this British colony: only at long intervals a cruising steamer stayed for a few hours and people came on shore with Kodaks and snapped – a vulture, the Governor's residence, a Negro woman rolling home from church in her Manchester cotton. But *their* films they kept for London: they didn't trust Billings, though he advertised 'Films developed in six hours'. Only an occasional prospector brought his pack – and a few prosperous blacks – a wedding in Wellesley Street, the opening of the Kru Town court.

And yet a stale smell of hypo always seeped out from under his door – from the dark room – lavatory – to mix and peter out in the fish smell from the market. If I were minister, Billings thought (so long as he didn't open the cable the news mightn't be so bad after all – the committee at home must need time for a decision), if I were minister . . . It meant nearly a pound a week from the collection, it meant his black suit, as it were, regularized, it meant marriage dues and baptisms and authority. In time he could even move out of the damp heat of the town to the European station.

He pushed the door open, and a mongrel puppy, hairless and pink, squirmed on its belly to his feet. It had misbehaved under the table and craved forgiveness, but he couldn't bother with it now. He stood among the advertisements for Kodak and Agfa and opened the cable. It was very short. 'B. Moss answering call. Arriving 16th. Please make arrangements.' He looked out of the window and saw a taxi bouncing down towards the harbour, the air was spotted with buzzards, they moved imperceptibly across the hot immaculate blue. He began to tear the cable up in very small pieces, his fingers worked faster and faster, the scraps fell round the plump and cringing puppy – an epileptic faintness seized him, he said, 'My God, my God,' and clutched the table-edge. The table shook, shook, shook: the heat flapped down on him. Then he was well again, facing life – the little stand of yellowed home-made picture postcards – a Negro woman in Manchester cotton, the Governor's residence – the smell of puppy and hypo – the sweat pouring down under the black cloth. Life for a moment had been frozen by failure, but now it thawed, it dripped on.

He became conscious that a Negro was watching him from the step. He said furiously, 'What do you want?'

'My pictures,' the man said, the voice hollow and toothless like a child's.

'They aren't ready. Come back tomorrow.'

To work, Billings thought, was to pray. He had to begin

praying all over again. He kicked the puppy and went on into the dark room – a wash-basin, a shelf, a lavatory seat, a red glass window. He hung his hat on a peg, unpacked a roll of film and bent over the shallow tray of chemicals. He had no interest in the dark strip of film: he weaved it to and fro through the hypo, until another person's life began to show in fits and starts – the negative life where black is white and right is left, but his own positive life shut him in with its unequivocal injustice. He couldn't be certain that B. Moss would ever require his help with the collection: another man might be asked to take it up.

He lifted the film out of the hypo too soon – the white faces of the blacks glowed faintly like transparent insects – and began to wash the negative. He worked absentmindedly (his pictures yellowed within a year) in the red glare of the window. Somebody knocked on his door, but he paid no attention. There were two places where he could be alone with his pride and his resentment – the chapel and the dark room. In the chapel he talked to God and in the dark room he spoke to his own past – the child flung into the water to sink or swim, the scared boy in the playground; he listened to voices saying, 'Creepy Billings' and a woman's appalling laughter. He did not pity himself: he brought up the images as a Jesuit may bring up the images of his Saviour's suffering – to steel himself. They were a discipline which one day would have its value. He would become impervious to contempt.

Again the knock on the door. He hung the negative up to dry and went out into the shop. 'Why,' he said and hesitated, 'it's Mr—'

'Five years ago,' the stranger said, 'and Anderson's store. Don't you remember, Billings, that night . . .'

'It's Hands,' Billings said without enthusiasm.

'I'm staying at the Grand.'

'The Grand?'

'I'm in the money now,' Hands said. He took off his big military-looking khaki sun-helmet and exposed himself for Billings' inspection – the new drill suit, the club tie. He said, 'What a crowd they are up there. Such starch. It might be Government House. I thought I'd slip away and see old Billings. Old Billings will have a bottle poked away.'

An odd expression twisted Billings' face: a sour taste, a happy memory, an unwelcome secret – you couldn't tell. 'Five years,' he said. 'A lot happens in five years.'

'Another window broken in the public library. Anderson sold out to Bates. They've put a pillar box in Gladstone Street. You can't tell me. I only landed this morning but I've been looking round.'

'Things happen to people,' Billings said.

'And here's the cupboard. Let's see what you've got.' He pulled it open – one empty dusty shelf, on another Agfa and Kodak films, a bottle of fruit, Heinz beans, sardines, a tin of Cambridge sausages. 'You don't say,' Hands said, 'you're out of it.'

'I found Christ,' Billings said. 'Didn't they tell you that at the Grand?'

Hands said uncomfortably, 'I didn't hear a word.'

'Of course,' Billings said, 'you never mentioned you were coming here. The street's empty, isn't it? Siesta time. You slipped along.'

'If you mean I'm ashamed—'

'You always were ashamed,' Billings said.

'I always liked you.'

'In secret.'

'Like you liked Christ,' Hands said. He shut the cupboard door. 'What the hell,' he said, 'don't let's quarrel the first minute. I came along,' he lied, 'to ask you to dinner – to meet Colley – you remember Colley – and Morrow, he's new . . .' He hesitated, 'And my wife.'

'You married?' Billings said.

'It's as you say – things happen to people.'

Again the secret look of misery or delight forked Billings' mouth. He said, 'It wouldn't be any harm to celebrate *that*.'

'You've got a bottle?'

'For medical purposes,' Billings said. He went through to his bedroom and fished under his bed, brought out a bottle of cheap brandy. 'I get the toothache,' Billings said. 'It's neuralgia. There's nothing a dentist can do. Sometimes it nearly makes me mad, grinding away. You'll excuse me if I've only got a cup to offer you, but I don't have many visitors.'

'What's happened to Cudlow?'

'He died of yellow fever back in '35.' Billings squinted up over his cup. 'He found Christ first.'

Hands laughed – uneasily.

'We ought to drink your wife's health, oughtn't we? What's her name?'

'Well, it's Ethel. But I call her Ethie.'

'To Mrs Hands.' They drank and Billings refilled the cups.

'She comes of a cultured family,' Hands said. 'You'll like her. You'll have a lot in common. You see her uncle is a photographer.'

'I know the sort of thing,' Billings said. 'Pictures for the *Tatler* – and *Vogue*. You make them lie on the ground and shoot from above while a gramophone plays. It catches on. Society.'

'Something of that sort,' Hands said. 'Could I have a drop more? Just a finger. Thanks.'

'And where's *your* money come from? From the wife?'

'I'm prospecting,' Hands said, 'for gold.'

'Where?'

'Across the border.'

'There's not enough to fill your teeth,' Billings said.

'I don't agree. Don't you remember that old Dutchman who came here? He said there was plenty in the Pandemai hills.'

'They had to ship him back third-class at the consul's expense.'

'But I've got money behind *me*. A whole expedition. Me and Colley – and a man called Morrow. We want servants – and carriers. That's why I came to you. You know the blacks.'

'You couldn't do better than Vandi for head man, but you'll get the carriers cheaper on the other side.' He poured out more brandy. 'I wish I were you. The bush is better than this place. You work and work – and then B. Moss gets the call.'

'Why don't you come? Colley's all right, of course, but I want someone I can *really* trust.' He said with importance. 'A leader has the hell of a lot of responsibility.'

'What's Morrow like?'

'A prig. You feel he's watching you.' He drank again. 'And Ethie – she's all right, but a man needs a man around. Sometimes I feel all a woman cares for' – he made a little shocked expression – 'is – you know – what. A leader's got to keep fit.'

'What I don't understand,' Billings said, 'is why they chose you.'

'Sometimes I wonder that myself.' The brandy surged like inspiration on his tongue. 'For years I used to imagine – you know big things. Perhaps it's fate. A man's sometimes kept – for the biggest things. Like Hitler. What was he?'

'I get that feeling too,' Billings said. 'I think of – all of us. A whole crowd who've never had a proper chance. Sneered at. Sacked. And then suddenly – the day comes, and it's we—'

'Is there a spot more brandy?'

'I've dreamed sometimes – of converting thousands. The father of the Negro. Those missionaries out there in the bush – they pamper the niggers with statues and holy medals. It's easy work changing one idol for another. But I'd like to give them – just God.' The cup clinked on the table. 'God bare.'

'By God,' Hands said, 'when you come to think of it, this is a big thing we're on to.'

'You don't have to take the name of God in vain.'

'I'm sorry. But you make me see things.'

'We'll be on our own. No officials nosing round.'

'It's history.'

They stared at each other with awe. 'I suppose,' Hands said, 'that's what made them choose me. They wanted someone – with imagination.'

'And faith,' Billings said.

Somebody knocked at the door. Billings opened it, and there was the blinding day and the buzzards on the rooftops, the little town and life going on. Colley said, 'I thought I'd find you here.' He came suspiciously in out of the glaring noon: and was like doubt in the heart to both of them. He said, 'Your wife's asleep, Hands. I didn't think she looked too good.'

'It's the heat,' Hands said. 'We all know that it takes getting used to.'

'Have you got some brandy there? I've got a thirst.'

'Sorry, old man, it's finished.'

Colley held the bottle to the sunlight, trusting neither of them. He wore a round white sun-helmet which was getting limp already with perspiration. He said, 'I took her up some orange-juice and left it outside her door. I didn't like to wake her.'

'Fine, old man. Where's Morrow?'

'Writing home.' He said with hatred, 'The Sunday letter. To papa.'

'Papa's dead.'

'Mamma then. Or little sister. If there's one thing I can't stand,' Colley said, 'it's priggishness. Thinking yourself better than the rest. That's why we are friends,' he said, turning the contents of the brandy bottle hopelessly into a mug, 'because we are all alike.' Hands and Billings watched him – with embarrassment as if they had been caught out in a crime or a falsehood . . .

Under the Garden

Part One

1

It was only when the doctor said to him, 'Of course the fact that you don't smoke is in your favour,' Wilditch realized what it was he had been trying to convey with such tact. Dr Cave had lined up along one wall a series of X-ray photographs, the whorls of which reminded the patient of those pictures of the earth's surface taken from a great height that he had pored over at one period during the war, trying to detect the tiny grey seed of a launching ramp.

Dr Cave had explained, 'I want you clearly to understand my problem.' It was very similar to an intelligence briefing of such 'top secret' importance that only one officer could be entrusted with the information. Wilditch felt gratified that the choice had fallen on him, and he tried to express his interest and enthusiasm, leaning forward and examining more closely than ever the photographs of his own interior.

'Beginning at this end,' Dr Cave said, 'let me see, April, May, June, three months ago, the scar left by the pneumonia is quite obvious. You can see it here.'

'Yes, sir,' Wilditch said absent-mindedly. Dr Cave gave him a puzzled look.

'Now if we leave out the intervening photographs for the moment and come straight to yesterday's, you will observe that this latest one is almost entirely clear, you can only just detect . . .'

'Good,' Wilditch said. The doctor's finger moved over what might have been tumuli or traces of prehistoric agriculture.

'But not entirely, I'm afraid. If you look now along the whole series you will notice how very slow the progress has been. Really by this stage the photographs should have shown no trace.'

'I'm sorry,' Wilditch said. A sense of guilt had taken the place of gratification.

'If we had looked at the last plate in isolation I would have said there was no cause for alarm.' The doctor tolled the last three words like a bell. Wilditch thought, is he suggesting tuberculosis?

'It's only in relation to the others, the slowness . . . it suggests the possibility of an obstruction.'

'Obstruction?'

'The chances are that it's nothing, nothing at all. Only I wouldn't be *quite* happy if I let you go without a deep examination. Not *quite* happy.' Dr Cave left the photographs and sat down behind his desk. The long pause seemed to Wilditch like an appeal to his friendship.

'Of course,' he said, 'if it would make you happy . . .'

It was then the doctor used those revealing words, 'Of course the fact that you don't smoke is in your favour.'

'Oh.'

'I think we'll ask Sir Nigel Sampson to make the examination. In case there is something there, we couldn't have a better surgeon . . . for the operation.'

Wilditch came down from Wimpole Street into Cavendish Square looking for a taxi. It was one of those summer days which he never remembered in childhood: grey and dripping. Taxis drew up outside the tall liver-coloured buildings partitioned by dentists and were immediately caught by the commissionaires for the victims released. Gusts of wind barely warmed by July drove the rain aslant across the blank eastern gaze of Epstein's virgin and dripped down the body of her fabulous son. 'But it hurt,' the child's voice said behind him. 'You make a fuss about nothing,' a mother – or a governess – replied.

2

This could not have been said of the examination Wilditch endured a week later, but he made no fuss at all, which perhaps aggravated his case in the eyes of the doctors who took his calm for lack of vitality. For the unprofessional to enter a hospital or to enter the services has very much the same effect; there is a sense of relief and indifference; one is placed quite helplessly on a conveyor-belt with no responsibility any more for anything. Wilditch felt himself protected by an organization, while the English summer dripped outside on the coupés of the parked cars. He had not felt such freedom since the war ended.

The examination was over – a bronchoscopy; and there remained a nightmare memory, which survived through the cloud of the anaesthetic, of a great truncheon forced down his throat into the chest and then slowly withdrawn; he woke next morning bruised and raw so that even the act of excretion was a pain. But that, the nurse told him, would pass in one day or two; now he could dress and go home. He was disappointed at the abruptness with which they were thrusting him off the belt into the world of choice again.

'Was everything satisfactory?' he asked, and saw from the nurse's expression that he had shown indecent curiosity.

'I couldn't say, I'm sure,' the nurse said. 'Sir Nigel will look in, in his own good time.'

Wilditch was sitting on the end of the bed tying his tie when Sir Nigel Sampson entered. It was the first time Wilditch had been conscious of seeing him: before he had been a voice addressing him politely out of sight as the anaesthetic took over. It was the beginning of the week-end and Sir Nigel was dressed for the country in an old tweed jacket. He had tousled white hair and he looked at Wilditch with a far-away attention as though he were a float bobbing in midstream.

'Ah, feeling better,' Sir Nigel said incontrovertibly.

'Perhaps.'

'Not very agreeable,' Sir Nigel said, 'but you know we couldn't let you go, could we, without taking a look?'

'Did you see anything?'

Sir Nigel gave the impression of abruptly moving downstream to a quieter reach and casting his line again.

'Don't let me stop you dressing, my dear fellow.' He looked vaguely around the room before choosing a strictly upright chair, then lowered himself on to it as though it were a tuffet which might 'give'. He began feeling in one of his large pockets – for a sandwich?

'Any news for me?'

'I expect Dr Cave will be along in a few minutes. He was caught by a rather garrulous patient.' He drew a large silver watch out of his pocket – for some reason it was tangled up in a piece of string. 'Have to meet my wife at Liverpool Street. Are *you* married?'

'No.'

'Oh well, one care the less. Children can be a great responsibility.'

'I have a child – but she lives a long way off.'

'A long way off? I see.'

'We haven't seen much of each other.'

'Doesn't care for England?'

'The colour-bar makes it difficult for her.' He realized how childish he sounded directly he had spoken, as though he had been trying to draw attention to himself by a bizarre confession, without even the satisfaction of success.

'Ah yes,' Sir Nigel said. 'Any brothers or sisters? You, I mean.'

'An elder brother. Why?'

'Oh well, I suppose it's all on the record,' Sir Nigel said, rolling in his line. He got up and made for the door. Wilditch sat on the bed with the tie over his knee. The door opened and Sir Nigel said, 'Ah, here's Dr Cave. Must run along now. I was just telling Mr Wilditch that I'll be seeing him again. You'll fix it, won't you?' and he was gone.

'Why should I see him again?' Wilditch asked and then, from Dr Cave's embarrassment, he saw the stupidity of the question. 'Oh yes, of course, you did find something?'

'It's really very lucky. If caught in time . . .'

'There's sometimes hope?'

'Oh, there's always hope.'

So, after all, Wilditch thought, I am – if I so choose – on the conveyor-belt again.

Dr Cave took an engagement-book out of his pocket and said briskly, 'Sir Nigel has given me a few dates. The tenth is difficult for the clinic, but the fifteenth – Sir Nigel doesn't think we should delay longer than the fifteenth.'

'Is he a great fisherman?'

'Fisherman? Sir Nigel? I have no idea.' Dr Cave looked aggrieved, as though he were being shown an incorrect chart. 'Shall we say the fifteenth?'

'Perhaps I could tell you after the week-end. You see, I have not made up my mind to stay as long as that in England.'

'I'm afraid I haven't properly conveyed to you that this is serious, really serious. Your only chance – I repeat your only chance,' he spoke like a telegram, 'is to have the obstruction removed in time.'

'And then, I suppose, life can go on for a few more years.'

'It's impossible to guarantee . . . but there have been complete cures.'

'I don't want to appear dialectical,' Wilditch said, 'but I do have to decide, don't I, whether I want my particular kind of life prolonged.'

'It's the only one we have,' Dr Cave said.

'I see you are not a religious man – oh, please don't misunderstand me, nor am I. I have no curiosity at all about the future.'

3

The past was another matter. Wilditch remembered a leader in the Civil War who rode from an undecided battle mortally wounded. He revisited the house where he was born, the house in which he was married, greeted a few retainers who did not recognize his condition, seeing him only as a tired man upon a horse, and finally – but Wilditch could not recollect how the biography had ended: he saw only a figure of exhaustion slumped over the saddle, as he also took, like Sir Nigel Sampson, a train from Liverpool Street. At Colchester he changed on to the branch line to Winton, and suddenly summer began, the kind of summer he always remembered as one of the conditions of life at Winton. Days had become so much shorter since then. They no longer began at six in the morning before the world was awake.

Winton Hall had belonged, when Wilditch was a child, to his uncle, who had never married, and every summer he lent the house to Wilditch's mother. Winton Hall had been virtually Wilditch's, until school cut the period short, from late June to early September. In memory his mother and brother were shadowy background figures. They were less established even than the machine upon the platform of 'the halt' from which he bought Fry's chocolates for a penny a bar: than the oak tree spreading over the green in front of the red-brick wall – under its shade as a child he had distributed apples to soldiers halted there in the hot August of 1914: the group of silver birches on the Winton lawn and the broken fountain, green with slime. In his memory he did not share the house with others: he owned it.

Nevertheless the house had been left to his brother not to him; he was far away when his uncle died and he had never returned since. His brother married, had children (for them the fountain had been mended), the paddock behind the vegetable garden and the orchard, where he used to ride the donkey, had been sold (so his brother had written to him) for building council-houses, but the hall and the garden which he had so scrupulously remembered nothing could change.

Why then go back now and see it in other hands? Was it that at the approach of death one must get rid of everything? If he had accumulated money he would now have been in the mood to distribute it. Perhaps the man who had ridden the horse around the countryside had not been saying goodbye, as his biographer imagined, to what he valued most: he had been ridding himself of illusions by seeing them again with clear and moribund eyes, so that he might be quite bankrupt when death came. He had the will to possess at that absolute moment nothing but his wound.

His brother, Wilditch knew, would be faintly surprised by this visit. He had become accustomed to the fact that Wilditch never came to Winton; they would meet at long intervals at his brother's club in London, for George was a widower by this time, living alone. He always talked to others of Wilditch as a man unhappy in the country, who needed a longer range and stranger people. It was lucky, he would indicate, that the house had been left to him, for Wilditch would probably have sold it in order to travel further. A restless man, never long in one place, no wife, no children, unless the rumours were true that in Africa . . . or it might have been in the East . . . Wilditch was well aware of how his brother spoke of him. His brother was the proud owner of the lawn, the goldfish-pond, the mended fountain, the laurel-path which they had known when they were children as the Dark Walk, the lake, the island ... Wilditch looked out at the flat hard East Anglian countryside, the meagre hedges and the stubbly grass, which had always seemed to him barren from the salt of Danish blood. All these years his brother had been in occupation, and yet he had no idea of what might lie underneath the garden.

4

The chocolate-machine had gone from Winton Halt, and the halt had been promoted – during the years of nationalization – to a station; the chimneys of a cement-factory smoked along the horizon and council-houses now stood three deep along the line.

Wilditch's brother waited in a Humber at the exit. Some familiar smell of coal-dust and varnish had gone from the waiting-room and it was a mere boy who took his ticket instead of a stooped and greying porter. In childhood nearly all the world is older than oneself.

'Hullo, George,' he said in remote greeting to the stranger at the wheel.

'How are things, William?' George asked as they ground on their way – it was part of his character as a countryman that he had never learnt how to drive a car well.

The long chalky slope of a small hill – the highest point before the Ural mountains he had once been told – led down to the village between the bristly hedges. On the left was an abandoned chalk-pit – it had been just as abandoned forty years ago, when he had climbed all over it looking for treasure, in the form of brown nuggets of iron pyrites which when broken showed an interior of starred silver.

'Do you remember hunting for treasure?'

'Treasure?' George said. 'Oh, you mean that iron stuff.'

Was it the long summer afternoons in the chalk-pit which had made him dream – or so vividly imagine – the discovery of a real treasure? If it was a dream it was the only dream he remembered from those years, or, if it was a story which he had elaborated at night in bed, it must have been the final effort of a poetic imagination that afterwards had been rigidly controlled. In the various services which had over the years taken him from one part of the world to another, imagination was usually a quality to be suppressed. One's job was to provide facts, to a company (import and export), a newspaper, a government department. Speculation was discouraged. Now the dreaming child was dying of the same disease as the man. He was so different from the child that it was odd to think the child would not outlive him and go on to quite a different destiny.

George said, 'You'll notice some changes, William. When I had the bathroom added, I found I had to disconnect the pipes from the fountain. Something to do with pressure. After all there are no children now to enjoy it.'

'It never played in my time either.'

'I had the tennis-lawn dug up during the war, and it hardly seemed worth while to put it back.'

'I'd forgotten that there *was* a tennis-lawn.'

'Don't you remember it, between the pond and the goldfish tank?'

'The pond? Oh, you mean the lake and the island.'

'Not much of a lake. You could jump on to the island with a short run.'

'I had thought of it as much bigger.'

But all measurements had changed. Only for a dwarf does the

world remain the same size. Even the red-brick wall which separated the garden from the village was lower than he remembered – a mere five feet, but in order to look over it in those days he had always to scramble to the top of some old stumps covered deep with ivy and dusty spiders' webs. There was no sign of these when they drove in: everything was very tidy everywhere, and a handsome piece of ironmongery had taken the place of the swing-gate which they had ruined as children.

'You keep the place up very well,' he said.

'I couldn't manage it without the market-garden. That enables me to put the gardener's wages down as a professional expense. I have a very good accountant.'

He was put into his mother's room with a view of the lawn and the silver birches; George slept in what had been his uncle's. The little bedroom next door which had once been his was now converted into a tiled bathroom – only the prospect was unchanged. He could see the laurel bushes where the Dark Walk began, but they were smaller too. Had the dying horseman found as many changes?

Sitting that night over coffee and brandy, during the long family pauses, Wilditch wondered whether as a child he could possibly have been so secretive as never to have spoken of his dream, his game, whatever it was. In his memory the adventure had lasted for several days. At the end of it he had found his way home in the early morning when everyone was asleep: there had been a dog called Joe who bounded towards him and sent him sprawling in the heavy dew of the lawn. Surely there must have been some basis of fact on which the legend had been built. Perhaps he had run away, perhaps he had been out all night – on the island in the lake or hidden in the Dark Walk – and during those hours he had invented the whole story.

Wilditch took a second glass of brandy and asked tentatively, 'Do you remember much of those summers when we were children here?' He was aware of something unconvincing in the question: the apparently harmless opening gambit of a wartime interrogation.

'I never cared for the place much in those days,' George said surprisingly. 'You were a secretive little bastard.'

'Secretive?'

'And uncooperative. I had a great sense of duty towards you, but you never realized that. In a year or two you were going to follow me to school. I tried to teach you the rudiments of cricket. You weren't interested. God knows what you were interested in.'

'Exploring?' Wilditch suggested, he thought with cunning.

'There wasn't much to explore in fourteen acres. You know, I had such plans for this place when it became mine. A swimming-pool where the tennis-lawn was – it's mainly potatoes now. I meant to drain the pond too – it breeds mosquitoes. Well, I've added two bathrooms and modernized the kitchen, and even that has cost me four acres of pasture. At the back of the house now you can hear the children caterwauling from the council-houses. It's all been a bit of a disappointment.'

'At least I'm glad you haven't drained the lake.'

'My dear chap, why go on calling it a lake? Have a look at it in the morning and you'll see the absurdity. The water's nowhere more than two feet deep.' He added, 'Oh well, the place won't outlive me. My children aren't interested, and the factories are beginning to come out this way. They'll get a reasonably good price for the land – I haven't much else to leave them.' He put some more sugar in his coffee. 'Unless, of course, you'd like to take it on when I am gone?'

'I haven't the money and anyway there's no cause to believe that I won't be dead first.'

'Mother was against my accepting the inheritance,' George said. 'She never liked the place.'

'I thought she loved her summers here.' The great gap between their memories astonished him. They seemed to be talking about different places and different people.

'It was terribly inconvenient, and she was always in trouble with the gardener. You remember Ernest? She said she had to wring every vegetable out of him. (By the way he's still alive, though retired of course – you ought to look him up in the morning. It would please him. He still feels he owns the place.) And then, you know, she always thought it would have been better for us if we could have gone to the seaside. She had an idea that she was robbing us of a heritage – buckets and spades and seawater-bathing. Poor mother, she couldn't afford to turn down Uncle Henry's hospitality. I think in her heart she blamed father for dying when he did without providing for holidays at the sea.'

'Did you talk it over with her in those days?'

'Oh no, not then. Naturally she had to keep a front before the children. But when I inherited the place – you were in Africa – she warned Mary and me about the difficulties. She had very decided views, you know, about any mysteries, and that turned her against the garden. Too much shrubbery, she said. She wanted everything to be very clear. Early Fabian training, I dare say.'

'It's odd. I don't seem to have known her very well.'

'You had a passion for hide-and-seek. She never liked that. Mystery again. She thought it a bit morbid. There was a time when we couldn't find you. You were away for hours.'

'Are you sure it was hours? Not a whole night?'

'I don't remember it at all myself. Mother told me.' They drank their brandy for a while in silence. Then George said, 'She asked Uncle Henry to have the Dark Walk cleared away. She thought it was unhealthy with all the spiders' webs, but he never did anything about it.'

'I'm surprised *you* didn't.'

'Oh, it was on my list, but other things had priority, and now it doesn't seem worth while to make more changes.' He yawned and stretched. 'I'm used to early bed. I hope you don't mind. Breakfast at 8.30?'

'Don't make any changes for me.'

'There's just one thing I forgot to show you. The flush is tricky in your bathroom.'

George led the way upstairs. He said, 'The local plumber didn't do a very good job. Now, when you've pulled this knob, you'll find the flush never quite finishes. You have to do it a second time – sharply like this.'

Wilditch stood at the window looking out. Beyond the Dark Walk and the space where the lake must be, he could see the splinters of light given off by the council-houses; through one gap in the laurels there was even a street-light visible, and he could hear the faint sound of television-sets joining together different programmes like the discordant murmur of a mob.

He said, 'That view would have pleased mother. A lot of the mystery gone.'

'I rather like it this way myself,' George said, 'on a winter's evening. It's a kind of companionship. As one gets older one doesn't want to feel quite alone on a sinking ship. Not being a churchgoer myself . . .' he added, leaving the sentence lying like a torso on its side.

'At least we haven't shocked mother in that way, either of us.'

'Sometimes I wish I'd pleased her, though, about the Dark Walk. And the pond – how she hated that pond too.'

'Why?'

'Perhaps because you liked to hide on the island. Secrecy and mystery again. Wasn't there something you wrote about it once? A story?'

'Me? A story? Surely not.'

'I don't remember the circumstances. I thought – in a school magazine? Yes, I'm sure of it now. She was very angry indeed and she wrote rude remarks in the margin with a blue pencil. I saw them somewhere once. Poor mother.'

George led the way into the bedroom. He said, 'I'm sorry there's no bedside light. It was smashed last week, and I haven't been into town since.'

'It's all right. I don't read in bed.'

'I've got some good detective-stories downstairs if you wanted one.'

'Mysteries?'

'Oh, mother never minded those. They came under the heading of puzzles. Because there was always an answer.'

Beside the bed was a small bookcase. He said, 'I brought some of mother's books here when she died and put them in her room. Just the ones that she had liked and no bookseller would take.' Wilditch made out a title, *My Apprenticeship* by Beatrice Webb. 'Sentimental, I suppose, but I didn't want actually to *throw away* her favourite books. Good night.' He repeated, 'I'm sorry about the light.'

'It really doesn't matter.'

George lingered at the door. He said, 'I'm glad to see you here, William. There were times when I thought you were avoiding the place.'

'Why should I?'

'Well, you know how it is. I never go to Harrod's now because I was there with Mary a few days before she died.'

'Nobody has died here. Except Uncle Henry, I suppose.'

'No, of course not. But why did you, suddenly, decide to come?'

'A whim,' Wilditch said.

'I suppose you'll be going abroad again soon?'

'I suppose so.'

'Well, good night.' He closed the door.

Wilditch undressed, and then, because he felt sleep too far away, he sat down on the bed under the poor centre-light and looked along the rows of shabby books. He opened Mrs Beatrice Webb at some account of a trade union congress and put it back. (The foundations of the future Welfare State were being truly and uninterestingly laid.) There were a number of Fabian pamphlets heavily scored with the blue pencil which George had remembered. In one place Mrs Wilditch had detected an error of one decimal point in some statistics dealing with agricultural imports. What passionate concentration must have gone to that discovery. Perhaps because his own life was coming to an end, he thought how little of this, in the almost impossible event of a future, she would have carried with her. A fairy-story in such an event would be a more valuable asset than a Fabian graph, but his mother had not approved of fairy-stories. The only children's book on these shelves was a history of England. Against an enthusiastic account of the battle of Agincourt she had pencilled furiously,

> And what good came of it at last?
> Said little Peterkin.

The fact that his mother had quoted a poem was in itself remarkable.

The storm which he had left behind in London had travelled east in his wake and now overtook him in short gusts of wind and wet that slapped at the pane. He thought, for no reason, It will be a rough night on the island. He had been disappointed to discover from George that the origin of the dream which had travelled with him round the world was probably no more than a story invented for a school magazine and forgotten again, and just as that thought occurred to him, he saw a bound volume called *The Warburian* on the shelf.

He took it out, wondering why his mother had preserved it,

and found a page turned down. It was the account of a cricket-match against Lancing and Mrs Wilditch had scored the margin: 'Wilditch One did good work in deep field.' Another turned-down leaf produced a passage under the heading Debating Society: 'Wilditch One spoke succinctly to the motion.' The motion was 'That this House has no belief in the social policies of His Majesty's Government'. So George in those days had been a Fabian too.

He opened the book at random this time and a letter fell out. It had a printed heading, Dean's House, Warbury, and it read, 'Dear Mrs Wilditch, I was sorry to receive your letter of the 3rd and to learn that you were displeased with the little fantasy published by your younger son in *The Warburian*. I think you take a rather extreme view of the tale which strikes me as quite a good imaginative exercise for a boy of thirteen. Obviously he has been influenced by the term's reading of *The Golden Age* – which after all, fanciful though it may be, was written by a governor of the Bank of England.' (Mrs Wilditch had made several blue exclamation marks in the margin – perhaps representing her view of the Bank.) 'Last term's *Treasure Island* too may have contributed. It is always our intention at Warbury to foster the imagination – which I think you rather harshly denigrate when you write of "silly fancies". We have scrupulously kept our side of the bargain, knowing how strongly you feel, and the boy is not "subjected", as you put it, to any religious instruction at all. Quite frankly, Mrs Wilditch, I cannot see any trace of religious feeling in this little fancy – I have read it through a second time before writing to you – indeed the treasure, I'm afraid, is only too material, and quite at the mercy of those "who break in and steal".'

Wilditch tried to find the place from which the letter had fallen, working back from the date of the letter. Eventually he found it: 'The Treasure on the Island' by W.W.

Wilditch began to read.

5

'In the middle of the garden there was a great lake and in the middle of the lake an island with a wood. Not everybody knew about the lake, for to reach it you had to find your way down a long dark walk, and not many people's nerves were strong enough to reach the end. Tom knew that he was likely to be undisturbed in that frightening region, and so it was there that he constructed a raft out of old packing cases, and one drear wet day when he knew that everybody would be shut in the house, he dragged the raft to the lake and paddled it across to the island. As far as he knew he was the first to land there for centuries.

'It was all overgrown on the island, but from a map he had found in an ancient sea-chest in the attic he made his measurements, three paces north from the tall umbrella pine in the middle and then two paces to the right. There seemed to be nothing but scrub, but he had brought with him a pick and a spade and with the dint of almost superhuman exertions he uncovered an iron ring sunk in the grass. At first he thought it would be impossible to move, but by inserting the point of the pick and levering it he raised a kind of stone lid and there below, going into the darkness, was a long narrow passage.

'Tom had more than the usual share of courage, but even he would not have ventured further if it had not been for the parlous state of the family fortunes since his father had died. His elder brother wanted to go to Oxford but for lack of money he would probably have to sail before the mast, and the house itself, of which his mother was passionately fond, was mortgaged to the hilt to a man in the City called Sir Silas Dedham whose name did not belie his nature.'

Wilditch nearly gave up reading. He could not reconcile this childish story with the dream which he remembered. Only the 'drear wet night' seemed true as the bushes rustled and dripped and the birches swayed outside. A writer, so he had always understood, was supposed to order and enrich the experience which was the source of his story, but in that case it was plain that the young Wilditch's talents had not been for literature. He read with growing irritation, wanting to exclaim again and again to this thirteen-year-old ancestor of his, 'But why did you leave that out? Why did you alter this?'

'*The passage opened out into a great cave stacked from floor to ceiling with gold bars and chests overflowing with pieces of eight. There was a jewelled crucifix*' – Mrs Wilditch had underlined the word in blue – '*set with precious stones which had once graced the chapel of a Spanish galleon and on a marble table were goblets of precious metal.*'

But, as he remembered, it was an old kitchen-dresser, and there were no pieces of eight, no crucifix, and as for the Spanish galleon . . .

'*Tom thanked the kindly Providence which had led him first to the map in the attic*' (but there had been no map. Wilditch wanted to correct the story, page by page, much as his mother had done with her blue pencil) '*and then to this rich treasure trove*' (his mother had written in the margin, referring to the kindly Providence, 'No trace of religious feeling!!'). '*He filled his pockets with the pieces of eight and taking one bar under each arm, he made his way back along the passage. He intended to keep his discovery secret and slowly day by day to transfer the treasure to the cupboard in his room, thus surprising his mother at the end of the holidays with all this sudden wealth. He got safely home unseen by anyone and that night in bed he counted over his new riches while outside it rained and rained. Never had he heard such a storm. It was as though the wicked spirit of his old pirate ancestor raged against him*' (Mrs Wilditch had written, 'Eternal punishment I suppose!') '*and indeed the next day, when he returned to the island in the lake, whole trees had been uprooted and now lay across the entrance to the passage. Worse still there had been a landslide, and now the cavern must lie hidden forever below the waters of the lake. However,*' the young Wilditch had added briefly forty years ago, '*the treasure already recovered was sufficient to save the family home and send his brother to Oxford.*'

Wilditch undressed and got into bed, then lay on his back listening to the storm. What a trivial conventional day-dream W.W. had constructed – out of what? There had been no attic-room – probably no raft: these were preliminaries which did not matter, but why had W.W. so falsified the adventure itself? Where was the man with the beard? The old squawking woman? Of course it had all been a dream, it could have been nothing else but a dream, but a dream too was an experience, the images of a dream had their own integrity, and he felt professional anger at this false report just as his mother had felt at the mistake in the Fabian statistics.

All the same, while he lay there in his mother's bed and thought of her rigid interrogation of W.W.'s story, another theory of the falsifications came to him, perhaps a juster one. He remembered how agents parachuted into France during the bad years after 1940 had been made to memorize a cover-story which they could give, in case of torture, with enough truth in it to be checked. Perhaps forty years ago the pressure to tell had been almost as great on W.W., so that he had been forced to find relief in fantasy. Well, an agent dropped into occupied territory was always given a time-limit after capture. 'Keep the interrogators at bay with silence or lies for just so long, and then you may tell all.' The time-limit had surely been passed in his case a long time ago, his mother was beyond the possibility of hurt, and Wilditch for the first time deliberately indulged his passion to remember.

He got out of bed and, after finding some notepaper stamped, presumably for income-tax purposes, Winton Small Holdings Limited, in the drawer of the desk, he began to write an account of what he had found – or dreamed that he found – under the garden of Winton Hall. The summer night was nosing wetly around the window just as it had done fifty years ago, but, as he wrote, it began to turn grey and recede; the trees of the garden became visible, so that, when he looked up after some hours from his writing, he could see the shape of the broken fountain and what he supposed were the laurels in the Dark Walk, looking like old men humped against the weather.

Part Two

1

Never mind how I came to the island in the lake, never mind whether in fact, as my brother says, it is a shallow pond with water only two feet deep (I suppose a raft can be launched on two feet of water, and certainly I must have always come to the lake by way of the Dark Walk, so that it is not at all unlikely that I built my raft there). Never mind what hour it was – I think it was evening, and I had hidden, as I remember it, in the Dark Walk because George had not got the courage to search for me there. The evening turned to rain, just as it's raining now, and George must have been summoned into the house for shelter. He would have told my mother that he couldn't find me and she must have called from the upstair windows, front and back – perhaps it was the occasion George spoke about tonight. I am not sure of these facts, they are plausible only, I can't yet *see* what I'm describing. But I know that I was not to find George and my mother again for many days . . . It cannot, whatever George says, have been less than three days and nights that I spent below the ground. Could he really have forgotten so inexplicable an experience?

And here I am already checking my story as though it were something which had really happened, for what possible relevance has George's memory to the events of a dream?

I dreamed that I crossed the lake, I dreamed . . . that is the only certain fact and I must cling to it, the fact that I dreamed. How my poor mother would grieve if she could know that, even for a moment, I had begun to think of these events as true ... but, of course, if it were possible for her to know what I am thinking now, there would be no limit to the area of possibility. I dreamed then that I crossed the water (either by swimming – I could already swim at seven years old – or by wading if the lake is really as small as George makes out, or by paddling a raft) and scrambled up the slope of the island. I can remember grass, scrub, brushwood, and at last a wood. I would describe it as a forest if I had not already seen, in the height of the garden-wall, how age diminishes size. I don't remember the umbrella pine which W.W. described – I suspect he stole the sentinel-tree from *Treasure Island*, but I do know that when I got into the wood I was completely hidden from the house and the trees were close enough together to protect me from the rain. Quite soon I was lost, and yet how could I have been lost if the lake were no bigger than a pond, and the island therefore not much larger than the top of a kitchen-table?

Again I find myself checking my memories as though they were facts. A dream does not take account of size. A puddle can contain a continent, and a clump of trees stretch in sleep to the world's edge. I dreamed, I *dreamed* that I was lost and that night began to fall. I was not frightened. It was as though even at seven I was accustomed to travel. All the rough journeys of the future were already in me then, like a muscle which had only to develop. I curled up among the roots of the trees and slept. When I woke I could still hear the pit-pat of the rain in the upper branches and the steady zing of an insect near by. All these noises come as clearly back to me now as the sound of the rain on the parked cars outside the clinic in Wimpole Street, the music of yesterday.

The moon had risen and I could see more easily around me. I was determined to explore further before the morning came, for then an expedition would certainly be sent in search of me. I knew, from the many books of exploration George had read to me, of the danger to a person lost of walking in circles until eventually he dies of thirst or hunger, so I cut a cross in the bark of the tree (I had brought a knife with me that contained several blades, a small saw and an instrument for removing pebbles from horses' hooves). For the sake of future reference I named the place where I had slept Camp Hope. I had no fear of hunger, for I had apples in both pockets, and as for thirst I had only to continue in a straight line and I would come eventually to the lake again where the water was sweet, or at worst a little brackish. I go into all these details, which W.W. unaccountably omitted, to test my memory. I had forgotten until now how far or how deeply it extended. Had W.W. forgotten or was he afraid to remember?

I had gone a little more than three hundred yards – I paced the distances and marked every hundred paces or so on a tree – it was the best I could do, without proper surveying instruments, for the map I already planned to draw – when I reached a great oak of apparently enormous age with roots that coiled away above the surface of the ground. (I was reminded of those roots once in Africa where they formed a kind of shrine for a fetish – a seated human figure made out of a gourd and palm fronds and unidentifiable vegetable matter gone rotten in the rains and a great penis of bamboo. Coming on it suddenly, I was frightened, or was it the memory that it brought back which scared me?) Under one of these roots the earth had been disturbed; somebody had shaken a mound of charred tobacco from a pipe and a sequin glistened like a snail in the moist moonlight. I struck a match to examine the ground closer and saw the imprint of a foot in a patch of loose earth – it was pointing at the tree from a few inches away and it was as solitary as the print Crusoe found on the sands of another island. It was as though a one-legged man had taken a leap out of the bushes straight at the tree.

Pirate ancestor! What nonsense W.W. had written, or had he converted the memory of that stark frightening footprint into some comforting thought of the kindly scoundrel, Long John Silver, and his wooden leg?

I stood astride the imprint and stared up the tree, half expecting to see a one-legged man perched like a vulture among the branches. I listened and there was no sound except last night's rain dripping from leaf to leaf. Then – I don't know why – I went down on my knees and peered among the roots. There was no iron ring, but one of the roots formed an arch more than two feet high like the entrance to a cave. I put my head inside and lit another match – I couldn't see the back of the cave.

It's difficult to remember that I was only seven years old. To the self we remain always the same age. I was afraid at first to venture further, but so would any grown man have been, any one of the explorers I thought of as my peers. My brother had been reading aloud to me a month before from a book called *The Romance of Australian Exploration* – my own powers of reading had not advanced quite as far as that, but my memory was green and retentive and I carried in my head all kinds of new images and evocative words – aboriginal, sextant, Murumbidgee, Stony Desert, and the points of the compass with their big capital letters ESE and NNW had an excitement they have never quite lost. They were like the figure on a watch which at last comes round to pointing the important hour. I was comforted by the thought that Sturt had been sometimes daunted and that Burke's bluster often hid his fear. Now, kneeling by the cave, I remembered a cavern which George Grey, another hero of mine, had entered and how suddenly he had come on the figure of a man ten feet high painted on the wall, clothed from the chin down to the ankles in a red garment. I don't know why, but I was more afraid of that painting than I was of the aborigines who killed Burke, and the fact that the feet and hands which protruded from the garment were said to be badly executed added to the terror. A foot which looked like a foot was only human, but my imagination could play endlessly with the faults of the painter – a club-foot, a claw-foot, the worm-like toes of a bird. Now I associated this strange footprint with the ill-executed painting, and I hesitated a long time before I got the courage to crawl into the cave under the root. Before doing so, in reference to the footprint, I gave the spot the name of Friday's Cave.

2

For some yards I could not even get upon my knees, the roof grated my hair, and it was impossible for me in that position to strike another match. I could only inch along like a worm, making an ideograph in the dust. I didn't notice for a while in the darkness that I was crawling down a long slope, but I could feel on either side of me roots rubbing my shoulders like the banisters of a staircase. I was creeping through the branches of an underground tree in a mole's world. Then the impediments were passed – I was out the other side; I banged my head again on the earth-wall and found that I could rise to my knees. But I nearly toppled down again, for I had not realized how steeply the ground sloped. I was more than a man's height below ground and, when I struck a match, I could see no finish to the long gradient going down. I cannot help feeling a little proud that I continued on my way, on my knees this time, though I suppose it is arguable whether one can really show courage in a dream.

I was halted again by a turn in the path, and this time I found I could rise to my feet after I had struck another match. The track had flattened out and ran horizontally. The air was stuffy with an odd disagreeable smell like cabbage cooking, and I wanted to go back. I remembered how miners carried canaries with them in cages to test the freshness of the air, and I wished I had thought of bringing our own canary with me which had accompanied us to Winton Hall – it would have been company too in that dark tunnel with its tiny song. There was something, I remembered, called coal-damp which caused explosions, and this passage was certainly damp enough. I must be nearly under the lake by this time, and I thought to myself that, if there was an explosion, the waters of the lake would pour in and drown me.

I blew out my match at the idea, but all the same I continued on my way in the hope that I might come on an exit a little easier than the long crawl back through the roots of the trees.

Suddenly ahead of me something whistled, only it was less like a whistle than a hiss: it was like the noise a kettle makes when it is on the boil. I thought of snakes and wondered whether some giant serpent had made its nest in the tunnel. There was something fatal to man called a Black Mamba . . . I stood stock-still and held my breath, while the whistling went on and on for a long while, before it whined out into nothing. I would have given anything then to have been safe back in bed in the room next to my mother's, with the electric-light switch close to my hand and the firm bed-end at my feet. There was a strange clanking sound and a ducklike quack. I couldn't bear the darkness any more and I lit another match, reckless of coal-damp. It shone on a pile of old newspapers and nothing else – it was strange to find I had not been the first person here. I called out 'Hullo!' and my voice went on in diminishing echoes down the long passage. Nobody answered, and when I picked up one of the papers I saw it was no proof of a human presence. It was the *East*

Anglian Observer for April 5th 1885 – 'with which is incorporated the *Colchester Guardian*'. It's funny how even the date remains in my mind and the Victorian Gothic type of the titling. There was a faint fishy smell about it as though – oh, eons ago – it had been wrapped around a bit of prehistoric cod. The match burnt my fingers and went out. Perhaps I was the first to come here for all those years, but suppose whoever had brought those papers were lying somewhere dead in the tunnel . . .

Then I had an idea. I made a torch of the paper in my hand, tucked the others under my arm to serve me later, and with the stronger light advanced more boldly down the passage. After all wild beasts – so George had read to me – and serpents too in all likelihood – were afraid of fire, and my fear of an explosion had been driven out by the greater terror of what I might find in the dark. But it was not a snake or a leopard or a tiger or any other cavern-haunting animal that I saw when I turned the second corner. Scrawled with the simplicity of ancient man upon the left-hand wall of the passage – done with a sharp tool like a chisel – was the outline of a gigantic fish. I held up my paper-torch higher and saw the remains of lettering either half-obliterated or in a language I didn't know.

I was trying to make sense of the symbols when a hoarse voice out of sight called, 'Maria, Maria.'

I stood very still and the newspaper burned down in my hand. 'Is that you, Maria?' the voice said. It sounded to me very angry. 'What kind of a trick are you playing? What's the clock say? Surely it's time for my broth.' And then I heard again that strange quacking sound which I had heard before. There was a long whispering and after that silence.

3

I suppose I was relieved that there were human beings and not wild beasts down the passage, but what kind of human beings could they be except criminals hiding from justice or gypsies who are notorious for stealing children? I was afraid to think what they might do to anyone who discovered their secret. It was also possible, of course, that I had come on the home of some aboriginal tribe . . . I stood there unable to make up my mind whether to go on or to turn back. It was not a problem which my Australian peers could help me to solve, for they had sometimes found the aboriginals friendly folk who gave them fish (I thought of the fish on the wall) and sometimes enemies who attacked with spears. In any case – whether these were criminals or gypsies or aboriginals – I had only a pocket-knife for my defence. I think it showed the true spirit of an explorer that in spite of my fears I thought of the map I must one day draw if I survived and so named this spot Camp Indecision.

My indecision was solved for me. An old woman appeared suddenly and noiselessly around the corner of the passage. She wore an old blue dress which came down to her ankles covered with sequins, and her hair was grey and straggly and she was going bald on top. She was every bit as surprised as I was. She stood there gaping at me and then she opened her mouth and squawked. I learned later that she had no roof to her mouth and was probably saying, 'Who are you?' but then I thought it was some foreign tongue she spoke – perhaps aboriginee – and I replied with an attempt at assurance, 'I'm English.'

The hoarse voice out of sight said, 'Bring him along here, Maria.'

The old woman took a step towards me, but I couldn't bear the thought of being touched by her hands, which were old and curved like a bird's and covered with the brown patches that Ernest, the gardener, had told me were 'grave-marks'; her nails were very long and filled with dirt. Her dress was dirty too and I thought of the sequin I'd seen outside and imagined her scrabbling home through the roots of the tree. I backed up against the side of the passage and somehow squeezed around her. She quacked after me, but I went on. Round a second – or perhaps a third – corner I found myself in a great cave some eight feet high. On what I thought was a throne, but I later realized was an old lavatory-seat, sat a big old man with a white beard yellowing round the mouth from what I suppose now to have been nicotine. He had one good leg, but the right trouser was sewn up and looked stuffed like a bolster. I could see him quite well because an oil-lamp stood on a kitchen-table, beside a carving-knife and two cabbages, and his face came vividly back to me the other day when I was reading Darwin's description of a carrier-pigeon: 'Greatly elongated eyelids, very large external orifices to the nostrils, and a wide gape of mouth.'

He said, 'And who would you be and what are you doing here and why are you burning my newspaper?'

The old woman came squawking around the corner and then stood still behind me, barring my retreat.

I said, 'My name's William Wilditch, and I come from Winton Hall.'

'And where's Winton Hall?' he asked, never stirring from his lavatory-seat.

'Up there,' I said and pointed at the roof of the cave.

'That means precious little,' he said. 'Why, everything is up there, China and all America too and the Sandwich Islands.'

'I suppose so,' I said. There was a kind of reason in most of what he said, as I came to realize later.

'But down here there's only us. We are exclusive,' he said, 'Maria and me.'

I was less frightened of him now. He spoke English. He was a fellow-countryman. I said, 'If you'll tell me the way out I'll be going on my way.'

'What's that you've got under your arm?' he asked me sharply. 'More newspapers?'

'I found them in the passage . . .'

'Finding's not keeping here,' he said, 'whatever it may be up there in China. You'll soon discover that. Why, that's the last lot of papers Maria brought in. What would we have for reading if we let you go and pinch them?'

'I didn't mean . . .'

'Can you read?' he asked, not listening to my excuses.

'If the words aren't too long.'

'Maria can read, but she can't see very well any more than I can, and she can't articulate much.'

Maria went kwahk, kwahk behind me, like a bull-frog it seems to me now, and I jumped. If that was how she read I wondered how he could understand a single word. He said, 'Try a piece.'

'What do you mean?'

'Can't you understand plain English? You'll have to work for your supper down here.'

'But it's not supper-time. It's still early in the morning,' I said.

'What o'clock is it, Maria?'

'Kwahk,' she said.

'Six. That's supper-time.'

'But it's six in the morning, not the evening.'

'How do you know? Where's the light? There aren't such things as mornings and evenings here.'

'Then how do you ever wake up?' I asked. His beard shook as he laughed. 'What a shrewd little shaver he is,' he exclaimed. 'Did you hear that, Maria? "How do you ever wake up?" he said. All the same you'll find that life here isn't all beer and skittles and who's your Uncle Joe. If you are clever, you'll learn and if you are not clever . . .' He brooded morosely. 'We are deeper here than any grave was ever dug to bury secrets in. Under the earth or over the earth, it's here you'll find all that matters.' He added angrily, 'Why aren't you reading a piece as I told you to? If you are to stay with us, you've got to jump to it.'

'I don't want to stay.'

'You think you can just take a peek, is that it? and go away. You are wrong – but take all the peek you want and then get on with it.'

I didn't like the way he spoke, but all the same I did as he suggested. There was an old chocolate-stained chest of drawers, a tall kitchen-cupboard, a screen covered with scraps and transfers; and a wooden crate which perhaps served Maria for a chair, and another larger one for a table. There was a cooking-stove with a kettle pushed to one side, steaming yet. That would have caused the whistle I had heard in the passage. I could see no sign of any bed, unless a heap of potato-sacks against the wall served that purpose. There were a lot of breadcrumbs on the earth-floor and a few bones had been swept into a corner as though awaiting interment.

'And now,' he said, 'show your young paces. I've yet to see whether you are worth your keep.'

'But I don't want to be kept,' I said. 'I really don't. It's time I went home.'

'Home's where a man lies down,' he said, 'and this is where you'll lie from now. Now take the first page that comes and read to me. I want to hear the news.'

'But the paper's nearly fifty years old,' I said. 'There's no news in it.'

'News is news however old it is.' I began to notice a way he had of talking in general statements like a lecturer or a prophet. He seemed to be less interested in conversation than in the recital of some articles of belief, odd crazy ones, perhaps, yet somehow I could never put my finger convincingly on an error. 'A cat's a cat even when it's a dead cat. We get rid of it when it's smelly, but news never smells, however long it's dead. News keeps. And it comes round again when you least expect. Like thunder.'

I opened the paper at random and read: 'Garden fête at the Grange. The fête at the Grange, Long Wilson, in aid of Distressed Gentlewomen was opened by Lady (Isobel) Montgomery.' I was a bit put out by the long words coming so quickly, but I acquitted myself with fair credit. He sat on the lavatory-seat with his head sunk a little, listening with attention. 'The Vicar presided at the White Elephant Stall.'

The old man said with satisfaction, 'They are royal beasts.'

'But these were not really elephants,' I said.

'A stall is part of a stable, isn't it? What do you want a stable for if they aren't real? Go on. Was it a good fate or an evil fate?'

'It's not that kind of fate either,' I said.

'There's no other kind,' he said. 'It's your fate to read to me. It's *her* fate to talk like a frog, and mine to listen because my eyesight's bad. This is an underground fate we suffer from here, and that was a garden fate – but it all comes to the same fate in the end.' It was useless to argue with him and I read on: 'Unfortunately the festivities were brought to an untimely close by a heavy rainstorm.'

Maria gave a kwahk that sounded like a malicious laugh, and 'You see,' the old man said, as though what I had read proved somehow he was right, 'that's fate for you.'

'The evening's events had to be transferred indoors, including the Morris Dancing and the Treasure Hunt.'

'Treasure Hunt?' the old man asked sharply.

'That's what it says here.'

'The impudence of it,' he said. 'The sheer impudence. Maria, did you hear that?'

She kwahked – this time, I thought, angrily.

'It's time for my broth,' he said with deep gloom, as though he were saying, 'It's time for my death.'

'It happened a long time ago,' I said, trying to soothe him.

'Time,' he exclaimed, 'you can —— time,' using a word quite unfamiliar to me which I guessed – I don't know how – was one that I could not with safety use myself when I returned home. Maria had gone behind the screen – there must have been other cupboards there, for I heard her opening and shutting doors and clanking pots and pans.

I whispered to him quickly, 'Is she your luba?'

'Sister, wife, mother, daughter,' he said, 'what difference does it make? Take your choice. She's a woman, isn't she?' He brooded there on the lavatory-seat like a king on a throne. 'There are two sexes,' he said. 'Don't try to make more than two with definitions.' The statement sank into my mind with the same heavy mathematical certainty with which later on at school I learned the rule of Euclid about the sides of an isosceles triangle. There was a long silence.

'I think I'd better be going,' I said, shifting up and down. Maria came in. She carried a dish marked Fido filled with hot broth. Her husband, her brother, whatever he was, nursed it on his lap a long while before he drank it. He seemed to be lost in thought again, and I hesitated to disturb him. All the same, after a while, I tried again.

'They'll be expecting me at home.'

'Home?'

'Yes.'

'You couldn't have a better home than this,' he said. 'You'll see. In a bit of time – a year or two – you'll settle down well enough.'

I tried my best to be polite. 'It's very nice here, I'm sure, but . . .'

'It's no use your being restless. I didn't ask you to come, did

I, but now you are here, you'll stay. Maria's a great hand with cabbage. You won't suffer any hardship.'

'But I can't stay. My mother . . .'

'Forget your mother and your father too. If you need anything from up there Maria will fetch it down for you.'

'But I can't stay here.'

'Can't's not a word that you can use to the likes of me.'

'But you haven't any right to keep me . . .'

'And what right had you to come busting in like a thief, getting Maria all disturbed when she was boiling my broth?'

'I couldn't stay here with you. It's not – sanitary.' I don't know how I managed to get that word out. 'I'd die . . .'

'There's no need to talk of dying down here. No one's ever died here, and you've no reason to believe that anyone ever will. We aren't dead, are we, and we've lived a long long time, Maria and me. You don't know how lucky you are. There's treasure here beyond all the riches of Asia. One day, if you don't go disturbing Maria, I'll show you. You know what a millionaire is?' I nodded. 'They aren't one quarter as rich as Maria and me. And they die too, and where's their treasure then? Rockefeller's gone and Fred's gone and Columbus. I sit here and just read about dying – it's an entertainment that's all. You'll find in all those papers what they call an obituary – there's one about a Lady Caroline Winterbottom that made Maria laugh and me. It's summerbottoms we have here, I said, all the year round, sitting by the stove.'

Maria kwahked in the background, and I began to cry more as a way of interrupting him than because I was really frightened.

It's extraordinary how vividly after all these years I can remember that man and the words he spoke. If they were to dig down now on the island below the roots of the tree, I would half expect to find him sitting there still on the old lavatory-seat which seemed to be detached from any pipes or drainage and serve no useful purpose, and yet, if he had really existed, he must have passed his century a long time ago. There was something of a monarch about him and something, as I said, of a prophet and something of the gardener my mother disliked and of a policeman in the next village; his expressions were often countrylike and coarse, but his ideas seemed to move on a deeper level, like roots spreading below a layer of compost. I could sit here now in this room for hours remembering the things he said – I haven't made out the sense of them all yet: they are stored in my memory like a code uncracked which waits for a clue or an inspiration.

He said to me sharply, 'We don't need salt here. There's too much as it is. You taste any bit of earth and you'll find it salt. We live in salt. We are pickled, you might say, in it. Look at Maria's hands, and you'll see the salt in the cracks.'

I stopped crying at once and looked (my attention could always be caught by bits of irrelevant information), and, true enough, there seemed to be grey-white seams running between her knuckles.

'You'll turn salty too in time,' he said encouragingly and drank his broth with a good deal of noise.

I said, 'But I really am going, Mr . . .'

'You can call me Javitt,' he said, 'but only because it's not my real name. You don't believe I'd give you that, do you? And Maria's not Maria – it's just a sound she answers to, you understand me, like Jupiter.'

'No.'

'If you had a dog called Jupiter, you wouldn't believe he was really Jupiter, would you?'

'I've got a dog called Joe.'

'The same applies,' he said and drank his soup. Sometimes I think that in no conversation since have I found the interest I discovered in those inconsequent sentences of his to which I listened during the days (I don't know how many) that I spent below the garden. Because, of course, I didn't leave that day. Javitt had his way.

He might be said to have talked me into staying, though if I had proved obstinate I have no doubt at all that Maria would have blocked my retreat, and certainly I would not have fancied struggling to escape through the musty folds of her clothes. That was the strange balance – to and fro – of those days; half the time I was frightened as though I were caged in a nightmare and half the time I only wanted to laugh freely and happily at the strangeness of his speech and the novelty of his ideas. It was as if, for those hours or days, the only important things in life were two, laughter and fear. (Perhaps the same ambivalence was there when I first began to know a woman.) There are people whose laughter has always a sense of superiority, but it was Javitt who taught me that laughter is more often a sign of equality, of pleasure and not of malice. He sat there on his lavatory-seat and he said, 'I shit dead stuff every day, do I? How wrong you are.' (I was already laughing because that was a word I knew to be obscene and I had never heard it spoken before.) 'Everything that comes out of me is alive, I tell you. It's squirming around there, germs and bacilli and the like, and it goes into the ground like a womb, and it comes out somewhere, I dare say, like my daughter did – I forgot I haven't told you about her.'

'Is she here?' I said with a look at the curtain, wondering what monstrous woman would next emerge.

'Oh, no, she went upstairs a long time ago.'

'Perhaps I could take her a message from you,' I said cunningly.

He looked at me with contempt. 'What kind of a message,' he asked, 'could the likes of you take to the likes of her?' He must have seen the motive behind my offer, for he reverted to the fact of my imprisonment. 'I'm not unreasonable,' he said, 'I'm not one to make hailstorms in harvest time, but if you went back up there you'd talk about me and Maria and the treasure we've got, and people would come digging.'

'I swear I'd say nothing' (and at least I have kept that promise, whatever others I have broken, through all the years until now).

'You talk in your sleep maybe. A boy's never alone. You've got a brother, I dare say, and soon you'll be going to school and hinting of things to make you seem important. There are plenty of ways of keeping an oath and breaking it in the same moment. Do you know what I'd do then? If they came searching? I'd go further in.'

Maria kwahk-kwahked her agreement where she listened from somewhere behind the curtains.

'What do you mean?'

'Give me a hand to get off this seat,' he said. He pressed his hand down on my shoulder and it was like a mountain heaving. I looked at the lavatory-seat and I could see that it had been placed exactly to cover a hole which went down down down out of sight. 'A moit of the treasure's down there already,' he said, 'but I wouldn't let the bastards enjoy what they could find here. There's a little matter of subsidence I've got fixed up so that they'd never see the light of day again.'

'But what would you do below there for food?'

'We've got tins enough for another century or two,' he said. 'You'd be surprised at what Maria's stored away there. We don't use tins up here because there's always broth and cabbage and that's more healthy and keeps the scurvy off, but we've no more teeth to lose and our gums are fallen as it is, so if we had to fall back on tins we would. Why, there's hams and chickens and red salmons' eggs and butter and steak-and-kidney pies and caviar, venison too and marrow-bones, I'm forgetting the fish – cods' roe and sole in white wine, langouste legs, sardines, bloaters, and herrings in tomato-sauce, and all the fruits that ever grew, apples, pears, strawberries, figs, raspberries, plums and greengages and passion fruit, mangoes, grapefruit, loganberries and cherries, mulberries too and sweet things from Japan, not to speak of vegetables, Indian corn and taties, salsify and spinach and that thing they call endive, asparagus, peas and the hearts of bamboo, and I've left out our old friend the tomato.' He lowered himself heavily back on to his seat above the great hole going down.

'You must have enough for two lifetimes,' I said.

'There's means of getting more,' he added darkly, so that I pictured other channels delved through the undersoil of the garden like the section of an ant's nest, and I remembered the sequin on the island and the single footprint.

Perhaps all this talk of food had reminded Maria of her duties because she came quacking out from behind her dusty curtain, carrying two bowls of broth, one medium size for me and one almost as small as an egg-cup for herself. I tried politely to take the small one, but she snatched it away from me.

'You don't have to bother about Maria,' the old man said. 'She's been eating food for more years than you've got weeks. She knows her appetite.'

'What do you cook with?' I asked.

'Calor,' he said.

That was an odd thing about this adventure or rather this dream: fantastic though it was, it kept coming back to ordinary life with simple facts like that. The man could never, if I really thought it out, have existed all those years below the earth, and yet the cooking, as I seem to remember it, was done on a cylinder of calor-gas.

The broth was quite tasty and I drank it to the end. When I had finished I fidgeted about on the wooden box they had given me for a seat – nature was demanding something for which I was too embarrassed to ask aid.

'What's the matter with you?' Javitt said. 'Chair not comfortable?'

'Oh, it's very comfortable,' I said.

'Perhaps you want to lie down and sleep?'

'No.'

'I'll show you something which will give you dreams,' he said. 'A picture of my daughter.'

'I want to do number one,' I blurted out.

'Oh, is that all?' Javitt said. He called to Maria, who was still clattering around behind the curtain, 'The boy wants to piss. Fetch him the golden po.' Perhaps my eyes showed interest, for he added to me diminishingly, with the wave of a hand, 'It's the least of my treasures.'

All the same it was remarkable enough in my eyes, and I can remember it still, a veritable chamber-pot of gold. Even the young dauphin of France on that long road back from Varennes with his father had only a silver cup at his service. I would have been more embarrassed, doing what I called number one in front of the old man Javitt, if I had not been so impressed by the pot. It lent the everyday affair the importance of a ceremony, almost of a sacrament. I can remember the tinkle in the pot like far-away chimes as though a gold surface resounded differently from china or base metal.

Javitt reached behind him to a shelf stacked with old papers and picked one out. He said, 'Now you look at that and tell me what you think.'

It was a kind of magazine I'd never seen before – full of pictures which are now called cheese-cake. I have no earlier memory of a woman's unclothed body, or as nearly unclothed as made no difference to me then, in the skin-tight black costume. One whole page was given up to a Miss Ramsgate, shot from all angles. She was the favourite contestant for something called Miss England and might later go on, if she were successful, to compete for the title of Miss Europe, Miss World and after that Miss Universe. I stared at her as though I wanted to memorize her for ever. And that is exactly what I did.

'That's our daughter,' Javitt said.

'And did she become . . .'

'She was launched,' he said with pride and mystery, as though he were speaking of some moon-rocket which had at last after many disappointments risen from the pad and soared to outer space. I looked at the photograph, at the wise eyes and the inexplicable body, and I thought, with all the ignorance children have of age and generations, I never want to marry anybody but her. Maria put her hand through the curtains and quacked, and I thought, she would be my mother then, but not a hoot did I care. With that girl for my wife I could take anything, even school and growing up and life. And perhaps I could have taken them, if I had ever succeeded in finding her.

Again my thoughts were interrupted. For if I am remembering a vivid dream – and dreams do stay in all their detail far longer than we realize – how would I have known at that age about such absurdities as beauty-contests? A dream can only contain what one has experienced, or, if you have sufficient faith in Jung, what our ancestors have experienced. But calorgas and the Ramsgate Beauty Queen? . . . They are not ancestral memories, nor the memories of a child of seven. Certainly my mother did not allow us to buy with our meagre pocket-money – sixpence a week? – such papers as that. And yet the image is there, caught once and for all, not only the expression of the eyes, but the expression of the body too, the particular tilt of the breasts, the shallow scoop of the navel like something carved in sand, the little trim buttocks – the dividing line swung between them close and regular like the single sweep of a pencil. Can a child of seven fall in love for life with a body? And there is a further mystery which did not occur to me then: how could a couple as old as Javitt and Maria have had a daughter so young in the period when such contests were the vogue?

'She's a beauty,' Javitt said, 'you'll never see her like where your folks live. Things grow differently underground, like a mole's coat. I ask you where there's softness softer than that?' I'm not sure whether he was referring to the skin of his daughter or the coat of a mole.

I sat on the golden po and looked at the photograph and listened to Javitt as I would have listened to my own father if I had possessed one. His sayings are fixed in my memory like the photograph. Gross some of them seem now, but they did not appear gross to me then when even the graffiti on walls were innocent. Except when he called me 'boy' or 'snapper' or something of the kind he seemed unaware of my age: it was not that he talked to me as an equal but as someone from miles away, looking down from his old lavatory-seat to my golden po, from so far away that he couldn't distinguish my age, or perhaps he was so old that anyone under a century or so seemed much alike to him. All that I write here was not said at that moment. There must have been many days or nights of conversation – you couldn't down there tell the difference – and now I dredge the sentences up, in no particular order, just as they come to mind, sitting at my mother's desk so many years later.

4

'You laugh at Maria and me. You think we look ugly. I tell you she could have been painted if she had chosen by some of the greatest – there's one that painted women with three eyes – she'd have suited him. But she knew how to tunnel in the earth like me, when to appear and when not to appear. It's a long time now that we've been alone down here. It gets more dangerous all the time – if you can speak of time – on the upper floor. But don't think it hasn't happened before. But when I remember . . .' But what he remembered has gone from my head, except only his concluding phrase and a sense of desolation: 'Looking round at all those palaces and towers, you'd have thought they'd been made like a child's castle of the desert-sand.

'In the beginning you had a name only the man or woman knew who pulled you out of your mother. Then there was a name for the tribe to call you by. That was of little account, but of more account all the same than the name you had with strangers; and there was a name used in the family – by your pa and ma if it's those terms you call them by nowadays. The only name without any power at all was the name you used to strangers. That's why I call myself Javitt to you, but the name the man who pulled me out knew – that was so secret I had to keep him as a friend for life, so that he wouldn't even tell me because of the responsibility it would bring – I might let it slip before a stranger. Up where you come from they've begun to forget the power of the name. I wouldn't be surprised if you only had the one name and what's the good of a name everyone knows? Do you suppose even I feel secure here with my treasure and all – because, you see, as it turned out, I got to know the first name of all. He told it me before he died, before I could stop him, with a hand over his mouth. I doubt if there's anyone in the world except me who knows his first name. It's an awful temptation to speak it out loud – introduce it casually into the conversation like you might say by Jove, by George, for Christ's sake. Or whisper it when I think no one's attentive.

'When I was born, time had a different pace to what it has now. Now you walk from one wall to another, and it takes you twenty steps – or twenty miles – who cares? – between the towns. But when I was young we took a leisurely way. Don't bother me with "I must be gone now" or "I've been away so long". I can't talk to you in terms of time – your time and my time are different. Javitt isn't my usual name either even with strangers. It's one I thought up fresh for you, so that you'll have no power at all. I'll change it right away if you escape. I warn you that.

'You get a sense of what I mean when you make love with a girl. The time isn't measured by clocks. Time is fast or slow or it stops for a while altogether. One minute is different to every other minute. When you make love it's a pulse in a man's part which measures time and when you spill yourself there's no time at all. That's how time comes and goes, not by an alarm-clock made by a man with a magnifying glass in his eye. Haven't you ever heard them say, "It's —— time" up there?' and he used again the word which I guessed was forbidden like his name, perhaps because it had power too.

'I dare say you are wondering how Maria and me could make a beautiful girl like that one. That's an illusion people have about beauty. Beauty doesn't come from beauty. All that beauty can produce is prettiness. Have you never looked around upstairs and counted the beautiful women with their pretty daughters? Beauty diminishes all the time, it's the law of diminishing returns, and only when you get back to zero, to the real ugly base of things, there's a chance to start again free and independent. Painters who paint what they call ugly things know that. I can still see that little head with its cap of blonde hair coming out from between Maria's thighs and how she leapt out of Maria in a spasm (there wasn't any doctor down here or midwife to give her a name and rob her of power – and she's Miss Ramsgate to you and to the whole world upstairs). Ugliness and beauty; you see it in war too; when there's nothing left of a house but a couple of pillars against the sky, the beauty of it starts all over again like before the builder ruined it. Perhaps when Maria and I go up there next, there'll only be pillars left, sticking up around the flattened world like it was fucking time.' (The word had become a familiar to me by this time and no longer had the power to shock.)

'Do you know, boy, that when they make those maps of the universe you are looking at the map of something that looked like that six thousand million years ago? You can't be much more out of date than that, I'll swear. Why, if they've got pictures up there of us taken yesterday, they'll see the world all covered with ice – if their photos are a bit more up to date than ours, that is. Otherwise we won't be there at all, maybe, and it might just as well be a photo of the future. To catch a star while it's alive you have to be as nippy as if you were snatching at a racehorse as it goes by.

'You are a bit scared still of Maria and me because you've never seen anyone like us before. And you'd be scared to see our daughter too, there's no other like her in whatever country she's in now, and what good would a scared man be to her? Do you know what a rogue-plant is? And do you know that white cats with blue eyes are deaf? People who keep nursery-gardens look around all the time at the seedlings and they throw away any oddities like weeds. They call them rogues. You won't find many white cats with blue eyes and that's the reason. But sometimes you find someone who wants things different, who's tired of all the plus signs and wants to find zero, and he starts breeding away with the differences. Maria and I are both rogues and we are born of generations of rogues. Do you think I lost this leg in an accident? I was born that way just like Maria with her squawk. Generations of us uglier and uglier, and suddenly out of Maria comes our daughter, who's Miss Ramsgate to you. I don't speak her name even when I'm asleep. We're unique like the Red Grouse. You ask anybody if they can tell you where the Red Grouse came from.

'You are still wondering why we are unique. It's because for generations we haven't been thrown away. Man kills or throws away what he doesn't want. Somebody once in Greece kept the wrong child and exposed the right one, and then one rogue at least was safe and it only needed another. Why, in Tierra del Fuego in starvation years they kill and eat their old women because the dogs are of more value. It's the hardest thing in the world for a rogue to survive. For hundreds of years now we've been living underground and we'll have the laugh of you yet, coming up above for keeps in a dead world. Except I'll bet you your golden po that Miss Ramsgate will be there somewhere – her beauty's rogue too. We have long lives, we – Javitts to you. We've kept our ugliness all those years and why shouldn't she keep her beauty? Like a cat does. A cat is as beautiful the last day as the first. And it keeps its spittle. Not like a dog.

'I can see your eye light up whenever I say Miss Ramsgate, and you still wonder how it comes Maria and I have a child like that in spite of all I'm telling you. Elephants go on breeding till they are ninety years old, don't they, and do you suppose a rogue like Javitt (which isn't my real name) can't go on longer than a beast so stupid it lets itself be harnessed and draw logs? There's another thing we have in common with elephants. No one sees us dead.

'We know the sex-taste of female birds better than we know the sex-taste of women. Only the most beautiful in the hen's eyes survives, so when you admire a peacock you know you have the same taste as a pea-hen. But women are more mysterious than birds. You've heard of beauty and the beast, haven't you? They have rogue-tastes. Just look at me and my leg. You won't find Miss Ramsgate by going round the world preening yourself like a peacock to attract a beautiful woman – she's our daughter and she had rogue-tastes too. She isn't for someone who wants a beautiful wife at his dinner-table to satisfy his vanity, and an understanding wife in bed who'll treat him just the same number of times as he was accustomed to at school – so many times a day or week. She went away, our daughter did, with a want looking for a want – and not a want you can measure in inches either or calculate in numbers by the week. They say that in the northern countries people make love for their health, so it won't be any good looking for her in the north. You might have to go as far as Africa or China. And talking of China . . .'

5

Sometimes I think that I learned more from Javitt – this man who never existed – than from all my schoolmasters. He talked to me while I sat there on the po or lay upon the sacks as no one had ever done before or has ever done since. I could not have expected my mother to take time away from the Fabian pamphlets to say, 'Men are like monkeys – they don't have any season in love, and the monkeys aren't worried by this notion of dying. They tell us from pulpits we're immortal and then they try to frighten us with death. I'm more a monkey than a man. To the monkeys death's an accident. The gorillas don't bury their dead with hearses and crowns of flowers, thinking one day it's going to happen to them and they better put on a show if they want one for themselves too. If one of them dies, it's a special case, and so they can leave it in the ditch. I feel like them. But I'm not a special case yet. I keep clear of hackney-carriages and railway-trains, you won't find horses, wild dogs or machinery down here. I love life and I survive. Up there they talk about natural death, but it's natural death that's unnatural. If we lived for a thousand years – and there's no reason we shouldn't – there'd always be a smash, a bomb, tripping over your left foot – those are the natural deaths. All we need to live is a bit of effort, but nature sows booby-traps in our way.

'Do you believe those skulls monks have in their cells are set there for contemplation? Not on your life. They don't believe in death any more than I do. The skulls are there for the same reason you'll see a queen's portrait in an embassy – they're just part of the official furniture. Do you believe an ambassador ever looks at that face on the wall with a diamond tiara and an empty smile?

'Be disloyal. It's your duty to the human race. The human race needs to survive and it's the loyal man who dies first from anxiety or a bullet or overwork. If you have to earn a living, boy, and the price they make you pay is loyalty, be a double agent – and never let either of the two sides know your real name. The same applies to women and God. They both respect a man they don't own, and they'll go on raising the price they are willing to offer. Didn't Christ say that very thing? Was the prodigal son loyal or the lost shilling or the strayed sheep? The obedient flock didn't give the shepherd any satisfaction or the loyal son interest his father.

'People are afraid of bringing May blossom into the house. They say it's unlucky. The real reason is it smells strong of sex and they are afraid of sex. Why aren't they afraid of fish then, you may rightly ask? Because when they smell fish they smell a holiday ahead and they feel safe from breeding for a short while.'

I remember Javitt's words far more clearly than the passage of time; certainly I must have slept at least twice on the bed of sacks, but I cannot remember Javitt sleeping until the very end – perhaps he slept like a horse or a god, upright. And the broth – that came at regular intervals, so far as I could tell, though there was no sign anywhere of a clock, and once I think they opened for me a tin of sardines from their store (it had a very Victorian label on it of two bearded sailors and a seal, but the sardines tasted good).

I think Javitt was glad to have me there. Surely he could not have been talking quite so amply over the years to Maria who could only quack in response, and several times he made me read to him from one of the newspapers. The nearest to our time I ever found was a local account of the celebrations for the relief of Mafeking. ('Riots,' Javitt said, 'purge like a dose of salts.')

Once he told me to pick up the oil-lamp and we would go for a walk together, and I was able to see how agile he could be on his one leg. When he stood upright he looked like a rough carving from a tree-trunk where the sculptor had not bothered to separate the legs, or perhaps, as with the image on the cave, they were 'badly executed'. He put one hand on each wall and hopped gigantically in front of me, and when he paused to speak (like many old people he seemed unable to speak and move at the same time) he seemed to be propping up the whole passage with his arms as thick as pit-beams. At one point he paused to tell me that we were now directly under the lake. 'How many tons of water lie up there?' he asked me – I had never thought of water in tons before that, only in gallons, but he had the exact figure ready, I can't remember it now. Further on, where the passage sloped upwards, he paused again and said, 'Listen,' and I heard a kind of rumbling that passed overhead and after that a rattling as little cakes of mud fell around us. 'That's a motor-car,' he said, as an explorer might have said, 'That's an elephant.'

I asked him whether perhaps there was a way out near there since we were so close to the surface, and he made his answer, even to that direct question, ambiguous and general like a proverb. 'A wise man has only one door to his house,' he said.

What a boring old man he would have been to an adult mind, but a child has a hunger to learn which makes him sometimes hang on the lips of the dullest schoolmaster. I thought I was learning about the world and the universe from Javitt, and still to this day I wonder how it was that a child could have invented these details, or have they accumulated year by year, like coral, in the sea of the unconscious around the original dream?

There were times when he was in a bad humour for no apparent reason, or at any rate for no adequate reason. An example: for all his freedom of speech and range of thought, I found there were tiny rules which had to be obeyed, else the thunder of his invective broke – the way I had to arrange the spoon in the empty broth-bowl, the method of folding a newspaper after it had been read, even the arrangement of my limbs on the bed of sacks.

'I'll cut you off,' he cried once and I pictured him lopping off one of my legs to resemble him. 'I'll starve you, I'll set you alight like a candle for a warning. Haven't I given you a kingdom here of all the treasures of the earth and all the fruits of it, tin by tin, where time can't get in to destroy you and there's no day or night, and you go and defy me with a spoon laid down longways in a saucer? You come of an ungrateful generation.' His arms waved about and cast shadows like wolves on the wall behind the oil-lamp, while Maria sat squatting behind a cylinder of calor-gas in an attitude of terror.

'I haven't even seen your wonderful treasure,' I said with feeble defiance.

'Nor you won't,' he said, 'nor any lawbreaker like you. You lay last night on your back grunting like a small swine, but did I curse you as you deserved? Javitt's patient. He forgives and he forgives seventy times seven, but then you go and lay your spoon longways . . .' He gave a great sigh like a wave withdrawing. He said, 'I forgive even that. There's no fool like an old fool and you will search a long way before you find anything as old as I am – even among the tortoises, the parrots and the elephants. One day I'll show you the treasure, but not now. I'm not in the right mood now. Let time pass. Let time heal.'

I had found the way, however, on an earlier occasion to set him in a good humour and that was to talk to him about his daughter. It came quite easily to me, for I found myself to be passionately in love, as perhaps one can only be at an age when all one wants is to give and the thought of taking is very far removed. I asked him whether he was sad when she left him to go 'upstairs' as he liked to put it.

'I knew it had to come,' he said. 'It was for that she was born. One day she'll be back and the three of us will be together for keeps.'

'Perhaps I'll see her then,' I said.

'You won't live to see that day,' he said, as though it was I who was the old man, not he.

'Do you think she's married?' I asked anxiously.

'She isn't the kind to marry,' he said. 'Didn't I tell you she's a rogue like Maria and me? She has her roots down here. No one marries who has his roots down here.'

'I thought Maria and you were married,' I said anxiously.

He gave a sharp crunching laugh like a nut-cracker closing. 'There's no marrying in the ground,' he said. 'Where would you find the witnesses? Marriage is public. Maria and me, we just grew into each other, that's all, and then she sprouted.'

I sat silent for a long while, brooding on that vegetable picture. Then I said with all the firmness I could muster, 'I'm going to find her when I get out of here.'

'If you get out of here,' he said, 'you'd have to live a very long time and travel a very long way to find her.'

'I'll do just that,' I replied.

He looked at me with a trace of humour. 'You'll have to take a look at Africa,' he said, 'and Asia – and then there's America, North and South, and Australia – you might leave out the Arctic and the other Pole – she was always a warm girl.' And it occurs to me now when I think of the life I have led since, that I have been in most of those regions – except Australia where I have only twice touched down between planes.

'I will go to them all,' I said, 'and I'll find her.' It was as though the purpose of life had suddenly come to me as it must have come often enough to some future explorer when he noticed on a map for the first time an empty space in the heart of a continent.

'You'll need a lot of money,' Javitt jeered at me.

'I'll work my passage,' I said, 'before the mast.' Perhaps it was a reflection of that intention which made the young author W.W. menace his elder brother with such a fate before preserving him for Oxford of all places. The mast was to be a career sacred to me – it was not for George.

'It'll take a long time,' Javitt warned me.

'I'm young,' I said.

I don't know why it is that when I think of this conversation with Javitt the doctor's voice comes back to me saying hopelessly, 'There's always hope.' There's hope perhaps, but there isn't so much time left now as there was then to fulfil a destiny.

That night, when I lay down on the sacks, I had the impression that Javitt had begun to take a favourable view of my case. I woke once in the night and saw him sitting there on what is popularly called a throne, watching me. He closed one eye in a wink and it was like a star going out.

Next morning after my bowl of broth, he suddenly spoke up. 'Today,' he said, 'you are going to see my treasure.'

6

It was a day heavy with the sense of something fateful coming nearer – I call it a day but for all I could have told down there it might have been a night. And I can only compare it in my later experience with those slow hours I have sometimes experienced before I have gone to meet a woman with whom for the first time the act of love is likely to come about. The fuse has been lit, and who can tell the extent of the explosion? A few cups broken or a house in ruins?

For hours Javitt made no further reference to the subject, but after the second cup of broth (or was it perhaps, on that occasion, the tin of sardines?) Maria disappeared behind the screen and when she reappeared she wore a hat. Once, years ago perhaps, it had been a grand hat, a hat for the races, a great black straw affair; now it was full of holes like a colander decorated with one drooping scarlet flower which had been stitched and restitched and stitched again. I wondered when I saw her dressed like that whether we were about to go 'upstairs'. But we made no move. Instead she put a kettle upon the stove, warmed a pot and dropped in two spoonfuls of tea. Then she and Javitt sat and watched the kettle like a couple of soothsayers bent over the steaming entrails of a kid, waiting for a revelation. The kettle gave a thin preliminary whine and Javitt nodded and the tea was made. He alone took a cup, sipping it slowly, with his eyes on me, as though he were considering and perhaps revising his decision.

On the edge of his cup, I remember, was a tea-leaf. He took it on his nail and placed it on the back of my hand. I knew very well what that meant. A hard stalk of tea indicated a man upon the way and the soft leaf a woman; this was a soft leaf. I began to strike it with the palm of my other hand counting as I did so, 'One, two, three.' It lay flat, adhering to my hand. 'Four, five.' It was on my fingers now and I said, triumphantly, 'In five days,' thinking of Javitt's daughter in the world above.

Javitt shook his head. 'You don't count time like that with us,' he said. 'That's five decades of years.' I accepted his correction – he must know his own country best, and it's only now that I find myself calculating, if every day down there were ten years long, what age in our reckoning could Javitt have claimed?

I have no idea what he had learned from the ceremony of the tea, but at least he seemed satisfied. He rose on his one leg, and now that he had his arms stretched out to either wall, he reminded me of a gigantic crucifix, and the crucifix moved in great hops down the way we had taken the day before. Maria gave me a little push from behind and I followed. The oil-lamp in Maria's hand cast long shadows ahead of us.

First we came under the lake and I remembered the tons of water hanging over us like a frozen falls, and after that we reached the spot where we had halted before, and again a car went rumbling past on the road above. But this time we continued our shuffling march. I calculated that now we had crossed the road which led to Winton Halt; we must be somewhere under the inn called The Three Keys, which was kept by our gardener's uncle, and after that we should have arrived below the Long Mead, a field with a small minnowy stream along its northern border owned by a farmer called Howell. I had not given up all idea of escape and I noted our route carefully and the distance we had gone. I had hoped for some side-passage which might indicate that there was another entrance to the tunnel, but there seemed to be none and I was disappointed to find that, before we travelled below the inn, we descended quite steeply, perhaps in order to avoid the cellars – indeed at one moment I heard a groaning and a turbulence as though the gardener's uncle were taking delivery of some new barrels of beer.

We must have gone nearly half a mile before the passage came to an end in a kind of egg-shaped hall. Facing us was a kitchen-dresser of unstained wood, very similar to the one in which my mother kept her stores of jam, sultanas, raisins and the like.

'Open up, Maria,' Javitt said, and Maria shuffled by me,

clanking a bunch of keys and quacking with excitement, while the lamp swung to and fro like a censer.

'She's heated up,' Javitt said. 'It's many days since she saw the treasure last.' I do not know which kind of time he was referring to then, but judging from her excitement I think the days must really have represented decades – she had even forgotten which key fitted the lock and she tried them all and failed and tried again before the tumbler turned.

I was disappointed when I first saw the interior – I had expected gold bricks and a flow of Maria Theresa dollars spilling on the floor, and there were only a lot of shabby cardboard-boxes on the upper shelves and the lower shelves were empty. I think Javitt noted my disappointment and was stung by it. 'I told you,' he said, 'the moit's down below for safety.' But I wasn't to stay disappointed very long. He took down one of the biggest boxes off the top shelf and shook the contents on to the earth at my feet, as though defying me to belittle *that*.

And *that* was a sparkling mass of jewellery such as I had never seen before – I was going to say in all the colours of the rainbow, but the colours of stones have not that pale girlish simplicity. There were reds almost as deep as raw liver, stormy blues, greens like the underside of a wave, yellow sunset colours, greys like a shadow on snow, and stones without colour at all that sparkled brighter than all the rest. I say I'd seen nothing like it: it is the scepticism of middle age which leads me now to compare that treasure trove with the caskets overflowing with artificial jewellery which you sometimes see in the shop-windows of Italian tourist-resorts.

And there again I find myself adjusting a dream to the kind of criticism I ought to reserve for some agent's report on the import or export value of coloured glass. If this was a dream, these were real stones. Absolute reality belongs to dreams and not to life. The gold of dreams is not the diluted gold of even the best goldsmith, there are no diamonds in dreams made of paste – what seems is. 'Who seems most kingly is the king.'

I went down on my knees and bathed my hands in the treasure, and while I knelt there Javitt opened box after box and poured the contents upon the ground. There is no avarice in a child. I didn't concern myself with the value of this horde: it was simply a treasure, and a treasure is to be valued for its own sake and not for what it will buy. It was only years later, after a deal of literature and learning and knowledge at second hand, that W.W. wrote of the treasure as something with which he could save the family fortunes. I was nearer to the jackdaw in my dream, caring only for the glitter and the sparkle.

'It's nothing to what lies below out of sight,' Javitt remarked with pride.

There were necklaces and bracelets, lockets and bangles, pins and rings and pendants and buttons. There were quantities of those little gold objects which girls like to hang on their bracelets: the Vendôme column and the Eiffel Tower and a Lion of St Mark's, a champagne bottle and a tiny booklet with leaves of gold inscribed with the names of places important perhaps to a pair of lovers – Paris, Brighton, Rome, Assisi and Moreton-in-Marsh. There were gold coins too – some with the heads of Roman emperors and others of Victoria and George IV and Frederick Barbarossa. There were birds made out of precious stone with diamond-eyes, and buckles for shoes and belts, hairpins too with the rubies turned into roses, and vinaigrettes. There were toothpicks of gold, and swizzlesticks, and little spoons to dig the wax out of your ears of gold too, and cigarette-holders studded with diamonds, and small boxes of gold for pastilles and snuff, horseshoes for the ties of hunting men, and emerald-hounds for the lapels of hunting women: fishes were there too and little carrots of ruby for luck, diamond-stars which had perhaps decorated generals or statesmen, golden key-rings with emerald-initials, and sea-shells picked out with pearls, and a portrait of a dancing-girl in gold and enamel, with Haidee inscribed in what I suppose were rubies.

'Enough's enough,' Javitt said, and I had to drag myself away, as it seemed to me, from all the riches in the world, its pursuits and enjoyments. Maria would have packed everything that lay there back into the cardboard-boxes, but Javitt said with his lordliest voice, 'Let them lie,' and back we went in silence the way we had come, in the same order, our shadows going ahead. It was as if the sight of the treasure had exhausted me. I lay down on the sacks without waiting for my broth and fell asleep at once. In my dream within a dream somebody laughed and wept.

7

I have said that I can't remember how many days and nights I spent below the garden. The number of times I slept is really no guide, for I slept simply when I had the inclination or when Javitt commanded me to lie down, there being no light or darkness save what the oil-lamp determined, but I am almost sure it was after this sleep of exhaustion that I woke with the full intention somehow to reach home again. Up till now I had acquiesced in my captivity with little complaint; perhaps the meals of broth were palling on me, though I doubt if that was the reason, for I have fed for longer, with as little variety and less appetite, in Africa; perhaps the sight of Javitt's treasure had been a climax which robbed my story of any further interest; perhaps, and I think this is the most likely reason, I wanted to begin my search for Miss Ramsgate.

Whatever the motive, I came awake determined from my deep sleep, as suddenly as I had fallen into it. The wick was burning low in the oil-lamp and I could hardly distinguish Javitt's features and Maria was out of sight somewhere behind the curtain. To my astonishment Javitt's eyes were closed – it had never occurred to me before that there were moments when these two might sleep. Very quietly, with my eyes on Javitt, I slipped off my shoes – it was now or never. When I had got them off with less sound than a mouse makes, an idea came to me and I withdrew the laces – I can still hear the sharp ting of the metal tag ringing on the gold po beside my sacks. I thought I had been too clever by half, for Javitt stirred – but then he was still again and I slipped off my makeshift bed and crawled over to him where he sat on the lavatory-seat. I knew that, unfamiliar as I was with the tunnel, I could never outpace Javitt, but I was taken aback when I realized that it was impossible to bind together the ankles of a one-legged man.

But neither could a one-legged man travel without the help of his hands – the hands which lay now conveniently folded like a statue's on his lap. One of the things my brother had taught me was to make a slip-knot. I made one now with the laces joined and very gently, millimetre by millimetre, passed it over Javitt's hands and wrists, then pulled it tight.

I had expected him to wake with a howl of rage and even in my fear felt some of the pride Jack must have experienced at outwitting the giant. I was ready to flee at once, taking the lamp with me, but his very silence detained me. He only opened one eye, so that again I had the impression that he was winking at me. He tried to move his hands, felt the knot, and then acquiesced in their imprisonment. I expected him to call for Maria, but he did nothing of the kind, just watching me with his one open eye.

Suddenly I felt ashamed of myself. 'I'm sorry,' I said.

'Ha, ha,' he said, 'my prodigal, the strayed sheep, you're learning fast.'

'I promise not to tell a soul.'

'They wouldn't believe you if you did,' he said.

'I'll be going now,' I whispered with regret, lingering there absurdly, as though with half of myself I would have been content to stay for always.

'You better,' he said. 'Maria might have different views from me.' He tried his hands again. 'You tie a good knot.'

'I'm going to find your daughter,' I said, 'whatever you may think.'

'Good luck to you then,' Javitt said. 'You'll have to travel a long way; you'll have to forget all your schoolmasters try to teach you; you must lie like a horse-trader and not be tied up with loyalties any more than you are here, and who knows? I doubt it, but you might, you just might.'

I turned away to take the lamp, and then he spoke again. 'Take your golden po as a souvenir,' he said. 'Tell them you found it in an old cupboard. You've got to have something when you start a search to give you substance.'

'Thank you,' I said, 'I will. You've been very kind.' I began – absurdly in view of his bound wrists – to hold out my hand like a departing guest; then I stooped to pick up the po just as Maria, woken perhaps by our voices, came through the curtain. She took the situation in as quick as a breath and squawked at me – what I don't know – and made a dive with her bird-like hand.

I had the start of her down the passage and the advantage of the light, and I was a few feet ahead when I reached Camp Indecision, but at that point, what with the wind of my passage and the failing wick, the lamp went out. I dropped it on the earth and groped on in the dark. I could hear the scratch and whimper of Maria's sequin dress, and my nerves leapt when her feet set the lamp rolling on my tracks. I don't remember much after that. Soon I was crawling upwards, making better speed on my knees than she could do in her skirt, and a little later I saw a grey light where the roots of the tree parted. When I came up into the open it was much the same early morning hour as the one when I had entered the cave. I could hear kwahk, kwahk, kwahk, come up from below the ground – I don't know if it was a curse or a menace or just a farewell, but for many nights afterwards I lay in bed afraid that the door would open and Maria would come in to fetch me, when the house was silent and asleep. Yet strangely enough I felt no fear of Javitt, then or later.

Perhaps – I can't remember – I dropped the gold po at the entrance of the tunnel as a propitiation to Maria; certainly I didn't have it with me when I rafted across the lake or when Joe, our dog, came leaping out of the house at me and sent me sprawling on my back in the dew of the lawn by the green broken fountain.

Part Three

1

Wilditch stopped writing and looked up from the paper. The night had passed and with it the rain and the wet wind. Out of the window he could see thin rivers of blue sky winding between the banks of cloud, and the sun as it slanted in gleamed weakly on the cap of his pen. He read the last sentence which he had written and saw how again at the end of his account he had described his adventure as though it were one which had really happened and not something that he had dreamed during the course of a night's truancy or invented a few years later for the school-magazine. Somebody, early though it was, trundled a wheelbarrow down the gravel-path beyond the fountain. The sound, like the dream, belonged to childhood.

He went downstairs and unlocked the front door. There

unchanged was the broken fountain and the path which led to the Dark Walk, and he was hardly surprised when he saw Ernest, his uncle's gardener, coming towards him behind the wheelbarrow. Ernest must have been a young man in the days of the dream and he was an old man now, but to a child a man in the twenties approaches middle-age and so he seemed much as Wilditch remembered him. There was something of Javitt about him, though he had a big moustache and not a beard – perhaps it was only a brooding and scrutinizing look and that air of authority and possession which had angered Mrs Wilditch when she approached him for vegetables.

'Why, Ernest,' Wilditch said, 'I thought you had retired?'

Ernest put down the handle of the wheelbarrow and regarded Wilditch with reserve. 'It's Master William, isn't it?'

'Yes. George said—'

'Master George was right in a way, but I have to lend a hand still. There's things in this garden others don't know about.' Perhaps he *had* been the model for Javitt, for there was something in his way of speech that suggested the same ambiguity.

'Such as . . . ?'

'It's not everyone can grow asparagus in chalky soil,' he said, making a general statement out of the particular in the same way Javitt had done. 'You've been away a long time, Master William.'

'I've travelled a lot.'

'We heard one time you was in Africa and another time in Chinese parts. Do you like a black skin, Master William?'

'I suppose at one time or another I've been fond of a black skin.'

'I wouldn't have thought they'd win a beauty prize,' Ernest said.

'Do you know Ramsgate, Ernest?'

'A gardener travels far enough in a day's work,' he said. The wheelbarrow was full of fallen leaves after the night's storm. 'Are the Chinese as yellow as people say?'

'No.'

There *was* a difference, Wilditch thought: Javitt never asked for information, he gave it: the weight of water, the age of the earth, the sexual habits of a monkey. 'Are there many changes in the garden,' he asked, 'since I was here?'

'You'll have heard the pasture was sold?'

'Yes. I was thinking of taking a walk before breakfast – down the Dark Walk perhaps to the lake and the island.'

'Ah.'

'Did you ever hear any story of a tunnel under the lake?'

'There's no tunnel there. For what would there be a tunnel?'

'No reason that I know. I suppose it was something I dreamed.'

'As a boy you was always fond of that island. Used to hide there from the missus.'

'Do you remember a time when I ran away?'

'You was always running away. The missus used to tell me to go and find you. I'd say to her right out, straight as I'm talking to you, I've got enough to do digging the potatoes you are always asking for. I've never known a woman get through potatoes like she did. You'd have thought she ate them. She could have been living on potatoes and not on the fat of the land.'

'Do you think I was treasure-hunting? Boys do.'

'You was hunting for something. That's what I said to the folk round here when you were away in those savage parts – not even coming back here for your uncle's funeral. "You take my word," I said to them, "he hasn't changed, he's off hunting for something, like he always did, though I doubt if he knows what he's after," I said to them. "The next we hear," I said, "he'll be standing on his head in Australia."'

Wilditch remarked with regret, 'Somehow I never looked

there'; he was surprised that he had spoken aloud. 'And The Three Keys, is it still in existence?'

'Oh, it's there all right, but the brewers bought it when my uncle died and it's not a free house any more.'

'Did they alter it much?'

'You'd hardly know it was the same house with all the pipes and tubes. They put in what they call pressure, so you can't get an honest bit of beer without a bubble in it. My uncle was content to go down to the cellar for a barrel, but it's all machinery now.'

'When they made all those changes you didn't hear any talk of a tunnel under the cellar?'

'Tunnel again. What's got you thinking of tunnels? The only tunnel I know is the railway tunnel at Bugham and that's five miles off.'

'Well, I'll be walking on, Ernest, or it will be breakfast time before I've seen the garden.'

'And I suppose now you'll be off again to foreign parts. What's it to be this time? Australia?'

'It's too late for Australia now.'

Ernest shook his brindled head at Wilditch with an air of sober disapproval. 'When I was born,' he said, 'time had a different pace to what it seems to have now,' and, lifting the handle of the wheelbarrow, he was on his way towards the new iron gate before Wilditch had time to realize he had used almost the very words of Javitt. The world was the world he knew.

2

The Dark Walk was small and not very dark – perhaps the laurels had thinned with the passing of time, but the cobwebs were there as in his childhood to brush his face as he went by. At the end of the walk there was the wooden gate on to the green which had always in his day been locked – he had never known why that route out of the garden was forbidden him, but he had discovered a way of opening the gate with the rim of a halfpenny. Now he could find no halfpennies in his pocket.

When he saw the lake he realized how right George had been. It was only a small pond, and a few feet from the margin there was an island the size of the room in which last night they had dined. There *were* a few bushes growing there, and even a few trees, one taller and larger than the others, but certainly it was neither the sentinel-pine of W.W.'s story nor the great oak of his memory. He took a few steps back from the margin of the pond and jumped.

He hadn't quite made the island, but the water in which he landed was only a few inches deep. Was any of the water deep enough to float a raft? He doubted it. He sloshed ashore, the water not even penetrating his shoes. So this little spot of earth had contained Camp Hope and Friday's Cave. He wished that he had the cynicism to laugh at the half-expectation which had brought him to the island.

The bushes came only to his waist and he easily pushed through them towards the largest tree. It was difficult to believe that even a small child could have been lost here. He was in the world that George saw every day, making his round of a not very remarkable garden. For perhaps a minute, as he pushed his way through the bushes, it seemed to him that his whole life had been wasted, much as a man who has been betrayed by a woman wipes out of his mind even the happy years with her. If it had not been for his dream of the tunnel and the bearded man and the hidden treasure, couldn't he have made a less restless life for himself, as George in fact had done, with marriage, children, a home? He tried to persuade himself that he was exaggerating the importance of a dream. His lot had probably been decided months before that when George was reading him *The Romance of Australian Exploration*. If a child's experience does really form his future life, surely he had been formed, not by Javitt, but by Grey and Burke. It was his pride that at least he had never taken his various professions seriously: he had been loyal to no one – not even to the girl in Africa (Javitt would have approved his disloyalty). Now he stood beside the ignoble tree that had no roots above the ground which could possibly have formed the entrance to a cave and he looked back at the house: it was so close that he could see George at the window of the bathroom lathering his face. Soon the bell would be going for breakfast and they would be sitting opposite each other exchanging the morning small talk. There was a good train back to London at 10.25. He supposed that it was the effect of his disease that he was so tired – not sleepy but achingly tired as though at the end of a long journey.

After he had pushed his way a few feet through the bushes he came on the blackened remains of an oak; it had been split by lightning probably and then sawed close to the ground for logs. It could easily have been the source of his dream. He tripped on the old roots hidden in the grass, and squatting down on the ground he laid his ear close to the earth. He had an absurd desire to hear from somewhere far below the kwahk, kwahk from a roofless mouth and the deep rumbling of Javitt's voice saying, 'We are hairless, you and I,' shaking his beard at him, 'so's the hippopotamus and the elephant and the dugong – you wouldn't know, I suppose, what a dugong is. We survive the longest, the hairless ones.'

But, of course, he could hear nothing except the emptiness you hear when a telephone rings in an empty house. Something tickled his ear, and he almost hoped to find a sequin which had survived the years under the grass, but it was only an ant staggering with a load towards its tunnel.

Wilditch got to his feet. As he levered himself upright, his hand was scraped by the sharp rim of some metal object in the earth. He kicked the object free and found it was an old tin chamber-pot. It had lost all colour in the ground except that inside the handle there adhered a few flakes of yellow paint.

3

How long he had been sitting there with the pot between his knees he could not tell; the house was out of sight: he was as small now as he had been then – he couldn't see over the tops of the bushes, and he was back in Javitt's time. He turned the pot over and over; it was certainly not a golden po, but that proved nothing either way; a child might have mistaken it for one when it was newly painted. Had he then really dropped this in his flight – which meant that somewhere underneath him now Javitt sat on his lavatory-seat and Maria quacked beside the calor-gas . . . ? There was no certainty; perhaps years ago, when the paint was fresh, he had discovered the pot, just as he had done this day, and founded a whole afternoon-legend around it. Then why had W.W. omitted it from his story?

Wilditch shook the loose earth out of the po, and it rang on a pebble just as it had rung against the tag of his shoelace fifty years ago. He had a sense that there was a decision he had to make all over again. Curiosity was growing inside him like the cancer. Across the pond the bell rang for breakfast and he thought, 'Poor mother – she had reason to fear,' turning the tin chamber-pot on his lap.

Publication History

'Dream of a Strange Land' was first published in the *Saturday Evening Post* in 1963 and collected in *A Sense of Reality* in 1963.

'The News in English' was first published in the *Strand Magazine* in 1940 and first collected in *The Last Word and Other Stories* in 1990.

'The End of the Party' was written in 1929, first published in the *London Mercury* in 1932, first collected in *The Basement Room and Other Stories* in 1935 and later collected in *Twenty-One Stories* in 1954.

'The Case for the Defence' was written in 1939, first published in the *Star Weekly* (Toronto) in 1940, first collected in *Nineteen Stories* in 1947 and later collected in *Twenty-One Stories* in 1954.

'The Basement Room' was written in 1935, serialised in five parts in the *News Chronicle* in 1935, first published in *The Basement Room and Other Stories* in 1935, first collected in *Nineteen Stories* in 1947 and later collected in *Twenty-One Stories* in 1954.

'A Day Saved' was written in 1934, first published in *The Basement Room and Other Stories* in 1935, first collected in *Nineteen Stories* in 1947 and later collected in *Twenty-One Stories* in 1954.

'Across the Bridge' was written in 1938, first published in *Britannia and Eve* in 1938, first collected in *Nineteen Stories* in 1947 and later collected in *Twenty-One Stories* in 1954.

'A Drive in the Country' was written in 1936, first published in the *Passing Show* magazine in 1936, first collected in *Nineteen Stories* in 1947 and later collected in *Twenty-One Stories* in 1954.

'The Innocent' was written in 1937, first published in *Tomorrow* in 1946, first collected in *Nineteen Stories* in 1947 and later collected in *Twenty-One Stories* in 1954.

'The Destructors' was written in 1954, first published in *Picture Post* and first collected in *Twenty-One Stories* in 1954.

'Men at Work' was written in 1940, first published in *The Penguin New Writing No. 9* in 1941 and then in the *New Yorker* in 1941, first collected in *Nineteen Stories* in 1947 and later collected in *Twenty-One Stories* in 1954.

'A Little Place Off the Edgware Road' was written in 1939, first published in *Nineteen Stories* in 1947 and later collected in *Twenty-One Stories* in 1954.

'A Visit to Morin' was first published in the *London Magazine* in 1957 and first collected in *A Sense of Reality* in 1963.

'The Hint of an Explanation' was written in 1948, first published in the *Month* and *Commonweal* in 1949 and first collected in *Twenty-One Stories* in 1954.

'Cheap in August' was first published in the *London Magazine* in 1964 and first collected in *May We Borrow Your Husband?* in 1967.

'The Moment of Truth' was first published in the *Independent* in 1988 and first collected in *The Last Word and Other Stories* in 1990.

'The Root of All Evil' was first published in the *New Statesman* and the *Saturday Evening Post* in 1964 and first collected in *May We Borrow Your Husband?* in 1967.

'A Branch of the Service' was first published in *The Last Word and Other Stories* in 1990.

'Two Gentle People' was first published in the *Weekend Telegraph* in 1967 and first collected in *May We Borrow Your Husband?* in 1967.

'Church Militant' was written in 1956, first published in *Commonweal* and the *New Statesman and Nation* in 1956 and first collected in *Collected Stories* in 1972.

'The Other Side of the Border' was first published in *Nineteen Stories* in 1947.

'Under the Garden' was first published in *A Sense of Reality* in 1963.

VINTAGE CLASSICS

Vintage Classics is home to some of the greatest writers and thinkers from around the world and across the ages. Bringing you not just the books you already know and love, but new additions to your library, these are works to capture imaginations, inspire new perspectives and excite curiosity.

Renowned for our iconic red spines and bold, collectable design, Vintage Classics is an adventurous, ever-evolving list. We breathe new life into classic books for modern readers, publishing to reflect the world today, because we believe that our times can best be understood in conversation with the past.